Hidden MERCIES

A NOVEL

SERENA B. MILLER

HOWARD BOOKS
A DIVISION OF SIMON & SCHUSTER, INC.

NEW YORK   NASHVILLE   LONDON   TORONTO   SYDNEY   NEW DELHI

Howard Books
A Division of Simon & Schuster, Inc.
1230 Avenue of the Americas
New York, NY 10020

First Howard Books trade paperback edition April 2013

HOWARD and colophon are trademarks of Simon & Schuster, Inc.

For information about special discounts for bulk purchases,
please contact Simon & Schuster Special Sales at
1-866-506-1949 or business@simonandschuster.com.

The Simon & Schuster Speakers Bureau can bring authors to your
live event. For more information or to book an event
contact the Simon & Schuster Speakers Bureau at
1-866-248-3049 or visit our website at www.simonspeakers.com.

Manufactured in the United States of America

10 9 8 7 6 5 4 3 2 1

Library of Congress Cataloging-in-Publication Data

Miller, Serena.
Hidden mercies : a novel / Serena B. Miller.
      p.   cm.
I. Title.
PS3613.I55295U53 2013
813'.6—dc23   2011035334

ISBN 978-1-4516-6035-7
ISBN 978-1-4516-6036-4 (ebook)

To Jacob "Wingman" Miller

IT specialist

Thank you, Son, for your limitless patience.

Acknowledgments

Deep gratitude to:

Dr. Elton Lehman: 1998 Country Doctor of the Year, who led the Amish community in building the Holmes County, Mt. Eaton Care Center—a freestanding birthing center for Amish and Mennonite women. Thank you for taking the time to talk with me about your work.

Katie Weaver: Lancaster County–trained Amish midwife. Your forty years of service to your people is an inspiration. As you said, "Childbirth is a holy thing."

Ivan Weaver: For supporting your wife's ministry, and for taking the time to teach us about your faith.

Mabel and Effie Miller, Old Order Amish sisters: For allowing me to share your poetry with my Amy.

Stephanie Miller and Marybeth Coriell, labor and delivery nurses: For taking the time to brainstorm, share your medical knowledge, and proofread.

Sandra L. Hess: For the in-depth information about your work as a certified professional midwife.

Lisa Morrison: For your prayers and allowing me to borrow your brilliant, eccentric horse, Copycat, for a few pages.

Tim Finley: For sharing your expertise about horses.

Jack Davis, Colonel United States Marine Corps, retired: For looking out for my two civilian kids when they were living in Hiroshima, patiently answering my questions, and for a lifetime of service to our country.

Remember not the sins of my youth, nor my transgressions: according to your mercy, remember thou me for thy goodness' sake, Oh Lord.

—PSALMS 25:7 (KJV)

Prologue

I n the seventeen years Claire Keim had been on this earth, she had seen only one movie—a horror film. It gave her nightmares for weeks. Her *Rumspringa,* her "running around" time, began and ended in one miserable night spent at the movie theater in the company of *Englisch* friends.

Yes, Claire had only seen one horror film—but at the moment, she felt like she was living in one.

"Where *is* that boy?" Aunt Beulah, hard of hearing and apparently under the impression that she was whispering to Claire's mother, was shouting the very question that was on everyone's mind.

Where on earth was her groom?

Enough food had been prepared to feed upward of three hundred people. Chickens, butchered at her uncle's farm, had been cooked to tender goodness. At the moment, carefully made stuffing baked in the ovens. Vats of potatoes boiled on the stoves, ready to be mashed by the dozens of women who, in order to finish preparing the food, would voluntarily miss the wedding that was to start in—Claire glanced at her mother's kitchen clock—that was scheduled to start right now!

She gazed out the living room window, willing Matthew to hurry up. From her vantage point, she could see the sea of black buggies that flooded her father's hay field. Two white sixteen-passenger vans, noticeably out of place, sat among them, hired to bring relatives all the way from upper New York State.

All of these people sacrificing time and money to get here now milled around the Keim farm. Some, ignorant of the fact that the groom had not yet arrived, were already seating themselves on the benches in the barn. From the window, she could see them through the maw of her father's dark red barn, men and women demurely facing one another. Waiting.

Her parents, not wealthy by any means, had sold some of the timber from the back of their farm in order to pay for this wedding. It was a sacrifice worth making, her mother said.

It *was* a sacrifice worth making. That is, assuming the groom ever showed up!

She intended to be a *gute Frau,* a good and obedient wife, but before the day was over, Matthew would be hearing her thoughts on being left to worry about whether or not he would come to his own wedding!

A clear, early-morning October sun broke through the fog, promising a lovely day. The threat of rain that had kept her awake all night had lifted.

She did not think she needed all that teaching in order to become a faithful wife to Matthew. A life without him was unimaginable. Even when they were apart, she spent every waking minute thinking about him. She knew they were going to have a wonderful future together. How could she not have a wonderful future with Matthew as a husband?

To an outsider, she would have looked like any other Amish girl; but this morning, she felt like a princess. Her dress was brand-new, handmade for this occasion by her grandmother, who had insisted on sewing it for her in spite of arthritic hands.

"Has that oldest boy of Jeremiah's run off?" Aunt Beulah shouted into her mother's ear, and thereby to everyone else sitting in the living room lined with older women. "What did he do, head back West? I told you those two were too young to get married."

Claire's face grew hot. The wall clock, which struck a chime every fifteen minutes, announced to everyone in the room that Matthew was now a full fifteen minutes late to his own *Hochzeit*.

This was unheard of. He should have been here before dawn helping her father, brothers, and uncles set up the church benches in the barn and taking care of any other last-minute things that needed to be done.

Matthew's father, a widower, was the most punctual man in their church, but he was not yet here, either. Nor was Matthew's brother, Tobias, or his little sister, Faye. It was not like Matthew's family to be late. Their buggy was always the first to show up on Sunday mornings.

"I'm going to saddle Pansy and ride over to their house to see what's holding them." Claire's older brother, Eli, patted her on the shoulder. "Someone should make certain they have not been in an accident."

"Thank you." Claire gave her brother's hand a squeeze. "I will pray that nothing bad has happened."

Claire dutifully did pray that everyone in Matthew's family was safe and sound, but in her heart she was beginning to wonder, along with Aunt Beulah, if Matthew had run off.

They had not gone together all that long. Their Swartzentruber church did not approve of long courtships, and with good reason—too much temptation. Could it be that Matthew had changed his mind? Could it possibly be that he had gone back West, to that ranch he had worked at last year? Sometimes his voice held a note of longing when he spoke of the great open spaces he had seen in Montana. Had she made a mistake in trusting him?

There had never been, in the collective knowledge of the people of their church, a groom who was late for his own wedding. She knew that to be a fact because Beulah, not only the deafest but also the oldest woman in their church, had just now trumpeted that particular piece of information to her mother.

The kitchen clock struck nine o'clock. The comfortable chatter that usually swirled around a bride died out. People were silent now, as the awful realization that something had gone terribly wrong settled over everyone. Claire saw one of her uncles take out his pocket watch and check the time.

Claire's twin sister, Rose, put her arm around her waist. "Henry is not here either," Rose said. "I'm worried about him as well."

Until this moment, Claire had not noticed that Henry, the boy who was courting Rose, had not arrived. He was supposed to stand up with them as a witness to her and Matthew's wedding.

Not for the first time, Claire wished their people were allowed to have a telephone shanty near their home. The liberal Old Order Amish thought nothing of having a telephone at the end of their driveway. Not her people, though. The Swartzentrubers would have excommunicated any member who attempted such a thing.

She stiffened. A lone rider, bent low, galloped toward her house. It was Matthew! He had come!

She ran out into the yard to greet him, overjoyed. Perhaps the ministers could shorten their sermons a bit so that everyone's dinner would not be late. She would soon be a married woman after all!

But it was not Matthew. It was Benjamin, a young neighbor of the Troyers, who leaped off the slavering horse.

"There's been an accident," he said. "The state patrol was just at the Troyer house. Jeremiah and Faye have gone to the hospital. Tobias and Henry are injured, and Matthew is"—he gulped for breath and her heart stopped—"Matthew is . . . gone."

"Matthew is gone? Where did he go?"

"He's . . . gone." Ben fidgeted, looking around at the crowd forming around them. "He was racing a new horse of Henry's and now he's dead. I don't know anything else."

"How badly hurt is my Henry?" Rose asked.

"I don't know. All they said was that it was bad."

Rose burst into tears.

Claire stared at her sister, wondering why she was crying. Certainly Rose knew that this was nothing more than a bad wedding joke. Matthew's friends loved playing pranks. No doubt they had "kidnapped" Matthew early this morning just to tease her. She smiled, relieved to have a reasonable explanation for Matthew's absence. In fact, if she knew Henry, he was probably at the bottom of this. Sometimes Henry took things a little too far. "Ben, go tell Henry and the others that this isn't funny," she said. "And tell him it's time to bring Matthew back. The bishop isn't going to be happy about this, and neither are my parents."

Ben looked at her and she saw real pity in his eyes. Oh, he was a good pretender, he was!

There was a long, long silence among the people grouped around her. She kept waiting for Ben to burst into laughter and for Matthew and Henry to come walking around the corner of the barn, but not one person moved. They all seemed to be waiting for something. Even Rose had quit crying and was now looking at her, puzzled.

Claire glanced around at her friends. She realized that she was the only one smiling. A knot began to form in the pit of her stomach.

"Henry!" she yelled. "You stop this right now! You bring Matthew out from wherever you're hiding him. I have worked too hard on this wedding for you to spoil it with your tricks!"

Once again there was nothing but silence. Many of her friends were staring at the ground. News had somehow traveled all the way up to the women preparing food, and they had stopped their work beneath the kitchen canopy. Everything seemed frozen in time.

"It is not a joke, Claire," Ben said. "With all my heart, I wish it was."

This comment infuriated her. How dare he continue to pretend about this! She had never realized before that Ben had such a streak of cruelty in him.

"Where is he?" She grabbed the front of his shirt in both hands and began to shake him. "Where is my Matthew? What have you done with him?"

Two hands grabbed hold of her and pulled her away from Ben. "Calm yourself, child," Bishop Weaver said, and gave her a slight shake. "The Lord has promised not to give you more than you can bear."

That was the moment she knew Ben's words were true. Bishop Weaver was the most humorless person she had ever known. He would never agree to be part of such a prank. This was not a joke. The unthinkable had happened. Her glorious, laughing, beautiful Matthew was dead.

Unlike Rose, Claire did not cry. Her emotions were too deep and tangled for her to be able to cry.

One of the *Englisch* van drivers volunteered to take her and Rose to the hospital. As he drove off, she pressed her face to the window and saw the women starting the process of putting the food away. There would be no wedding feast today. Instead, the stalwart people of their church would begin preparations for a funeral.

chapter ONE

Twenty-seven years later . . .

Time had slowed to a crawl for Captain Tom Miller. The minute hand on the hospital clock seemed to take forever to make it around the clockface. Finally the big hand hit eight o'clock, and he congratulated himself for having made it through another hour. The almost imperceptible tick-tick-tick of the clock had become a constant companion, ticking away the seconds of his life.

The nurse kept her eyes averted as she fussed with taking the lids off the various containers of his breakfast tray. He didn't blame her. There was a mirror on the underside of his bed tray. He had seen the damage. If he were her, he would keep his eyes averted, too.

Evidently it had fallen on her to feed him today. She must have drawn the short straw.

"The weather?" His voice was raspy. Inhaling the heat from the explosion had caused damage.

The nurses had learned to have the answer ready to that question before they came through the door in the morning. The weather had become a small obsession with him. It reassured him that the outdoors still existed.

7

"Cold and snowy," she said.

"How cold?" he asked. "How snowy?"

"Maybe four or five inches fell overnight," she said. "I don't know the exact temperature, but it was so cold this morning, I had to wear my heaviest coat."

From his room at the Walter Reed Army Medical Center, he could see the sky . . . but only the sky. There had been a heavy layer of nimbostratus clouds yesterday evening, and he had silently predicted that there would be anywhere from three to six inches of snow accumulation before morning. It gave him a small feeling of pride that he had predicted correctly. A man didn't spend as many hours in the air as he had without being able to read the clouds.

"We have some yummy peach yogurt today."

The nurse was young. She had no idea how emasculating the word *yummy* sounded to him. He shoved his pride down as she tucked a napkin beneath his chin. He was forty-four years old. A captain in the U.S. Marines. A decorated war hero. He had been trained to withstand torture and avoid capture, and had the skills to escape if incarcerated. The one thing necessary to his survival that he had *not* been taught was how to keep his ego intact while being fed like a baby.

His hands were still bandaged from instinctively shielding his face when the bomb detonated. His body was covered with multiple shrapnel wounds, and he'd had reconstructive surgery on his left jaw and cheekbone.

"Do you want a sip of milk?" The nurse opened a carton and inserted a straw into it.

Actually, he would prefer a cup of hot, black coffee, but that was not an option. The chances of getting scalded by some clumsy nurse were too great, and he refused to sip his coffee through a straw. Instead, he swallowed the milk and waited for a spoonful of—what was it she'd said? Peach yogurt?

Good grief.

Eggs and bacon would have been his first choice. Fried crisp. The eggs scrambled in real butter. Half a loaf of homemade bread, toasted, with a pot of his mother's good strawberry jam. Now, *that* would be a breakfast, but until his throat healed, he was reduced to eating only those things that were easy to swallow.

The nurse glanced over her shoulder at the silent television hanging on the wall. "Do you want me to turn it on for you?"

He had been asked that question so many times.

"No."

"It would make time go faster."

"No."

She shrugged and scraped the last bit of yogurt from the plastic container. "Suit yourself."

The television had been blaring when he first came to this room. At the time, his throat had not healed enough to tell them to turn it off. He had lain there, fighting against the most intense pain he had ever felt, wondering if he would live, wondering if he *wanted* to live, while being forced to listen to the canned laughter of some silly sitcom when nothing was funny.

The first whispered, raspy words out of his mouth had been "Turn that thing OFF!"

Post-traumatic stress disorder. That's what the hospital shrink called it. PTSD.

He didn't buy it.

In his opinion, PTSD was one of those catchphrase mental illnesses that the medical establishment used to pigeonhole and categorize people. Wrap up all the pain, shove it into a neat file folder, and tie it up with a bow.

Oh, that guy? The one with all the bandages. The one sensitive to noise. He has PTSD. Classic symptoms. Understandable under the circumstances. Okay, next patient.

He did not believe that he had PTSD. What he had was a perfectly reasonable desire for quiet. Raised voices, canned laughter, stupid commercials—noise of any kind made his nerves fizz with anxiety and irritation.

Now, at least, he could lie in blessed silence—or as close to it as a hospital could get—dozing in a drug-induced stupor after the morphine shots, enduring the minutes after it had worn off until the next shot was due.

He did not complain. Marines did not complain, and even though he was battered and broken, what was left of him was still every inch a soldier.

He was not a man who often prayed unless the helicopter he was flying was under fire. Then he would toss off a quick prayer during evasive maneuvers. More often than not, that prayer included a few curse words.

Since the explosion, a set of very specific prayers began running through his head.

If you'll pull me through this, Lord, I promise to go back home and make things right with my father and Claire. Please let me live. Please let me heal. Please let me walk out of here on my own two feet. Then a scrap of Scripture, vaguely recalled. *Remember not the sins of my youth.*

chapter TWO

A valentine, a man's work handkerchief, and a lock of hair. After twenty-seven years, that's all she had left to remember Matthew by. She touched each item gently, remembering.

If she were *Englisch,* she would have old photos. There would be an engagement picture clipped out of the local newspaper, perhaps a yellowed wedding dress hanging in the closet, maybe an engagement ring.

As much as she wished she had a picture of Matthew, she did not disagree with their Amish leaders' decision to forbid cameras. *Graven images,* they called them, and had she owned a photo of him, it probably would have become a graven image for her. Something to worship. Something to hold close to her heart.

"You aren't asleep yet?" Her sixteen-year-old niece, Maddy, stood in the open doorway in her long nightgown, brushing her hair.

Claire's first instinct was to shove the items out of sight, but she stopped herself. With her husband, Abraham, gone now, there was no one left to hide them from. She had been a good wife to Abraham. He had no cause to be jealous of Matthew—but he would have been furious had he ever come across her looking at these things.

11

She did not pull them out often, but every once in a while she took them out just to reassure herself that Matthew had actually existed—that he had not been some glorious figment of her imagination.

"Sure," Claire said. "Come in."

"What are those?" Maddy sat down on the bed beside her.

"Some things I probably should have thrown away a long time ago."

Maddy picked up the valentine and read it. "Who is Matthew?"

Claire hesitated. "Matthew was Levi's father."

"Oh."

Claire could tell that Maddy wasn't sure how to respond. Many in the community still struggled with the fact that Levi had been born out of wedlock.

"Did you love him a great deal?"

"When I was seventeen, I thought I could not take a breath without him." Claire folded the handkerchief into a neat square. "Then one day I learned that I had no choice."

"Is that a lock of his hair?"

"The day he died, I asked the nurse at the hospital for a pair of scissors. I wanted something of him that I could keep with me always."

"But you had Levi to remember him by." Maddy's voice was tentative, as though she didn't know whether or not this was a forbidden topic.

"I did not know that at the time."

It was not the Amish way to speak of intimate things with children—or even with other adults, if it could be avoided, and yet, as a midwife, Claire believed there were things Maddy should know. The girl had just turned sixteen. Her *Rumspringa* would be starting soon. She needed to be taught that there were consequences to decisions.

"Levi was conceived two days before Matthew and I were to be married. We loved each other very much, and with the wedding so close, we thought it would be . . . safe." She brushed a strand of loose hair behind Maddy's ear. "Until one is married in the eyes of man and of God, it is not right to express one's love too passionately. Do you understand what I'm saying?"

"Yes." Maddy glanced down at her hairbrush, as though embarrassed. Claire wondered if she had said too much. The girl was still so innocent, and yet . . . Claire was trying to raise her brother's two girls with as much wisdom as she could muster. There was more to her responsibility to them than just food and clothes.

"Why did you keep the handkerchief?" Maddy asked.

"I cut my foot on a jagged rock one day. A group of us were having a picnic. It was summer and I was barefoot. There were others about, but it was Matthew who knelt, took this handkerchief out of his pocket, and bound up the cut. He was so tender and kind. That is when I fell in love with him."

"He sounds wonderful."

"He was."

"What do you keep to remember Abraham by?"

The girl's question was innocent, and yet it hurt. The truth was, her marriage to Abraham had not been a success, but Maddy did not need to know that.

She smiled brightly. "I have this house, and this farm, and my four other children to remember Abraham by."

"Didn't you want a lock of his hair?"

"I was fighting for my life when he died. It did not cross my mind." The random intruder who two years earlier had shot and killed her husband and deliberately wounded her had ripped all their lives apart.

"Do you ever get scared that something bad like that might happen again?"

She pondered the question. It was understandable why the girl asked. But she had determined early on that she would not allow the evil they witnessed that day to define who they were.

"No. By the grace of God, I do not fear that will ever happen again."

It was true. It had taken a great effort of will and much, much prayer, but by God's grace, she no longer trembled every time she heard a vehicle pull into her driveway.

For a moment, there was only silence as Maddy pondered her words. Then Maddy's head lifted. "Was that the telephone?"

They both grew silent and listened—yes, the phone in their outdoor phone shanty was ringing. It was faint, but they could hear it. This late at night, a phone call usually meant only one thing.

"Whose baby is due?" Maddy asked.

"Nancy and Obed's."

"I will get your birthing bags." Maddy, a veteran of many late-night phone calls, rushed out the door.

Claire grabbed her birthing dress and pulled it on over her head. She had been expecting this call. Thank goodness she and Maddy had been awake and heard the phone ring. With all her heart, she wished she didn't have to rely on such an unreliable form of communication between her and the women she served. The shanty was far enough away from her house that she often missed calls altogether. Too many times, fathers had had to leave their laboring wives to come pound on her door.

By the time she had pinned up her hair, rushed outside to check the message on the answering machine, returned Obed's call to assure him that she was on her way, and hitched Flora up to the buggy, Maddy had placed her birthing bags and a few sandwiches in the backseat of the buggy.

"I put fresh batteries in," Maddy said, handing Claire a flashlight. "Be careful."

Claire put a foot on the one metal step attached to the buggy and sprang in. "What would I ever do without you?"

"The question is," Maddy answered, "what would Amy and I do without you?"

Claire clucked to the horse, and the buggy lurched forward.

"I will be gone awhile."

"I will be praying for you."

"Please do so," Claire said. "I'm afraid this birth might be difficult."

As she drove the three miles to Nancy and Obed's, she gave thanks once again for the gift of each of her children. Her two nieces, competent and kind Maddy and thirteen-year-old Amy, who was crippled in the same accident that had taken their parents. Her oldest, Levi, now grown and living next door with his new wife. And the four precious little souls who were the fruit of her marriage with Abraham. There had been hints lately about a couple of available men in two other nearby church districts, in whom she had adamantly expressed no interest. She could not imagine ever wanting to marry again. Her children were her life. To watch after and care for them was all she asked. The fact that she had a skill, with which she could support them and help others, was a gift from God.

She prayed again for Nancy and Obed and hurried down the road.

Claire could not wait to tell her sister, Rose, about the baby girl she had just delivered. This had been a special birth, indeed! Nancy and Obed, both in their forties, had been married eighteen years. Until today, only a succession of heartbreaking miscarriages marked their desire for a family. Claire had held her breath these past nine months, doing everything in her power as a midwife to make this a safe pregnancy, praying daily that it would be God's will for Nancy to carry this baby full term.

It had been a long and difficult labor, lasting nearly nineteen hours, but late this afternoon, the Lord had allowed her to hand that deserving couple a perfect, healthy, safely delivered baby girl!

All children were miracles, but this babe was maybe a little bit more of a miracle than most. Rose would want to know this wonderful news, and Claire was dying to share it with someone.

The way home from Nancy's took Claire directly past Mrs. Yoder's restaurant in Mt. Hope. It was Rose's night to work, and Claire knew that no one at the restaurant would mind if she stopped in to tell her sister about the successful birth. It was that kind of a place—a true family restaurant.

As she tied her horse to the railing provided, she wondered again why Rose had taken this job. Henry had inherited a fine farm and was healthy and strong.

As she went in, two plump, gray-haired women tourists were leaving the restaurant. One was wearing bright yellow shorts, a top printed with purple roses, and yellow hoop earrings. The other woman had on plaid shorts, a cherry-red blouse, and white-rimmed sunglasses. Compared to the subdued shades Claire was used to seeing, this clothing almost hurt her eyes. The two women seemed unaware of the jarring effect of their colors. Each had a big smile, and they were obviously having a grand time visiting Amish country.

"Get the special," the woman in yellow shorts confided on her way out. "The pot roast is to die for."

"Thank you." Claire was amused. It was not exactly a secret that Yoder's had delicious slow-cooked pot roast. "I will remember to do that."

It usually took a couple visits to Holmes County for out-of-town *Englisch* to figure out that it was okay to speak to the Amish. This must not be these women's first trip here. Claire was startled by a sudden whoosh of air behind her and saw a large, chartered bus opening its doors. Several more tourists walked out of the restaurant and piled into the bus.

It made Claire happy to know that Gloria Yoder's gamble in establishing a restaurant in this small village was giving people so much pleasure. It had certainly been a boon to the town. Money coming in from the outside world was a welcome thing, indeed.

Margaret Hochstetler, the hostess for the night, greeted her with enthusiasm. "Claire! It is good to see you!"

"And how is our little James doing?" Claire had delivered three of Margaret's children. The last one, tiny James, had been especially tricky.

Margaret, a robust Old Order matron, laughed. "Not so little anymore," she said. "He is helping his father plow this spring. Four horses at a time, that boy can handle."

"And him only ten," Claire marveled.

"His father says he is a born farmer." Margaret grabbed a menu. "Are you eating with us or have you come to see Rose?"

"I was hoping for a minute with her."

"That is no problem. Now that the bus has left, we are not so busy tonight." Margaret lowered her voice. "I saw Rose taking some aspirin a few minutes ago."

"I hate to hear that," Claire said. "My sister has dealt with a bad back ever since giving birth to her first child."

"Oh, the poor thing," Margaret said.

Claire agreed. It wasn't as though Rose enjoyed the work. She had always fought lower back pain, and carrying those heavy trays of food took a toll on her. She acted tired all the time these days—weighed down, instead of her usual happy and confident self.

And Rose didn't look like herself these days either. She had always dressed well, making her dresses from the best grade of fabric that she was allowed within the confines of their church *Ordnung*. She bought new shoes more often than Claire thought necessary. In fact, Rose had always stepped a little close to the sin of pride, but not anymore. Now her shoes were worn, scuffed and run down at the heel. Some of her dresses had been worn until they were beginning to fade. Either her sister no longer had the money to purchase the things she needed, or she had simply stopped caring about her appearance. Claire's attempts to talk to her about it had not been welcomed.

Claire saw her sister wiping off a table and went over to her. "Do you have a minute? I have something wonderful to tell you."

Rose winced as she straightened up.

"Is that old back bothering you again?" Claire put her hand on the small of her sister's back, wishing she could make the pain go away. She hated to see anyone hurting, but especially Rose.

"I'm fine," Rose answered, but Claire knew she was lying.

There was a time when Rose would not have pretended to be fine with her. These days it seemed like her sister was pretending most of the time. Others probably couldn't tell—but she certainly could.

"Rose, please tell me what is wrong."

"I said I am fine." Rose's voice warned her to leave the subject alone. "What is it you want to tell me?"

Claire saw that it would be unwise to press her sister any further, at least here and now. Instead, she hoped that telling

Rose the good news might make her sister feel more cheerful. It was certainly making her own heart sing!

"Nancy just had her baby. Obed is over the moon."

A soft, happy smile bloomed on Rose's face—the first Claire had seen in far too long.

"What did she get?"

"A baby girl. Full term. Eight pounds, ten ounces."

"Ach!" Rose said. "And Nancy no bigger than a mouse."

"She did well," Claire said. "Obed was a great help. I think he will make a good father, and he is such a good provider. That is one child who will never want for clothes or food."

She saw a shadow pass over Rose's face, and wished she could take back her words.

"I hope, for Nancy's sake, that you're right," Rose said. There was a hint of bitterness in her voice as she bent to finish wiping off the table.

"I will leave you to your work now," Claire said. "Come visit soon. I will make that clover and mint tea you like so well."

There was a slight glitter of tears in Rose's eyes. "I would like that very much. I—I am sorry for being sharp with you. I am not myself these days."

"You must not try to be anything special for me," Claire said. "You know that, no?"

"*Jah,* I know." Rose glanced away. "But I must get back to work now."

As Claire left the restaurant, she wished she could hold on to that good feeling she got after each successful birth, but it had evaporated into a cloud of worry about her sister.

Squinting at the foggy road was taking a toll on Tom. Staying hair-trigger-ready to swerve every time he saw a piece of trash or a dead animal took an even bigger toll. No matter how hard he tried, he could not turn off the training that reminded him not to let down his guard for a second.

The doctors at the hospital had warned him that he might struggle with this. They told him that a lot of returning soldiers battled the need to be ultravigilant when they came home. They told him to try to relax.

Easy to say. Hard to do. He had been hardwired to suspect anything on the road to be booby-trapped. Inattention could be deadly. Underpasses were especially threatening. He swerved abruptly as he passed beneath one. A truck driver honked at him, but in Afghanistan and Iraq, a soldier never knew when someone would be hiding there, primed to fire at you.

The Honda Civic that the rental place had given him felt small and insignificant compared to the heavily armored troop transport vehicles he was used to. He planned to turn it in when he got to Holmes County and buy something more substantial. With any luck, Moomaw's over in Sugarcreek would still be in business. He intended to check them out in a day or two and see what they had in stock.

When the bright lights of a gas station appeared to his right, he pulled in, grateful for a chance to fill his tank with gasoline and his body with coffee. He needed a stiff shot of caffeine to counteract the stupefying effect of the painkillers he had taken to make it this far. The stronger the coffee, the longer it had simmered on the burner, the better.

Talking his doctor into discharging him early and placing him on convalescent leave was not the smartest thing he had ever done, but his doctor had seen that he had reached a point when he could not stand one more day of being there. His irritation had grown with every day he got stronger. There came a moment when he could not abide one more nurse, one more question, or one more bland hospital meal.

He never dreamed that driving from Bethesda, Maryland,

to Mt. Hope, Ohio, would be so taxing, but he did not want to stop. After an absence of more than two decades, he felt like a crippled homing pigeon winging its way back, but he had no intention of stopping until he reached his destination.

He sat the coffee on the counter and handed his credit card to the multipierced, gum-chewing cashier. She glanced up from a magazine and caught a glimpse of his face. Her eyes widened at the damage she saw there.

"You shoulda seen the other guy," Tom joked.

The cashier did not seem to think the comment was funny. Perhaps it was because he wasn't smiling. He needed to remember to smile next time.

"It was a bomb," Tom said. "Afghanistan. I asked the plastic surgeon to make me look like George Clooney, but he said no one was that skilled." This time he remembered to smile.

Still staring at him, the clerk automatically started to blow a bubble, thought better of it, and sucked it back into her mouth.

Ever since he'd left the hospital two days ago, he'd found that a joke and a quick explanation made it a little easier on the civilians he interacted with. They could file the information neatly away in their brain, probably along with a new determination never to let a relative of theirs set foot inside of Afghanistan for any reason whatsoever.

"Sorry." The girl ran his credit card through the machine, handed him a receipt, then studiously went back to her magazine.

The plastic surgeon had said that the scars would fade with time. He wished the fading would hurry. He was not a vain man, nor had he ever considered himself particularly handsome, but having people steal sideways glances at him wherever he went got old real fast.

Hunger was gnawing at his stomach by the time he neared

his hometown. This was not the kind of hunger that could be filled at the window of a drive-through. As he got closer to home, he began to crave a meal that would fill the emptiness in his heart as much as his stomach.

He wanted comfort food—Holmes County soul food. Homemade egg noodles. Slow-roasted chicken. A custard pie with a crust so light it melted in your mouth. Whipped potatoes that didn't come out of a box. Gravy made from honest-to-goodness meat drippings. Home-canned green beans seasoned with onions and bacon. A mile-high apple pie topped off with a piece of the best-tasting cheddar cheese in the world—prize-winning cheese made with milk produced right there in the heart of Ohio.

If he was lucky, every bite would be seasoned with the soft, comforting sound of Pennsylvania Deutsch being spoken all around him. It would be a nice contrast to the Farsi he was used to hearing until the day he had been flown out of Afghanistan with an IV in his arm and a sling holding his jaw in place.

As he drove through Mt. Hope, he was a little surprised to discover that a large restaurant had been built in the middle of the small village. Mrs. Yoder's Kitchen, the sign said. He wondered exactly *which* Mrs. Yoder had decided to start this establishment. The name was so common here, it could have been any one of a hundred Mrs. Yoders.

It was exactly the kind of place he'd been hoping for, and the minute he walked in, he knew he was finally home. Many of the patrons were Amish, and he knew that the Amish spent their hard-earned money only at restaurants where they knew the food to be good and plentiful.

The specialties appeared to be broasted chicken and slow-cooked roast beef. He ordered the chicken, asparagus with cheese and bacon sauce, and bread dressing.

The Amish waitress brought his order, and he sat at a table near the window, consuming crispy, moist chicken, along with homemade bread slathered with his people's favorite condiment, *Lattvarick,* slow-cooked apple butter. He had healed enough to swallow real food again, and was grateful for every bite.

The sight of buggies trotting past the front windows brought on a wave of homesickness so strong it nearly took his breath away.

"Can I get you anything else?" The waitress laid the bill down on his table. There was something familiar about her. He took a good look at her face.

He realized the tired-looking, worn-around-the-edges waitress was Rose. He had known her since they were both in diapers. She was Claire Keim's twin. They'd come within hours of being in-laws. He almost greeted Rose by name, but some instinct stopped him.

"I'm trying to decide between the pies." So many memories he had of Rose and Claire. He remembered playing baseball with them during recess. Those two girls had been able to run bases like colts, even in their long dresses.

"The Dutch chocolate looks good—but I'm also partial to custard. It's hard to decide."

"They're all good." She showed no sign of recognition, nor did she show any interest in his order. She seemed to be a woman from whom the drudgery of life had stolen all signs of the high spirits he remembered when they were young.

"Custard, please."

Without a word, Rose headed back to the kitchen.

Not once, through the entire exchange, did she show any sign that she knew him. To her, he was just another tourist wandering through Amish country. It was a little disturbing to discover that the change in his appearance was that profound.

He had not considered the possibility of coming back to Holmes County and not being recognized. From Rose's reaction, it appeared that he might have a choice whether or not to reveal his identity.

Rose brought the pie, and as he cut through the thick custard with his fork, he noticed that a woman had come in and was talking to Rose as she wiped off tables. The woman was the same age and height as Rose. She turned just enough that he could see the side of her face. It was Claire. It had to be Claire. So she was still here.

He had driven all the way here to talk with her, but he couldn't do it here. There were questions to ask, and apologies to make, but not yet. Not until he had rested and washed the long trip from his body.

In fact, his need for rest right now was so great, it was making him a little light-headed. He needed to pay his bill and concentrate on getting to the hotel. This was not the time or the place to talk with the woman who had haunted his dreams for most of his life.

In a few days he would go see Claire. If Claire would speak to him, he would tell her that he had once been Tobias Troyer, the younger brother of the man she had expected to marry. He would explain that he had spent a lifetime regretting his part in his brother's death. Most important of all, he would ask forgiveness for having made her a widow before she could become a wife. Maybe, if he was very lucky, she would make it possible for him to meet his brother's son.

He also planned to check in with his father and sister, assuming that either of them were willing to speak with him. There was no guarantee they would. He did not hold out a lot of hope that his uncles, aunts, and cousins would talk with him. They would probably simply follow his father's and sister's lead. When Swartzentruber Amish banned someone, they were banned indeed.

If he was very lucky, she would grant him the forgiveness he'd craved for a lifetime. Or she might unleash all the words she had saved up all these years to say to him.

That would be her decision. All he knew was that in order to live the rest of his life with any measure of peace, he had to tell the people he cared about how sorry he was for causing such pain.

Claire noticed a tall, broad-shouldered man rising from his table as she talked to Rose. His hair was short. There was an angry scar running along the entire length of his jaw, and another one directly above his left cheekbone. As he pulled money from his billfold for a tip, she saw that he used his hands with some difficulty—hands that appeared to have been badly burned—and when he walked away, he walked with a limp.

She knew of poultices that might draw some of the pain from those wounds. Had the man been Amish, she would have considered approaching him and offering a suggestion or two, but he was not Amish. In fact, there was something about him that made her think he might have been a soldier at one time.

No, she would not be talking to that man anytime soon. Of all professions, that of soldier was one of the most alien to her culture. Quickly, she turned away before he caught her staring.

chapter THREE

Room 214 of Hotel Millersburg had a king-size bed, an antique desk, and three large windows that overlooked the historic hotel's brick-lined courtyard. The brochure said that live entertainment would perform there during summer months, but in May, the only entertainment Tom could see was two hardy little sparrows quarreling over a scrap of bread.

He smiled when the drab little female won and flew off, the male following close behind her.

He was contemplating the possibility of driving somewhere for lunch when there was a soft knock on the door.

"Housekeeping," a voice called.

He unlocked the door. A worried-looking woman stood on the other side. The sixtyish housekeeper, her gray hair done up inside a white prayer *Kapp,* apologized.

"I am sorry to disturb you. It's just that . . ."

"I need to let you do your job," he said. "I'll go get some lunch and give you time to do whatever you need."

He knew that she would change the sheets, open the windows to the spring air, and give the room the kind of good cleaning any self-respecting Amish woman would.

He had missed his people.

Once he got on the road, he realized that his leg had started to throb again. He fumbled in his pocket, brought out a small pill bottle, flipped open the lid, shook out four pills, tossed them into his mouth, and swallowed, chasing them down with a swig of cold, leftover coffee.

Soon, the pills began to work their magic and he could relax a little and enjoy the scenery. He marveled at the timelessness of the area. No electricity poles or wires marred the sky. No mobile homes dotted the landscape. Silos thrust up from the earth as though they were organic things growing straight out of the soil. The very number of them was a witness to the richness of the land.

Farmers walked behind their patient, glistening workhorses, their boots and homemade denim pants stained with the earth from which they wrested a living.

The smell of that earth being split open with steel plow points, now exposed to the air and sunshine, wafted in through his open window and tickled his senses. He well knew the feel of leather reins in his hands, the tug of the horses, the smell of horse sweat. It almost made him want to stop the car and ask to plow a few rows.

Almost.

Nostalgia aside, he had no desire—no true desire—to trudge along staring at the rear end of a horse.

He turned his mind back toward his goal. Perhaps today he would see Claire and apologize for having killed the father of her child.

Maddy was sweeping the porch when Claire arrived home from her second birth that week.

"You're back from Kathleen's so quickly?" Maddy greeted her. "That was a short labor."

"Four hours," Claire said. "She even fixed me a cup of tea before I left."

"You let her do that?"

"She insisted. Oh, and she had a basket of boys' pants sitting beside the bed so that she could mend them while she was in labor. Kathleen does not allow any grass to grow under her feet."

Maddy grinned. "She is a bit of a show-off, that one is."

"True."

Maddy's competent presence freed her to take on more maternity clients than she could have managed otherwise—especially with two-year-old Daniel at home. In her opinion, taking in her brother's two orphaned daughters had been an even greater blessing to her than to them.

"I cautioned Kathleen about trying to do too much too soon." Claire stepped out of the buggy and began to unhitch old Flora. "I doubt she will listen."

Her married son, Levi, appeared in the doorway of the nearby workshop wiping his hands on a rag. "I'll do that for you, *Maam*."

"*Denke*, Son." She gathered the two shoulder bags in which she kept the supplies she needed to attend a birth and headed for the house.

Amy, Maddy's thirteen-year-old sister, looked up from a small table on the porch where she was busy practicing her newest hobby, calligraphy. "We had some tourists stop by today."

"Oh?"

"They saw the signs down by the road and came in to buy one of Levi's baskets. The woman said one of his big ones would be perfect for storing the quilts they had purchased."

Amy, with her freckled face and sweet smile, tried hard to be enthusiastic about life, in spite of being confined to a wheelchair. Claire appreciated the girl's valiant spirit. It would have been hard on everyone if Amy gave in to the despair Claire knew she sometimes felt.

"Is that all they wanted?"

"No. Once they got inside the house and saw all the jars of honey and maple syrup on the shelves, they bought some of that, too. And . . ." Amy liked to draw good news out and savor it. "The wife saw the greeting cards I made and bought all of them!"

"All of them?" Claire said.

"Every last one. I had a dozen made up at two dollars apiece. She gave me two twenties and refused the change because she said my cards were worth more than I was charging. She and her husband were from Arizona. They were nice."

"Did you mark it on your map?"

"The *Englisch* lady did it for me," Amy backed her wheelchair away from the table and maneuvered it to a large map of the United States tacked to a board. She pointed out where the woman lived. "And she told me all about their hometown. She says it's very dry there right now."

"So what are you going to do with your riches?" Claire asked.

"I'm going to save up until we can go to Walmart and get more supplies. I'm in great need of card stock and a fine-point paintbrush."

Claire had not loved the idea of setting up a corner of her living room as a store, but it did give Amy an outlet for her homemade greeting cards and a steady stream of new people to talk to. In spite of her disability—or perhaps because of it—the girl was usually as sociable as a puppy. Every day was an adventure for Amy as long as someone came to purchase something. One customer had been thoughtful enough to send her a postcard of a Florida beach, which now adorned the wall of the bedroom she shared with Maddy.

She supposed the little store—really just some shelves Levi had put up in one corner of the front room—was the equivalent to Amy of what a television would be to an *Englisch* child, except the store brought in a small stream of cash.

Maddy joined them on the porch. "I'm glad you're home. Rose is down in the back worse than usual, and the restaurant gave her permission to see if I could come in and take her place. Do you mind?" Maddy worked at Mrs. Yoder's Kitchen a few hours a week, and the income she brought in was very much appreciated.

Claire sat on the porch swing, took off her shoes, and massaged the arch of her right foot. Standing for hours, helping a laboring mother-to-be, took its toll. "If you like, as soon as Flora has a short rest, it would do you good to get out."

At that moment, little two-year-old Daniel toddled in from his favorite napping place, the front-room couch. He did not like being tucked away upstairs in his bed because he was too afraid of missing something. He reminded her of a hummingbird, buzzing here and there all day, involved in everything, until he would suddenly stop and nap, and then get up and start buzzing around again.

"And how is my Danny?" she asked, as he climbed up onto her lap for a quick cuddle.

He held up one little finger with a Band-Aid on it.

"Ah, you put your finger where you should not?"

Maddy laughed. "No, I nicked myself on a knife and when he saw me putting a Band-Aid on my cut, he had to have one, too."

Claire kissed the nonexistent hurt. Oh, how she loved this child that she had come so close to losing!

Daniel, having received all the attention he desired for now, clambered off her lap, scooted carefully down the porch steps, and was off and running in the front yard. One of the chickens had gotten out, and Daniel thought it was his duty to catch it. The chicken thought otherwise.

"Shouldn't the boys and Sarah be home from school by now?" Claire asked.

Amy looked up from the swirls of her calligraphy practice. "Albert and Jesse brought Sarah home and then went back to help the teacher clear some big limbs that fell yesterday during that thunderstorm."

Twelve-year-old Albert, stalwart and steady, could be trusted with as much responsibility as most adults. He would watch out for Jesse, who, at ten, with his quicksilver laughter and tendency to be distracted by a passing butterfly, was not quite as trustworthy. Fortunately, Albert would watch out for his little brother and Sarah.

"I am pleased they are being helpful, but I wish they were home."

The sweeping finished, Maddy hung the broom in its wooden holder in a corner of the porch.

"They are obedient children, and will be careful, as you have taught them."

"Oh, I trust the boys, but you never know when a car might come around a curve too quickly."

"Then we will trust the Lord with their safety," Maddy reminded her.

She needed the reminder. The older she got, the more protective she felt about her family. She had seen enough bad things happen in her forty-four years that she had lost the blind optimism of her youth.

"Where is Sarah now?"

"Grace came by to get her," Amy said.

"Grace?"

Claire was not thrilled with Levi's choice of a wife. Grace

was a good person, but . . . she was *Englisch*. "What did she want with Sarah?"

"She said that she was learning how to bake cookies from scratch today and needed a child to practice on."

"Well, Sarah won't mind that," Claire said.

"Yes . . . if she does not come home with a tummy ache."

The expression on Maddy's face was studiously innocent, but Claire hid a smile. Her niece's gentle dig at the quality of Grace's cooking was as close as the sweet girl would ever come to saying anything negative about someone.

"Grace tries to embrace our culture," Claire said. "It's a shame she will not go all the way and actually become one of us."

"She tries so hard to act Amish, without becoming Amish, Amy and I have made up a new name for her."

"Oh?"

"We call her our Old Order *Englisch* relative."

Claire chuckled. "That well describes our Grace."

"She sent over some beef stew this morning with Levi."

"Have you eaten any of it?"

Maddy paused. "I thought perhaps I would wait. I would hate not to share Grace's efforts with the rest of the family."

"Ah. You prefer that we all face it together. Who knows, perhaps it has turned out well this time."

"One can hope."

Now that all of her chicks were accounted for, Claire could relax. She knew where each of her children was, exactly what they were doing, and all was well.

Six was such a nice, full number of children with which to fill a home. She hoped she would never have to live in a house that did not ring with the sound of children's laughter.

"I need to go inside, change my clothes, and shower," Claire said.

She found herself savoring the word *shower*. It had been only a little over a year since Levi put in plumbing for her. Leaving the conservative Swartzentruber Amish sect for the Old Order Amish had been an agonizing decision, but it had allowed some amazingly welcome additions to her life—like a bathroom, and a windshield on her buggy for when it rained.

"Supper is on the stove," Maddy said. "I made chicken stew."

"If your hands prepared it," Claire said, "I know it will be wonderful good."

She had started up the stairs to her room, when she heard a man's voice on the front porch. It was the kind of voice that sounded rough, as though ruined by too many years of smoking cigarettes, and it held no hint of the Germanic lilt of her people.

She did not mind the women tourists who stopped. They were almost always polite and considerate, but a lone man worried her.

The shower would have to wait until the man was safely gone. It was comforting to know that Levi was only a few yards away, in the workshop.

She hurried into the front room as Amy wheeled herself into the house. A tall man with short, salt-and-pepper hair held the door for her. This was the person she had seen at Mrs. Yoder's a few days earlier.

"Can I help you?" she asked.

The moment the stranger saw her, his expression changed. There was a look of recognition there that disturbed her.

Once, long ago, when she was a young woman, she had received many unwanted glances from men. Now, as a middle-aged Amish woman, she was used to being overlooked, nearly invisible, which was something she fervently welcomed. No decent Amish woman wanted to attract the notice of an *Englisch* man.

In spite of the recent scars, the man still somehow managed to be attractive. He was well built and held himself straight, but she did not like the pallor that she saw coming over him. When sweat suddenly popped out on his forehead, the healer in her grew concerned.

"Are you all right?" she asked. "You do not look well."

"I'm—I'm sorry." He dropped into the nearest chair. "I've only been out of the hospital a few days. I honestly thought I was stronger than this."

From the looks of him, she was half afraid this strange man was about to faint.

"Put your head down." She was no longer afraid of him. A man so weak he couldn't stand up was not a threat. He leaned over, both elbows on his knees.

"Shrapnel." He answered a question she had not asked.

Ah. That explained much. This man was a soldier, as she had thought two days ago when she'd seen him at Mrs. Yoder's.

She remembered his limp—it was his left leg that he favored—and the way he struggled to extract some bills from his wallet with damaged hands. In fact, in her opinion, she remembered him just a little *too* well. Why would she bother to memorize so many details about an *Englisch* man?

Then he slumped and completely lost consciousness. She found herself bearing the full weight of this stranger, trying to keep him from hitting his face on the linoleum of her front room floor.

Maddy walked into the front room, ready to go work for Rose, and stopped dead. "What's going on?"

"Get Levi, Maddy. Quick! We have *Druwwel*."

"Levi," Maddy yelled as she ran out the door, "come quick! We have trouble!"

chapter FOUR

Tom awoke, disoriented, in a room as bare of decoration as an army barracks. More bare, actually. Sometimes there were pinups in a barracks.

A dark blue curtain was swagged to one side of the window in front of him. He moved his head slightly to see where he was. That slight movement brought an angel to his side.

Not an angel, of course. He blinked to clear his head. An Amish woman in a light blue dress and a white head covering.

The fog cleared a little. This wasn't just any Amish woman. It was Claire. She held a pill bottle in front of him. "How many of these did you take?"

He squinted at the bottle, trying to remember. "Four."

"When?"

"Maybe a half hour ago. On my way here."

"That's more than double the dose." Claire's voice was laced with disapproval.

"I'm sorry." He tried to push himself up off the couch that he had no memory of lying down upon. "I'll go now."

Yet again, this was not the sort of situation in which he wanted to apologize for that fateful night. Not like this, lying on his back, barely able to string two thoughts together.

"You"—she looked at the pill bottle label—"Mr. Tom

Miller, passed out cold in my front room and scared me and my girls out of our wits. I'm trying to decide whether or not my son should take you to the hospital."

"No, please," he said. "I'll be fine."

To prove it, he gave a great effort and sat up. He intended to go straight into a standing position, but all he could manage before succumbing to the dizziness again was to push himself upright. It didn't last. He found himself sliding back down onto the pillows.

The last thing he needed was to be taken to the hospital for what would be marked as an accidental drug overdose.

Her voice softened. "How long ago did you eat?"

He thought about it. "Last night."

"*Ach.*" She clicked her tongue. "An empty stomach and morphine is not a good combination. You will have some soup now."

Even in his misery, he smiled at the take-charge tone in her voice. She didn't ask if he would like some soup. She told him that he was going to have some.

Claire had always been a little bossy—but only for the good of others. He and his older brother, Matthew, thought it was cute. Matthew, already a man, had delighted in her while Tom quietly and painfully worshipped from afar—as only a teenaged boy could.

The young girl he had met outside on the porch now maneuvered her wheelchair to a spot near the couch and peered down at him. "Hi. I'm Amy. You are a first, you know. We almost had a woman give birth in our kitchen once, but we never had a tourist faint in our front room." She paused for a breath. "What happened to your face?"

"Leave the man alone, Amy," Claire called from another room from which he could hear the clatter of dinnerware. "I am sure he does not feel like answering your questions right now."

He turned his head. Through a connecting doorway, he saw Claire busy in the kitchen, an older girl at her side. Both were bustling about, lighting the gas stove, opening a mason jar of what looked like vegetable soup, slicing bread. His almost-sister-in-law had changed a little. Her blond hair, what he could see of it, had streaks of gray. Her body had grown slightly heavier—perhaps with childbearing.

As his head cleared further, he noted that Claire was barefoot, and her skirt stopped several inches above her ankles. This was a surprise. No Swartzentruber Amish woman showed that much skin. They wore their dresses completely down to the tops of their shoes, and the fabric was darker and heavier. Claire's dress was light blue, and the material thinner. He glanced down at the floor. Linoleum. It even had a small pattern. No Swartzentruber church would allow something that fancy. It was wooden floors for them. Period. Even the finish used on the wood floors was prescribed.

Either the Swartzentruber Amish had drastically changed their ways or she had become Old Order Amish. That was practically unthinkable. The ultraconservative Swartzentrubers considered the Old Order Amish too modern even to have fellowship with them. If Claire had become Old Order Amish, that meant that she would have been excommunicated by the church where she had grown up.

"Did you get hold of your wife, Levi?" she called from the kitchen.

"Yes," a man's voice answered from a place near Tom's feet. "Grace was at the grocery store with Sarah, but she should be here any minute."

Tom had to raise his head slightly to see who had spoken. It was a familiar-looking young man sitting in a chair with a rosy-cheeked toddler on his lap. He thought there was the look of his brother, Matthew, in Levi's features, but it had been a long time since he'd seen his brother, and it wasn't as though he had any photographs to keep the memories fresh.

Not that he didn't have clear memories of Matthew. The last night of Matthew's life was emblazoned in his mind in ways that made him wish he *could* have stuffed it in a photo album and shoved it in a drawer somewhere, instead of having it lodged forever in his brain.

"I am Levi Troyer," the young man said. "We are pleased to see you come back to consciousness. My wife will be here, soon. She is a nurse practitioner and will know what to do with you."

"Thank you . . . Levi."

Tom knew exactly who Levi was. He had thought about that little boy ever since he had read about his existence in *The Budget,* the Amish newspaper printed in Sugarcreek, Ohio, which collected news from all over the world from various Amish and Mennonite church districts. Every now and then, a copy would catch up with him, and he would read every word. Each issue was a bittersweet experience, giving him a small window into what was going on back home. *The Budget* took the place of the letters from home that were never written or received.

When he read about the birth of his brother's child, he was surprised at first. Matthew had not mentioned a pregnancy to him. Chances were the pregnancy was still so new that even Matthew didn't know. It was possible Claire also had not known then.

For a long time after that, all he could think about was how hard it must have been for Claire to bear a child out of wedlock exactly nine months after a wedding that, thanks to him, had not taken place. Matthew had been killed around four o'clock on the morning of what was supposed to have been their wedding day. He and Claire would have said their vows about noon. The girl had been only eight hours away from being a married woman.

Pregnancy was tough on any woman. He remembered the morning sickness and swollen ankles his mother had endured with his little sister, Faye, but he hated to think about how hard an unwed pregnancy must have been on Claire, stranded as she was within the ultraconservative Swartzentruber sect. He hoped that, under the circumstances, their people had been understanding.

Several years later, another copy of *The Budget* mentioned that she had married Abraham Shetler, who owned the farm next door to his father's. This had been as great a surprise as the announcement that his brother had fathered a child.

He had known Abraham, but he'd never particularly liked the man. It surprised him that Claire had chosen to marry him. Unless—and this thought made him feel half sick—she been offered no other marital option.

He would have come home and married her himself if he'd had the slightest inkling that she would have considered it. The problem was, he knew she would never consent to live the life of a military wife, and there was no chance that he would ever go back to living the life of a Swartzentruber. He had loved Claire Keim as long as he could remember—but the thought of going back to being a Swartzentruber was unbearable. He'd seen and experienced too much in the intervening years. He could not possibly put himself back into that tightly closed box.

After that, he didn't read *The Budget* anymore.

"Geili!" the little boy on Levi's lap demanded. *"Geili!"*

"You want another horsey ride already?" Levi chuckled. "You will give me leg cramps."

Levi sat the toddler astride his right leg and began

pretend-trotting as he sang a nursery rhyme that Tom had forgotten existed.

> *Reide, reide Geili,*
> *halb Schtund de Meili,*
> *Geili schpringt da hivvel nuff*
> *Boomp—fallscht du nunner!*

Tom closed his eyes. It seemed like a hundred years ago that he'd been trotted on his father's knee to the words of exactly the same nursery rhyme.

> Ride, ride a horsey,
> Half an hour a mile.
> Horsey runs up the hill,
> Bump—you fall down!

As he lay in Claire's house, with her family nearby, he wondered if he should tell her who he was yet. Like her sister, Rose, there had been no hint of recognition in Claire's voice or eyes. It was strange to know that he could walk among his people with complete anonymity if he wished.

Funny, he had always assumed his people would recognize him if he ever came home, but how could they? He had grown another three inches after he left home, and gained at least forty pounds of muscle after joining the Marines. Instead of the below-the-earlobes bowl haircut that every other Swartzentruber man wore, his hair was now cut close to the scalp. The shrapnel had left one side of his jaw permanently scarred. He knew that not even his voice was recognizable. The heat from the blast had left him with a permanent hoarseness.

There was every reason to believe that he could remain in the area without having to reveal his identity unless he chose. This was a novel idea. And tempting. He had planned to move on after making his apologies. Perhaps he wouldn't have to.

Maybe he could go see his father without being tossed out on his ear after a few sentences. Perhaps the physical changes were profound enough that his own sister and *daed* would not recognize him.

His *daed*. There were so many mixed feelings and emotions tied up with Jeremiah Troyer.

"It should have been you!" That was the sentence that had reverberated down the hallways of his life. "It should have been you."

Why did *Daed* have to say those words to his sixteen-year-old son? No parent should say that to a boy at the grave site of his brother. No boy should ever have to hear it, no matter what the circumstances.

His father was right, of course. It should have been him who died that night. But *Daed* didn't have to destroy him when he was already riddled with guilt and grief over his brother's death.

The horsey ride now over, the toddler began to fidget on his big brother's lap.

"I think it might be time to get this little one to a bathroom," Levi said. "Our Daniel has not been long without diapers." He hurried out of the room, holding the child at arm's length.

Claire came in with a cup of hot soup. "You should sip this slowly until it cools."

Up close, without a hint of makeup, Claire was still one of the most beautiful women he had ever seen. She had the sort of classic features that even a twenty-seven-year absence could not erase.

As he studied her face, he was glad to see laugh lines around her eyes. It gave him pleasure to think that she had had reason to laugh over the years.

He would have told her right then and there who he was, were it not for the presence of Amy and the older girl. This conversation, when it took place, needed time and privacy. He did not know how much anger she might still hold against him. The Amish were a forgiving bunch, but he wasn't sure even Claire was that holy. For a young Swartzentruber girl to raise an out-of-wedlock child would have been unbelievably difficult. It would be impossible for there not to be a deep well of resentment toward him within her.

"What happened?" She inspected the bad side of his face. "To cause all this damage?"

"I was in Afghanistan and got too close to a suicide bomber."

Levi came back in holding a much more content Daniel.

"A suicide bomber hurt this man." Claire addressed her son, using the form of German peculiar to Holmes County Amish that many people referred to as Pennsylvania Deutsch. No doubt she assumed Tom could not understand a word. "What is a suicide bomber?"

"That is when someone places a bomb on their own body," Levi responded in German. "And then detonate it. They turn their bodies into a sort of weapon. Grace told me all about it. They do that sort of thing in the Middle East. Tom must be military."

"*Ach.* Another military one!"

Tom understood every word of the German they were speaking, but he gave no sign.

"They are coming out of the walls, these soldiers," Claire said. "So many returning from that dangerous place—that Afghanistan."

This comment made absolutely no sense to Tom. Holmes County wasn't exactly a military destination.

Levi immediately took offense. "Good thing for *you* that they are, *Maam*!"

Now Tom was totally confused, and it wasn't entirely the fault of the pain meds.

"That is not the point," Claire said. "It is not an easy thing to have an *Englisch* daughter-in-law who cannot cook, sew, or drive a buggy. Being a soldier is not a good training ground for a wife."

"No," Levi said evenly. "But she can suture a wound, cool the fever in a sick child, and she saved your life and Daniel's."

"That is not much comfort when my oldest son's belly is crying out for a decent pot of bean soup."

Levi, exasperated, suddenly switched to English. "Elizabeth makes an excellent bean soup, mother. I don't go hungry."

"Your wife's name is Elizabeth?" Tom felt safe in participating now that they were speaking English.

"Oh, no, no." Claire also switched to English. "Grace is Levi's wife. Her grandmother's name is Elizabeth and she lives with Levi and Grace."

"Actually," Levi said, "we live with her. The house belongs to Elizabeth."

"You could have lived here with me," Claire said.

"And you would have bossed Grace around like you do me—and she would have bolted."

"See? A good Amish wife—you would not have to worry about her running away."

"If I had married anyone except Grace, I wouldn't have cared if they *did* run away."

Tom got the feeling that this was a conversation that had taken place many times between these two. Neither Amy nor the other girl was paying any attention to it.

Claire gave up on this particular argument and turned her attention to looking out the window. "Albert and Jesse should be home by now."

"They are helping their teacher, and you know that Rhoda will watch after them," Levi said. "That girl is part mother hen. She's almost worse than you at keeping track of her chicks."

"I hope Rhoda gets married when I turn sixteen," Amy said. "I would like to teach at that school. I think I would be good at it."

"You would," Levi said. "But I've heard that Bessie Mueller is next in line for the job, if Harold Keim doesn't get around to proposing to her first."

Tom had forgotten this aspect of being Amish. They were so intimately connected and had so many people in their lives, it was nearly impossible for an outsider to keep track of all the names they tossed around as a matter of course. His head had begun to throb, and he rubbed his temples. He was starting to feel worse.

"I'm sorry," Claire said. "Here we are, talking about people you do not know, and you are not well. Are you sure you do not want Levi to take you to the hospital?"

"No. No hospital." He tried to get up again. "A few more minutes, and I'll . . . leave."

"You cannot drive. I am sorry, but you cannot. Where are you staying?"

"I have a room at Hotel Millersburg."

"Well, then. Open up, please." She surprised Tom by spooning a mouthful of hot vegetable soup into his mouth.

"Were you headed somewhere?" Levi asked. "Or was Holmes County your actual destination?"

"I—I used to live around here. This seemed like a good, quiet place to come while I heal." At that moment, a young, pregnant woman burst through the door. She was about Levi's height, with blondish hair twisted up in a clip, wearing a long, plain, maternity shift-like dress. He was no expert in pregnancy, but she didn't seem to be very far along. A small, blond Amish girl trailed behind her with a half-eaten cookie in each hand. The little girl looked exactly the way he remembered Claire at that age.

In spite of the woman's matronly appearance, there was an air of professionalism about her. No doubt this was Levi's wife. That would make her his niece by marriage. His family was getting larger by the minute, even though no one but him knew it.

"Hello," she said. "You must be the tourist my husband called me about. My name is Grace, and I'm a nurse practitioner. If you don't mind, I'd like to check your vitals."

"I don't mind."

"Good." She dropped a specially made basket onto a chair, went to the kitchen sink, and thoroughly washed her hands. Then she pulled a clean dishcloth out of a drawer, dried her hands, reached into the basket, and drew on a pair of rubber gloves.

"Levi says you're military." She bent to examine his face, touching the still-healing wounds with her fingertips. "Looks like you took some hits over there."

"A few."

"These are not completely healed. What did you do? Drive yourself all the way from Walter Reed?"

"Yes."

She pulled a thermometer out of her bag and stuck it in his mouth. "Do you have a name?" He started to take the thermometer out to answer, but she hooked his dog tags out from beneath his shirt collar.

"Captain Tom Miller," she read. She glanced at his face. "I knew a Tom Miller once. A helicopter pilot. Were you stationed at Bagram by any chance?"

He nodded.

"I was there, too, for a while and I remember your name," she said. "You flew on several medevac missions when we needed a gunship escort."

Now Claire and Levi's tense conversation made sense. Levi's wife had also been in the military. He could only guess at the drama that had taken place here before the marriage. Having an *Englisch* daughter-in-law was every Amish mother's nightmare. Evidently, from what Levi had said to his mother, Grace had been involved in saving Claire's life in some way.

He tried to remember seeing Grace's face, but there had been so many troops and faces over the years. Thousands.

She took the thermometer out of his mouth and glanced at it. "One hundred two point four," she said. A look passed between her and Claire.

"He must have an infection," Claire said. "That is not good."

"No." Grace put the thermometer away and pulled off her gloves. "It is most definitely not good. I can get him some antibiotics, but I don't think it's wise for him to be left alone right now."

Strange. He knew he felt bad, but had not known he felt *that* bad. Perhaps the relief of being home again, or his nervousness over seeing Claire again, had kept him from realizing how sick he was.

"Do you have any family here?" Claire asked.

"No." It was true. He had no family here—at least not in the sense that Claire meant—someone who would be willing to take him off their hands.

Help from his father didn't bear thinking about. The old man would never accept him back. Not unless he showed up in a windowless buggy with an untrimmed beard and a commitment to living the rest of his life in the 1800s.

Grace came to a decision. "Levi, I want to put Captain Miller in the downstairs bedroom at our house for a few days. He needs care, but not badly enough to take him to the ER. At least not yet. He just needs someone to keep an eye on him."

Levi frowned. "You think taking a stranger into our home is a good idea?"

"Yes, Levi. This man is no stranger. His name was well known to everyone on the base. He saved many lives with his skill and courage. One of them was mine." Grace pulled off her gloves. "Probably more than once. Tom Miller could get into and out of places lesser pilots could not. Our medevac helicopter was not armed, and it made us sitting ducks more than once. When bullets started flying, we knew that pilots like Tom would come in with guns blazing, buying us those extra thirty seconds we needed to get a wounded soldier loaded. His crew laid down gunfire more than once to give us a chance to pull combat soldiers out without becoming casualties ourselves. Helping this man isn't just the right thing to do—it is an honor and a privilege."

"I have a room in Millersburg," Tom mumbled. He was feeling worse and worse. "I did not come here to be cared for."

"And how lonely is that?" Grace said. "You can be our guest for a few days and heal, or you can go it alone until you end up hooked to IVs in some veterans' hospital. I know you're a tough guy, Tom, but I strongly suggest you stay with us."

"Yes." Levi rallied from his surprise at Grace's making such a snap decision. "You must come home with us."

Tom no longer had the strength to argue. Staying with his nephew and his nephew's nurse-wife for a few days would beat lying alone and unconscious on the floor of his hotel room.

"I will pay you."

"No, you won't," Grace said. "But Levi will need the key to your room so he can gather your things and check you out. Do you have it on you?"

He fished it out of his pocket and handed it to her. Even that small gesture took effort. No, it was evident that he did not need to drive back to the hotel.

"That poor man," Amy said as soon as everyone had gone. "He has been hurt very bad. I think in many ways."

Claire agreed, and in spite of the annoyance she frequently felt toward her son's wife, she was enormously grateful for Grace's presence today.

"What man?" Ten-year-old Jesse and his brother clattered into the kitchen, home from school.

Claire was always amazed at how disheveled this particular little boy could get in so few hours. The clean clothes she had sent him to school in this morning looked like he had rolled around in the school yard all day instead of sitting at a desk and then helping the teacher pick up windblown limbs.

"We had a wounded helicopter pilot fall down on our floor today," Amy told him, all important with her firsthand eyewitness information. "Grace and Levi took him home with them."

"A helicopter pilot?" Jesse was entirely too impressed for Claire's comfort. "A real one? A man who flies these things?"

At that, he began to whirl around the room with his arms outstretched, making putt-putt-putt noises.

"That will be enough," Claire admonished him. "We do not need for you to knock something over. If you think you want to be a helicopter, you must go outside."

Twelve-year-old Albert was uninterested. He had other things on his mind. "May I go check on my chickens now?"

he asked. "I want to see if that new feed I'm trying has made a difference in their egg output."

"Of course," Claire said. With some relief, she noted that Albert's clothes looked exactly as they had when she sent him out the door this morning. He would probably be able to wear them again tomorrow.

Albert had a mind only for his animals and for learning how to care for the farm. She felt at ease in her mind about Albert's future. He would be content with his life as long as he could plow and plant and have livestock to care for.

Jesse was another story. Jesse, with those big ears of his, wanted to know everything.

It was good that Tom was at Levi's and no longer in her front room. He and Grace could talk about soldier things to their hearts' content. She did not want that sort of talk around her children—especially Jesse, who was entirely too suggestible. It was bad enough that Amy had to hear about such things as suicide bombers!

How could such things exist? How could the human mind come up with a terrible idea like that? Apart from *The Budget,* she read no newspapers or worldly magazines, nor did she watch television or listen to the radio.

This dribble of toxic knowledge that had come into her life today had made her especially grateful for the wisdom of their Amish leadership, which forbade such things. She did not want thoughts of war touching her children.

"I'm hungry." Jesse had lost interest in pretending to be a helicopter.

"Of course you are," Claire said. "You are a growing boy. There is some beef stew in the refrigerator. Ask Maddy to heat it up for you."

Claire felt only a slight twinge of guilt about suggesting the stew for Jesse's after-school snack. Grace's last attempt at stew had gotten scraped out into the pig's trough, after dark, when she thought there was no chance Grace would see or know. Her daughter-in-law had a fondness for adding strange spices to her cooking. Perhaps Jesse would be too hungry to notice.

"You may have as much as you want," she encouraged. "You do not have to hold back."

While Maddy served Jesse, Claire went upstairs to her bedroom. She had not slept for a very long time. Not only had she helped Kathleen have her baby, she had sat up all night with Amanda Hershberger, who turned out to be having false contractions.

She changed out of her good birthing dress and into an old choring dress. She had chosen the birthing dress material, designed and sewn it with much thought. It was a lighter blue than she would have normally worn—an Amish compromise for a white nurse's uniform. She had also taken the liberty of modifying her church's prescribed dress pattern slightly by setting in loose, elbow-length sleeves instead of full-length, so her sleeves did not get in the way when she needed to catch a baby. Her apron was white, and she always took an extra one along with her when she attended a birth. She had made three of these outfits, because she never knew how many times she might get called out in a week, and she did not want to get caught without a clean birthing dress and apron.

The washing of clothes was more complicated for her and her girls than for the *Englisch*. She could not simply toss a dress into a washer and then a dryer and have it come out ready to wear with no thought to whether it was raining or the sun was shining. She had to plan ahead.

Her bed beckoned. There was nothing she wanted more right now than to fall into it and sleep for a long, long time, but she could not. She had chores. Always so many chores. With Abraham gone and Levi having both farms on his shoulders now, she tried to help him as much as possible. It was a heavy load along with the midwifery and the ever-present work that went with raising a family.

She looked at the bed again. Oh, it was enticing! The soft pillow, the snowy sheets, the lovely, worn wedding-ring quilt passed down from Abraham's grandmother. It would feel so good to lie down and close her eyes for a few blessed minutes.

Perhaps if she could catch a short nap, she would have the energy to push through the rest of the evening.

No. She shook it off. The time to sleep would come to-night. Not a minute of daylight hours could be wasted. Approximately two hundred people would be having church at her house in the late summer, and with all she had to do, she needed every spare minute to get ready for it. Walls had to be washed. Drawers turned out and sorted. The kitchen could use a new coat of paint, as could the girls' upstairs bedroom. The garden needed to be weeded, the yard raked, the barn cleaned . . . the list was endless. She wanted to plant several more flower beds, enough to make an impressive display. For the past two years, since Abraham's death, her church had not expected her to host, and with everything else she had to do, she had relaxed a little too much about keeping up her house.

She would wait until nightfall to rest—and hope that no one else went into labor tonight!

chapter FIVE

T om's fever did not abate for several hours that night. He tossed and turned on the bed in Levi and Grace's downstairs guest room until he barely knew when he was awake and when he was asleep. Scenes from his past found their way into his dreams, becoming nightmares so realistic, it was as though he were reliving each one in detail.

The worst one of all involved his final day in Afghanistan. *"A towering confection of culinary perfection,"* Vicki Kenworth texted him. *"Deep, rich chocolate with enough coffee-flavored caramel frosting to make it decadent."*

Vicki had been a pastry chef before coming to work for USAID. If she said his birthday cake was perfection, it was. In an often brutal and disheartening environment, Vicki was a bright ray of decency and kindness.

He pulled up to the gate of Green Village in Kabul and was passed through on foot by the Nepalese guards. The name of the compound was a joke. Like the rest of Afghanistan, there was little that was "green" about Green Village. The best that could be said about it was that it was well guarded.

As Tom strode toward Vicki's office, he saw George, an old Marine buddy who had been hired to help train the Afghan army. George sat in the shade of an office building, his chair tilted back against the cooler side of the wall.

Vicki stepped out of the office building where she worked and gave him a big smile. "Happy birthday, Tom. The coffee is ready. You two go on in. I'm heading to the bakery for the cake. George has been eager to help you celebrate."

"I'm touched, George," Tom joked.

"We're talking birthday cake, buddy," George said. "I'd celebrate Groundhog Day for a slice of whatever it is that Vicki's concocted."

"Hey, guys, check out my party clothes." Vicki turned around in a circle so they could get the full impact of her outfit. "I dressed up for the occasion."

She wore garish orange slacks and a bright pink blouse. Oversize sparkly earrings peeked out from behind her shoulder-length blond hair. A multicolored scarf was draped around her neck. It was a deliberately silly outfit, but it was nice to rest his eyes on a woman wearing something other than desert camouflage and olive green.

"Y'all go on into my office," she said in that sweet, Southern Tennessee accent of hers. "I'll be right back."

They found that she printed out a banner saying HAPPY BIRTHDAY TOM and attached it to the wall of her office. Somewhere, she'd managed to dig up three sad-looking balloons, which hung from the ceiling.

"That boyfriend of hers back home is a lucky man," George observed.

"I hope she gets to go home soon," Tom said. "That girl does not belong here."

They'd barely walked inside her office when there was a deafening explosion. The ground shook beneath their feet, the walls of the office building trembled, and he heard screams.

He awoke with a start. His teeth were chattering and he was chilled to the bone. Where was he? Whose bed was he lying in? This was not Green Village.

A pregnant woman materialized and tried to give him a pill. He wouldn't take it from her. She disappeared and then came in again, wiped his arm with something cold, and gave him an injection. He tried to fight it, but he was so weak. A man held him still so she could do this thing, and it shamed him that he was too helpless to fight.

"You go on to bed," the man said to the woman. "I will call if you are needed."

"The meds should take hold in a few minutes," she said. "If this fever doesn't break soon, I'll want to get him to the hospital where I can start an IV."

"You rest." There was kindness in the man's voice. "I will watch over him."

The man had his brother's face. That was strange. Matthew was dead. He knew this for a fact, because he had been the one who killed him.

The shot began to take effect, and he started to sink into a spiraling oblivion, until the nightmare started up again. He thrashed around, trying to regain consciousness. Then, when he could no longer fight and began to slip back into that dark place, the movie that had been playing started back up again—like a movie projector over which he had no control.

He had spent enough time in the Middle East to know that an explosion that big could only mean one thing—a VBIED—a vehicle borne improvised explosive device, better known to the world and the media as a car bomb.

Glass shattered all around them. George dropped his *Field & Stream* on the floor as they rushed to the window. A black cloud rose from the front gate—the very gate through which Tom had walked minutes before.

The compound had been compromised. Sirens wailed. Noncombatants were heading to safety.

"Move it, man!" George shoved Tom out the door. "Let's get inside a bunker. You aren't gonna do any good with that little peashooter sidearm you're carrying, and neither am I."

The compound had erupted with more explosions. AK-47s were rat-a-tatting all around them. Tom could hear grenades and suicide bombers detonating. George was right—he needed to get himself to the bunker. He was a pilot, not a ground pounder. Those Nepalese guards were in charge of protecting the compound and they were a lot better trained at hand-to-hand combat than he.

The problem was, where was Vicki? The girl was a civilian. She was not combat trained. Even worse, the bakery where she had gone was near the front of the compound—next door to the main explosion.

"We have to find Vicki!" Tom yelled.

"Right. Let me lead," George responded. "I have more ground combat experience."

Ducking low, they headed directly toward the bakery. Tom kept scanning the personnel scurrying past him—hoping he'd see her.

"Here!" A German policeman tossed both of them AK-47s from an armload he was handing out.

They passed several bunkers where office workers, technicians, and experts in everything from carpentry to proper waste management were sheltering. Even though none of these people was military, all the bunkers had guns pointing outward, ready to be the last line of defense if the guarded perimeter did not hold.

As they passed each one, Tom shouted for Vicki, hoping she'd made it to safety. Each bunker led them closer and closer to the intense fighting at the front gate.

They reached the bakery. Its sides were riddled with bullet holes.

He made a run for it, dove headfirst through the bakery door, and hugged the floor. George slammed the door behind them for the little protection it afforded.

He saw a stainless steel work table topped with a chocolate cake that had been blown to bits. Vicki was lying, motionless, in her festive orange slacks and pink blouse on a floor littered with cake. He checked for a pulse. It was weak, but it was there.

Tom did not know how long the fighting continued. He remembered only pieces of what happened later.

He had a memory of running with her in his arms, carrying her to the safety of the nearest bunker. He saw a Taliban fighter step around a wall. He was wearing a suicide vest and the stupid grin from the drugs they had to take in order to have the courage to go through with their grisly task. George, still leading, was slightly ahead of him.

Later, he had a vague recollection of two German medics working over him. He tried to crawl to Vicki's body, but the medics held him down. One punched a shot of something into his arm. Slowly, his will to fight faded.

When he awoke, he was being flown to the States. George, they told him, was wounded but stable. Vicki had not survived.

All because of his birthday cake.

The damage to his body was great. The damage to his soul was greater. The black hole in his heart grew until he did not know if he could bear it. He cursed the Taliban for being so brutal, God for allowing this terrible thing to happen, and himself for allowing that sweet girl to bake a birthday cake in the midst of a war zone. For three days, the hospital staff quietly placed him on suicide watch.

• • •

"How is he?" the pregnant woman asked. "Did he sleep?"

"Yes, but it was restless," the man said. "I would not have wanted to be inside his mind tonight. I do not think it would be a good place to be."

"There are probably wounds within him that we cannot see, Levi."

"I think his fever may have broken," the man said. "He began to sweat a few minutes ago."

"Open, please." She stuck a thermometer in his mouth.

"Yes, it has begun to go down," she said a few moments later. "When he fully awakens, if he's strong enough, it would be a good idea for him to take a shower while I change those sweaty sheets. Will you help him, Levi?"

"For a man who saved my wife's life," the man said, "I would do much."

Levi had to help prop him up while the shower washed the dried sweat from his body. The clean sheets felt fresh against his skin. He was as weak as a kitten, but he thought the worst might be over. How grateful he was for the kindness of his nephew and his wife, as well as Elizabeth, who would come in from time to time and put a hand on his forehead, a gesture he remembered his mother doing when he was a small child.

His sleep, when it came this time, was healing. For once, there were no nightmares. The movie forever reeling through his subconscious had finally shut off. For now.

As Claire sorted laundry in the dim early-morning light, she was deeply troubled in her soul. The man who had passed out in her front room yesterday was not a man easily forgotten.

She'd seen the haunted look of near-desperation in his eyes when he'd fully awakened, and yet he had tried his best to refuse help. Had Levi and Grace not insisted, he would have tried to drive himself to the hotel in his feverish state. Lord only knows what might have happened to him.

The long scars along his left jawline and beneath his eye spoke of some serious reconstructive surgery. The scarring on his hands had been extensive—as though he'd thrown up his hands to protect his face.

He had lived in such an alien world to her, a world entirely different from the one in which she lived, and yet the man had not seemed foreign to her at all. There had been a strange, visceral feeling of recognition that she could not explain.

This could not be. Her circle of *Englisch* acquaintances was very small. Grace and Elizabeth at the farm next door. A few tourists who dropped by to purchase something from Amy's little store. The *Englisch* driver, Annette, whom she hired from time to time to drive her to clients homes too far away to be reached by buggy. A few salesclerks at the *Englisch* stores where she shopped. Nowhere had she ever met anyone remotely like this Tom Miller.

She had never experienced this kind of familiarity before, but she sorted through the *Englisch* people she had known, trying to figure out why Tom seemed known to her, and she got so lost in her head that she tossed a pair of Jesse's denims onto a pile of whites and had to grab them back out. This would never do. She had too many responsibilities to allow herself to be so distracted as to nearly ruin an entire load of clothes.

After starting the motor of her old Maytag wringer washer, she left the first load agitating, grabbed a notebook and pen, and sat on the back porch steps to start making a list of all the projects she needed to finish before the Sunday she was to host church. *That* ought to make her stop thinking about Levi and Grace's wounded soldier.

chapter SIX

T om sat in the swing on the back porch of Levi and Grace's home. It was his third day here. That first bad night, he had been barely conscious. The next morning and all day yesterday, he had been conscious but too weak to be on his own. This morning, he had regained enough strength to go back to the hotel. It was four-thirty in the morning, too early for the rest of the family to be up, too early to leave without saying good-bye, too early to simply drive away.

He had awakened at four and had taken Grace up on her invitation to make himself at home, by fixing a pot of coffee for himself and Levi, who would awaken at five.

He had also taken the liberty of scrambling some eggs and making toast for both himself and his nephew. Levi had done this for himself yesterday, but this morning, Tom had felt well enough to take over the job.

In the three days he had been here, he had decided that Levi, like Matthew, worked way too hard. He had also come to the conclusion that his brother's son was a good man. He was glad to know this because, to his utter surprise and shock, Tom had become a wealthy man a year earlier—a wealthy man with no heir.

For the past twelve months, his bank statements had

shown that he had more money than he could, in all good conscience, spend. At least not with his Spartan tastes. And it hadn't happened on a soldier's pay. A buddy of his had a computer geek for a little brother. The kid had a crazy idea about some sort of business he wanted to start that was connected to computers. Tom didn't know much about computers at the time, but he pooled some savings, along with four other unmarried Marines, to help the kid get his business off the ground.

Not one of them expected anything to come of it. From the beginning, he figured he was throwing away his hard-earned money. He, like the others, had just wanted to encourage the kid.

Three years later, the company took off like a rocket.

When the money started coming in, the other four men got out of the service as fast as possible. He didn't know what to do with himself if he wasn't flying, so he stayed, changed nothing, and the money had grown. Unlike the other four soldiers, he had no wife or children to spend it on.

He had pondered the possibility of buying a big house or a fancy car or a nice suit, or going on a long trip—but nothing he could think of had excited him all that much.

While lying in the hospital, it bothered him that if he died, the government would decide what to do with the money. He preferred making that decision himself. So far, the top contender was Levi.

He also liked what he saw of Grace. Like Levi, she also worked too hard. She would awaken at seven, have a carton of yogurt, and spend a full day in the ER at Pomerene Hospital.

Grace's grandmother, Elizabeth, would get up any old time she felt like it and eat anything from chocolate cake to leftover spaghetti for breakfast if she felt so inclined. He had seen her do this.

He would move on soon, but not quite yet. Being here and

getting to know his nephew felt like a gift from God. It had been a long, long time since he'd had family in his life. Now that he was close to his father's farm, he kept thinking about going to see him. It would not be an easy meeting. First he wanted to grow a little stronger.

For many years, he had not been what most people would consider a religious man. He had most definitely avoided serious commitment to any established church, but he still believed in God, and believed that sometimes God intervened in people's lives.

He had seen hundreds of military nurses come and go on various bases, in various countries over the years, so it wasn't too great a coincidence to find one married to his nephew—but still—he wondered if God had chosen to bring this about. If so, he was grateful. Claire had come by only twice, once with some homemade tomato soup, the next day with a rhubarb pie. She seemed in a hurry and didn't stay long. Not long enough to have a private conversation with her.

Elizabeth came out onto the back porch in her robe and slippers. "You're up early. Mind if I join you?"

"Not at all."

He liked Grace's grandmother. The old woman had wandered in and out of his room that first nightmarish night, and her presence had comforted him. Levi and Grace had felt alien, but as Elizabeth had clucked and worried over him, she had gotten mixed together in his mind with his own mother. When he had come fully awake, he'd been surprised to discover Elizabeth wearing a bright pink jogging suit and orange Crocs instead of an Amish dress and prayer *Kapp*.

"I see you set breakfast out for Levi." She sank down onto the wicker chair beside the swing. "You'll spoil the boy. Grace had just about gotten him trained to fix it for himself."

"I'm sure she needs her sleep," he said.

"It hasn't been an easy pregnancy." Elizabeth took a sip of coffee and made a face. "Is this some kind of special Marine coffee?"

"Is it too strong?"

"Too strong?" She opened her eyes wide and batted them a couple times. "Maybe a tad. I'm definitely awake now!"

He made a stab at conversation. "What are your plans for the day?"

"Plans?" Elizabeth contemplated. "Well . . . this morning I'm going to paint the upstairs bedroom and tear down that derelict corncrib out back. Then I think I'll do a few calisthenics and have lunch. After lunch, I plan to climb Mt. Everest, compete in a bathing beauty pageant, and run for Congress. What are your plans?"

Elizabeth was so deadpan as she said this, at first he'd thought that she was experiencing a little dementia, but eventually realized that her off-the-wall comments were part of Elizabeth's supersharp intellect.

"What am I doing?" He tried to answer along the same vein. "I thought I'd see if I could write another *War and Peace* this afternoon."

Elizabeth gave this comment consideration. "Your delivery is getting better, but you could stand to be more imaginative."

"Writing *War and Peace* isn't a good choice?"

"Too predictable and no real humor. Me entering a bathing beauty contest—now, *that's* funny."

"You're entering a bathing beauty contest?" Levi came out onto the porch with a plate of scrambled eggs in one hand and a cup of coffee in the other. He sounded confused. "What is a bathing beauty contest and why would you want to enter it?"

"For the scholarship, of course." She winked at Tom. "And world peace."

Levi shook his head and started shoveling food into his mouth. "I don't understand half of what you say, Elizabeth."

"I'm yanking your chain, Levi," Elizabeth said. "My real plans for the day are to finish the crossword puzzle I started last night, take a walk, nap, write a letter, take another nap, and finish a good book I started yesterday. Age has its rewards. What about you, Tom?"

"Now that my fever is gone, I thought I might walk to Amy's little store. I think I can manage a quarter mile, and if I remember right, I think there was some homemade fudge."

"That's one of Maddy's contributions," Elizabeth said. "Amy will probably try to sell you one of her poems, too."

"Amy writes poetry?"

"Reams of it. If you make a fuss over it, she'll be your BFF."

"BFF?"

"Best Friend Forever," Elizabeth said. "You need to keep up, Tom."

He thought this over. "I guess I could use a friend."

"Most of us can," Elizabeth agreed. "I think walking down to Amy's store would do you some good. She'll love the company, and whatever you buy will provide a small blessing to that family's bank account."

"They seemed to have quite a variety of signs out front."

"You can say that again. It started out with a few of Levi's baskets. Then Claire's nieces came to live with her, and it kind of mushroomed from there."

Levi, who had steadily been plowing his way through his plate of food, spoke up. "Amy wanted a way to sell her little cards, so I put a sign up for her. We didn't think there would be many people stopping, but tourists have caught on to the fact that buying some of the things they see advertised at private homes will give them a glimpse of Amish life they wouldn't get otherwise."

Elizabeth nodded. "That's true. Then, once they saw that people would stop for Amy's greeting cards, the children coaxed Levi into installing some shelves in a corner of the front room. Then they *all* got into act. That cluster of handmade signs at the end of the driveway represents quite a mixture of talents."

"It is good for children to work," Levi said as he drained the last dregs of his coffee cup. "Albert keeps chickens and sells fresh eggs. *Maam* taught Jesse how to forage for sassafras in the woods, and how to dry and package the root chips for a medicinal tea. Albert helps me with the beehives, and I let him sell whatever honey we can't use. Maddy keeps a supply of her homemade fudge ready, and sells quart jars of any extra produce she and *Maam* can. *Maam* taught Sarah how to make little pot holders, so now even Sarah is part of things."

"It sounds like a busy house."

Elizabeth broke in. "Oh, I just remembered. Maddy has recently started making those intricate prayer *Kapps* that all the Amish women wear. The mother of one of her girlfriends taught her how. She really has a knack."

"Daniel helps out, too," Levi said.

"I didn't know that," Elizabeth said. "What can a two-year-old contribute to the store?"

"Daniel's job is to be Amy's legs," Levi said. "He runs to get whatever item she needs. He takes great pride in it and she pays him a few cents each week. *Maam* gave him a jelly jar to keep his earnings in. It is good for the children to help out now that Abraham is gone."

That last sentence knocked the entire pleasant conversation completely out of Tom's head.

Abraham was gone? Claire's husband was dead? This fact had not come up even once in the past two days. He fought not to let it show how shaken he felt by this news.

"I'd better go. I'll be in the back field, and I'll have my cell phone on me if anyone needs me for anything," Levi called as he went out the door.

"Thank you, Levi," she said. "You are a very good boy."

Tom saw Elizabeth's eyes watch Levi as he left. She had a worried look on her face.

"Is something wrong?" he asked.

She turned her attention back to him. "Have you ever been married, Tom?"

"No."

"Then you have no way of knowing that in a new marriage there is almost always some little thing wrong."

"Why do you say that?"

"Levi and Grace had to jump a lot of hurdles to be together. They were in love almost from the moment they met. He didn't know it, and she didn't know it, but I could see it and it scared me. It was not possible for two people to come from two such different cultures and not have problems. He was Swartzentruber Amish. You can't find a stricter, or a more isolated sect among the Amish. And there was poor Grace, coming home to take care of me after my heart attack two years ago, never knowing that she was going to discover the man of her dreams living next door."

"What did they do?"

"Levi eventually decided to leave the church and they got married and lived happily ever after. At least that's the way it would be if it were in one of those romance novels Grace likes to read. Happily ever after." She snapped her fingers. "Just like that. Overcome the obstacles, get married, and life is rosy forever and ever. Those two didn't have a clue how hard it was going to be for them to carve out a marriage together."

"And they've been living here with you the whole time."

"Yes, they've been living here with me ever since. In spite

of the *Daadi Haus* Levi built for me last year, I can't help but notice how much they fuss at each other. It worries me."

"I'm sorry to hear that."

"He doesn't want her to work after the baby comes." She began to tick off items on her fingers. "It is positively unthinkable to him, raised in the Swartzentruber church, that his wife work outside the home after the baby comes. Grace is too good at what she does to walk away from it—besides, she earns a whole lot more than he does."

"I can see where that would be hard on a man."

"Which brings up another problem. He thinks the husband should be in complete control of the finances, because he thinks it's his job to take care of her. Grace is about as likely to give over total financial control of her money as she is to cut off her own leg. That's for starters. I could go on."

"It's a shame." He was barely listening. The news that Claire was a widow had changed everything. All this time he thought he was coming home to make his peace with a woman who was long married.

"It's foolish—that's what it is," Elizabeth said, heatedly. "Those two have no idea how brief life is, or how much they'll regret fighting over such petty things when one of them is standing over the other one's grave or the grave of one of their children. Trust me, I know. I've had to endure both. Then the career and the pride and the precious hours they spent fighting with each other will feel like such a ridiculous waste of time."

"No doubt."

"Take it from an old lady who has made her own mistakes," she said. "There are only two things that matter in life—those you love and those who love you. Nothing else, except the good Lord, Himself, is worth a hill of beans."

chapter SEVEN

As Tom slowly walked the quarter mile to Claire's, Elizabeth's words rang in his ears.

There are only two things that matter in life—those you love and those who love you.

He did not yet feel strong enough to risk his father's rejection, but he could at least go talk to Claire if she was home.

The little white handmade signs at the end of Claire's driveway took on a new meaning to him as he thought of the children behind them: Fresh Eggs. Homemade Fudge. Wild Sassafras Root. Greeting Cards. Honey. Pot Holders. How industrious Claire's children were!

The little girl in the wheelchair was not outside on the porch when he arrived. It occurred to him that even though he'd been up for several hours, it was still quite early. She was probably still in bed.

He would have turned around and gone back, but the walk had been a little longer than he'd realized, and he needed to rest a bit before he attempted to go back.

At that moment, Claire walked around the corner of the house with an empty clothes basket on her hip. She stopped the moment she saw him.

"Well, hello," she said. "It is good to see you up and about. How are you feeling today?"

She was so very lovely in her light green dress that looked like it had been made especially for spring. Her choring kerchief was a bright white against the early morning sky. Her feet were bare in spite of the dew-drenched grass. He wished he had a painting of her as she was right now—timeless.

She had no husband. The thought flooded back into his brain. Loving her was one of his earliest childhood memories. But even if it were at all possible for her ever to care for him, the weight of a five-hundred-year-old culture stood between them. He knew she would never leave it, and that he knew he could not endure it.

Should he tell her who he was and why he had come? He dreaded it. He dreaded finding out if she hated him.

Not yet, he told himself. Not yet.

"I'm much better, thanks," he said. "I thought I'd give walking here and back a try, but I'm even more out of shape than I realized. I hope you don't mind if I rest a few minutes before I go back."

"Of course not. You look like you could use a drink of water, too."

"I would appreciate that."

"I will be right back."

She returned with two glasses of water and sat down on the porch steps a few feet away from him.

"Thank you, Claire."

Early morning. No children stirring yet. It was the perfect opportunity to tell her who he was and why he had come.

He had almost convinced himself to speak when the phone rang.

"Excuse me." Claire ran to the end of the driveway where a phone shanty stood.

He could not hear the conversation, nor did he want to. Her life was none of his business.

"One of my mothers-to-be had to change her home checkup appointment," Claire said as she came back. "I am so glad I was out here where I could hear the phone. Otherwise I might have driven all the way to her house just to find out she was gone."

"It must be difficult to run a business without a phone in the house."

"It is not so difficult." She bristled a little at what she must have interpreted as pity. "I do have a phone now, and Levi installed an answering machine for me. That is a very big help."

"I'm sure it is."

He realized now that she was proud of having a phone at all—even if it was at the end of her driveway. She must have left the Swartzentrubers fairly recently. It was not difficult to figure out why. With Levi determined to marry Grace, his mother must have had a terrible time deciding what to do. Stay within the safety of the church where she'd grown up and be forced to shun her own son, or become Old Order Amish and be allowed to have contact with him.

He was impressed that she had chosen her son over the only church she had ever known. Not every Swartzentruber parent made that choice. He was painfully aware of that fact.

"Actually." She was gazing pensively at the phone shanty. "Even with the phone shanty, it is difficult. Last Sunday I was in church when a mother went into labor, and the father had to send his *Englisch* neighbor to come get me. It was very disruptive. Grace suggested I ask the leaders of our church for permission to have a pager."

"Have you done so?"

"I have." Her forehead creased in worry. "I do not think the chances are good."

Once again he tried to steel himself to tell her who he was—but he simply could not make himself say the words. He was enjoying the chance to talk to her. The minute he told her, he was fairly certain that their conversation would be over. Probably for good.

Instead he brought up the other subject that he couldn't stop thinking about.

"I found out this morning that your husband passed away a couple years ago. I am sorry for your loss."

"My husband did not 'pass away,'" she said, evenly. "Abraham was murdered."

He was startled. Violence was not unknown among the Amish, but it certainly was not common.

"How?"

"In the words of my children, a 'bad' man came into our home with a gun and killed their father and wounded me. I was carrying Daniel at the time. The man did not know us. He had nothing against us. He simply wanted money and was very unhappy that we did not have more."

"*Unhappy* is not the word I would use." Tom could feel his blood begin to boil. Someone had shot Claire? How *dare* they hurt this good woman! "*Crazy* is more like it."

She shrugged. "Sometimes Annette, my *Englisch* driver, uses a phrase to describe things that she cannot control. Annette will say, 'It is what it is.' I prefer to believe that the God who created the universe will somehow bring triumph out of tragedy."

"And has God created triumph out of tragedy for you?"

"I have no idea," she said. "But what I do know is that when my brother, Eli, and his wife, Martha, became victims of a low-flying logging truck, I was able to take their two daughters in, even though the accident left Amy crippled."

"How did your husband's death have anything to do with them?"

"Abraham was a good farmer, and he was respected by our community for his steadiness, but he would not have been willing to take those girls into our home. Abraham would have counted the cost and would have thought it too great. He and I would have struggled over it and I would have had to give in because I needed to respect his authority."

"You were able to make your own decision."

"And it was a good decision," she said. "Understand this, I would not have had such a terrible thing happen to my husband if I could have prevented it—but I would be lying if I said that I did not see the good of being able to offer a loving, safe home to two orphans."

"Those girls are blessed to have you."

"No. I am the one blessed." She changed the subject. "Do you plan to stay long?"

He could not derive any meaning from that casual question. Was she hoping he would leave soon, or was she hoping he would stay?

"Long enough to get a little stronger." He looked down at his fingers and flexed them. "Long enough to figure out what to do next with my life."

"Will you go back to your war?"

"I doubt that I would be allowed to," he said. "The helicopters I flew were expensive. The government would not risk assigning such a valuable asset to a pilot who is not in peak form."

"Then perhaps you should look for a different job," she said. "Sometimes the Lord closes one door and opens another that we did not expect."

"Unfortunately, flying is the only thing I've ever been good at."

"Flying is the only thing you know how to do?"

She sounded incredulous. He realized that in an Amish woman's eyes, a real man was a jack-of-all-trades.

"The Marines trained me in mechanics before I became a pilot."

"And what does that mean?"

"It means I can fix a broken helicopter as well as fly it."

"Oh." She nodded approval. "That is good, then. If your helicopter plane fell out of the sky, you could fix it!"

"Something like that." He wondered if she realized that being around to fix it after it fell from the sky might not be an option. A woman who had never seen television or a news program would probably have no idea how quickly a helicopter could plummet to the ground.

"Claire!" Their conversation was cut off by a small voice from inside the house.

"What do you want, Amy?" Claire called.

"I'm up. Can you please come help me get dressed?"

"I'll be right there." Claire shot him an apologetic look. "Our Amy gets very impatient once she's awake. I should go help her."

"You don't have an easy life, do you, Claire?"

"No," she said. "But I am walking the path that God chose for me, and that is enough."

As she helped Amy get ready for the day, she wished the child could have slept a few more minutes. She had been enjoying her conversation on the porch. She usually conversed only with her children, about children's things, or with pregnant women about their needs. It was interesting to glimpse inside this soldier's mind.

How would an *Englisch* man support himself if he could no longer do the only job for which he was trained?

He was nothing like she would have expected an *Englisch* soldier to be. There was no gruffness or impatience in his voice as they had spoken. In spite of their very different lives, he had listened to her with interest. Unlike the few other *Englisch* men with whom she had dealings, he did not seem to be uncomfortable around her because she was Amish.

Her guess was that there was a world of interesting things that he could tell her. She wished she could hear about the different countries he had been to and the people he had met. Under normal circumstances, she would never have allowed herself to chat so long with an *Englisch* man she barely knew, but he had not seemed anxious to leave, and she did not want him to think she was put off by his disfigurement. Actually, although the battle wounds he bore were unfortunate, she had found that the intelligence in his eyes and the kindness in his voice somehow made the scars less noticeable.

Of course, he would be leaving soon—which was just as well. She felt that there could be a friendship between them, but of course, under the circumstances, that would be highly inappropriate.

"I heard voices outside. Who were you talking to?" Amy asked, as Claire helped her remove her long nightgown.

"Tom Miller walked to our house from Levi's. He is getting stronger but the walk tired him out and he needed a rest and a drink of water."

"What did you talk about?"

Claire brought a fresh dress from the closet and handed it to her. "He is afraid he will not be allowed to fly his helicopters anymore."

"I wonder what it would be like to go up so high."

Claire busied herself tidying the top of Amy's dresser. The child liked to do as much as possible for herself and did not like being watched while she struggled to get her dress on.

"I don't know, but when I was little," Claire said, "I climbed a very tall tree and I did not like it much."

"What happened?"

"I was like a small kitten, climbing from one branch to the next until I ran out of branches. The ground was so far away it made me dizzy. Like a kitten who has climbed too far, I could not figure out how to get back down."

"What did you do?"

"I clung to the tree, calling out for help. A friend of mine came to my rescue. A little boy named Tobias who had been playing in the barn with my younger brother. He heard me and came running. Our parents were inside the house, visiting. Instead of going for an adult, he climbed up and told me each step to take and each branch to grasp and encouraged me until I finally got my feet on firm ground."

Amy began unplaiting her hair. "How old were you?"

"About seven."

"Why did he not just go get your *daadi*?"

"Because he knew I would get in trouble." Claire picked up a hairbrush from the bedside table and began to brush Amy's hair. "Little girls in dresses were not supposed to climb trees when other people were around."

"Why did you do it, then?"

"Because Rose had hurt my feelings." Claire laughed, remembering. "She wanted to play with Tobias's little sister, who was just a baby. Tobias and Matthew were off playing with my brothers. Since I was feeling left out, I decided to show them all by climbing that tree."

"That makes no sense."

Claire smiled. "Having sense was not a talent of mine back then."

"Did you ever try to climb that tree again?"

"No. That experience left me with a fear of heights and a

lifelong gratitude that I would never be expected to climb the tall barn frames that men had to whenever our church had a barn raising. I was content to work alongside the women with my feet firmly on the ground."

"Mommi?" Sarah raised her head from her bed next to Amy's.

"Good morning sleepyhead." Claire handed the hairbrush to Amy and walked over to Sarah's bed. "Did you have good dreams last night?"

Sarah was still half asleep and did not want to talk. She simply reached her arms up for a morning hug. Claire sat down cross-legged on the bed and gathered her littlest girl into her arms. Cuddling a sleepy child was the thing she loved most. She kissed Sarah's forehead, where tendrils of nearly white-blond hair lay, mussed from bedcovers and sleep. Sarah closed her eyes and snuggled closer.

Claire leaned against the headboard. She breathed in the clean little-girl scent of this child for whom she would gladly give her life and watched Amy rebraid her hair. The sun had risen just high enough that a slice of sunshine divided the room.

She had three home visits to make today to check on women in various stages of pre- and postpregnancy. Maddy had asked if she could take Daniel with her so that she could have some freedom to replenish their supply of prayer *Kapps*. The little boy could not seem to keep from touching the pristine white fabric with fingers that might not be clean. There was a never-ending round of chores and responsibilities that would keep her busy until she fell into bed tonight. But the laundry was hung, there was a breakfast casserole cooling on the stove, her children were all healthy, and there was a little extra money in the bank.

As Tom had said, her life was not easy. Her days were long

and hard and she frequently despaired of getting through them. It was not an easy thing to raise a large family while trying to make a living to support them.

But she had learned a secret.

Englisch people seemed to think that love was simply about feelings. In her opinion, that was one of Grace's problems—the girl had gotten married on feelings alone, and was now having trouble adjusting to the reality of day-in and day-out marriage. Amish people tended to emphasize the idea of love being an action. She had learned that love was more than either of these things.

Love was a fuel.

It was love that fed the flame in her to keep trying. It was love that fueled her resolve to work until she dropped, if necessary, to care for these children. It was love that helped her rise before dawn so that she could take a good run at the day before anyone else in the house stirred.

Claire knew that some people wondered if she would remarry, but there was already enough love in her life to keep her going for a long, long time. She had known women who did not seem to think they could exist without a man in their life and would do much to attract one. Even though she knew she was spiritually free to remarry, and two men from neighboring Amish churches had expressed interest, Claire wondered where she would get the energy even to care.

Besides, she strongly suspected that they were more attracted to the fact that she would come with eighty acres of valuable Holmes County farmland than they were to the middle-aged widow with six children still living at home.

And yet . . .

Those few minutes alone with Tom on the porch had been charged with something that she could not define and that she wasn't sure she wanted to examine. It was probably not wise to be alone with that man. She would avoid doing so in the future.

"So," Elizabeth said, as he came through the door, "did you bring me any leftovers of Maddy's fudge? I've been thinking about it ever since you left."

"Fudge?"

"That's why you walked down to Claire's," she said. "You were going to get some fudge at Amy's store. I know I didn't make that up."

The last thing on his mind when he'd been talking to Claire was fudge.

"What happened down there? Were they out?"

"I have no idea," he confessed. "It was too early for Amy to be up, and Claire was hanging out wash when I got there. She brought me some water, and we sat on the porch and talked awhile."

"Really," Elizabeth said. "You and Claire. Sitting on the porch. Talking."

"Yes." He didn't know why he should feel defensive about such an innocent act—but as Elizabeth turned her laser beam of attention on him, he was distinctly uncomfortable.

"Good heavens," she said.

"What?"

He expected for her to say something about how he had spent the morning, but she didn't. Instead she got up and went back to her *Daadi Haus,* shaking her head the whole way. Before the screen door slammed behind her, he distinctly heard her say, "Uh-oh."

chapter EIGHT

Claire nervously plied her crochet hook. It was a no-church Sunday. This was a day she usually enjoyed, what with the tradition of visiting friends and relatives, or simply resting and doing small chores. But this particular no-church Sunday was different.

Bishop Schrock, their two ministers, and the deacon were meeting to talk about . . . her. It felt so strange to know that the leaders of her church were meeting specifically to discuss her request for a pager. She knew there were a few in the Old Order church who privately bent the rules a little and owned cell phones. One was a mother who bought the phone to keep track of her four children, who were all on *Rumspringa* and all owned cell phones. If it was done quietly, there were seldom ramifications.

But even if Claire wanted to, she couldn't "cheat" and then hand out her cell phone number to all her expectant mothers. She was a professional, and she had a business. The point was for people to be able to get hold of her. She wouldn't have done such a thing, even if she thought she could get away with it.

She knew there was no chance that her leaders would or could approve a cell phone, but she thought they might allow her a pager, so a desperate mother or father could contact her.

This was not a decision for the church to take lightly. The leaders were concerned that allowing her to openly carry a pager would be a slippery slope that would lead to others wanting the same convenience. There was a danger it would eventually lead to all their congregation feeling free about openly carrying cell phones in their pockets. If that sort of thing happened, their church might as well join those liberal Beachy Amish and start driving cars and using computers!

"Don't worry," Maddy said, as she kneaded the rolls they would have for dinner. "I think they will allow it. It is a reasonable request."

"The Lord's will be done." Claire glanced at the clock. Her statement, she knew, was a little hypocritical. On this issue, she didn't want the Lord's will to be done unless it mirrored her own. A pager was not for her own selfish purposes—it was for the good of her mothers and their babies. Recently there had been two instances when a young husband had the options of staying with his laboring wife, leaving a message on Claire's answering machine and praying she heard it, or streaking out on a horse to bring help, leaving his wife alone and untended.

The pager could save lives. It could also save a nine-year-old from having to help her mother deliver a baby, a regrettable situation that had happened a few months ago. Children, in Claire's opinion, should be shielded from such things until they were old enough to understand. An innocent childhood was a gift she wished all children to have.

She glanced at the clock. The men should be finished with their discussion by now. She hoped one of them would ride over and let her know what they had decided so she wouldn't have to wait on pins and needles any longer.

As the soft wool slipped through her fingers, she thought about how there had seemed to be a swell of births among their Amish community lately. She had almost run out of these tiny newborn hats that she liked to personally crochet for each of her babies. The Mueller girl was due to deliver anytime now, and it would be a sorry thing if Claire didn't have a tiny warming cap ready.

Some midwives simply bought the caps, and there was nothing wrong with that, but Claire's grandmother had been the one who had trained her and given her the skills with which she now supported her family. It had been her grandmother's habit to crochet these little caps, and doing so now made her feel as though her grandmother was still with her.

"Someone is coming." Jesse stopped playing checkers with Albert and went to the window to look.

Claire heard them now, too. The sound of buggy wheels on gravel.

Jesse craned his neck to look down the driveway. "It's the bishop."

Claire had just enough time to put away her crocheting before Bishop Schrock was knocking at their door.

Their church was blessed to have a godly and kind man as their bishop. She not only respected him, she liked him, and his wife was a good friend.

No matter how kind a bishop might be, however, friendship took a backseat to the good of their religious community. As logical and rational as she felt her desire for a pager was, there was still a good chance that it would be turned down.

"Please come in, Bishop." Claire hoped that she did not sound too nervous.

"I can make tea, Bishop," Maddy offered.

"*Denki,* but I can't stay," the bishop said. "Two of my sons have gone over to Pennsylvania to visit family, so I have extra chores this evening. Still, I thought you would like to know our decision before you sleep tonight."

"I am anxious to hear," Claire said.

"It was not a decision easily made."

His expression was so solemn, she felt her heart plummet. The leaders were going to turn her down. She would have to continue to rely on her answering machine for word from her clients. That meant she would continue to nervously make a dozen or more trips out to her phone shanty every day for fear there would be someone who needed her and she would not know.

Still—if that was the decision of their leaders, she would accept it. At least they had heard her out and given it consideration. In her old church, the Swartzentruber church, she would never even have broached the subject.

"There are many small businesses within our church, as you know," the bishop said. "Many of our people are self-employed and would enjoy the freedom that a cell phone or a pager would give them to allow customers to contact them."

Claire knew for certain now that she would be turned down. They could not prioritize her needs over the others, even if her work was not like theirs. It really wasn't fair. An order for lumber could wait a day. A question about a quilt was not a matter of life or death. But her women had no control over when a baby would decide to come.

She did not protest, but bowed her head to await the verdict.

"Yours is a special situation," the bishop said. "There is a chance that a baby or a mother's life could be lost if a mother has no way to reach you. We value our families too much to allow that to happen. God has given you a special gift, Claire. We have come to the conclusion that it would not be wise or in the best interests of our church to quench that gift."

She could hardly believe her ears. Was he saying what she thought he was saying?

"It was unanimous," the bishop said. "You may have your pager. We will let our church know our reasoning on the matter during church next Sunday."

Claire felt her heart lift with this good news. Oh, God was so good!

"Thank you," she said. "So very much."

"Your faithfulness and devotion to the Lord, in addition to your work, has been noted. We know you will use it wisely." The bishop rubbed his hands together. "Now, while I am here, are you and the children doing all right? Are there any needs that have not been met that our church needs to see to?"

Claire knew this was his way of asking her if she had enough money for herself and her family.

"We are by necessity frugal," she said, "but we are able to care for our needs. Levi, of course, shares a portion of the income from the farm with us, and with my work, and the children's store, we are all right."

"You are a wonderful good steward," the bishop said. "But you will let me know if things ever become not 'all right'? The Bible teaches us to take care of our widows and orphans. That is our first financial responsibility as a church. You know this, Claire."

She lifted her chin, and looked him straight in the eyes. "By the grace of God, I am able to provide for my family."

The bishop smiled. "I am pleased with your strength."

Six words that meant the world to her. Such high praise from their bishop.

"Have you written any more poems?" he asked Amy, who, along with the other children, had been listening wide-eyed to the conversation.

Amy put her hand on a stack of small notebooks. "I have

so many poems," she said. "I can hardly make cards fast enough to use all of them."

"That reminds me," the bishop said. "My wife asked me to pick some more cards up for her since she knew I would be stopping by here."

"She's out already?"

"My wife loves sending them to people. She says they are like mailing a piece of art to someone. Do you have any left?"

"Oh!" Amy started gathering up several that had been scattered around her little worktable. "These are the ones I finished this week."

Claire's heart smiled as she watched the bishop get down on one knee beside Amy's craft table. Soon, his and Amy's heads were close together, bent over the small stack of cards, discussing the merits of each one.

Claire knew that it would never occur to Amy that men his age would not really be interested in her little poems. This man who had been chosen by God to be their bishop was a true shepherd to their church and he had the heart and wisdom to care about something so important to one of the church's children.

After he had carefully selected five cards, he stood and drew out a twenty-dollar bill from his wallet. Amy happily made change from her money box.

"Your wife might like to have some sassafras tea, too," Jesse pointed out.

"And some fresh eggs?" Albert added helpfully.

"I am so grateful that you pointed these things out to me," the bishop said. "I am quite sure my wife is in need of these things—and a jar of honey, too."

"I make pot holders," Sarah said, shyly.

"Oh, little one," the bishop said. "I'm sorry. How could I have overlooked such fine pot holders? I know my wife would want me to bring her a couple."

"Does she like fudge?" Maddy asked.

The bishop laughed out loud. "Yes, as a matter of fact, she likes fudge, and Maddy, unless I miss my guess, she's probably in need of a new head covering as well."

"I just finished two new ones."

After paying for the other items, he told Jesse and Albert that the bass were getting big over in his pond and invited them to come catch some. Then he put his packages in his buggy and drove on. Claire marveled at the feeling of warmth and security he left behind. He had stayed no more than fifteen minutes, and yet the whole atmosphere in the room had changed. Their church was blessed indeed.

chapter NINE

Elizabeth was at church. Grace was working a double shift at the ER, and he wasn't sure where Levi was. What he was sure about was that it was time for him to leave.

The old adage that fish and guests start to stink after three days was one he had seen played out in more than one culture. This morning would make three and a half days that he had stayed with these good people. It was time to go.

He found an envelope, put three hundred dollars in—a hundred for each night—and wrote a heartfelt thank-you note to go with it. Leaving would be easier this way. He did not want to go through the awkwardness of their polite insistence that he stay.

He still had unfinished business here in Mt. Hope, but he could do it just as well from Hotel Millersburg. He would stop back in a few days.

There wasn't anything to pack. He was on his way to throw his duffel bag in the trunk of his rental car when he heard a loud yelp and a metallic thunk coming from a small barn. That did not sound good, and he hurried there as fast as he could.

He slid open the door and found Levi sitting, dejected, on a bale of hay, nursing one bloodied hand against his chest.

Both hands were also stained with black grease, as was his shirt. Levi did not look happy to see him.

"What happened?"

"I just broke off a spark plug trying to remove it from the block. The motor has a bad miss and I'm trying to get some new spark plugs and wires on this motor. The man I bought it from said it ran good, but it might need a tune-up. But now I've got a major problem with this plug broken off in the block."

"What's that?" Tom pointed to a book lying open beside him.

Levi glanced down at bright-colored book. *"How to Rebuild and Restore Ford Tractors."*

"You're trying to learn tractor mechanics from a book?"

"How else am I going to learn?" Levi said, with a touch of bitterness. "The only people I know are Grace, Elizabeth, and some Swartzentruber men who will no longer speak to me."

Tom's heart melted. How he identified with the young man! He'd been in his nephew's boots before, trying to enter the *Englisch* world with only 1800s technology knowledge to draw from. At seventeen, when *Englisch* boys were busy fixing up old jalopies, he was shoeing horses. Strangely enough, in spite of that, he had somehow scored high in mechanical ability on the aptitude test he took upon entering the Marine Corps. The mechanics of a tractor were nothing compared to the mechanics of a helicopter. He could help Levi, and he wanted to.

"How bad is that hand?"

"I don't know. I just now hurt it."

"Let's get it cleaned up and tended to, and then I'll help you fix that tractor."

"You can do that?"

"Yes." He dropped his duffel bag on the ground. "If you don't mind."

Once they got all the grease off Levi's hand, the injury

turned out to be not much more than some badly skinned knuckles. He felt bad for Levi, who he soon discovered had no working knowledge of combustion engines at all.

"How on earth do you keep your car running?" he finally asked.

"Grace takes care of that." Levi sounded a little embarrassed. "Grace takes care of a lot of things."

"I'm sure having a competent wife is a good thing."

"Oh, it is," Levi said. "But it is hard to figure out how to be the leader in my home when my wife knows so much more than me that she has to teach me how to change a lightbulb."

"I'm sure there are things you could teach her."

"Like what? How to weave a basket? How to harness a horse? How to fix a buggy wheel?" Levi's voice rose and Tom could tell that he had been distraught over this for a long time. "These are not skills that Grace needs or wants. I even had to depend on her to teach me how to take her out to a restaurant and how to purchase tickets at a movie house."

"Does she mind?"

"She says she doesn't. But she complains about other things."

Tom didn't ask what, but Levi seemed determined to tell him.

"She says I compare her cooking to my mother's."

"Do you?"

There was a long pause. "Maybe."

Tom tightened a screw on the motor. "Perhaps you could buy her a cookbook."

"Have you seen Grace angry?"

"Not yet."

"Then don't suggest she buy a cookbook. I already tried that. It did not go well." Levi shook his head. "She talks about not having gotten a necessary gene to make her as good a cook as the Amish, but when I tried to help her by buying her a cookbook for our anniversary, she blew up."

"I'm sorry, Levi."

"If I would allow it, she would live in jeans and T-shirts. She says they are comfortable, but I think she does not know how much they show off her body. I do not see a need for other men to see that. I think it is not unreasonable for me to ask her to wear dresses. After all, I don't dress the way I used to either. And it is my job as head of our home to take care of the finances. I am very good at figures and she is not. But will she accept my headship? No. She insists on paying bills, and makes a mess of our checkbook."

Evidently Levi had been building up a head of steam for a long time. Tom was not enjoying this conversation, but he thought perhaps he was helping Levi depressurize a little.

"She wants to fight me on not going back to work after the baby is born—but everyone knows a woman should not work after she has children."

Tom thought about all the women he knew who managed to balance both—including Levi's own mother—but thought better of it. Let Levi get it all off his chest.

"And even though we agreed before we got married that we would not watch television, now she complains about missing it. She says she just wants to watch a program every once in a while. Sometimes I know she sneaks over to Elizabeth's *Daadi Haus* to watch it there. I love her, but I do not know what to do with her."

Tom couldn't help but think of the men who would think that they had died and gone to heaven if they had a wife like Grace, but telling Levi that would do no good. In fact, he had no idea what to tell Levi. But in all the things he had told him, there was one he thought might be an easy fix.

"I know how to fix this motor, and I can teach you—but

do you want some advice about your marriage from a man who doesn't have a clue what he's talking about?"

Levi sat back and didn't say anything for a moment.

"I will listen to what you have to say."

"If I were you, I'd go buy the woman a television. You don't have to listen to it. Just let her watch it sometimes. Maybe she'll ease up on the other stuff then."

"I will give thought to what you say."

"Good, now, then, come here and give me a hand. I will teach you about motors if you want to learn—but you'll have to do most of the work. I don't have the grip I used to."

"Grace says I paid too much money for an old tractor that I don't know how to keep running."

"Yeah, well, let's prove her wrong."

"I have one more favor to ask."

"Anything, Levi."

"Would you stay a few more days?"

"Why?"

Levi gave him a sheepish grin. "There are other motors around here that I do not know how to fix."

Tom knew exactly how to get a broken spark plug out of an engine block. It was a pleasure teaching his nephew, who was so quick to learn, how to accomplish this tricky task. Levi had just successfully replaced the broken spark plug, and Tom was in the process of giving his nephew an awkward high five, when Elizabeth walked in.

"What are you boys up to?" She was wearing a purple dress, a rope of pearls around her neck, a big quilted purse, and white tennis shoes.

"I thought I was supposed to come and get you," Levi said.

"Hazel brought me home instead."

"I think it might start now," Tom said. "Give her a crank."

Levi hopped onto the seat, turned the ignition, and the

tractor roared to life. The grin on Levi's face was worth every second Tom had spent helping him. He grew even more satisfied when Levi drove it out of the barn, down the driveway, and toward Claire's without mishap.

"I saw your note inside the house," Elizabeth said. "It said you were leaving, but you are still here."

"I'm sorry about that," he said. "I really was leaving, but Levi was having trouble and I stayed to help him."

"Have we done something to offend you?"

"No. Of course not. It's just that I'm stronger now, and I don't want to intrude any longer."

"That's the happiest I've seen that boy since he bought that piece of junk from old Harold Givens. I could have told him that Harold would try to take him—and he did—but Levi was trying so hard to act like he knew what he was doing that he wouldn't listen to me. Came home with that mess that he'd paid too much for. It made Grace mad when she saw it and she said some things that hurt him. He's been tinkering with it ever since. Looks to me like you kinda handed him his manhood back. It might help if you'd stay around and teach him how to do some things he doesn't know how to do."

Tom scratched his head. "Levi did ask me to stay."

"And I'm asking you to stay, too."

"But Grace . . ."

"Grace is either working, puking, or fussing at Levi. She won't hardly notice whether you're here or not. Besides, it's my house and there's plenty of room." She handed him the envelope with the money still in it. "Now that you're feeling a little better, it will be good for Levi to spend some time with you. It's been hard on him trying to transition. Frankly, it's been hard on me having to watch him. Having you here has been a relief."

How well he understood. If it hadn't been for an understanding commanding officer and some Marine buddies, he would have been in sad shape himself.

"I guess I could stick around for a few more days."

"I'd appreciate it," Elizabeth said. "And I'm sure Levi would, too."

"Do you miss it?" Grace asked.

They were in the living room. She was sorting some baby clothes a coworker at the hospital had given her. Elizabeth was working on a class for her Wednesday-evening Bible study, and Levi was still out plowing, even though it was getting dark. Apparently he was so thrilled with having a tractor that worked, he did not intend to come in until it was too dark to see or he ran out of gas.

"Miss what?" Tom glanced up from filling in the remaining blocks of one of Elizabeth's innumerable half-finished crossword puzzles.

"Flying. Being in a war zone. Helping people."

"I miss flying. Being in a war zone not so much. Why?"

"I felt so . . . necessary over there." Grace's voice was wistful. "Do you know what I mean?"

"All I did was fly shotgun for some of the medevac crews that went out. I didn't actually hold lives in my hands, not like you and the others."

"I was good at what I did."

"I'm sure you still are." He tried to go back to the crossword. Grace did not take the hint.

"Do you think cooking and cleaning and canning and gardening are as important as saving lives?"

Elizabeth looked up sharply. He was definitely walking on thin ice here. "I think they are *as* important."

She shot him a look. "No you don't."

True. He had to admit it. Canned peaches could be purchased in a grocery store for pocket change. People with Grace's skills were rare.

"Levi has no idea what I did over there, or who I was, or even what I do at the ER. I could be working overtime trying to save a grandfather from going into heart failure, but all Levi sees is an empty place at the supper table."

"There is no way I'm going to weigh in on this."

"Nor should you have to," Elizabeth said. "Grace, that's enough."

It was the sharpest he'd ever heard Elizabeth speak to her granddaughter.

Being in a house divided felt awkward. As a Marine, he was trained how to dodge bullets—not how to deal with a young woman's marital woes.

Grace ignored her. "I've given up the clothes I like to wear, because he doesn't like me to wear jeans anymore, and I *hate* wearing dresses. I've grown my hair out until it is driving me nuts. He doesn't approve of TV, so I have to sneak over to Grandma's even if I just want to watch the news. We're having a child sooner than I wanted because he was afraid we might not have time to have a large family if we waited any longer. He doesn't like the church Grandma and I were going to—but he hasn't found anything else he likes better—so most Sundays we don't go anywhere anymore."

"Grace!" Elizabeth said. "Enough! If you spent as much time praying about your marriage as you do complaining about it, you might be a happier woman."

Grace looked at her grandmother as though she had just been slapped.

Then she got up and rushed out of the room, in tears. Tom decided that he would rather face a firing squad than have to deal with a crying, pregnant woman.

"I apologize. It's just the pregnancy hormones talking. At least, I hope that's all it is." Elizabeth glanced toward the kitchen door and acted startled. "Oh. Levi. When did you come in?"

Levi was standing in the doorway. He was weary, and looked far too old for a man only in his twenties. He was staring at the door Grace had just gone out.

"Maybe we should never have married," Levi said. "I am afraid that our child will pay the price for it."

Then he turned on his heel and left.

chapter TEN

"Having trouble sleeping?" Elizabeth asked. "Me, too."
It was after 2 a.m. Tom found himself once again on the back porch. Levi had not come home yet. He could hear Grace crying herself to sleep upstairs, directly over where he lay. He'd dozed, but felt worse for it. Just when he thought he had beaten the nightmares, another one had hit. Matthew had been in it. Actually, it had not been a nightmare, which in some ways made it worse to endure. It was a dream that Matthew was alive again, a good dream, in which Matthew was living with Claire and surrounded by children. He had been so happy to see his brother again. Then he'd awakened, and realized that it had been nothing more than a cruel joke that his subconscious had played on him.

It had broken his heart. Again.

Allowing Levi and Elizabeth to talk him into staying longer had been a mistake. Being here with Levi, who looked and acted so much like Matthew, as well as talking with Claire again, was not wise. Not when his nerves were already shot.

Now he was half afraid that if he went back to sleep, he'd be visited with the birthday cake–suicide bomber nightmare again. He decided it would be better to stay awake than to chance it, and had come out here where it was cool and peaceful. "Yes, I'm having trouble sleeping."

"Nightmares again?" Elizabeth asked.

"How did you know about the nightmares?"

"I heard you talking in your sleep the first night you came here."

"Yes. I've been having nightmares again."

"Do you want to talk about it?"

"About the nightmares? No. That wouldn't help."

"I'm not talking about nightmares. I'm talking about the other thing that is bothering you."

"What other thing?"

"Whatever it is that you're wrestling with."

"It's just nightmares and a little insomnia. Nothing to worry about."

"I was an educator for many years, Tom. I know the look on a child's face when they are keeping a secret that is eating them up. You have that same lost look. Do you think you might be able to sleep if you talked about it with someone?"

Could he trust her?

"And yes, in case you're wondering, you can trust me."

"What are you, Elizabeth?" He tried to laugh. "A mind reader?"

"If you live long enough, and pay close enough attention, after a while it gets pretty easy to read faces."

"It's a long story."

"I'm sure it is. Neither of us is going to get any sleep tonight. Tell me what's bothering you, son."

He did not know whether or not he could trust her, but what he did know was that he desperately needed to talk to someone. She was right. His secret was eating him up. And even though he was a grown man in his forties, and she looked nothing like his Amish mother, there was still something about Elizabeth that reminded him of her.

"My given name is not Tom Miller. That is my legal name."

"Okay, that's a good start. Who are you?"

"Tobias Troyer. I had my name changed the day after I turned eighteen."

Elizabeth pulled her legs up under her on the cushioned porch chair, as though settling in for a long session. "One of our neighbors, Jeremiah Troyer, had a son with that name."

"I know."

There was a long silence as his and Elizabeth's eyes locked, and she digested the impact of what he had revealed.

"That makes you Levi's uncle. The one who left and never came back. Why didn't you tell us?"

"I intended to explain who I was the minute I introduced myself to Claire. Then I fell ill again, and the next thing I knew, Grace had stuck a thermometer in my mouth, read my dog tags, and drawn her own conclusions. I felt too bad at the time to go into a long explanation."

"That's understandable. You've even told the truth after a fashion. You legally are Tom Miller. But why on earth did you change your name?"

"I was hurt and angry at my father for a long time. It seemed like a good way to strike back at him—to deliberately get rid of even the name he gave me. Miller was a family name of my mother's. I wanted to make a completely fresh start."

"I know very little about you as Tobias Troyer," Elizabeth said. "Except for the fact of your existence."

"That's probably just as well."

"So what happened? Why did you leave?"

"I was the cause of my brother's death."

"That's it? You ran away because you felt responsible?"

"No. It was something my father said to me at the funeral."

"And what was that?"

"I tried to tell him how sorry I was." Tom swallowed hard before he could get the words out. "But all *Daed* said was, 'It should have been you.' Then to make sure I understood exactly what he was saying, he said, "I wish it had been you."

"What a horrible thing to say!" Elizabeth said.

"I agreed with him, though," Tom said. "I still do."

"Oh, honey. You shouldn't feel that way."

"Maybe not—but I still think it."

"You weren't formally banned, though, were you?" She said. "I mean, you were only seventeen. You hadn't been baptized into the church yet."

"Actually, I had been baptized. Before Matthew came home, I thought I might have a chance with Claire. She was one of those girls who felt so sure of her religion that she chose to be baptized the summer she turned sixteen. I followed right along and was baptized early, too. I thought it would help my chances with her, and she was the only girl I had ever wanted. So, yes, when I ran away, I was most definitely banned."

"Now you wonder if your father will receive you?"

"I doubt he'll even meet with me. You've lived here. You know how strict the Swartzentrubers can be. A stricter *Meidung* was the main reason they split from their Old Order church in the first place."

"So why are you here?"

"It feels . . . I don't know . . . like I'm stuck right now and I can't get on with my life until I find out how he'll react to me after all these years. Frankly, I'm wondering the same about Claire."

"Are you still in love with her?"

"No. Of course not. That would be foolish. So much time has passed, I don't really even know her. I just want to apologize to her about what I did to her life. I also wanted to meet Matthew's son."

"Well, now that you have, what do you think of him?"

"I think Matthew would be proud of him," Tom said. "I hate for him to think I have been deliberately lying to him. That was not my intent."

"You know," she said, "I think that the Lord has given you an opportunity many people never get."

"What's that?"

"I think you need to go see your father—as Tom Miller, the person you are today. You can tell him that you are a helicopter pilot. You are *Englisch*. You used to live around here. All of that is true. Tell him you were friends with his son Matthew— which is also true. Give your father a chance to get to know you as the man you are today. Give yourself a chance to get to know your father as the man he is today. Then, if you want, you can decide whether or not to tell him who you used to be."

"The church will discipline him if he has anything to do with me."

"You know, Tom?" she said. "I like Jeremiah. He's been a good neighbor to me for many years. He accepts the fact that I'm *Englisch* and we get along fine. I think the two of you might enjoy spending a little time together, and after all the two of you have been through, you deserve that. I am not all that convinced that his bishop needs to know everything right now. I have had some dealings with Bishop Weaver, and he is not an open man. Let your father get to know you as Tom Miller. Then someday, when he finds out who you are, he will have those memories of talking with you, without having to feel guilty for having done so."

"You don't think this is underhanded?"

"No," Elizabeth said. "I think it is being kind to an old man who has been through way too much."

"Should I remain silent about who I am to Levi and Claire?"

"It might be wise for now. Let them get to know you as the person you are now without all that other baggage you'll need to work through with them later. If they get upset, I'll take the blame. I'll tell them that I twisted your arm and forced you to be quiet. Frankly, Tom, I think you need to drive down and see your father tomorrow. That's a meeting that is way overdue."

One twenty-five-pound bag of chicken feed, $18.75.

Claire tapped her freshly sharpened pencil on the desk that Abraham had made. She'd done the math. Although her chickens scratched in the dirt for a living, their diet also had to be supplemented. She'd discovered that it cost more for her to raise her own eggs than it did to buy them at the grocery store.

The problem was, the bright orange-yoked eggs her own chickens laid were infinitely superior in taste and nutrition to the cheap, pale-yolked ones that came from the store. Good nutrition was important to growing children. She would keep her laying hens. The extra price was worth it. The chicken feed would stay.

Veterinarian bill and medicine, $150. That was for the case of mastitis her little Jersey cow had developed. It might be cheaper to buy store-bought milk, but at around three dollars a gallon, she doubted it. Hopefully, the cow would stay well now. Seven gallons a day that little cow gave. Plenty of butter and cream, too. The cow most definitely earned her keep.

Cloth for Amy's new dress, $15.10. They'd gotten a good deal on that material.

Cough syrup for Sarah's bad cough, $9.21. It had helped, but next time the little girl caught a cold, Claire was determined to mix up a batch of her own elderberry cough and cold syrup. She could find elderberries along the roadside for free.

The expenses mounted up, even when it felt like she wasn't buying anything at all.

Her biggest financial worry of all, however, was the age of her standardbred horse. At twenty, Flora was simply too old to pull the buggy much longer. Claire tried to keep the buggy as light as possible and to go only short ways with plenty of rests in between, but she needed a new horse badly.

If only she could become a certified midwife! Then she could work under the doctor who oversaw the midwives at the famous Mt. Eaton Care Center, the birthing center that Dr. Lehman had spearheaded when Barb, the saintly Amish woman who had taken laboring mothers into her home, couldn't handle the hard physical work any longer.

Her church district would never allow her to become certified. She'd heard that a few New Order Amish church districts were beginning to allow some of their midwives to become certified—but even allowing her to have a pager was a stretch for hers.

Becoming New Order was, of course, out of the question. Leaving the Swartzentruber Amish for Old Order was a big enough leap for one lifetime.

In the meantime, as long as she didn't charge any money, she could legally continue to function as a lay midwife. She could only take donations. The problem was, she was entirely on her own. There was no cozy birthing center available to her, no comfortable office for patient visits so that she didn't have to pay an *Englisch* driver to take her to all these far-flung farms. Although she was grateful that she had work, the donations she received from her midwife jobs were barely enough to keep the wolf from the door. Her income depended upon how many babies she delivered in a month, and there were occasional dry spells.

She had heard that *Englisch* midwives sometimes charged as much as three thousand dollars to see a mother through a pregnancy, but the norm among Amish midwives was not even close to that. Her fee, as she told clients, was whatever they could afford. Most knew that the standard donation for an Amish midwife was four to eight hundred dollars, and that included monthly checkups.

Her clients also knew that if they could not pay, she would still take care of them. So far, even the Swartzentrubers, who tended to have far less income than the other Amish sects, always paid her, even if it came in at a few dollars at a time. She could not imagine refusing help to a pregnant woman who needed her.

Still, unless there was a sudden rash of babies, the need for a new horse was a great worry.

Normally, Levi would have figured out a way to help her take care of this problem, but the boy was so preoccupied figuring out how to be married to his new *Englisch* wife, he was letting many things slide, and she hated to nag.

Maddy peeked over her shoulder. "Money problems?"

"Not so much money problems as spending problems," Claire said.

"The church will help," Maddy said. "You know they will."

"And I will ask for and accept that help with gratitude if necessary. It does help me sleep at night knowing that I have a church willing to care for my family. But as long as I am able-bodied and possessed of some skill, we will continue doing the best we can."

"I have been thinking of working more hours at Mrs. Yoder's." Maddy picked up the calculator and fiddled with it.

"Rose has not been able to come in much lately. They are offering to let me work more hours. That would help."

Claire wanted to refuse, but the truth was that extra hours would be quite helpful. "I don't want you to feel like you have to."

"I know," Maddy said. "But I enjoy it and it's close enough that I can walk to work until winter sets in."

It was not unusual for a sixteen-year-old girl to clerk or work part-time in a restaurant, but Maddy was not just any sixteen-year-old. She was unusually beautiful—which was never, ever a good thing, especially not when the world put such a high value on beauty—but what Maddy was suggesting was reasonable. Most families expected a child to start working for a salary at some point after they got past the eighth grade. Even more, they expected that child to hand over their salary for the good of the family until they turned twenty-one, or got married. Whichever one came first.

"If that is what you want," Claire said. "And, Maddy?"

"Yes, Claire."

"I do appreciate your help."

Maddy smiled. "I know. I'm happy to help. I live here, too, you know."

Claire returned to her book work, grateful for her good children and her good life. It struck her that even though she had to be careful, at least she didn't have to force herself to work a job she hated—like Rose.

chapter ELEVEN

I t was time.

    He'd waited a lifetime.

As Tom approached his old home, his pulse began to beat faster. He passed Claire's home, topped a small rise, and saw the house where he had been raised. An older man was plowing in a side field.

Jeremiah Troyer had aged, but Tom would have recognized him anywhere.

He drove past, but his father did not look up. Everything within him screamed to keep driving and not risk rejection, but it was as though a magnet was attached to the new Impala he'd purchased at Moomaw's that morning.

He stopped, turned around, and drove back.

It took all the courage he had to pull into his father's dirt driveway, get out, close the door, and walk over to the fence. After all he had done. After all he had experienced as a pilot, it struck him as strange that he was having trouble catching his breath. There was certainly no physical danger in being here, and yet he was practically trembling with nerves.

Jeremiah Troyer was in his late sixties, but his appearance was that of a much older man. While Tom had been turning the car around, his father had decided to give the plow horse a rest, and was now sitting in the shade of a maple tree, the very same tree that Tom had once fallen out of, breaking his arm.

"Good morning," Tom said.

"Guten Morgen." His father showed little interest in the "stranger" who stood before him. He was unscrewing a battered blue thermos that Tom recognized. Like his father, it was much older, and worse for wear, but still functioning. His father was nothing if not frugal.

"I was wondering if you could direct me to Jeremiah Yoder's home."

"I am Jeremiah Yoder." Those sharp blue eyes that Tom remembered so well pinned Tom with a penetrating stare. "What do you want with me?"

No pleasantries. There never had been. Not with an *Englisch* stranger.

"My name is Tom," he said. "I used to know your son, Matthew, a long time ago."

"What business do you have with Matthew?"

"I was passing through town and thought I'd check in on some old friends."

"You were friends with my Matthew?" Suspicion dripped from the old man's voice.

"I knew him." Tom was testing the waters, but if his father recognized him, he gave no sign. "There was also a brother named Tobias, if I remember right."

His father poured black coffee out into the lid of the thermos and then took a sip, but said nothing. Tom decided to try again.

"I hired on one summer to help bale hay over at the Dennison's. He was an *Englisch* farmer over in . . ."

"I know who Clyde Dennison was," his father interrupted. "Matthew worked for him. Dennison was a fair man. He paid well."

His father would know exactly what Dennison paid, because both he and Matthew had handed their father every penny the day they got it. This was not unusual, just the way things were among the Amish—no one ever questioned it. Jeremiah had fed and sheltered his sons for many years and it was considered a reasonable thing for them to pay him back. The only recompense either of them received for their labor was some pocket money his father doled out to them, with an admonition not to spend it all.

Tom had hired out that summer along with Matthew, although he was only fourteen and his muscles not yet as hardened as his older brother's. Matthew had seen that Tobias did not have quite enough strength to do the job, but instead of gloating about his greater strength, he quietly made allowances for it, taking some of Tobias's work on himself when he saw that his younger brother was about to falter.

That was the kind of brother Matthew was.

Jeremiah took a cookie wrapped in waxed paper out of his front pocket. Tom saw that it was oatmeal raisin, and remembered that it was his father's favorite. Jeremiah broke the cookie in two and stared down at the pieces. "Matthew went home twenty-seven years ago."

"Home?"

"My son passed."

"I'm so sorry." Even though he knew the truth of it, hearing it from his father's lips still felt like a blow, but he felt the need to press on. He wanted to hear what his father would say. "How did he die?"

"An accident." His father, instead of eating the cookie, crumbled it between his fingers.

Tom did not ask what sort of accident. He knew more about it than his father did. He had entirely too much knowledge, so much knowledge that it had weighed him down for years.

Then he asked the question he had been aching to ask.

"What of the younger brother, the one named Tobias?" He held his breath. Like a child wanting his parent's approval and love, even when he'd done something wrong, he longed to hear some hint of love for him. Some longing. Some molecule of regret in the old man's voice.

Instead, Jeremiah's voice hardened. "I have no son named Tobias."

Tom tried again, a part of him desperately wanting his father to acknowledge him. "But I distinctly remember . . ."

"I have no son named Tobias," his father repeated.

Jeremiah poured the leftover coffee back into his thermos, tucked the waxed paper back inside his front pocket, and rose. "What is your name again?"

"Miller. Tom Miller."

He waited. Something inside of him cried out for his father to recognize him.

Jeremiah looked up at the sky, distracted. "Lots of Millers around here."

"Yes." Tom glanced up as well. There was nothing but cloudless blue. It was Jeremiah's way of shutting him out.

Jeremiah's eyes continued to peruse the sky. "You related to any of them?"

Tom considered this question. His father had just informed a complete stranger that his son Tobias did not exist. Things didn't get much clearer than that. "No," Tom said, with resignation. "I'm not related to any of the Millers around here."

Claire was surprised when she saw a shiny, new black car pull into her driveway and Tom climbing out. He was so deep in thought as he approached the house, he didn't even see her sitting there on the swing with mending in her lap until she spoke.

"Hello, are you back for some of Maddy's fudge?" she teased. "Elizabeth tells me you forgot to buy some the other day."

He did not seem startled by her presence, nor did he answer her question. Instead, he sat down on the top step and leaned against the porch railing.

"Do you mind if I ask you a question?" he said.

She bit off the thread she had used to sew a patch on one of Jesse's shirts. "You may ask me anything you like."

"I've never been a parent," he said, "so I don't know what it is like to raise a child. Could any of your children do anything bad enough to cause you to hate them?"

"Of course not." She was appalled. "There is nothing my children could ever do to make me hate them. I would sorrow for them, and pray for them, but I would never stop loving them."

"So that's what a normal parent would do, then?"

"I can't say. I only know what I would do."

"I thought that is what you might say."

"What is wrong, Tom?" She was getting concerned. This man who had endured so much physical pain seemed to be having some sort of emotional battle. Everything within her wanted to reach out to him.

"Would you forgive that child in addition to loving him?"

"How could I not? How could I expect my Father in heaven to forgive me if I could not forgive my own child?"

Tom seemed to drink in every word. "You believe in forgiveness, then."

"Of course. Without forgiveness, love cannot exist. Not with God, not with a family, not with a church."

"Thank you." He stood up, ready to go.

"What is bothering you, Tom?"

It seemed as though he desperately wanted to tell her something, but what, she had no idea. His life had been so different from hers, she could not imagine what went on inside of him. There was no way she could anticipate his next question.

"What do you want out of life, Claire?"

"What do you mean?"

"Some people want to achieve great things, some want to amass great wealth, some simply want to be loved. What do you want?"

"Peace." She did not even have to stop to think about it. "I want peace. In my home. In my life. I have had enough turmoil to last me a lifetime."

"I imagine you have." His voice was kind, but she could tell their conversation was over. "Thank you, Claire. I hope you find that peace, and I hope no one will ever take it away from you again."

As he drove away, she wondered what had just happened. That was one of the strangest conversations she'd ever had. Somehow, she felt as though her words had disappointed him—but she couldn't imagine why.

She had been so compassionate, so understanding. For a few minutes it had been on the tip of his tongue to tell her who he was, and to ask for that very forgiveness of which she spoke.

Then came the comment that all she wanted in life was peace. The information he had almost given her would not give her peace, it would bring more turmoil into her life—the last thing she needed.

He was not selfish enough to try to erase his own heartache by unloading all that pain on her. The woman had enough to deal with. He was quite certain that she did not need Matthew's long-lost brother rising out of the ashes.

Let sleeping dogs lie. That was something his father had often said. There was another saying of his father's that was a little more earthy. *The more you stir a pile of horse manure, the worse it stinks.* In other words, leave it alone. Let it lie. Keep quiet. If you've got a mess, don't go stirring it all up again.

He was grateful now that he'd been gifted with the choice of anonymity. Claire didn't need Tobias in her life, and his father didn't *want* Tobias in his life. Elizabeth had been wise in cautioning him about revealing his identity too soon. Right now, he doubted that he ever would be able to reveal it.

chapter TWELVE

That afternoon, Tom and Elizabeth were having lunch when Levi astonished them by carrying in the largest flat-screen TV Tom had ever seen.

"When did you get that?" Elizabeth said. They both followed him into the living room as Levi unboxed the giant screen along with a TV mount, and promptly began attaching them to the wall.

"This morning. Walmart."

"Why?" Elizabeth asked.

"Because I am trying to make Grace happy. It is not such an easy thing, making Grace happy."

"I thought she had agreed not to have a television in the house," Elizabeth said.

"We did agree." Levi searched in a bucket of tools for the correct size wrench. "But I have changed my mind. I think Grace's moods will get better if I buy her a nice, big television. We are not Amish. We can have this in our house if we want. I have been unreasonable keeping this from her."

"Boy, when you change your mind, you really change your mind!" Elizabeth surveyed the gargantuan object with interest. "Although it does seem to be a little overkill to put that in a house that only gets three stations."

"I will allow Grace to get satellite or cable."

"You will 'allow' me to get satellite or cable?" Their heads all swiveled to see Grace coming down the stairs. "You will 'allow' me to get them?"

There was a look in Grace's eye that made Tom pity Levi. The poor man had no idea who this woman was that he had married. Tom had seen the determination that was in the hearts of the military nurses who flew into the valleys and mountains of Afghanistan. They did not back away from a fight, no matter how great the danger. They *ran* to the helicopters when a call came in and then flew right into the mouth of it!

Elizabeth and Tom took one look at each other and by mutual, unspoken agreement, melted into the kitchen.

"I am so sick of this." Elizabeth went to the sink and filled the teakettle with water. "I apologize to you. Here you are, a guest trying to recuperate in our home, and there is no peace in this house. It's about all I can stand to live here myself— and I genuinely love those two." She sat down and sighed. "It seemed like such a good idea for me to give up the house and move into that nice, new little *Daadi Haus* Levi built right beside them. I envisioned dandling babies on my knees and having cozy chats with Grace and Levi in the evenings on the porch." She shook her head. "But it is not turning out to be anything like I'd envisioned. Instead, most of the time my *Daadi Haus* just feels like a place to duck and take cover."

It pained him to see the feisty older woman looking so frail and emotionally exhausted.

"If I had not gotten sick," Elizabeth said, "then Grace would not have come home and we wouldn't be having all these problems. Levi would have married some nice Amish girl, Grace would be happily bandaging someone somewhere, and I would be left in peace."

"From what I understand," Tom said, "if you hadn't gotten sick, then Grace wouldn't have been here to save Claire's life."

"Yes," Elizabeth agreed. "That is true. And those children of hers would have been motherless *and* fatherless. That man would still have come into their home, whether Grace was here or not."

"I'll tell you what," Tom said, as the voices in the living room rose one pitch higher. "Let's me and you take a walk."

Relief etched itself across Elizabeth's face. "I would like that."

The loud voices receded somewhat as they walked out into the overgrown yard. Getting away from all that tension was a relief.

"I guess maybe you have to be Amish for a *Daadi Haus* to work," she mused, as they watched Levi storm out of the house. He slammed into his car and spun gravel as he took off toward town. "I warned her not to fall in love with him. But did she listen? No. Now Grace is having the worst pregnancy I've ever seen. Hormones all over the place. Trust me, you are *not* seeing the real Grace. I thought the girl had more to her than what I'm seeing. I thought Levi did, too. Never would I have guessed that their marriage would turn out this way. Lord help the child who comes into it if those two don't get things sorted out in the next few weeks. I'd hate for even a newborn to have to listen to that mess."

"I'm sorry, Elizabeth," he said. "But I really think it is time that I found someplace else to recuperate." He wished he could grab his duffel and bolt right now—but he hated to abandon Elizabeth.

"Heavens, no. Don't do that. You aren't the problem. *They're* the problem. Levi can't help sticking his foot in his mouth, and Grace is too emotionally unstable right now to deal with things well. I'd leave right now myself if I didn't want to be here when my other granddaughter, Becky, comes home for the summer from college. She would feel so rootless if she didn't have this old place to come home to."

"Tell me about Becky." Tom hoped talking about her other granddaughter might distract her from the drama that was happening in the house.

Elizabeth brightened. "She's such a sweetheart. For a long time it was just me and Becky here while Grace was in the service. Becky was my buddy. Until I had my heart attack, we did everything together. She's only a sophomore in college, but she's going to be studying law."

Elizabeth's back had been hunched from all the conflict, as though she were trying to protect her middle from a blow. Now, talking about Becky, he watched her straighten up. "She's one bright little penny, our Becky. Got her sights set on law school at Ohio State once she graduates. With her straight-A's, I'm sure she'll get in."

They heard doors slamming inside the house and Elizabeth's shoulders slumped again.

"Both my granddaughters are smart as tacks," she said. "But that's not saying that the oldest one has a lick of sense right now!"

A buggy trotted from the direction of the Shetlers'. It pulled in and stopped not far from the bench where they sat. Tom felt his heart lighten when Claire stepped down from the buggy.

"Beautiful day for a ride," Elizabeth called. "Are you on your way to deliver a baby?"

"Not today. Although I have a mother who should be going into labor in the next week or so," Claire said. "I'm on my way to visit Rose. Maddy has been baking and wanted me to bring you some—"

She broke off as another door slammed shut inside the house. Then came what sounded like a muffled oath.

"—fresh bread."

The sound of glass shattering came next. Tom hoped it wasn't the plasma TV. It would take an awfully good corn crop to pay for that thing.

"What's going on?" Claire asked. "Where did Levi go?"

"I don't know. He just drove off. Levi and Grace have been having a fight," Elizabeth said. "And it has definitely *not* been pretty. Grace is letting off steam. They'll get over it. I hope."

"I am very sorry to hear that." Claire frowned as she laid a fresh loaf of bread, wrapped in a clean dish towel, in Elizabeth's lap.

"Thanks," Elizabeth said. "Maybe this bread will calm Grace down a little. I've noticed she does better when she gets a load of carbohydrates in her."

Claire crossed her arms and stared at the house. "And what was this fight about?"

"Looking back," Elizabeth spoke up, "I think Levi was on solid ground when he bought that TV for Grace, but he blew it when he said he would 'allow' her to get either cable or satellite."

"But why is she upset about that?" Claire asked. "My son was trying to give her a gift that an *Englisch* girl would like. I don't understand the anger I hear coming from that house."

"Listen to me closely when I explain again. Levi said he would 'allow' Grace to get either cable or satellite. Emphasis on the world 'allow.'" Elizabeth made quotation marks in the air.

"Your granddaughter is too strong-willed," Claire said. "She should have been taught that the Bible says that the husband is the head of his house."

Tom could feel Elizabeth bristle at this comment. It was obviously one thing for Elizabeth to criticize Grace, but a whole other ball game for Claire to do so.

"I understand the biblical teaching about a husband being the spiritual leader in his home," Elizabeth said. "I've read the fifth chapter of Ephesians many times, very closely, and I see nothing giving a man permission to spiritually bludgeon his wife with the twenty-second verse. Any man who does that is skating on thin ice with me, and I would wager he is with the Lord, as well."

"My Levi would never—"

"He doesn't mean to," Elizabeth said. "It's bred into him, Claire. That's exactly the way Abraham treated you. Forbidding you to be a midwife while you were married to him—even though that was your great love and passion. Forbidding you to allow Levi the books he loved to read. Now Levi is 'forbidding' Grace to work a job she loves. And 'forbidding' her to wear the clothes she's comfortable in. And 'forbidding' her to wear her hair any way except in a bun. I love your Levi as though he were my own. I think he's one of the finest men I've ever met in my life, but right now I'm not so thrilled with him. He seems determined to change everything about Grace. It's as though he married one woman and is trying to mold her into an entirely different one. I honestly don't know how much more of this I can stand—or that Grace can. She's tried so hard to please him, but she's been so upset lately, I'm about half afraid she'll bolt."

"But she is carrying my grandchild!"

"And my great-grandchild."

They heard another crash inside the house.

"Is that Grace breaking china?" Claire sounded appalled.

"Probably," Elizabeth said. "Don't worry, though, I sold all my good china in the auction we had two years ago. She's smashing garage-sale stuff now. I suppose she feels like it's a better outlet than smashing Levi's jaw when he gets back."

Claire's eyes were beyond shocked. "Your granddaughter would resort to violence against my son?"

"I don't think so. That's why she's smashing china. But if I were Levi, I'd step softly for a while when he gets back. She's had martial arts training and even though she's pregnant, I think she might be able to take him."

"Do you understand a woman who would act like this, Tom?" Claire surprised him by turning to him for support.

"You're asking me?" Tom couldn't help but laugh. "Claire, if I understood women, I would have married one by now."

This caught her interest. "So you have never been married. Ever?"

"No."

"Why?"

He had often pondered that question himself. It wasn't as though he hadn't dated lots of attractive women. He had received plenty of hints that a marriage proposal would be welcomed. Finding women was not a problem. A Marine uniform always turned heads. The problem was, one of the things he had never been able to shake about being raised Amish was a bone-deep conviction that marriage was for life. That conviction had always brought him up short—especially when his ideal woman happened to be an Amish woman with blond hair, no makeup, and more integrity than all the women he had every dated combined.

He told Claire none of this, of course.

"I just never found the right one, I guess."

"I thought the *Englisch* married and divorced easily, without much thought."

"Actually, for most there is a lot of thought—and tears."

He felt a little defensive about his *Englisch* buddies. Two of his friends in particular had gotten word from their wives that they were divorcing them while the men were still in a war zone. He'd always wondered what was so important that the wives couldn't wait until the men were safely home. A distracted soldier was a dead soldier.

"I will talk to my son," Claire said. "He should not expect his *Englisch* wife to change so much. He knew who she was when he chose to marry outside his faith."

"Amen, sister," Elizabeth said.

That was Claire. Rigid in her own beliefs, but willing to allow someone else leeway in theirs. Willing to do what she could to save her son's marriage—even if it meant counseling him from an entirely different point of view than the one in which she had been raised.

Elizabeth's comment about Abraham bothered him. He had forbidden her to work as a midwife? That told him more about her husband than anything else he'd heard—and he didn't like it.

"I should go," Claire said.

"Are you in a hurry?" Elizabeth said. "You're welcome to stay and visit. You can keep us company while we wait to see how this latest bit of drama between Levi and Grace turns out."

Claire glanced worriedly at the house. "It is best that I do not. After I visit my sister I am meeting my *Englisch* driver at Mrs. Yoder's. Today is Annette's birthday, and I am treating her to dinner."

"Well now, that sounds nice," Elizabeth said. "You go enjoy yourself and don't worry about those two young'uns of ours. They'll work things out." A note of doubt colored her voice as she said again, "I hope."

"If I'm ever stuck on a desert island"—Annette slipped a quarter rack of ribs, dripping homemade barbecue sauce, onto her plate—"Friday-night buffets at Mrs. Yoder's restaurant is what I'll fantasize about. Would you just look at this? These ribs are so tender, they're falling off the bone."

Claire preferred the battered shrimp, but she was glad that the birthday dinner she was treating her driver to was turning out to be a success. Annette had been a good friend to their family for many years, and the woman definitely loved barbecued ribs. Actually, Annette loved pretty much everything on the buffet.

"And these baby pickled beets!" Annette put four on her plate, speared one with her fork, and put it in her mouth. "They are to die for!"

Claire glanced around the restaurant, hoping no one had seen that. Sometimes Annette could be a bit too enthusiastic about her food. Eating while standing in line at the buffet was something the restaurant discouraged.

Rose was ill, and had to stay home again tonight. That meant Maddy was working here yet once again. Claire was unhappy with this for several reasons. One, she was worried that the reason Rose was ill was a combination of worry and poor nutrition. Second, with Maddy having to work, she'd had to ask Grace and Levi to watch the children while she took Annette for her birthday dinner. And third—well, she had never been entirely comfortable with Maddy's working here—and right now she was downright upset about it. The problem was, Maddy had grown into a stunner, and in this large dining room crowded with Friday-night customers, Claire could clearly see that she wasn't the only person who had noticed. Unlike most Amish girls, she had been blessed with raven-black hair that came down into what the old folks called a widow's peak. Neatly parted in the middle, and swept back beneath the snowy-white head covering, it framed Maddy's heart-shaped face perfectly. Her eyebrows were perfectly arched, matched by lovely long eyelashes. Her teeth were as white as fresh cow's milk, and she was so healthy that her cheeks and lips had a naturally rosy hue that most *Englisch* girls would have to use makeup to achieve.

Quick to laugh, blue eyes that sparkled with fun, and one deep dimple on her cheek—Maddy was as beautiful as any movie star gracing the glossy magazines that Claire tried not to look at when standing in line at the grocery store. This was decidedly not a good thing, especially now that her niece was working out in the world.

There were some who would never consider Mrs. Yoder's Kitchen a worldly place. It was a family restaurant that employed many Amish girls. The clientele tended to be middle-aged tourists or local people. It was not unusual for a table to be filled with Old Order Amish, especially during the buffets.

Maddy was, of course, dressed in her modest, Amish clothing. And yet Claire knew that it would be obvious to even the most casual eye that she was beautifully formed.

The problem was, Claire had a suspicion that some of the men's eyes in the crowded dining room weren't all that casual. Her young niece was still too innocent to realize that her good-natured smile and quick laughter as she brought food out from the kitchen and dished it into the buffet warming trays could be misinterpreted.

"Have you ever tried the breaded mushrooms?" Annette asked as she neared the end of her meal. "These things are delicious."

Distracted, Claire chewed a piece of feather-light whole wheat bread spread with Amish peanut butter and honey.

"Yes, they are."

"You didn't even get any," Annette pointed out. "Is something wrong?"

"I'm worried," Claire admitted.

"What about?"

Claire nodded meaningfully at a scene she was watching unfold over Annette's shoulder. A group of young men—decidedly not Amish—were bantering with her niece over what sort of toppings to put on the sausage they were putting onto their plates from the buffet.

Claire was not as innocent as Maddy, and the snickers she heard after some of the boys' remarks made her think that their comments held a double meaning her young niece appeared to be oblivious to.

Annette looked over her shoulder for a few seconds and listened. "Yes, they are trying to draw her into dirty talk, and no, she doesn't have a clue," Annette said, reading her mind. "Do you want me to deal with it, or do you?"

Annette was not a small person. As a younger woman, she had played college basketball. She towered over Claire a good four inches, and when riled, she used words that made Claire cover her ears.

Claire did not know if it was wise to unleash the full fury of Annette's wrath on the boys, and she did not want to embarrass Maddy, who had done nothing wrong.

"I'll take care of it." She rose and strode over to the counter.

"Isn't your shift about finished?" she asked Maddy. "Our driver is ready to leave."

Maddy looked puzzled by Claire's interruption. "I suppose I can leave as soon as I finish up in the kitchen."

"Good." Claire took the time to look each of the boys straight in the eye. "Our driver and I will be waiting."

Annette had arisen to her full six-foot height, her arms crossed across her chest, watching. Claire saw the boys glance at Annette, and their smiles dimmed. Claire was pleased. The boys now knew that Maddy was not alone. She had people who cared about her and were watching out for her.

Maddy obediently gathered her things, and Annette and Claire flanked her as they ushered her out of the building.

"Was I doing something wrong?" Maddy asked the moment they were outside.

"You did nothing wrong, little one," Claire said.

"Nothing except being pretty as a picture," Annette said, "and you can't help that."

"Those boys were just being friendly," Maddy said. "They come in all the time."

Claire wished she could agree, but she was suspicious that the boys' words and intentions had not been nearly as innocent as her niece's heart.

chapter THIRTEEN

"That's it," Tom encouraged. "Just ease that bolt off."

"Like this?"

"Not if you want a faceful of motor oil," Tom said. "Like this."

He was lying on his back, beneath Levi's car, which they had up on blocks. With his damaged hands, it was awkward, but he could still demonstrate the proper way to do an oil change.

After they successfully finished the task, Levi ran into the house and brought back two ice-cold Cokes and handed one to him.

"Thanks."

They sat in companionable silence, two grungy men who had just completed a dirty job, enjoying the sweet reward of a cold soft drink together. He had never had a son, and had no idea how much satisfaction he would get out of teaching one something as simple as how to do an oil change. Levi was such a quick study. A few more weeks and the boy would be a regular mechanic.

"How long do you get to stay?" Levi asked.

"You mean here?"

"No. I mean away from the military. Your sick leave or whatever soldiers call it."

"From the moment I left the hospital, I had thirty days of sick leave coming to me."

"How much of that is gone?"

"A little over a week."

"What happens when those thirty days are up?"

"I'll have to make a decision." He took another swig of Coke. "Depending on how I feel three weeks from now, I can petition Marine headquarters and the hospital commander for a formal extension of my convalescent leave . . . or I can retire."

"Retire?" Levi said. "Aren't you a little young to retire? What are you? Midforties?"

"Forty-four, and no, I'm not too young. I have twenty-five years in, which makes it an option. I just never thought I'd have to face the decision this soon."

"What happens if you ask for an extension?"

"I'd probably get it. I'm an officer and I have years of honorable service behind me. They would give me time to fully recuperate before I come back. The problem is, unless I get an awful lot better, there's no guarantee I'd ever be allowed to fly again. More than likely, I'll just end up with a desk job."

"You would hate that."

"Yes, I would definitely hate that."

"What would you do if you retire?"

"I'm not sure. A couple buddies have offered me jobs. They own small private helicopter companies—the kind that fly executives from one place to another or get rented to take kids up for a joy ride on prom night."

"They would let you fly when the military wouldn't?"

"Piloting a Cobra while under fire takes a whole different skill level than taking people up from time to time in good weather in a commercial helicopter."

There was a long silence as Levi thought this over.

"You would hate that, too."

"I would."

"You could stay here, maybe," Levi said. "And help me."

There was a wistful note in his voice that grabbed Tom's heart and held it. He already loved this young man. There was an innocence to him, a goodness that one didn't find every day. He wondered if the trust Levi felt for him would dissipate when he learned that he was his father's brother, only pretending to be a stranger.

"That's the best offer I've heard yet," Tom said. "But I've stayed here with you and your family way longer than I ever intended."

"What if you had your own apartment? I know of one. Grace suggested it the other day as a possibility."

"Where is it?"

"Over the workshop at my mother's. I lived there before Grace and I were married. It isn't big, but it's furnished. *Maam* uses it for overnight guests sometimes. It might be a good place to stay while you make up your mind about what you're going to do and where you're going to go. *Maam's* house doesn't have electric, but the apartment does, and I put a bathroom and shower in a couple years ago." Tom hoped that Levi's offer was given out of true friendship, and not just because the hydraulics on his tractor needed a complete overhaul.

The idea of living that close to Claire was tempting. Just being able to look out his window and see her going about her chores would be enjoyable. He might even be able to help her out a little from time to time if she would let him.

"Wouldn't your mother object to having someone like me living that close to her?"

"She's so busy taking care of the children and birthing babies, I doubt she'd even notice," Levi said. "Besides, a lot of the Amish rent out cabins to tourists. I don't see how this would be any different."

"I'd insist on paying rent."

"Well, that would definitely catch her interest." Levi said. "Let me talk it over with Grace and see what she thinks."

"You and Grace are on speaking terms again?"

"We are today. Last time I checked." Doubt crept into his voice. "As far as I know."

"How long would he stay?" Claire asked later that night when Levi came proposing that Tom move into his old apartment. The very idea was a worry to her.

"I don't know," Levi said. "Not so long. Just until he gets his strength back. He says there's a commercial piloting job in Toledo he's considering taking if he decides not to go back to the military. I doubt he'll be staying here more than a few weeks, but Grace floated a number to him that I thought was unreasonable, and he took it with no hesitation."

"How much?" Claire asked.

"Four hundred dollars."

"A month?"

"A week."

"A week!" Claire blinked. "That is a lot!"

"Grace says that it's a lot less than renting a hotel room during tourist season, which is what he originally intended to do."

"I suppose." Claire was doubtful.

"You don't have to say yes."

"I have children," Claire said. "Sometimes I'm gone."

"He's a good man," Levi said. "I trust him. Grace said that back on the base, he had a reputation for integrity as well as skill. She says that he would fight to protect anyone who even thought about harming you or one of your children."

"I—I suppose I could consider it," Claire said. "The money would be welcome."

"I'll go check out the apartment and make sure everything is turned on and working. It's been awhile since I was up there."

As Levi left, Claire did the math. Four hundred dollars a week! She could hardly believe the man had agreed to such an amount! If he stayed a couple months, she might be able to afford a new buggy horse! What a help that would be!

It seemed to Claire that she had recently been a bigger bother to her bishop than she ever intended. First the pager, and now the apartment.

It was a little embarrassing even to approach him about it, but at least it was a decision the bishop could make without consulting the other leaders, because it did not involve going against the *Ordnung* in any way.

The bishop was working in his barn when she drove Flora in. He heard her and came out. That was a blessing. She didn't want to go knocking at the door asking for him, which would make his wife feel like she needed to invite her in for some sort of refreshment. Even though the bishop's wife was a kind woman, Claire had two home visits to make today, and she wanted to get this conversation over with, not have it turn into a social call.

"Good morning," the bishop said. He had a broken harness in his hand, and it appeared that he'd been engaged in mending it.

"Good morning, Bishop," she said. "I am sorry to interrupt your work."

"I am not sure I want to do this work," the bishop said. "I'm coming to the conclusion that there are times when one needs to stop mending and simply purchase new."

"Sometimes that is necessary," she agreed.

"So what brings you here?" he asked. "Are you or the children in need?"

"I am in need, Bishop," she said. "Of your counsel."

"Oh?"

"My son and daughter-in-law have taken in a soldier, a man Grace says she heard many good things about when she was working as a nurse in Afghanistan. He recently got out of the army hospital for some serious wounds he received. He came to Mt. Hope to recuperate."

"Why did he come here instead of someplace else?" the bishop asked. "This seems a strange place for a wounded soldier to choose."

"He says he used to live near here."

"And what is the name of this man?" The bishop was already frowning.

"Tom Miller."

"You say he is *Englisch* and that Grace and Levi have taken him in?"

"Yes. He was quite ill and Grace nursed him back to health rather than make him spend any more time in a hospital. She knew him in Afghanistan. She said she owes him her life."

"And what is it you need to ask me about this Tom Miller?"

"He is looking for a small place to rent, temporarily. Levi thought his old apartment might be a good place."

"Levi approves of this plan?"

"Levi says he trusts this man." She hesitated and then told the bishop what was practically burning a hole in her heart. "He has offered to pay four hundred dollars a week."

"Four hundred dollars a week?" The bishop whistled. "For that much, I would be tempted to rent him my bedroom!"

"It is a great deal of money," Claire agreed.

"And much needed, unless I miss my guess?"

"It could be put to good use."

"Do you have any feelings for this man?" the bishop asked.

Claire gave his question careful thought. "I've only barely met him. Our conversations have been short."

"Does he look good to your eyes?"

Claire considered. "No. He has been much hurt, and is slightly disfigured."

"And he is an honorable man, even though he is *Englisch*?"

"Grace says he has much integrity."

"And it is only temporary," the bishop mused. "I see no reason you cannot make this extra money for you and the children, but I will caution you strongly against forming a relationship with this *Englisch* man."

"I have no desire for any man, Bishop," Claire said. "My children are my only earthly concern now—them and the mothers I serve."

"You will not go into his apartment for any reason unless he is gone. If he is there, one of your children must accompany you."

"Yes, Bishop, that won't be a problem."

"You say that now, but you are still young. Some *Englisch* men see a virtuous Amish woman as a challenge."

"I will be very careful, Bishop," Claire said. "Thank you for your permission and your wise counsel."

"One more thing," the bishop said. "Remember that some people will pay more attention to what you do than if you were . . . someone else."

"You mean because of Levi?"

"Yes." He looked embarrassed. "I'm sorry. Our people should have shorter memories than that, but sadly, they do not."

Her face burned, and she wished she was not having this conversation with him. "Thank you. I will be mindful of that."

As she left, she couldn't help but think about all the years of faithful service to her family and the Lord—and her people still had things to say about her.

On the whole, the Amish were terrible gossips. They knew better, and they didn't mean anything cruel by it, it was just that they were so extremely interested in one another's business.

She was quite aware that she had become the cautionary tale with which local Amish mothers warned their daughters not to assume that they were "as good as married" until their union had been blessed by both the church and God.

As she drove, she contemplated the bishop's words of warning. Yes, she was intrigued by Tom Miller, and puzzled over the haunted look she saw in his eyes from time to time. She sometimes wondered at the feeling of familiarity she had when she was around him. But what the bishop did not understand was that she was the last one in the world to be tempted by yet another man. The grief of loving and burying Matthew, and then enduring a marriage to Abraham, had been enough challenge for one lifetime. Deep in her heart, though, she knew that the bishop was right. It would not be wise for her to spend any time alone with Tom Miller. It wasn't about giving the gossips fodder—it was about protecting her heart.

She had dreamed one night this week that in the middle of the overgrown garden that was her life, filled with the large, familiar blossoms of concerns about her children and her work, she had discovered a tiny bright flower growing. It was a delicate flower that she had never seen before, and she kept wondering how this exotic plant had gotten here. She had certainly not planted it. She knew she should pluck it out—but leaving it there to come upon from time to time gave her pleasure.

The dream had been so vivid, she had lain and pondered it in the gray dawn before anyone else stirred. It had not taken her long to recognize the truth her mind was trying to tell her. Tom was so alien from anything she had ever known, so exotic compared to her humdrum existence, she had allowed a small fascination with him to develop.

She was grateful for the dream and for its warning. The last thing she needed was to have feelings for an *Englisch* man. It had been hard enough watching her son go through that agony and the disastrous marriage that had ensued. Unlike Levi, she would consider leaving the Amish church for no one. She needed to be very careful. The last thing she needed was a broken heart.

chapter FOURTEEN

T he apartment above the workshop was clean, sparse, and exactly what he needed.

He'd been a little worried about climbing the steps, but by using the handrail, he could make it. Levi carried his duffel bag up. Grace had gone to the grocery store and bought a few things so that he could have breakfast in the morning. Elizabeth had baked some cookies to take with him.

It was nice to have a family.

He soon saw that he wouldn't lack reading material while he lived here. The walls of Levi's old apartment were absolutely lined with books!

"Sorry about all the books." Levi sat Tom's duffel on the bed. "I got a little carried away after I left the Swartzentrubers."

"Have you read all of these?" Tom asked.

"Most," Levi said. "After I left, it seemed like there weren't enough books in the world. I was starved for knowledge."

"It's an impressive collection."

"Actually, I'm ashamed," Levi said. "A man should have better things to do with his time than read. I am afraid reading is a great weakness of mine."

"I wouldn't count that as a weakness," Tom said. "Have you ever considered getting a more formal education?"

"I took a few classes at a nearby community college after I got my GED."

"Did you enjoy it?"

"Very much."

"What kind of classes did you take?"

"The basics. I had the foolish notion of someday becoming a teacher."

"Then why did you stop?"

"I could no longer justify taking college classes once we were expecting a child. I will soon have a family to support."

Levi lovingly ran his hand over the spines of the books nearest him. "My stepfather would be turning in his grave if he knew that there were this many books on his property."

Claire walked in, a quilt folded over her arm. "He could not help the way he was. Abraham was only doing what he thought best. That is the way he was raised."

"That's true," Levi said. "I'm sorry. I should not have criticized him."

Claire waved off his apology and laid the folded quilt across the foot of the bed. "Here is extra warmth if you need it. I hope you will be comfortable here."

"I appreciate your hospitality," Tom said.

Claire merely gave a curt nod and went back down the steps.

He was a little surprised at the lack of warmth. Claire was usually more personable than that.

"Is she okay with me being here?" Tom said.

"She seemed fine with it when we talked," Levi said. "*Maam* gets a little preoccupied when she has a client who is close to birth. She will be fine. I'm going to be working downstairs for a while today. Come down whenever you're settled and I'll show you around my shop. And there's this broken chain saw . . ."

"I'll take a look at it, son."

"Thanks."

Levi headed down the stairs, unperturbed by Tom's slip of tongue. It wasn't unusual for an older man to refer to a younger man as "son." Tom knew that, but what shook him was that he had nearly meant it literally. He had met Levi only a week ago, but it would be easy to love him as a son.

Realizing this, he pondered the question that he had posed to Claire a few days earlier. Was there anything Levi could do that would make him stop loving him? Could make him hate him? He came up with the same answer Claire had—no. He might be disappointed, or hurt, or angry—but to stop loving him? He honestly did not think it was possible.

He wondered what it was about him that had made it possible for his father to hate him so much that he would pretend he no longer existed.

Claire

~~Grace~~ hid those first four hundred-dollar bills that Tom gave her for rent beneath a rug in her bedroom. This was the start of her new horse fund, and she was absolutely determined not to dip into it. Flora had been wheezing yesterday when she came home, even though it was a fairly short trip to the bishop's.

Today was going to be a good day. She had no appointments, no one ready to go into labor, and Maddy wasn't at work today. And it was Saturday, so the younger children were not at school, and the sun was shining. The only thing she had to do today was start working on her house so she could host church without embarrassment. Her plan was to make a list of jobs for each of the children and take a good hard run at that mountain of work she had to do. Even Amy could do some dusting and sorting out of drawers, especially if she had Sarah's and Daniel's help. Albert and Jesse could start shoveling out the stables. Hopefully Levi could help with that. She and the older girls could begin washing the walls upstairs. It was not looked down upon to have a "work frolic" the week before hosting church, but the family was expected to do as much as possible in the weeks leading up to it.

She had gathered her children together around the kitchen table and was handing out assignments when her sister, Rose, knocked on the screen door with a basket over her arm.

A visit with Rose was always welcome. Perhaps, if her back was feeling better, she could stay and help with the impromptu work frolic she and the children were having. What fun that would be!

Her hopes about her sister staying were soon crushed.

"Can I talk to you privately on the porch?" Rose asked after a brief greeting.

Rose's face was pinched with worry, and she seemed thinner.

"Of course." An ominous feeling was stirring in the pit of Claire's stomach as she followed Rose to the far end of the porch.

Rose had a bad habit of chewing her fingernails when she was upset, even when she was small. For years, Claire had accurately judged her sister's emotional state by glancing at her fingernails. Well-shaped, healthy nails were a sign that things were going well in Rose's world.

As her sister drew back a towel to reveal several fine pieces of china in her basket, Claire saw her fingers and stifled a gasp. Rose had practically gnawed her fingernails off. Even her cuticles were ragged and bleeding.

"You mentioned that you liked this dinnerware set the last time you came over," Rose said. "I—I'm getting rid of some things. I wondered if you might like to take them off my hands. I wouldn't charge you very much."

This behavior was so out of character, coming from her generous sister, that Claire could hardly believe it. In the past, Rose would have given her first choice of anything she no longer wanted, and refused any mention of pay.

"What's going on, Rose?" Claire said. "I'm your sister, you can tell me."

Rose feigned nonchalance. "Oh, we're a little short on cash this month. I thought I'd sell a few things that I was planning on getting rid of anyway."

"You loved this set," Claire said. "It was a tenth anniversary gift from Henry. I'm going to ask again—what is going on?"

"If you don't want to buy them, it's okay." Rose tucked the towel back over the dishes and attempted to leave. "I won't bother you anymore."

Claire blocked her way. "You aren't leaving this porch until you tell me exactly what is going on in your life."

She knew a battle was going on inside of Rose. Her sister was torn between loyalty to her husband, her own pride, and great need. She knew the instant when the battle stopped, because what light there had been in Rose's eyes went out.

"We have no food in the house," Rose said. "My children are hungry."

Those words felt like the kick in the stomach she had once received from an irritated milk cow.

"What about all of that canned produce you put up last summer?" Claire asked. "Even we have not eaten all we grew yet."

"What do you think we've been living on the past few months, Claire? It's gone."

The idea of a good Amish family having no food in their house was unbelievable. She could hardly imagine it. No one went hungry in Holmes County. At least no one who was

Amish. A family might be a little ragged, their shoes worn, but the land was rich and generous, and help from neighbors was plentiful when there was need.

"Don't you have any livestock left?"

"I butchered the chickens, one by one. We've eaten the pork from our pigs—even though it was the wrong time of year to butcher. Henry has crops in the field, but it will be many weeks before harvest."

"The church has not helped you?"

"Henry will not ask." Rose lifted her chin. "And I will not dishonor my husband by going behind his back. The children have been living on leftovers that I have taken home from the restaurant, but on the days I'm unable to work, they have nothing."

Claire looked at her sister's emaciated body. "You've been going without food, too."

"My children's need is greater than mine."

Claire's mind flew to the four hundred dollars she'd so carefully tucked beneath the braided wool rug in her bedroom. She had vowed not to touch it until she'd saved enough for a horse. But now the need for a new horse, as great as it was, paled in comparison to what was going on in Rose's home.

"Stay right here," Claire said. "I'll be right back."

She flew to her bedroom, extracted the money from beneath her rug, emptied her purse of every dime, put it all into a ziplock bag, and ran back to the porch.

"Where are you going, *Mommi*?" Sarah asked. "Why are you and Rose staying out on the porch?"

"Don't worry, little one," Claire said. "Just some grown-up talk."

"Is Rose going to have a baby?" Sarah asked.

The question brought Claire up short until she realized

that sometimes when women clients came to her home, she would tell Sarah to go outside and play so that she could have grown-up talk.

"Not that I know of," she said as she hurried outside.

"Sarah wants to know if you're pregnant," she asked.

"No chance of that," Rose said.

"Really?"

"Henry has been a little . . . distracted for the past several months."

"What do you think is going on with him?"

"I do not know," Rose said. "He will not talk to me anymore. Not about finances, not about the farm, not about where he goes. He used to leave only on Saturday. Now he is gone for two or three days a week. He gets angry if I ask him where he is gone to all that time. It's like I am living with a stranger."

"How is he able to farm if he's gone so much?"

"He isn't. The children and I are keeping the livestock fed. We never know when he will be home and when he will be gone. Even when he is with us, it is as though he is someplace else in his head. It is to the point that it is easier around our home when he is gone. He left early today. He might not come home until tomorrow or the day after. That happens sometimes."

"You know the leaders of our church will have to get involved if things don't change soon."

"I know," Rose said. "But I can't face going to them yet, and I'm praying hard that whatever is eating at Henry will go away."

Claire decided that even though there was nothing she could do about Henry, she could help feed her sister and her sister's children.

"I still have jars of vegetable soup in my cellar yet, and

much applesauce and other things. Come help me fill your buggy. Oh, and here's money for groceries." She handed Rose the ziplock bag.

Rose stared at the bag for a long time without reaching for it.

"You would do it for me, and you know it," Claire said.

"I would," Rose said. "I would not have to think about it for a second."

"Nor do I."

"But I have a husband and you do not."

"True—but from where I stand, your Henry is not much use to you these days."

Rose took the money and tucked it into her pocketbook. Then they carried some of Claire's surplus of canned goods up from the cellar to the buggy. It wasn't until Rose drove out of sight that Claire realized her sister had deliberately left the basket of lovely dinnerware behind.

Somehow, the joy had gone out of cleaning her house today. Having things in perfect order for church no longer seemed all that important.

Tom watched the pitiful little scene unfolding below him. Neither Claire nor Rose seemed to be aware that their voices were carrying. They were so engrossed in their own drama, they weren't aware that he was sitting on the small landing outside Levi's apartment.

He had been tempted to run in and add whatever cash he had in his billfold to what Claire gave her sister, but he doubted it would be welcome, especially considering how hard it had been for Rose even to confide in her sister.

He and Rose's husband had not seen each other since they were boys. Henry wouldn't recognize him as anyone connected to the family. There was a chance he could help Rose find out where Henry had been going.

He had been needing a project to keep him occupied—one that did not require physical strength. This was a good one. At that moment, he vowed to find out where it was that Henry was going. One thing he remembered about his people was that auctions were an Amish man's favorite form of entertainment. It was rare for an Amish farmer to miss out on a good local auction. He decided he would go to every auction he could find, hoping to run into him and hopefully strike up a friendship. Henry had never been a complicated man. The same topics he'd enjoyed as a young man—baseball, good food, pretty women, favorite beers, and fine horseflesh—were probably still topics he would enjoy discussing. An *Englisch* man with a decent knowledge of any one of these things could probably easily win Henry's friendship—and it could possibly result in some confidences being shared. He hoped so and would do his best. He didn't have much use for a man whose wife had to beg to feed her children.

chapter FIFTEEN

"You are *Englisch*," Claire said when she showed up on his doorstep on Monday afternoon with a basket over her arm.

That was an odd statement, coming from her.

"I am."

She seemed nervous. "Would you be willing to do a small favor for me?"

"Of course," he said.

"At church yesterday, I heard that our neighbor, Jeremiah Troyer, is ill. I am worried about him. He is my Levi's grandfather and he lives alone on the other side of our . . ."

"I know who Jeremiah Troyer is."

"Oh, good. I have made him a basket of food, but he will not take it from my hand or Levi's."

"Why won't he?" Tom knew the answer, but he wanted to hear what she would say.

"It is hard to explain, but I will try. When my son was banned from our Swartzentruber church, I was expected to ban Levi from my life, also. I could not do that. Especially since he was innocent of the thing of which he was accused. Instead, I accepted the sting of the *Meidung* of my own church and joined with the Old Order Amish so that I could freely fellowship with him. It was not an easy change, and I gave up many friendships, but it was the right thing to do. Now I am banned from ministering to my neighbor unless it is a true emergency. I know it is a hard thing for you to understand, but it is our way."

If you only knew, Tom thought, if only you knew how well I understand. He decided to play along. "Why would he take it from my hand and not yours?"

"Because you are *Englisch* and you do not count."

Oh, the bluntness of the Amish. He almost laughed. Of *course* he didn't count. He was *Englisch*!

She seemed blissfully ignorant of how rude her comment sounded. "The food will need to be taken to his springhouse. Jeremiah has no other refrigeration, and this chicken and dumplings will not keep for long without it."

"I understand. I'll do it."

She looked at him with those innocent blue eyes that he remembered so well. "Thank you."

"One question, Claire. If Jeremiah has shunned you, why do you feel the need to care for him?"

"Even after Matthew died, Jeremiah was kind to me for a very long time, and he liked my chicken and dumplings so much," Grace said. "This is my way of letting him know that I care for him still, even if I am not allowed to set foot over his doorstep."

It was not hard for Tom to imagine his father being kind to Claire. Jeremiah had always had more patience with his daughter, Faye, than with his two boys.

"I'll be happy to take it."

After she left, Tom tried to convince himself that he didn't care one way or the other. He meant nothing to Jeremiah, and Jeremiah meant nothing to him.

It didn't work. His pulse was pounding as he carried the basket of food to the car.

Tom had many good memories of being a boy on his father's farm. Eating his mother's baked oatmeal each morning in a kitchen kept warm with a woodstove. Arm wrestling with his brother, Matthew, for the last piece—and Matthew letting him win. His little sister's face shining from their mother's washcloth, her brown hair tightly braided and held with many hairpins, all covered by a minuscule prayer *Kapp*. He missed many things from his former life. Not all of it had been bad. Only those last few days.

Going to his father's home now was like picking up crumbs from the kitchen floor when one craved a full meal. His father would be as polite to him as he would be to any stranger. That was the most he could expect. His father had made it clear that he had no son named Tobias. There would be no Prodigal Son ending to this story. There would be no loving father waiting and watching, running to greet *him* with gladness in his heart.

The only way he would ever receive a prodigal welcome was if he came home willing to blindly accept a culture and rigid belief system that he knew he would not be able to tolerate.

And yet he could not turn down Claire's request. It was such a simple thing she had asked of him. Drop off a basket of food for a neighbor who wasn't feeling well. She had no idea how complicated this small task felt to him.

His father was plowing with a two-horse team when Tom arrived.

As he approached the fence, he held up Claire's basket for Jeremiah to see. His father tied the reins to the plow handle and walked over the raised furrows to where Tom stood. "What is that?"

"Supper."

"Supper? Why are you bringing me supper? Aren't you

that Miller boy that was here a few days ago asking about my Matthew?"

"Yes. I'm renting an apartment from Claire Shetler. She asked me to bring this over to you. She is under the impression that you are ill, and that you need nourishment."

"One visit to the doctor and a few heart pills, and everyone starts talking," Jeremiah grumbled into his beard.

"I'll let Claire know you're feeling better."

Jeremiah spat a stream of dark red tobacco juice at a weed near the fence. "How do you come to be renting from Claire?"

Tom had almost forgotten the Swartzentruber affection for tobacco. His father's ability to nail any target at which he aimed had fascinated him as a child. No longer. He wondered if that lifelong habit had anything to do with his father's need for heart medication.

"I ran into Grace and Levi the other day. She and I discovered we used to work together in Afghanistan. I was looking for a place to rent, and they recommended Levi's old apartment."

"In what way did you work together?"

"She was a medevac nurse. Most of the helicopters she flew on were unarmed, but the enemy fired on them anyway. I flew a Cobra gunship alongside of them when they had dangerous extractions."

Jeremiah's face never changed expressions. "War is a bad business."

"I could not agree with you more."

A wind had kicked up, and the leaves on the tree above them began to rustle.

"Looks like we're in for some rain. This is good. The crops have been thirsty," Jeremiah said. "Are you in a hurry?"

"No. Why?"

"Come inside." Jeremiah nodded toward the horizon where

rain clouds were scudding toward them. "We will *katsche und schmatze*. Talk and eat. Claire always did make too much."

There was a hint of kindness in Jeremiah's voice, and it reminded him of the father he had once known, before his mom passed.

There had been a time when Jeremiah had been a man much given to hospitality, who had delighted in having a table filled with relatives and friends. Tom remembered sitting on his father's knee as a child, leaning against his strong chest, basking in his embrace, falling asleep, while the adults' laughter and voices swirled around him, flavoring his small world with a feeling of contentment and safety.

What would it be like to enter that door again?

"I would like that."

He knew he would end this charade soon and tell his father who he was, but, as with Claire—not yet. For now, he wanted a chance to pretend, just for a few minutes, that he was truly welcome at his father's table.

Soon, Tom was standing in his mother's kitchen, trying to fully absorb the fact that he was here, in his childhood home, and his father was heating up Claire's chicken and dumplings for their dinner.

It was hard trying to pretend to be a stranger in a house where he knew every nook and cranny right down to the spot in the kitchen, next to the table, that still had a squeak in the floorboard.

"Been meaning to fix that," his father said, as he placed two bowls on the table.

Tom was tempted to smile at that comment. His father was a hardworking man, but he had been meaning to fix that squeak for the past thirty years.

The house that had once been filled with voices was now painfully quiet. The giant table that could seat a family of twenty had only two places set at right angles to each other at the far end.

After they had a silent prayer, he lifted his head to find his father looking straight at him.

"Do they hurt?"

"What? These?" Tom instinctively touched his face. "Yes, but they're getting better."

"I have a salve that might help."

This felt so familiar. The Amish had salves and potions for everything.

His father rose from the table and left the room. He came back in a few minutes with a large white bucket with a yellow label.

"This is B and W salve," Jeremiah said. "Betcha never saw it before. I use it for my livestock."

No surprise there either. He remembered once when his *daed* dosed himself with antibiotics he'd purchased for his cows, trying to rid himself of a bad case of bronchitis.

The Amish were so vested in alternative medicine that they would probably choose a chiropractor over going to a hospital even if they were in the middle of a massive heart attack.

His father went to the cupboard and pulled out a clean jelly jar, which he filled half full of a substance the color of beeswax with the consistency of axle grease.

"There. Take that home with you and use it. " Jeremiah sat the jelly jar in front of him. "It cleared up a bad place on one of my cows last week when she cut herself on an old nail."

"What is in it?"

"Honey mostly, and a few healing herbs. Supposed to be for burns and wounds. That's the reason for the B and W name on the label. Some Amish man developed it after his child got burned. A lot of our people swear by it. Says it helps take away scarring, too. Some soak burdock leaf in sterile water and use it as a bandage over it. Burdock is supposed to be healing, too—but I never set much stock in it."

Tom had trouble visualizing himself walking around with a wet burdock leaf on his face, but he would definitely try the salve, even if he already had been cared for by the finest surgeons at the Army's disposal. He knew there was no way this little jar was going to make the scars disappear, but he would use it anyway—just because his father had cared enough to give it to him.

"That's kind of you," he said. "I'll try it tonight."

"Might help." Jeremiah shrugged. "Might not. Probably won't hurt. If you like it, you can come by and get more. Most of us with livestock keep a bucket of it around. Cheaper that way, instead of buying it in the little bitty jars they sell at the whole foods place in Mt. Hope. Sometimes it saves us the cost of a vet bill."

Jeremiah ladled chicken and dumplings into Tom's bowl and then his own. Aromatic steam rose from the homemade wooden bowls.

Tom tasted it and discovered that Claire had seriously undersalted it. Probably in case Jeremiah had to be on a salt-restrictive diet.

Fortunately, he didn't have to be quite that careful yet. He reached for a jar of salt sitting on the table, took a pinch, sprinkled it over his food, and tasted it. Perfect.

He ventured a question. "Do you happen to know a Henry Miller?"

"I do, why do you ask?"

"Claire is concerned for her sister. From what I gather, Henry has been neglectful of his family of late."

"I have heard that an *Englisch* driver picks him up on Tuesdays right outside Lehman's Hardware and takes him to where no one knows."

"You've given me some valuable information, thank you."

"So you fly the helicopters, huh." Jeremiah was obviously finished with the subject of Henry. His father had never been a gossip. "Why?"

"The mechanics of flight have always interested me."

This was a true statement, and the explanation he always gave.

What he never told anyone was that he simply loved to fly. Being in the sky brought him a rush of freedom he never experienced on land. There was a purity in being so high in the air that buildings and traffic and people disappeared and it was just he and his machine waltzing with the clouds or following mountain streams through canyons. Even the unforgiving valleys of Afghanistan held a rugged beauty from the air. On foot, however, the poverty was so great, he often had to deliberately switch off any human feelings of compassion in order to function.

The rain that Jeremiah had predicted began to beat against the tin roof of the farmhouse as his father gazed off into the distance. "My youngest boy was interested in flight. He would lie on his back as a child and look up into the sky for hours, watching barn swallows swoop and soar, hoping for an airplane to fly by."

Tom did not remember doing that. It surprised him that his father had locked that memory away.

"He used to fold bits of paper into airplanes and try to fly them from the top of that maple tree out front. He was always good at making up his own toys."

Tom's throat had suddenly gotten so tight he had to clear it in order to speak. "Is that Tobias you're talking about?"

"Jab."

"I thought you said you didn't have a son by that name." His heart was in his mouth as he waited for the answer. Could there possibly be something redemptive his father might say about him?

"Tobias ran off when he was seventeen."

Tom decided to step carefully around the next question, but he had to know. " I heard a rumor that your son had been banned from your home."

"He was," Jeremiah said. "We were instructed by our bishop to have nothing to do with him—not even to eat with him or take a cup of coffee from his hand." The old man looked straight at Tom and spoke the words that shattered his heart. "That didn't mean I didn't care about him. I never stopped loving my boy or worrying about him. There isn't a day goes by that I don't pray for my Tobias."

The words brought a lump to Tom's throat so huge he could barely swallow. It was all he could do to keep from breaking down completely and confessing everything to his father. But the stakes had gotten too high. He wanted more time with this man, but if his father knew who he was, he would be obligated to kick him out unless he promised to live a faithful life from that point on.

A faithful life, by their definition, was being a Swartzentruber. Returning to the Swartzentruber faith would mean taking on the full regalia of legalistic dos and don'ts, in addition to never being allowed to fly again under any circumstance.

It was too great a sacrifice to contemplate.

Hearing his father say that he loved and prayed for him every day was a balm to his soul that he would cherish for the rest of his life. Those words alone had been worth this entire trip. Someday soon, he would tell his father and accept the consequences, but not now. For now, he wanted to savor the unexpected gift of this evening.

While life-giving water pelted the sturdy old house, they talked of many things. As a pacifist, Jeremiah was not interested in hearing about the military. Instead, he wanted to hear stories about the countries Tom had traveled to and the various customs he had witnessed. The time passed so quickly, Tom was surprised when the old windup clock struck eight o'clock. He glanced at his watch, then back at his father's wall clock.

"My watch says it's nine o'clock," he said. "Is your clock slow or is my watch wrong?"

"Our people do not observe the world's 'fast time.'"

He'd forgotten that the Swartzentrubers refused to accept daylight saving time. Everyone else in the United States might be "springing forward" in the spring and "falling back" in the fall, but not his father's people. The Swartzentrubers plodded on, keeping the same time all year long, never adjusting to anyone else's frivolous notions of moving time around.

"It is getting late." Jeremiah yawned and picked up a kerosene lantern from a side table where it had made flickering shadows on the wall all evening. "I will go to bed now. Milking time comes early."

"I know." He well remembered getting up at four in the morning, even on school days, to help his father milk.

"You have knowledge of milking?"

"I used to help my father."

"Four o'clock is early, *ja*?" Jeremiah's voice sounded almost hopeful.

"I don't know anymore. I seldom sleep that long. My dreams bother me."

"You have seen much battle?"

"Too much."

"So that is how it is, then." Jeremiah looked at him, as though weighing something in his mind. "You are welcome to come milk whenever your dreams awaken you early. All those early-morning hours should not be wasted."

"I appreciate that, Jeremiah," Tom said. "I'll probably take you up on it."

"Good. Milking is sometimes tiresome, but it has never given me bad dreams." Jeremiah picked up the lantern. "I will walk you to your car. You *Englisch* are not used to the darkness."

The hard rain had stopped.

"The crops will grow good, now," Jeremiah said as Tom got into his car. "You be careful out there on the road. There are many fast cars these days."

Tom waited, illuminating his father's path to the house before he backed out of the driveway. He watched until he saw the lantern light glowing through the window of his father's bedroom. There were no secondary lights at this farm, no porch lights outside, no city streetlights. When it was dark, it was dark, unless the moon and stars were out. Tonight, they were not.

It was at that point that he rolled down the windows, turned off the motor, laid his head back against the headrest, and absorbed the intense darkness and quiet of his father's farm.

Tonight had been as healing to his soul as the rain had been to the parched ground.

By the time Tom got back from his father's, his leg was acting up. Getting up the stairs was an effort. When he got inside, he went into the bathroom, shook two pain meds capsules into his hand, thought better of it, and put one back in the bottle.

He had come close to becoming dependent on these things before and would not allow that to happen again.

There was an inviting weathered Amish rocker out on the small upstairs porch. Tom decided to sit outside until the medication kicked in enough for him to sleep.

His father loved him, and he had no idea what to do about it.

Jeremiah Troyer was no lightweight when it came to obedience. If Tom went to him and confessed who he was, Jeremiah would feel honor bound to tell the bishop of the return of his erring son. If the bishop instructed him to have nothing to do with him, his father would respect the bishop's wishes. Jeremiah was not Claire. He would never leave his church in order to have fellowship with him.

The only way Tom could see his way clear to spending time with his father again was to continue to pretend he was someone else. He could lie and be part of his father's life or tell the truth and lose the small bit of contact he had.

He heard a noise and realized that one of Claire's upstairs windows was slowly opening. A small flashlight shone in the window for a second, then switched off. Even though it was dark, he could see a slim figure climb out of the window, shimmy down a tree, and then sprint off across a field.

It had to be Maddy. There was no one else in Claire's house it could be. She was exactly the right age to be sneaking out. He wondered where the party was being held tonight, because undoubtedly there was a party somewhere. There were so many isolated barns around the countryside to drink beer in, and there were always a few Amish parents willing to turn a blind eye if that's what it took to keep their children at home instead of running off to become *Englisch*.

She would grow out of it. Most of them did. Claire might even know where she was headed. Some parents kept closer tabs on their children than the kids realized.

He realized that his leg wasn't aching quite as badly now. The pain pill had kicked in, and it was a perfect evening and a perfect place to savor the amazing fact that his father loved him and prayed for him. Every day.

Jeremiah was no liar. If he said he prayed for his Tobias every day, that's exactly what he did.

Tom wondered how many near misses there had been over his lifetime because of his father's prayers.

chapter SIXTEEN

That night, Tom was hopeful that perhaps this reconciliation of sorts with his father signaled the end of the worst nightmare of all, but he was wrong. His subconscious had a world of its own, and its own agenda.

Someone was tossing handfuls of pebbles at their bedroom window. The sound was as startling as buckshot in the deep stillness of the night.

"Who is it?" His older brother, Matthew, propped himself up on one elbow as Tobias threw off a quilt, padded over to the window, and opened it.

It was to be their last night of sleeping in the same room. Tomorrow, by noon, Matthew would be a married man.

"Come down," a voice called up to their open window; the man stood in the shadows beneath. "I want to show you something."

"It's Henry," Tobias said.

"What time is it?"

Tobias lit a lamp and checked the windup clock on the wall. "One thirty."

He heard a muttered oath as Matthew flopped back onto the bed they shared. "Doesn't he realize I have to be up in a few hours to go to Claire's? I need to help her family finish preparing for the wedding."

Tobias leaned out the window. Swartzentrubers did not use window screens, which annoyed him a great deal in the summertime when his choices were suffocating in an airless bedroom or being inundated with flies. There were always plenty of flies on a working farm.

"What do you want?" he called down.

He had to admit, he was curious. Henry was his first cousin on his mother's side, and enjoyed fast cars a little too much to join the church yet.

"Just come down," Henry said. "I can't tell you, I have to show you."

The night was warm for late October, and there was a headiness in the air—almost as though the earth itself was rejoicing over the abundance of rich crops filling the barns and silos.

"What's so important that you need wake us up in the middle of the night?"

Henry grinned up at him. "I got something sweet to show you."

"When did you get home?" Tobias knew his cousin's father had been saving for years to improve their stock. Henry's father's dream was to breed foals valuable enough to support their family. It was an unusual dream for a Swartzentruber man—but Henry's father was not a particularly good farmer. His great love was horses. The bishop had given him permission to try his hand at this new venture as long as he gave everything beyond a modest living back to the church. Having a slightly different occupation could be tolerated if it kept the family on the farm, where God intended man to live. "We got home a couple of hours ago," Henry said. "Do you want to see what we got down there in bluegrass country?"

Tobias was now wide awake and curious. "I'll be right down."

"Henry's dad brought a new horse from Lexington," he told his brother. "I'm going to go see it."

Tobias jerked on some clothes. He decided he wasn't going to get any sleep tonight anyway, so he might as well go see his cousin's new horse.

"You aren't going without me." Matthew jumped out of bed, pulled on his pants, and hitched up his suspenders. "Not if there is a horse involved."

Tobias enjoyed the drive through the October air in Henry's car with the windows open and rock music blaring. It felt wild and free, and soothed some of the ache in his heart over losing Claire to Matthew.

Not that he resented his brother. Matthew was a better person than he in every way, and Claire deserved the best.

Henry slid open the barn door as soon as they got to his parents' farm. "Here he is."

All three of them went in and hung over the stall's gate, but with only a lantern for illumination, it was hard to see the black Thoroughbred standing in the shadows.

"I thought you were going down there to buy two horses, a stud and a mare," Matthew said.

"The mare's over there. She has good bloodlines, but Ebony Sky is a prize. When Daed saw the horse, he had to have him, even if Ebony did cost every dime we have. He's past his prime as a racer, but he has some champions in his lineage." Henry unlatched the stall. "Here, let me take him out where you can see him better."

The sleek, black horse that Henry led out was like nothing Tobias had ever seen up close. There was speed written in every line of that animal's body. He whistled softly. "Man, I don't care if he is past his prime. An animal like this didn't come cheap."

"We were in luck. The horse farm was in financial trouble. Bad management. They needed to sell some stock off fast. We were at the right place at the right time, and Daed had cash."

"I wonder how fast he can go," Matthew said.

"I'll bet he's still got some speed in him." Henry dredged a flask

out of his back pocket and took a long swig, then remembered his manners. "You want some?" he asked, holding out the flask.

"Sure," Tobias answered. Drinking alcohol was not against their Ordnung, but he had not drunk anything stronger than cider. He took a big swallow and it burned its way down his throat.

Matthew didn't even bother to acknowledge the offer. His eyes were drinking in something much more intoxicating to him—Ebony Sky. Matthew had never seen a piece of horseflesh that he didn't want to touch or couldn't ride.

"You are a beauty." Matthew ran his hand over the horse's glossy coat. Ebony Sky shied away at first, but Matthews's reassuring words soon calmed the horse to the point that it was practically leaning toward him. Tobias didn't blame the horse—Matthew had that effect on every living thing he touched.

"You want to ride him?" Henry swayed ever so slightly as he handed the flask back to Tobias. It was then that Tobias realized his cousin had crossed over the line to being drunk.

He decided that he didn't mind joining him and took another gulp of the noxious liquid, hoping it would take the edge off his dread of having to pretend that his heart wasn't breaking at tomorrow's wedding.

"Only professional jockeys ride horses like this," Matthew said.

"Aw, come on, you know you want to," Henry said. "I bet you twenty dollars you can't stay on him."

Tobias saw a light in Matthew's eyes and he knew that there was nothing his brother wanted more than to climb upon the back of that horse.

"What do you think, Tobias?" Matthew said. "Should I try?"

Tobias thought was there probably was no horse alive that Matthew couldn't ride.

It was at that moment that he spoke the words he would regret *for the rest of his life.* "I'll take that twenty-dollar bet, Henry. My brother can ride anything."

Matthew didn't bother with a saddle. He simply took the reins from Henry's hands and led Ebony Sky out beneath the night sky, walking the horse around in circles, talking to him, calming him, the horse's black coat glistening in the moonlight. Then suddenly, before either he or Henry knew what was happening, Matthew was upon the horse's back.

"I'll take that twenty now," Tobias said.

"Nope, the bet was for riding him, not just sitting on his back. I tell you what . . ." Henry frowned. "The road crew just got done grading this road and there isn't a pothole for two miles. Let's see how fast Ebony can go."

"Are you up for that?" Tobias asked his brother.

"I don't know . . ." Matthew stroked the horse's mane as he sat astride him bareback.

"Hey," Henry said, "give it a try. I want to see him in action, find out if we got our money's worth."

"Maybe just a quarter of a mile," Matthew said. There was longing in his voice.

Barefoot, shirtless, perfect in physical form, he looked magnificent in the moonlight astride that great horse. Tobias had never been prouder of his brother—or more envious. No wonder Claire preferred Matthew to him. Compared to his brother, Tobias knew he would always come in a poor second.

"You'll need some light," Henry said. "We'll follow you with the headlights on."

"You shouldn't be driving," Tobias cautioned as Henry stumbled toward the car.

Henry, who was always good-natured, laughed and tossed him the keys. "Yeah, I'm pretty wasted. Daed and I picked up some Kentucky bourbon on the way home to celebrate. Here, you take over."

Tobias had been behind the wheel of Henry's car only once before, but he knew even a Thoroughbred couldn't go much past thirty miles per hour. It shouldn't be too hard to keep control of a car going that slow.

He started the engine while Matthew got the horse into position. When Henry said, "Go!" Ebony Sky took off like a shot.

Watching his brother leaning low, clinging to that horse like a burr as he rode flat out, was one of the proudest moments of his life. He pressed down on the accelerator to keep up.

"Check it out!" he shouted to Henry as the speedometer hit thirty, then thirty-two, and finally thirty-five miles per hour. "That's good riding! You owe me twenty dollars!"

Matthew had ridden a full mile at top speed and was starting to slow down when a huge, antlered deer darted across the road right in front of the car.

"Look out!" Henry yelled and grabbed the steering wheel.

Tobias managed to swerve and miss it, but lost control of the car when the wheels hit the loose gravel at the side of the road. Neither he nor Henry had bothered with seat belts. Buggies didn't have seat belts.

He missed the buck, managed to jerk the car back onto the road, overcompensated, attempted to hit the brakes, misjudged, accidentally stomped on the accelerator, and rammed an electric pole head-on. The last thing he remembered was Henry flying through the windshield and Ebony Sky rearing up as broken electric lines flashed in the sky.

The police said later that it was a miracle that he and Henry lived through the accident. The doctors said it was amazing that Tobias, with a fractured leg, had managed to walk to the nearest house where an elderly Englisch widow lived. He had collapsed on the porch, while she dialed the sheriff's department.

None of the boys had any ID on them. It was several hours before things got sorted out enough to contact their families.

When Tobias woke up, he was informed that his brother had died, electrocuted by the wires that had fallen upon him and the horse.

Some kind souls whispered that it was a blessing the brothers' mother was not alive to face such heartache. Some tsked over the boys' foolishness that had caused such a tragedy. Others bemoaned the fact that Henry's father had lost a prize stallion for which he had saved a lifetime to own.

He knew what they said, because he heard the words being whispered in the corridors outside the hospital room where he lay, grieving, angry, and humiliated that he had allowed himself to be pulled into doing such a stupid, stupid thing.

What had he been thinking, encouraging Matthew to ride such a valuable and high-strung animal? What had he been thinking when he'd accepted Henry's offer of Kentucky bourbon? What had he been thinking, getting behind the wheel of an automobile when he had next to no experience and was half intoxicated?

Tobias knew the answer. Pride and a twenty-dollar bet had destroyed his brother . . . and himself.

chapter SEVENTEEN

T om was shocked awake when he fell, bruised, flat onto the floor. His covers were thrashed halfway off the bed. He was not surprised. Fighting one's way out of a wrecked car with a broken leg was not a passive act. Even if it was all in his mind.

Unless this stopped, he would never want to go to sleep again.

He looked around. It was still as black as sin outdoors, but unless things had changed, his father would be milking a small herd of Guernsey cows this morning before the sun came up. The milk would be picked up by one of the local cheese factories. Farming was a hard job. Levi had told him that there were fewer and fewer Amish farmers in Holmes County. That was a shame. He respected men like his father and Levi who stayed on the land, even when nearby factories provided an easier way of making a living.

His desire to sleep was gone. Falling out of bed could do that to you.

He pulled on his clothes and went to the kitchenette to make a pot of coffee. As the coffee brewed its homey scent into the air, he tried to decide what to do so early in the morning. He could always read, but he realized that in the

160

emotional fallout of reliving the night that Matthew died, the one thing on earth he wanted to do right now was walk out into that inky blackness and help Jeremiah Troyer milk his cows. It felt slightly miraculous that he could do so with some expectation of being welcome.

When he arrived in the barn, Jeremiah greeted him warmly.

"What is this *Englisch* man doing up at this time of the morning?" Jeremiah said. "Are you here to take pictures of this old Amish man going about his early-morning chores?"

The tease in Jeremiah's voice was gentle. He seemed pleased to see Tom walk in, flashlight in hand.

"I was never much good at taking pictures," Tom replied. "But I'm pretty good at milking cows. Or at least I used to be."

He flexed his hands, the scar tissue tight across his knuckles. He wasn't entirely sure that he was capable of milking. His hands were not what they had been—not since the accident—but he wanted to try.

"*Ach,* I am always grateful for an extra pair of hands," Jeremiah said. He nodded toward a galvanized bucket lying upside down on a shelf covered with a clean, white cloth.

Tom grabbed the bucket, washed off the udder of a cow that had not yet been milked, and then began the process at which he had once been proficient.

It did not go well.

His fingers were even stiffer than he had realized. It was almost impossible for him to squeeze tight enough to produce any milk at all. As he struggled to grip hard enough to even get a few drops out, he heard the rhythmic sound of Jeremiah's milking pinging against the side of his bucket.

Jeremiah finished with the cow he was milking and took over another one while Tom struggled to do a job he had spent so many hours at when he was a boy. Sweat broke out on his brow as he fought against the pain, and he realized that his physical therapist back at the hospital had not pushed him hard enough. Bringing a fork or cup to his mouth had never created the need for him to use his hands to this extent.

Dressing himself, fumbling with buttons, all of these things he had mastered after a while. Driving an automatic shift car had not been a problem—but now he was whipped. His hands burned and ached, his body felt like he had run a marathon, and all he had to show for a half hour of intense effort was a quart of milk.

Jeremiah came to look over Tom's shoulder. "I am sorry. This is hard for you because of the burns. Do you want me to finish it for you?"

"Please." Tom stood, his arms trembling from the effort he'd put out. "I keep thinking I'm getting stronger, but until this morning, I didn't realize how weak I still am."

Jeremiah took his place on the milking stool and soon he heard the rhythmic sounds of milk hitting tin again.

Tom looked down at his fingers, concerned. "I won't be able to fly a helicopter unless I can regain some strength in my hands."

Jeremiah rose, having already stripped the cow's udder. The bucket of milk sloshed against the sides of the bucket.

"Maybe you should help me with the milking until you become strong again."

"That is a kind offer, but I would be useless to you."

"That is true," Jeremiah conceded. "You are useless as a milker, but I do not think the cow minds so much if you practice on her."

They both glanced at the cow, who was placidly chewing her cud.

"You were a friend of my boys, and I have no boys left. Having you here might ease the missing of them a little.

You will be welcome to come and try every morning if you want."

"I would like that. This is even tougher than some of the therapy I got in the hospital."

His father held the lantern up so that he could see, then he reached for his hand and inspected the scarring. "These fingers will become strong again, I think—and then you will be able to drive your *Englisch* helicopters again."

Claire got home just as Maddy was setting out dinner for the younger children. The girl was competent, and whenever she wasn't working at the restaurant, she seemed content to stay at home, gardening, working, and watching over the younger children. Claire did not know what she would have done without her these past months. Still, there were dark circles beneath her eyes. The girl was obviously working too hard. She was young, and she should have some nice, healthy, young-people fun.

Claire slipped her shoes off the minute she sat down. She disliked wearing shoes, especially now that it was getting warmer. "Aren't you going to the singing tonight?"

"I wasn't planning on it," Maddy said.

"You should go. You should have chances to be with other Amish youngies."

The image of those *Englisch* boys eying Maddy was fresh in her mind. She made a resolution to encourage her to go to as many singings as possible. She needed to find a good, honest Amish boy to marry.

"How did work go this morning?" Maddy set a pitcher of water on the table.

"It was fine." Claire lifted her black bonnet off her head, sat it on the kitchen table, then pulled the straight pins out of the white prayer *Kapp* beneath. "I told Martha Keim—Caleb's Martha—that she needs two week's bed rest. Her due date is soon, and I am certain she is carrying twins. The poor woman can barely walk."

Maddy glanced at her in concern. "Is she in danger of losing the babies?"

"I don't think so, but that husband of hers is not as thoughtful as he could be. He expects her to work in the fields with him. Martha can't even tie her own shoes—let alone do heavy farmwork."

"Is her husband mean?" Amy asked.

"No, not at all. But he can be thoughtless. Prescribing bed rest will give her a chance to gather her strength before the babies come."

"How can you tell for sure and for certain that it's twins?" Amy asked.

"I heard two separate little heartbeats with my stethoscope last week when I checked on her."

"Aww," Amy said. "Can I go see the babies when they get here?"

"If all is well with them and their mother and father."

Maddy started pulling tins of bread out of the oven, quickly dumping them out onto the snowy white kitchen towel. The girl was so smart. Claire was of the opinion that Maddy knew more about cooking than many women twice her age. She had bread down to a science. It was cheap and filling and they ate a lot of it.

"That looks and smells so good," Claire said.

Maddy took a serrated knife and began to cut thick, crusty slices from the nearest loaf.

"I've been growing a sourdough bread starter the past few days," Maddy said. "This is my first batch with it."

Sarah brought a pot of honey from the pantry, while Claire

pulled a pitcher of cold milk and a crock of butter from the refrigerator. Albert brought butter knives from a drawer. Jesse set plates around the table. Sarah got drinking glasses. Amy folded napkins and gave them to Daniel who managed, by standing on tiptoe, to place one at each place.

Everyone knew their job. This was a routine they indulged in once a week, always on Maddy's baking day.

Then each one took their seat, and all bowed their head in silent prayer. Claire gave heartfelt thanks for God's tender care, asked Him to take care of her children and her sister. She also added a new name to her list. Tom Miller. If anyone needed prayer, that man did. Unfortunately, praying for Tom led her to thinking about him—which was not a wise thing to do. She became so engrossed in her thoughts about how she should *not* be thinking about him that she couldn't keep from thinking about him—and ended up forgetting to lift her head until Jesse cleared his throat. She glanced up and smiled serenely—as though she had been deep only in prayer, instead of letting her mind wander to the interesting soldier next door.

Oh, what a hypocrite she was! "Shall we enjoy God's bounty, children?"

That was the signal they had been waiting for. They all dug in; the smell of baking bread had made everyone ravenous.

The seven of them began spreading butter on the warm bread, and then slathering it with their own golden honey, flecked with tiny pieces of honeycomb, from Levi's bees. All of it was washed down with ice-cold milk.

Claire loved this part of the week—their no-cook day, when she and the children surfeited themselves on Maddy's fresh bread. She couldn't even remember when they had begun this tradition. It had just developed. Not only was it delicious, it was also thrifty—which was always a good thing.

"I think this is the best bread you've made yet," she told Maddy. "I would save that recipe. It is wonderful. Did you make extra for Rose and her children?"

"I did," Maddy said. "And you know I don't mind, but I don't understand why we're taking food to Rose all the time."

"It is hard for me to explain, just trust me when I say I believe it is the Lord's will that we do so."

"Can I have another piece?" Albert asked.

"Of course." While Maddy sliced another loaf, there was a knock on the door.

"I'll answer it." Jesse jumped up and ran to the door.

Claire paused a moment in her enjoyment of Maddy's culinary expertise to listen. It was probably a customer wanting to purchase something from the store. If so, Amy could handle it, but the next thing she knew, Tom Miller was standing in the doorway with a familiar-looking basket in his hand, and it was filled with strawberries.

"Oh!" Claire was surprised. "It is you."

It came out sounding ruder than she intended, but she was surprised to see the man she found herself thinking about entirely too much, standing here in her kitchen.

Tom smiled his crooked smile. "Jeremiah asked me to bring these over in payment for the dinner you sent."

This information struck her as odd. "That was two days ago. How does Jeremiah now know you so well that he asks you to do this thing?"

"I've helped him milk."

"Jeremiah asked you to help him milk?"

"No." Tom flexed one hand. "He's allowing me to help him as a sort of physical therapy."

"Really." This caught her attention. "Is it helping?"

"Actually, it is. I'm definitely gaining a little strength and flexibility."

"That is good. I am surprised, though. Jeremiah is an admirable man, but warmth toward *Englischers* is not his strong suit."

"He's an old man and he's lonely," Tom said. "I guess I was better than nothing."

"That's true. Both of his sons and his wife are gone, and his only daughter moved away about a year ago."

"Yes, he told me about that."

"When?"

"While we were milking. We were talking about places that we'd been and he mentioned having a daughter and son-in-law who moved to the Gallipolis, Ohio, area with some other Amish."

"You ate with him?"

"Yes," Tom said. "We had a good visit."

That stung. Jeremiah had not said more than two words to her since she left the church. She had even stopped lifting her hand in a silent wave to him when he rode by because he never acknowledged her with so much as a nod.

Even though she knew what she was giving up when she joined the Old Order church, it was still a shock to her how completely she had been cut off from people she had once thought loved her.

That was the power of the *Meidung*. It brought people back into the church by breaking their hearts. Sometimes those hearts needed breaking. Hers had not. "Would you have supper with us?"

"Thanks, but I'm not hungry."

"Some coffee, then? There's still some warm on the stove."

"I would not say no to that."

"Albert, would you get him a cup?"

The minute Tom sat down at the table, Jesse began an interrogation.

"Are you really a helicopter pilot?"

"I was at one time."

"Levi says you flew a gunship." Jesse had stopped eating and was totally focused on Tom. "He said it was a helicopter called a Cobra and that you kept bad guys from hurting people like Grace."

"That is enough, Jesse," Claire said.

Goodness! A flying vehicle named Cobra of all things! Even the very name gave her the shivers. Shooting people from the air. That is what the helicopter Tom flew had been used for.

How could such a kind-acting man have done such things? How could the fact that he had killed people not be written in his eyes? She was going to have a talk with Levi about telling Jesse such things. The child was far too impressionable. "That sounds very scary," Amy said.

"It was." Tom glanced apologetically at Claire, as though he realized how inappropriate it was to discuss such things here in her home. "It was often very scary."

Claire was torn. She had to protect her children's ears, and would, but deep down, she wished the children were not here right now so that she could hear every word that came out of his mouth without having to monitor the conversation for her children's good. He had traveled around the world and seen and done things she couldn't even imagine, and she wanted to know much, much more about his life.

What all did he have to go through to be trained enough to fly these big, expensive Cobras? Why did a man like himself choose to be a warrior instead of something safer, such as a banker? What did he think about when he was flying around up in the clouds? And most important—why had a man like him never married? Even with the scars, there was something about him that attracted her, though she was determined to fight that attraction. There had to have been many women over the years who would have been more than willing to become his wife. *Englisch* women, of course—she reminded herself. A good Amish woman would never, ever allow herself to be interested in an *Englisch* soldier.

"I bet it was exciting, though," Jesse said, a little too eagerly. "Being up in the air, flying wherever you wanted to go. What do clouds look like up close? Do they look as cottony up there as they do down here? Have you ever been in a crash?"

This had gone on long enough. The one thing Claire did not want was Tom's presence putting ideas in Jesse's head. The child was hard enough to rein in.

"Now, Jesse—"

To her surprise, Tom cut her off. "May I deal with this?" She wasn't thrilled with the idea, but she nodded.

"Jesse, there was a time when all I could think about was getting skilled enough to fly something like one of those Cobras," he said. "But when you find yourself flying every day over mountains and valleys where there are people constantly trying to shoot you out of the sky, it isn't exciting, and it isn't fun. It's a dangerous job where you know that every mission could be your last."

"Will you ever get to fly one of those again?" To Claire's dismay, Tom's reply didn't seem to have made a dent in Jesse's eagerness to talk about things an Amish boy shouldn't even be thinking about. On the other hand, Claire found herself holding her breath as she waited to hear his answer. Would he be going back to his work? Back to that war? Part of her knew it would be better for her and the children if he left. Part of her wished he would stay.

"I doubt it."

"Why?"

Tom held up both hands. "Right now, these hands can't even milk a cow properly. The instrument panel of a helicopter is a lot more complicated than a cow."

"Were you the only person who got hurt by that bomb that hurt you?" Amy asked.

"No." Tom didn't enlarge on that statement, and Claire was glad.

Amy wouldn't leave it alone. "Are those other people who got hurt all right now?"

"No," he said gently. "They are not all right."

Amy cocked her head to one side. "Were they your friends?"

Claire had long ago given up on understanding the reason behind some of Amy's questions. Her niece had intuition and curiosity that went beyond her thirteen years.

He didn't hesitate. "They were my very good friends."

"Amy, that is enough for now." She could not let this interrogation continue. "Tom, I apologize for my children's inquisitiveness."

"There is no reason to apologize," he said, with a smile. "I am not that fragile."

That was debatable, but concern for him could not be her highest priority. The look of avid curiosity on Jesse's face was worrying her. That was one little boy who did not need to have so much admiration in his eyes when he listened to a soldier.

Then again, neither did she.

chapter EIGHTEEN

In Claire Shetler's eyes, Dorcas was little more than a child. At eighteen, her body was not yet completely developed, her bones not properly set. And yet she was having a baby. And it was coming soon.

"Make it stop!" Dorcas cried. "It hurts!"

She tried to coax the girl from the fetal position that, in spite of her big belly, she was trying to curl herself into.

"Dorcas," Claire soothed, "you can do this."

The contraction ceased long enough for her to get Dorcas to scoot off the bed Abel had set up in the kitchen and walk a few steps. Then it hit again, and she bent over, calling out for her mother.

Claire wished with all her heart that Dorcas's mother was here to encourage her, but Lilly Beachy had gone to her Maker only two weeks earlier—while giving birth. This had terrified Dorcas beyond reason.

Claire thanked God that she had not been the midwife at that birth. It was every midwife's nightmare, losing a patient. So far, all of the babies she had delivered had lived, as had their mothers.

Abel stood beside his wife's head, a frightened look in his eyes. It was obvious that the young man wanted to bolt but knew the manly thing to do was to stay in that room. He was only twenty, but looked younger. She gave him points for standing his ground, even if he was completely useless.

"*Mommi,*" the girl cried as another wave of contractions washed over her. "I want *Mommi*."

"Please do something!" Abel pleaded. "I do not believe my wife can stand this much longer."

The young husband's terror had grown with each hour as his wife's labor intensified.

"First babies are seldom easy," Claire said. "Be patient. Trust the Lord. The child will come."

"It hurts!" Dorcas pleaded with her. "I want it to stop."

Not for the first time, she wished she could take the pain of a young mother upon herself. At least she understood the birthing process.

Claire knew what it felt like to be young and scared while bringing a baby into the world. She had been only seventeen when her eldest was born and she well remembered her own terror at the strange pains ripping through her body.

It worried her that Dorcas was losing heart and control. This labor had been particularly intense. Although the Swartzentruber Amish were a stoic bunch, Claire could tell that her young client was close to going into a complete panic.

Claire used her calmest and most reassuring midwife voice. "Dorcas, you are doing so *gut*. You can do this."

"You are doing so *gut*." Abel echoed Claire's words while patting his wife's shoulder over and over. "You can do this."

His nervous, repetitious patting grated on his wife's nerves.

"Stop that!" Dorcas snapped at him.

Claire hid a smile at the startled look on Abel's face as he jerked his hand away. Under normal circumstances, this sweet, obedient Amish wife would never use such an angry tone when speaking to her husband, but these were not normal circumstances. She was going through the transition period of labor, those final minutes when the baby entered the birth canal. It tended to make even the most docile woman a bit testy.

"Do you think the water has cooled enough?" Claire asked the young father. "I want to get her into the birthing tub. It will help relieve some of the pain."

He had been given the job of heating enough buckets of water on the couple's woodstove to fill the portable birthing pool that she had brought with her. Unfortunately, he had been a little overzealous, overfilling the tub with too hot water. She'd been waiting these few minutes for the water to cool.

Had she been in an Old Order home, it would have been so much easier to prepare for this moment. She would have had access to hot and cold water straight from the faucet. Delivering a baby in a birthing pool in a Swartzentruber household where there was no running water presented a much greater challenge. The task of drawing water from a well, carrying it to the woodstove, and getting it hot was time-consuming. It did, however, give the husband something practical to do.

Abel tested the temperature of the water. "I think it is ready."

Looking at his callused fingers, Claire felt doubtful about his ability to judge the temperature. She dipped her elbow in to check. "It is ready. You did a fine job. Now help me get her into the water."

The contractions were coming so quickly, there didn't seem to be enough time between them for Dorcas to shuffle the few steps to the birthing pool. Abel swept his wife up in his arms and gently slipped her into the water. Even pregnant, the girl weighed so little in the young farmer's arms that he didn't so much as grunt. Her loose, white nightgown covered her just well enough for Claire to do what was needed without embarrassing the father.

The contraction eased, and Dorcas's eyes widened as she settled onto the small, soft seat built into the bottom of the birthing pool. The water reached just above her waist.

"The warmth will ease some of your pain," Claire explained. "And the water will soften your skin so that it will be more pliable when the baby comes. You will be holding that sweet babe in your arms soon."

There had been a time when Claire had not believed the words of an *Englisch* midwife who told her that being in warm water eased the pain of childbirth. Then one of her more experienced mothers expressed a willingness to try it. The mother had climbed into a bathtub filled with warm water and later remarked that this baby had been delivered with much less pain than her other eight children.

Claire immediately ordered a birthing pool from one of her catalogs and had been encouraging her clients to use the birthing pool ever since.

Grace had expressed surprise that Claire would use such a modern invention as a portable birthing pool. This had greatly annoyed Claire, although she tried to hide it. The fact that she was Amish did not mean she would withhold good ideas that would give her clients comfort! It was not as though warm water was some sort of new technology!

Dorcas went into a contraction so strong that it left her gasping when it was over. Abel stood aside, his big fists dangling helplessly at his side, a terrified look in his eyes. Claire had seen that look in expectant fathers' faces before. It was the expression of a man on the verge of bolting. The poor boy was trembling with the effort it took him to remain in the room.

"Oh, this feels so *gut*!" Dorcas sighed after another contraction had passed and she relaxed back into the comfort of the warm water.

"You are doing *wunderbar,*" Claire said. "The baby will be here soon."

She wished she had a nickel for every time she had used those exact words to a laboring mother. Encouragement and praise, she had found, were needed every bit as much as having someone present to catch the baby.

Only a few seconds passed before yet another teeth-clenching contraction rippled through Dorcas's body. She grabbed her husband's rough hand and gripped it so tightly that Claire saw him wince. Swartzentruber women were not weaklings.

"We are almost finished, little one," Claire soothed. "You are very courageous. Your *maam* would be so proud of you!"

Dorcas's eyes were grateful. "Do you truly think so?"

"Oh, yes. I—"

At that moment, Dorcas obeyed the deep primal call within her and began to push. Claire had not told her do so. There was no need for her to give Dorcas instructions at this point. Something within the girl's body was forcing her to push.

Claire never ceased to marvel at the intricate clockwork the Lord had installed within a woman's body. The act of childbirth was a miraculous symphony of natural chemistry.

She had heard that there were highly educated *Englisch* people who actually believed that this process had evolved spontaneously, with no Creator involved. She found this puzzling. The delicate mechanisms and hormones necessary to bring new life into the world were so intricate and a work of such genius that she thought perhaps the people who believed this might have spent a little *too* much time getting educated.

She glanced at the kitchen table, where she had laid out all of her supplies. Everything was in place. Scissors, a handheld scale, a small oxygen tank in case the baby needed a whiff, clamps for the umbilical cord. She had a device to suction the phlegm from its throat, but she seldom used it. In most cases she'd found it unnecessary. Her experience was that babies who could expel the phlegm naturally with the help of a crook of her finger nursed more quickly and strongly.

As she waited for nature to take its course, she prayed for the baby and for this young couple just starting out in life.

The contraction passed. Dorcas lay back, panting from the effort, and then she began to strain again, so hard that a high keening sound came from her mouth. Oh this girl was a strong one! For her slight build, their Dorcas was a fighter!

"I'm thirsty," Dorcas gasped as the contraction eased.

The young husband practically fell over his own feet in his hurry to get water for his wife.

Abel might be young, but Claire liked him. He had stayed in this room with his laboring wife all this time, leaving only once to care for their livestock, when many men would have run for the hills.

Claire hoped that remembering his wife's pain would give him the discipline to see that she did not give birth again too soon! Swartzentruber families tended to have more children than the other Amish sects. It was not uncommon for Swartzentrubers to have twelve children or more. Only last month, she had delivered a Swartzentruber mother's eighteenth child. She did not have ironclad numbers, but she would estimate that the more moderate Old Order families averaged around seven children per family.

Abel carried in a homemade tin cup dripping with cold water from the well. She noticed that the cup had been made from the bottom half of a tin can upon which someone had soldered a handle. The Old Order Amish were excellent stewards of their own resources, but by necessity, the Swartzentruber Amish were even more so.

"Just a few sips." Claire wished she could have ice chips for the girl, but a Swartzentruber house did not have such things as refrigerators or freezers. "Now is not a good time to fill your belly with water."

Dorcas obeyed. Then another contraction began. She dropped the cup and began to strain again.

"Get behind her, Abel," Claire instructed, "and support her back."

Abel did not hesitate. He put his strong arms around his wife, providing a living wall into which she could lean while pushing their baby out into the world.

And then came the moment for which Claire lived and breathed—that holy moment when a precious new little soul came into the world, straight from the heart of God.

"You have a son!" Claire lifted the baby from the water. "A healthy little boy."

"Praise *Gott!*" the husband exclaimed.

Dorcas relaxed against her husband's chest, panting from the effort.

Claire's hands flew as she checked the time, cleared the baby's throat with her finger, clamped and cut the umbilical cord, and then laid the infant high on Dorcas's belly. She would weigh him later. Her eyes softened when she saw the husband tentatively stroke the newborn's cheek while the red-faced infant squalled.

"A son." There was awe in his voice. "We have a son."

Ach. That was as it should be. She had no respect for husbands who treated this moment as though it were nothing.

"Thank you for this great gift, my wife."

Dorcas smiled up at her husband, relaxed and happy now that it was over. Her face was aglow with the look of triumph that every woman wears after successfully bringing new life into the world.

It was an intimate moment, one that did not need to be shared with an outsider. While they acquainted themselves with their first child, Claire gave them a measure of privacy by going to the woodstove and taking a little more time than necessary pulling out one of the receiving blankets she had placed in the stove's warming oven.

She glanced around the tidy kitchen, giving thanks to God that this young couple had been given the chance to purchase a small farm where they could nurture this child. Too many Amish families were being forced off the land because of the high cost. She knew that at least half of the young people from this particular church had moved to away in search of more affordable property.

She thanked God that Abel's grandparents were wise and generous people. Lilly had told her that Bess and Leroy were selling this homestead to Abel and Dorcas for barely a fourth of its value.

Had Bess and Leroy sold their property for what it was worth, they would be considered well-off by the world's standards, but the Amish had always measured worth by a very different yardstick. Many parents and grandparents put more value on having their children living close, with the ability to support themselves at least partially from the land, than on putting "paper money" in the bank.

She respected Leroy and Bess for having sacrificed a small mountain of "paper money" for the sake of this young couple and for this precious life that had just fought his way into the world.

She brought the blanket, lifted the infant off its mother's belly, and wrapped it in the blanket's warmth. She would bathe the baby later.

"Here." She handed the tiny, snug package to Abel.

Then came the other moment she loved. The baby, quieted by the secure tightness and warmth of the blanket, gazed up at his father for the first time, and Abel, so young that his husband beard was still thin and scraggly, gazed down into his little son's wide-open eyes. It seemed to her as though the newborn was memorizing his father's face.

Still gazing at his father, the baby worked his arm out from beneath the blanket and noisily began to suck his fist.

"He is a hungry one," the new father said, proudly.

There was always a moment when, after a successful birth, she she felt a sort of euphoria—a lightness and happiness over having used her skill and knowledge to help a mother come safely through the most intense moment of a woman's life.

For the first time since meeting Tom, she found herself wondering if there was any chance that this was how he felt when he flew his helicopter to protect people like Grace who went onto battlefields to save the lives of wounded soldiers.

If so, it would be a hard thing to walk away. It had certainly broken her heart when Abraham forbade her to do this holy work.

As Claire kneaded Dorcas's slack belly to help expel the afterbirth, she noticed Abel surreptitiously wiping away tears. Oh, this was very good! That boy would be a loving father . . . like his father before him, and his grandfather before him.

Claire felt the weight of her forty-four years as she realized that counting the new babe, she had known four generations of this family.

As Claire prepared to help Dorcas learn how to nurse her sweet-smelling little boy, Abel left to once again tend his livestock. She smiled when she glanced out the window and saw the new father striding out to the barn with such a spring to his step that his boots were barely touching the ground!

Dorcas was a lucky girl—only eighteen, with a farm, a house, a healthy son, and a good, steady husband with love in his heart for both her and his child. In Claire's opinion, a better life was not possible on this earth.

A very small part of her—a part she would have been ashamed to admit existed—felt a sharp stab of envy.

If Matthew had lived, she would have been like Dorcas, with a fine, young husband, a precious baby boy, and the homestead that Matthew had rented for them.

There would have been no shame to endure. Instead, she would have had memories of a joyous wedding and a man who truly loved her. It would have been a much easier life.

Who would she have become had Matthew not died?

For one thing, she would not be the kind of woman who, for Levi's sake, had to put away her grief long enough to convince herself to marry Abraham. At ten, Levi needed a man to lead him into adulthood. He did not need to learn how to cook and clean and sew—the skills she knew. He needed to learn how to plow and plant and harvest, like Abraham, who had been a skilled and canny farmer. Abraham could teach her son the intricacies of mending fences and harnesses. He could explain the breeding of cattle and rotation of crops.

The fact that Abraham was thirty-three and still unmarried should have warned her that there was a reason other women had turned down his proposals.

She had married for her son's sake—and, truth be known, because she wanted more children—thinking she could learn to love a frugal farmer who owned his own farm and went to church regularly. There had been little courtship. He had been the only one who asked—and she had accepted.

Six weeks after their marriage, she had heard the whipping in the barn. The sound of Levi's sobs—such a good little boy always, so quick to try to please—made her want to take a pitchfork and run it through her new husband.

Instead, she waited until Abraham came out of the barn, and humbly asked what Levi's great sin had been to deserve such a punishment. Abraham's answer? The little boy had wept over the fact that his hands were cut and bleeding from trying to learn the skill of basket weaving from his new stepfather.

What kind of woman would she be now, if she had not been forced to fight not just to love her new husband but for the discipline to not hate him?

Levi was a quick child. He learned how to avoid his stepfather's anger, and she helped him know how. She learned that the more subservient she became, the less Abraham felt the need to take his frustration with her out on her child. He became the best-fed man in their church, with the cleanest clothes and the tidiest house. These things kept him reasonably happy.

The whippings grew infrequent.

She often wondered what Grace would think if she knew that most of Claire's expertise as a cook and homemaker had been developed out of sheer desperation to keep Abraham content enough to keep his temper down.

Grace would never know. Nor would Levi. Nor would anyone else. She would be too ashamed to tell anyone. She would also be ashamed to tell anyone how much she enjoyed the freedom of sitting down to a no-cook dinner of bread and milk, or of the pleasure she took in sometimes allowing the house to grow so messy that it would have sent Abraham into a rage.

Still, she acknowledged that she had received four important blessings from her years with Abraham. Her children. Her mortgage-free farm. Levi's knowledge and ability to make a living as a farmer. And her own strength. These were things she could, and did, often thank God for.

Sometimes she remembered the intense fires of anger she had felt after Matthew's death. She had fought those flames down, also. There had been no choice. She had to come through those fires, and over to the other side of forgiveness, in order to have enough peace to survive.

Oh, those foolish young boys! How their foolishness had impacted so many people's lives!

Tobias drinking and driving, Henry showing off his father's valuable horse, Matthew racing an unfamiliar horse in the middle of the night. She could imagine it all so clearly, the high spirits, the illusion of youthful invulnerability, the exuberance Matthew must have felt flying through the night on a champion racehorse, faster than any animal he had ever ridden. That night had practically destroyed her life, as well as Jeremiah's. Henry's father had lost heart when his lifetime of working and saving for a chance to buy a horse like Ebony Sky went up in smoke. And then there was Tobias.

She often wondered what had happened to Tobias in the intervening years. No one, to her knowledge, had ever heard from him again after the funeral. It could not have been easy on him, just a kid completely on his own in the world. No ID, no driver's license, no Social Security number, no education, no acquaintances outside the Swartzentruber community.

They had been such good friends growing up together. He had been one of the kindest young men she had ever known. She could hardly imagine how hard his part in his big brother's death had hit him. Tobias had worshipped Matthew. They all did.

She hoped with all her heart that someday, before her life was over, Tobias would find his way back home so that she would have a chance to tell him that she understood. That she didn't blame him for what had happened. If she knew Tobias, however, he had probably spent the intervening years blaming himself for everything that had happened.

She hoped that wherever he was, he had found a measure of peace.

Ever since the night that Rose had come to Claire's trying to sell her anniversary china, Tom had been keeping an eye out for Henry. Mt. Hope was so small, the odds were good that he would run into him if he just paid attention. He wasn't sure what he would do if he did see him—he certainly was in no shape to give Rose's husband a threshing, although he would have been happy to give it a try if it would help her and the kids.

Then it happened. He was headed to Lehman's Hardware to pick up a part for an old lawn tractor Levi had gotten hold of. He'd planned on going there anyway, and it was Tuesday, the day Jeremiah had heard that Henry was picked up there by an *Englisch* man. At first, he wasn't sure he would recognize Henry after so many years, but then he saw a man who looked like an older copy of Henry, standing right in the heart of Mt. Hope, on the very corner where Lehman's Hardware was situated—just as his father had described. Older, paunchy, balding—but it was definitely Henry. He was pacing the sidewalk beside the hardware store.

Tom paused at the stop sign and watched. Every so often, Henry would stop pacing and look up the road to the north, as though he were waiting for someone. He was wearing his dress-up clothes, or as close to dress-up clothes as an Amish man got. Black pants. Black vest. Black coat. White shirt. A straight-brimmed, black felt hat. An Amish man would wear the same dress outfit for church, weddings, funerals, or . . . wherever it was that Henry was going.

In a few minutes, a dark sedan pulled up, stopped, and Henry got in. Tom watched as they sped off toward the south.

Tom had no desire to play detective, but the memory of Rose's desperation sent him speeding south behind them, trying to catch up.

It was no trick to close the distance between them. An Amish buggy had slowed them down to a crawl. From that moment on, Tom followed as Henry's driver, or perhaps friend, proceeded southwest, carefully driving the speed limit.

When he had heard of Rose's plight, he had worried that Henry had found another woman. Infidelity was rare among married Amish men who had been raised from birth to be faithful husbands and fathers, but people being what they were, he was certain things like that happened. Henry had possessed quite a roving eye when they were young. Perhaps he regretted settling down with Rose as early as he did.

If Henry was bent on destroying his family because of some other woman, Tom wanted to know. Perhaps he could talk some sense into his cousin. If that didn't work, he would be forced to mention it to the bishop. Or even better, he would tell Claire whatever he found out and let her deal with it. He trusted her instincts better than his own in this instance.

He followed them for over an hour, until he saw that his gas gauge was getting dangerously low. There weren't many gas stations on these roads, so he was forced to pull in at the first one he saw. He knew there might not be any more for several miles. By the time he'd filled his tank, they were long gone. When he didn't catch up with them during the next ten miles, he reluctantly turned back, knowing little more than he had an hour ago.

chapter NINETEEN

He had fallen into a sort of daily routine. He liked routines—a carryover from the military. He especially needed routines now. They gave him a hook upon which to hang his days.

He arose promptly at 4 a.m. every morning, and after eating a quick breakfast, he would join his father and attempt, once again, to force his fingers to squeeze hard enough to extract milk from the most patient cow in his father's small herd. Yesterday morning, he had gotten almost a half bucket before his fingers would not grasp anymore. So there was improvement.

Tom knew he was little help to Jeremiah. His fingers were so stiff and sore, his hands so slow, that more than once a cow turned her head and looked at him, still chewing her cud, as though to say, "You about done, there, fella?"

His hands burned from the stretching he was doing. He hoped it was the right thing to do. Milking had not exactly been on the list the physical therapist had given him.

As he milked, he thought how odd it felt to pretend to be an outsider around people he knew so well that he could have recited their birthdays and food preferences.

His father had a strong dislike of cabbage. It was almost

unthinkable with his Germanic background, and something his father tried to hide.

Claire never met a vegetable she didn't like, but her meat had to be cooked so thoroughly, it was almost a family joke.

"Better burn Claire's a little more," her brother, Eli, used to say when someone was grilling hamburgers at church outings.

Tom was also working on stamina. After the milking was finished, he had started taking a long walk. He would go as far as he could, then he would rest on whatever was available, a fallen tree, a rock, whatever—until he regained some strength—and then walk back.

This morning was no exception. He was feeling stronger and thought maybe he could go a full mile before having to take a rest. After he had showered the smell of cow off, he planned to go into town and rent a post office box. He wasn't expecting a lot of mail, but it would give the military a place to forward something if it did show up.

He was on his way back when he saw a freshly painted sign at the end of Claire's driveway that had not been there earlier when he passed. It was advertising home-canned to-mato juice, sauerkraut, peaches, and baked goods.

For some reason, home-canned tomato juice sounded wonderful—yet another thing he had not had in longer than he could remember. He had seen the little store in Claire's front room the one time he had been inside. Evidently the girls had decided to expand their little business.

Suddenly, a quart of tomato juice sounded like the only thing in the world he wanted. It almost amounted to a crav-ing. His desire to have an excuse to see Claire had nothing to do with it whatsoever.

Except she was outside working in her flower garden, and

it was a lovely spring day, and he was tired of having only Jeremiah and a cow to talk to.

"Good morning," he said.

She glanced up, and it was as though the sun had suddenly broken through the clouds. Her smile was so ravishing, he forgot to breathe for a moment. "Good morning!"

It took him a moment to compose himself. "I saw the sign. That's new, isn't it?"

"Maddy put it up a little while ago. It appears that we are going to have a bumper peach crop this year, so we are selling last summer's bounty."

"Do you mind if I go in and purchase something?"

"More fudge?" she teased.

"I'll try not to forget to buy some this time."

She sat back on the grass and looked up at him with a mischievous grin. "Elizabeth says for me to remind you of her great sweet tooth every time you come to purchase something from the store."

"Elizabeth has a strange sense of humor."

He went inside, purchased a quart jar of tomato juice and a small packet of fudge from Maddy, who was busy rolling out piecrust. Then he went back out to the porch and sat down on the steps near where Claire was working.

"Do you mind if I drink this here?" he asked. "Before I head home?"

Claire looked at the mason jar. "I would not mind having that jar back."

"Of course." He shook up the contents of the jar, twisted off the canning ring, and pried off the lid with his thumbnails. Then he began to drink the salty red juice.

It filled something deep within him, as though his body had been crying out for it all along. Half the jar was gone before he took a breath.

Claire had stopped weeding and now sat back on her haunches, looking at him curiously. "You like it that well?"

He wiped his mouth. "I like it—but it feels more like my body is craving it."

"Juice is healing," Claire said. "The garden gives us many of the medicines we need."

"The way this is tasting to me right now, I think I might end up buying your whole supply."

"Well, at least you won't have far to come!"

"That's true." He rummaged in his pocket and brought out four folded, crisp hundred-dollar bills and started to hand them to her. "I almost forgot. I picked this up from the bank yesterday. It's for next week."

"Thank you." Claire took the money and tucked it away in a pocket. "Have you given any thought as to how much longer you will be staying with us?"

"I have been giving it a great deal of thought."

The longer he stayed here in the Mt. Hope area, the more he wanted to stay. This had not been his intent. He had planned to see his father, apologize to Claire, meet Levi— and then get the heck out of this place that held such painful memories. Instead, he had found himself being embraced by these decent people living ordinary, decent lives. It was exactly what he had fought for—that they might have that right.

Now, instead of aching to leave, he found that he had been drawn into the rhythm of their lives.

He didn't want to lose the ability to walk over to his father's. He didn't want to forfeit the hours he spent with Levi, teaching and being taught by him. He didn't want to walk away from the valiant and troubled Grace, or the eccentric wisdom of Elizabeth.

He especially didn't want to walk away from Claire and her houseful of children. Only yesterday he had helped Albert repair a chicken fence after a rooster had escaped, had helped extricate Amy when one of her wheels got caught by a crack in the porch floor, and had talked Jesse out of jumping off the barn roof with a makeshift parachute made from a bedsheet. He'd also seen Maddy sneaking out of the house again and was debating whether or not to talk to Claire about it.

In so many ways, he wanted to stay, but he couldn't imagine retiring at such a young age. Strength was slowly coming back to his hands. If he worked hard at it, he might be able to achieve the level of expertise he'd had before the explosion. He wasn't there yet, but if he could get another month of sick leave, he thought he might be able to become fully functional as a pilot again.

"My thirty-day sick leave will be up shortly," he said. "I'm going to contact Marine headquarters and start the paperwork for another month. If you don't mind, I'd like to rent that apartment for a few weeks longer."

At that moment, both heard something buzz. She jumped, startled. A vision of a rattlesnake flashed through his mind.

"Oh!" she said. "It is my pager. I am not used to it yet. This must be one of my mothers."

She checked the number and frowned.

"Is something wrong?" he asked.

"I do not know," she said. "I hope not."

Brushing her hands off, she ran to her telephone shanty at the end of the driveway.

He drained the jar of tomato juice and set it beside the front door. It was time to leave, but she seemed worried, and he was a little hesitant to leave until he found out if everything was okay.

He walked toward the phone shanty as he headed back home, hoping he could find out if anything was the matter before he actually left.

When he got to the phone shanty, he saw that she was frantically dialing a number. She listened for the length of several rings, then hung up.

"Is something wrong?" he asked.

"One of my clients has gone into labor. It is sooner than we expected. She has many small children, and her husband is not at home. The oldest daughter was the one who called, and she is only ten."

"You need to get to her."

"Yes, but she lives too far away to take the buggy, and my driver is not answering her phone." She picked up the receiver and began to push in numbers again.

"Who are you calling now?"

"There is another driver I know, but she lives further away."

"Let me take you."

She stopped in mid-dial. "What?"

"I have a car and nothing to do today. Let me take you."

"Oh, yes, please!" She made her decision in an instant. "Go get the car while I grab my bag."

"Maddy!" she shouted as she headed for the house. "Start gathering my things!"

It took him less than three minutes to get to his car, back it out of his driveway, and pull up to her house—but she had already changed into a light blue dress and a white apron, and was standing on the porch holding what looked to be an oversized diaper bag.

Maddy must have had everything ready before Claire even made it through the door. The girl might be sneaking around at night, but at least she was competent when it came to helping Claire.

He got out and opened the passenger door for her. In spite of her hurry, she looked at him, head cocked, then ignored the open door and got into the backseat instead.

Midwife on a journey of mercy or not, she obviously didn't want to be seen driving around the countryside while sitting in the front seat of a strange *Englisch* man's car.

"Tell me where we're going," he said.

She gave him directions and he drove as fast as he considered safe on a road where any curve might have a slow-moving buggy hidden behind it.

"Why didn't she call an ambulance if she thought she was in labor?"

"They have eight children under the age of ten." She met his eyes in the rearview mirror. "The father has been ill and unable to work until this past week. The cost of a hospital stay is not something they need to be burdened with." She looked away. "They will have enough trouble coming up with the money to pay me—and I will care for them whether they can pay me or not."

He was not surprised, but he was impressed. "They are lucky to have such an understanding midwife."

"Luck has nothing to do with it," she said. "This is my ministry, the holy work God gave me. If I never got paid a penny, I would still help these women. Making a living for my family is a side benefit, not my sole goal."

"I stand corrected," he said. "So how did you get into this? How did you get the training for this skill?"

"My grandmother was a midwife. She was trained in Lancaster, Pennsylvania, in the old ways."

"What are the old ways?"

"Roots and herbs. Tinctures to make a pregnancy safer or labor easier. Preparations to help a woman hold on to a baby that is trying to come too early or to hurry a baby that wants to come too late."

He had known her grandmother, a woman he remembered as having swollen knuckles and legs that did not work well. She had used a special cane to get around, and he had a vague memory of her coming to their home when his little sister, Faye, was born.

"So your grandmother taught you how to be a midwife?"

"Yes. Levi's father was killed before he was born. I was quite young, but my grandmother was wise enough to see that I needed a profession if I was to raise my child, and I wanted to learn from her. After she passed on, I inherited her practice. I used the old ways, but I tried to incorporate the best of the new ways, too."

"Like what?"

"Some babies need a whiff of oxygen when they first come into the world. I always carry a small tank with me. I do a lot more than simply show up at a mother's home when she's ready to have a baby. I make certain there are monthly checkups. I monitor her blood pressure and girth. I talk to her about nutrition and make sure she's eating the things she needs to build a healthy baby. I do everything in my power to discover potential problems long before they get out of hand, and if I have the slightest hint that there might be problems serious enough that they need to be taken care of by a hospital, I make certain that she gets the kind of medical help I cannot provide."

"How many babies have you delivered?"

"Three hundred and forty-four," she said.

"You keep track that closely?"

"Of course. Every life is precious. I record names and dates and weight and height in a notebook, and sometimes, late at night after all the chores are done, I pray over those names, for those babies to grow strong in body and in the Lord."

"Have you ever lost one?"

"By the grace of God, I never have—and I hope I never will."

Within minutes they had traveled a distance that would have taken more than an hour in a horse and buggy. He pulled into a rutted driveway and had barely come to a full stop before Claire had gathered her things and was opening the door.

"The oldest child is the one who called me," Claire said. "The father was not home when she called. Perhaps you could help keep the children out of the room?"

"Of course."

The bareness of this Amish home was even more severe than most he had been inside—bare of everything except children. Several were playing with a small kitten. Two were rolling empty thread spools back and forth. A worried-looking girl, about ten years old, had let them in. She was carrying a baby boy on her hip. The baby looked to be about a year old and too heavy for such a skinny little girl to be toting around.

"*Daed* is gone." She seemed overwhelmed with relief that Claire had arrived. "Grandma is real sick. *Maam* had written your number on the phone shanty wall." She nodded toward the stove. "I put some water on to heat while I waited for you to come."

"You did so well, little one." Claire hurried into the mother's bedroom.

As the door closed, Tom glanced down and saw several pairs of little eyes looking up at him. Only the oldest girl spoke.

"Who are you?"

"I'm a neighbor of Claire's."

"Annette is always her driver." The little girl hitched the big baby a little higher on her hip.

"Annette was gone."

"What's your name?"

"Tom."

"Tom?" She glanced down at the children playing on the floor. "We have a Thomas. He's that one." She pointed at a tow-headed child barely out of diapers.

"It's a good name."

"My name is Laura Mae."

"Hello, Laura Mae." The children were playing so quietly, he could hear Claire's voice behind the closed door.

"I am here now, it is safe to push. We will have this baby here in no time," Claire said. "You are doing so *gut*!"

"The little ones aren't supposed to be hearing this," Laura Mae informed him. "Annette always took us outside or to Grandma's when she and Claire came."

Tom knew that Amish parents tried to keep the other children away when there was a birth. Ideally, they were taken to a relative's house and then brought home later to discover that God had gifted them with a new baby brother or sister in their absence.

Still, he didn't want to be out of earshot of Claire's voice if she needed him.

"Let's go outside."

All the children besides the baby were old enough to walk, although one curly-headed little doll baby insisted on holding her big sister's hand to steady herself. Laura Mae was barely able to hold on to the baby with both skinny little arms, let alone use only one.

"I'll take the baby," Tom offered.

"Thank you." Laura Mae's eyes were grateful. "He was getting kind of heavy."

As Tom swung the infant up into his arms, he marveled that she could carry him at all. The little guy was a chunk.

Getting them all outside was a production. The kitten had to be taken outside, too, and there was a slight disagreement about who would have the honor, but after a few short words from Laura Mae in German, one of the two children let go, and the other snuggled the kitten beneath her chin.

The problem was what to do with them when he got them outside. He didn't want anyone wandering off, and there were almost too many to keep an eye on. No longer encumbered with the baby, Laura Mae took over with as much authority as an adult. There was a low swing hanging by two long ropes tied to a large tree in the front yard. She got the children in line, then set about pushing them one by one in turn.

An old, tired collie wandered out, flopped down, and immediately became entertainment for two of the girls who petted and made a fuss over her. The dog's eyes rolled back in its head in sheer ecstasy when it rolled over and they began to scratch its belly.

One little guy became absorbed in some pebbles and created his own private game with them, the rules of which Tom could not discern.

With everyone occupied, Tom sat down on a weathered bench and watched these Amish children who could entertain themselves with so little. These little ones were particularly engaging. There were things about being raised Amish that never left a person, a value system that became so deeply embedded that it was next to impossible to shed. Claire, with her careful speech and her modest, plain clothes, was more appealing to him than any of the *Englisch* women he had dated. The fact that she was a respected midwife impressed and intrigued him. This was not a shallow woman.

Claire had set a high standard in his mind—even while still in her teens—and no other woman had ever come close. Age had served only to increase her appeal.

And all he had to do for a chance to have her as his own

was to voluntarily throw off everything about himself that was *Englisch*—including his hard-won profession. Forget he had ever driven a car, or owned a cell phone, or listened to jazz, or worn a pair of Levi's.

There was also the small matter of not knowing how she would react when he told her who he was. Add his physical limitations and disfigurement, and he didn't think there was a chance that she would ever care for him.

For all he knew, she would stop speaking to him entirely.

And yet, now that he had seen her, he knew he couldn't leave. Not now. If he could hang on to his anonymity, he could at least be able to see and talk with her from time to time. That would be better than nothing.

He remembered being a lovesick teenager, thinking about Claire constantly, wanting to keep her in his life forever.

Now here he was. Twenty-seven years older, and still pole-axed whenever he was around her.

Maybe he should leave.

He felt caught between two worlds, paralyzed by his own training and background. The Amish part of him had always wanted a family. Being part of the "Marine" family was no substitute for what Claire had with her rollicking houseful.

A small boy tugged at his pants and said something in German. Tom caught himself in time not to let on that he understood exactly what the little boy was saying.

"He wants to see inside your car," Laura Mae interpreted.

That was a reasonable enough request. Swartzentruber children seldom got a chance to ride in a car. To do so would mean their parents having to get special permission from their bishop. That permission would not be given unless the need for nonbuggy transportation was great.

"Sure." Still holding the baby, he took the little guy's hand

and led him over to the car. Unfortunately, the moment the door was opened, several pairs of curious little eyes followed him—and then all of them wanted to join their brother.

He saw no real harm in allowing them to try out the soft seats. With the keys safely hidden in his pocket, he allowed one little boy the honor of sitting in the driver's seat, grasping the steering wheel.

"What is this?" One of the older children said, holding up a bag they had found on the backseat.

He had forgotten the bag of candy he had put there. Jeremiah had mentioned having a sweet tooth, and he had purchased some peppermint that he knew his father liked and had planned to take to him tomorrow morning.

He knew these children did not often get treats, and decided that he would buy more candy for Jeremiah at a later time.

He doubted that candy, children, and cars would be a good mix, so he was enticing the children out of the car with the candy in his hand when he heard the clip-clop of a horse's hooves nearing the house.

An Amish man pulled into driveway behind his car.

"Get out of that car!" He spoke in German to the children. "And why are you taking candy from this stranger?" He climbed down out of the buggy and strode toward Tom. In English, he demanded, "Who are you and why are you here?"

The father was a large man, and wore heavy, sweat- and work-stained clothing. Tom had a feeling that he would do anything to protect his children.

"I'm Tom Miller. I drove Claire Shetler here. She asked me to bring the children outside."

"You are a driver of the Amish?" the father asked.

"No," Tom answered. "I am a neighbor to Claire."

"Claire Shetler? The midwife?" The man's aggressive attitude changed immediately. "Already?"

"Yes. Apparently, your wife is giving birth," Tom said. "That is why I brought the—"

"It is too soon!" The man strode off toward the house before Tom finished his sentence.

The buggy horse, reins loosely tied, wandered toward the barn. Tom decided to leave it alone. The father knew exactly where his horse was and would be out soon enough to take proper care of it.

In the meantime, while the horse slurped water from the trough, Tom felt some water himself. The baby, who had been wearing cloth diapers covered by a tightly knit wool "soaker," had urinated all over the *Englisch* man holding him.

Fortunately, Tom was wearing jeans and a plain black T-shirt. Nothing fancy that couldn't be thrown into the wash. He wasn't entirely certain of what to do. He didn't want to leave the children to go back inside the house, where he was fairly sure things were becoming more and more intense. On the other hand, he wasn't thrilled with the idea of spending the next half hour or so holding a wet infant.

Evidently the infant wasn't thrilled with being wet, either, and set up a howl.

About that time, a boxy black sedan came lumbering down the road and pulled in. A woman with a gauzy prayer *Kapp* and a dress dotted with sprigs of flowers climbed out.

"Nora!" Laura Mae sang out. "You got my telephone message!"

"I did!" the ruddy-complexioned woman said. She was holding a large black purse on her wrist and wore black leather Nikes on her feet. They seemed incongruent with the pastel, flower-sprigged dress she was wearing, but Tom was no fashion expert. He saw a competent Mennonite woman to whom he could turn these children over.

"Who are you?" Nora asked, her hands planted firmly on her hips. "And what are you doing to that baby?"

"Tom Miller. A neighbor to Claire Shetler. Annette wasn't able to come, so I brought her. It sounded like an emergency," he amended. "The only thing wrong with the baby is that it is wet."

Clucking her tongue, she carefully removed the dripping infant from his arms. With the warmth of the little body removed, his wet jeans and shirt felt cold against his side.

"You can go home now, Mr. Miller," she said. "I'm here."

"I thought I would wait around for Claire to finish up here."

"I'll bring her home," the woman stated firmly.

Tom was not reluctant to go home and change his baby-soaked shirt and pants, but he hated to leave Claire without checking in first. "I'll go in and let her know I'm leaving."

"She might be a little too busy to talk to you," Nora said. "I'll be happy to give her a message."

Tom wasn't sure he liked this woman. It was good to have someone competent and female coming into the house, but she seemed awfully eager to take charge.

He was trying to decide whether to go or leave when all of them heard a newborn baby's cry from inside the house. Laura Mae gasped and a beatific smile spread over her face. The baby jumped, startled, and began to cry even louder.

"She'll be needing me to help now," the woman said, and barged in. "Keep the children out here for a few minutes longer."

"Wonder if it's a boy or a girl," Laura Mae said to him.

"What were you hoping for?" he asked.

"A girl to even things out a little," Laura Mae said. "We've only got two girls in the family, and all these boys. *Daed* says he needs workers in the field, but *Maam* says she could use some more girls around the house." Then she glanced at the paper bag in his hands. "The little ones would probably like some of that candy right about now." She looked at the candy with a wistful expression on her face.

He had forgotten about it. "Of course." He began to hand it out. The children were polite and all thanked him before they began to suck on the peppermint sticks. Laura Mae pretended that she didn't need any candy, she just wanted her little brothers and sister to have some, but it didn't take much to persuade her to take one.

That occupied them until about a half hour later, when the father came out onto the porch and motioned for them to all to come in. "You, too, *Englisch,*" he said. "Come see the new baby the Lord has given us!"

The man's joy was real and contagious, and yet Tom wondered how he could be so joyful when it was so obvious that they were practically overwhelmed with children as it was. And yet . . . he envied the man.

The baby had been wrapped up like a tiny cocoon and now lay in its mother's arms. The children gathered around as the father proudly introduced them to their new baby brother. The mother glanced up at him. "Thank you for watching the children."

"They were very good."

Claire, he saw, was quietly sitting in the corner in a wooden rocker. Her face was flushed, and a few damp tendrils had fallen out of their neat pinnings—something one did not see often in Amish women. It was obvious that she had worked very hard to help this baby come into the world.

"And thank you for bringing Claire to me," she said. "I

did not want for Laura Mae to have to deliver this baby. She's too young."

"Do you want me to take you home?" he asked Claire. "Or will you be staying?"

He did not expect her to be ready to leave—but she glanced up at Nora. "Can you care for her?" she asked.

"Of course I can," Nora huffed.

"Then I'd like to go home, if you don't mind waiting, Tom. I need to gather my things."

"I don't mind in the slightest, Claire."

Nora's quick glance at him made him wonder if he'd allowed a little too much feeling to creep into his voice.

chapter TWENTY

"Everything went well for you in there?" he asked, as he drove home with Claire in the backseat.

"Thanks be to God. I appreciate your help with the children."

"Eight kids under the age of ten," he said. "That's nearly one per year. Do you think there's any chance this baby will be the last?"

"I would be surprised," she said. "That's a Swartzentruber family. They are more likely to be farmers, but it is not easy to make a living in the old ways. They need large families and lots of unpaid, willing hands to make it work. Most Old Order farmers are getting out of the business, except for their large gardens and a cow or two."

"I hate to hear that."

"I have seen some signs that are encouraging, though."

"Oh?"

"A few are getting into hydroponics. They've had some commercial success in growing salad vegetables out of season. I've heard that a modest living can be made on as little as five acres that way, with the right equipment and knowledge. One young farmer, a teacher at one of our schools, raises organic chickens and sells them to specialty markets."

"And yet some men, like Jeremiah, still farm in the old way."

"Yes, but Jeremiah is wearing down," she said, "and his one daughter married and moved away. Our people help him when extra hands are needed, but it is hard on a man like Jeremiah to have good rich ground and no sons to work it. Many people have made Jeremiah offers on his farm, but he will not sell, and he kills himself trying to make it work."

"Why does he do this?"

"I believe it is because he lives in hope that his remaining son will someday return and take over."

This comment felt like an ice pick to his heart. His father could not possibly be trying to preserve the farm for *him*. Could he?

"Are you talking about Tobias?"

"Yes. For many years, Jeremiah has set a place at the table for his youngest son every day. Some Amish people whose children have left the church do that. It is a silent way of grieving their absence, as well as a sort of prayer that someday they will come back. Didn't you notice?"

"I saw a few dishes sitting at the opposite end of the table from where we ate. I thought it was simply a few items he'd not bothered to put away. I had no idea what they were there for."

"He washes those dishes once a week, and then resets Tobias's place. If I know Jeremiah, he will not stop until he dies or Tobias comes back. It annoys his son-in-law. He has asked Jeremiah not to do that when they are visiting. He says that it upsets Faye, but I do not think it upsets Faye."

"Why would the son-in-law even care?"

"Because Faye's husband has a greedy streak. I believe he hopes that his wife will inherit property worth many dollars someday and does not like the idea of sharing."

"And does Jeremiah obey his son-in-law's wishes?"

"Jeremiah?" She chuckled. "No, he is a very stubborn man.

When his son-in-law comes to visit, Jeremiah adds a few extra dishes to Tobias's place setting."

Tom's strength was coming back in small bits and pieces. He continued to go to his father's early every morning, but recently he had begun to walk there and back, one mile round-trip, and the walk did not tire him. His milking ability was still negligible, but his attempts—although painful—were bringing about a little more flexibility in his hands every day. Getting up that early was not a challenge. His body seemed determined to wake him at 4 a.m. every morning anyway. It felt more productive to dress and go to his father's barn than to force himself to lie in bed a few more hours.

In addition to bringing about some strength and flexibility, there was a deep emotional comfort in engaging in this daily routine. The flicker of joy he saw in his father's eyes each morning when he arrived, always accompanied with a bit of gentle teasing about his *Englisch*-ness.

There was comfort in the sounds, sights, and smells of this old barn that had played such a large part in his childhood. In this familiar place, the ultravigilance he had developed in the Middle East lessened. It was unimaginable, even to his touchy subconscious, that an enemy would want to secrete an explosive device in this place.

Jeremiah encouraged Tom in his efforts to regain his strength and seemed to take a great deal of personal satisfaction out of every small milestone, measured by how much milk was in the bucket when they finished each morning. Tom had no illusions about being any real help, but he appreciated the old man's enthusiasm.

After whatever other light chores he could help his father with, he would walk back, stopping long enough to purchase yet another quart jar of Claire's tomato juice. To make sure he had a good supply, the girls had stopped putting it on the shelves of their little store. Now Maddy went down into the cool cellar and brought up a fresh jar for him every morning.

As he rested on Claire's porch steps with a quart jar of that ruby-red liquid in his hand, it felt like he was drinking pure sunshine and that his body had been ravenous for it. Amy, always happy for company, would show him her latest creation and would prattle on about her small world. Talking to Amy always left him smiling. It was impossible not to love that little girl.

A bonus to this routine was that Claire would frequently be employed in some outdoor chore at that time of the morning, when it was still cool. She would be sweeping off the porch, or hoeing in her vegetable garden, or hanging up wet clothes. She would inquire about his health or ask about Jeremiah. Then he would find out some small snippet about her plans for the day. She would mention the new dress material she planned on sewing up for one of the girls or a new recipe she'd tried at the house of a friend that she was going to try out. He felt honored the morning that she chose to confide her worries about her sister's plight. From what he could tell, it appeared that Claire was pretty much singlehandedly keeping that family in groceries, while Henry stayed away more and more.

He did not tell her about having tried to follow Henry that day, but he did resolve to find reasons to linger around Lehman's Hardware a little more often. He also resolved to keep his gas tank filled so that he could follow Henry all the way to wherever the destination was that was destroying him and his family.

Each afternoon, he spent long hours reading from Levi's copious library, interspersed with more walks. Sometimes he would wander over to Levi and Grace's. They were seldom around during the day, but Elizabeth was always up for a visit. It was good to have one person with whom he could talk freely about the experience of being around his father and Claire under these circumstances. Elizabeth continued to counsel caution. She said that God would let him know when the time was right.

He confided to Elizabeth about his unexpected windfall, and how it worried him that he could think of nothing he wanted to buy or do with it. He was afraid it was another symptom of that PTSD diagnosis the doctors had been determined to pin on him. She told him there was a good chance the Lord had something else in mind for that money and to wait until God showed him a purpose. This thought appealed to him and was a relief.

He frequently stopped to talk to old Flora. She had grown to depend on an apple always being in his pocket and would come to the fence to get a treat and a good scratching behind her ears. Flora was definitely showing her age. Claire was aware of this and had begun hiring a driver more and more often.

He found great comfort in the company of Claire's animals. The soft clucking of the hens as they sat on their nests eased something in his chest. Like Albert, he had been in charge of the chickens and eggs when he was young. One of the barn cats had a litter of kittens. He had never liked cats all that well, but in this new quiet in which he was living—this unhurried cocoon of time—he allowed himself to sit in the barn for hours, simply watching and enjoying the antics of those kittens tumbling and playing about.

Most days were good, though some days were a struggle. But one overcast day, when every bad thing he'd experienced or seen in the Middle East was jockeying for position in his mind, God sent him a gift.

He was sitting on the steps of his apartment that evening,

watching the barn swallows flit and glide—ever the accomplished aerial acrobats—when he saw a dog lurking on the edge of the field.

The dog was larger than a German shepherd and it had matted, shaggy white fur.

He looked at the dog, and the dog looked at him.

"Are you lost, boy?" he said.

The dog took a few tentative steps toward him, then lost heart and retreated.

"It's okay, I'm not going to hurt you."

The dog whined and came a few steps closer, head down, its tail swishing back and forth.

Even though it was almost dusk, he could tell that the animal was pretty beat up. As it drew closer, he could see that it was male and had been in several dogfights.

"Whatsa matter, Rocky," he said, thinking of the multiple fight scenes when Sylvester Stallone was the underdog and came out swinging. "You lose a few?"

The dog had gotten down on its belly now, and was crawling slowly toward him. It didn't take someone who was fluent in dog body language to see that it was afraid to trust, but its need to be petted, to have human contact, was even greater than its fear. There were scars above its eye and several on its neck and body.

"I'm not going to hurt you, Rocky." He held his hand out, palm up.

He held his hand out for a long time until the dog screwed up its courage, raised its head, gave his hand a sniff, and then gently licked it. The touch of its tongue was so quick, so light, he could barely feel it—but it was there. They were friends. He gently chucked it under the chin.

"You're a good dog, aren't you, buddy?"

At that moment, it did something he'd never seen a dog do

before in his life—it stood, came close, and laid its head in his lap, sideways, and then closed its eyes.

It was such a trusting, tender thing to do, like a tired child lying its head in the lap of a trusted adult.

The gesture brought a lump to his throat. He identified with the dog. He was pretty beat up himself, and some days it felt like he'd crawled on his belly all the way to Holmes County, hoping to have contact with gentle people who would treat him well.

For a few minutes, they sat like that, on the bottom step, dog and man, both battle scarred and weary. He smoothed his hand over the dog's matted hair, and the animal gave a deep sigh of contentment as though he knew he was finally home.

As he ran his hands down over its sides, he could feel the ribs. The long hair hid an emaciated body. Rocky was not well fed. There was no dog food here, but he did have a package of hot dogs.

"You hungry, Rocky?"

The dog lifted his head and looked at him with such anticipation, he would have sworn the animal understood exactly what he'd said.

He made his way up the stairs with Rocky at his heels.

"Sorry, buddy. You can't come in with me, but I'll be right back out." The animal immediately sat down on the small landing outside the door. Tom came back out and fed hot dogs to him one by one.

After eating eight all-beef hot dogs, Rocky lay down on the landing and fell asleep. Tom went to bed, hoping the white dog would still be there when he got up in the morning. He could use a good friend, and unless he was mistaken, Rocky could use a good friend, too.

· · ·

It was growing dark and Claire had already put the smaller children to bed. Maddy had gone to a singing with some friends, Albert and Sarah were sound asleep, as was Amy. Jesse was reading under the covers with a flashlight and thought she didn't know. His thirst for knowledge was as great as his older brother Levi's.

She walked out onto the porch, intending to sit on the swing for a few minutes. Since the weather had gotten warmer, it had become her habit to say her nightly prayers out there. She found that praying in bed after a hard day of work was too conducive to falling asleep!

She'd been sitting there in the shadow of a trellis of morning glory vines when Tom walked down the stairway of his apartment and sat down on the bottom step. She didn't move for fear he would see her. Chatting with him outdoors in broad daylight with the children running about was one thing. A conversation with him in the dark was entirely too intimate an act, and she did not want to be put in the position of pointing that out to him.

Then she saw the stray dog tentatively coming out of the shadows. She sat, transfixed, as Tom gently encouraged it to come to him. She watched as the dog crawled on its belly to him. Watched Tom coax it toward him. Tears sprang to her eyes when she saw it lay its head trustingly in his lap. She held her breath, hoping he would not frighten it away. Then she let it out when she saw him gently pet it, talking to it softly. She smiled when she saw him feeding it hot dogs.

The dog would obviously be a permanent inhabitant now. She supposed some people in her position would insist that her renter get rid of the dog—but she didn't feel that way. The healer in her saw the probability of Tom and the stray dog finding solace in each other.

It was her opinion that you could tell a lot about a man

by how he treated an animal. Her trust ratcheted up a couple notches when she saw Tom responding so gently to the stray. It bothered her that he was a soldier—a profession of which she heartily disapproved—but there was a lot of goodness in that man's heart.

She watched as Tom went back into his apartment, and she stayed put until the light went out. At that point she knew it was safe to get up and go inside her house without him thinking she'd been deliberately spying on him.

"You decided to stay, did you, boy?" Tom was delighted when he opened the door the next morning. Rocky was lying so close to the screen door that Tom had to nudge it to get the dog to move.

Even though his nudge was gentle, Rocky was up like a shot, backing into the corner of the small porch, looking at him with worried eyes.

Tom came outside, sat down on the top steps, and whistled a soft invitation. Rocky wagged his tail and came close enough for Tom to ruffle the fur on top of the dog's head.

"Did you sleep good, boy?" he said. "Did those hot dogs lie okay on your stomach? If I'd eaten a whole package for supper, I'd have been up half the night."

He could almost swear that Rocky grinned at him.

"Come here," Tom said, gently pulling the dog closer. "Let me take a closer look at you.

"You're pretty beat up, aren't you, fella? Did someone make you do this? You don't seem to be the kind of animal that would deliberately pick a fight with another dog."

Rocky whined softly and lay down, his muzzle on his paws.

His best guess was that there were some illegal dogfights

going on somewhere in the state and Rocky had managed to get loose.

The thoughts of forcing dogs to fight one another made Tom's stomach turn, but he knew it happened.

That one wound on the back of his neck needed to be looked at. A dog could lick a wound on its body and keep it clean enough to heal, but Rocky couldn't reach this one.

Tom remembered the B&W ointment his father had given him. He'd been rubbing it into his own scars and—though it might be wishful thinking on his part—he thought it was helping.

"Stay right where you are, buddy." Tom rose and went into the apartment.

He didn't have any more hot dogs, but he did have some leftover bacon grease, which he mixed in with a bit of leftover cooked oatmeal. Then he broke a couple raw eggs over it, poured in some milk, and gave it all a good stir. It wasn't gourmet, but it would feed the hollow inside of Rocky long enough to let him go for the morning milking and then to the store for dog food.

Rocky didn't complain about the unusual meal set before him, he just gobbled it up. Then came the tricky part—trying to smear the B&W ointment on Rocky's open wound.

He let the dog smell the ointment, then he let it watch him put a dab on his own neck.

"See?" he said. "Good stuff."

Rocky cocked his head, watching him come closer with a dollop of ointment on his fingers.

It took time, and a lot of softly spoken encouraging words, but Tom did manage to cover the wound with the healing ointment without Rocky sinking his teeth into his arm, a risk Tom knew he was taking with a strange dog.

He started back inside to wash off his hands, and Rocky stuck his nose in the door as though expecting an invitation.

Tom hesitated. It wasn't that he minded having a dog in the apartment, but he wasn't sure Claire would approve. After all, it was her property. He glanced over at her house and saw that the lamps were already lit in the kitchen. Claire was an early riser, too.

"Let's wait a bit on that, Rocky." He blocked Rocky's entrance. "I think I need to talk to the lady who owns this place first."

Rocky sat down on his haunches and stared through the screen door until Tom had washed off his hands, gathered his car keys and wallet, and came back outside.

"Gotta go introduce you to Claire and see if you can stay, buddy," he said as he walked across the driveway to Claire's kitchen door.

He had no idea what he would do with the dog if she said no.

She had a spatula in her hand when she came to the door. She was dressed for the day, with her prayer *Kapp* already firmly in place.

"Good morning, Claire," he said. "I wanted to ask if you'd mind if I keep this stray?"

Claire came out onto the porch and took a good look at the dog.

"The poor thing has seen better days."

"I'm hoping I can rectify that."

"He will need a good bath."

"I'll take care of it."

"I don't want any fleas in the apartment."

"I'll get a flea collar—or whatever the vet recommends. It's been a long time since I owned a dog."

"Well . . . I would not mind having a good dog around, as long as it gets along with the children."

"If it shows even the slightest sign of aggressiveness toward you or the children, I won't keep him."

"Yes, I cannot have an aggressive animal around." Her voice was doubtful, and there was a worried frown on her face. "I don't know, Tom. He looks like he could be very vicious if provoked."

For a moment, Tom thought he would have to find another home for his dog, when Rocky stepped forward and gave Claire's hand a quick lick. Then he sat down on his haunches, looked up at her and whined, as though asking to be given a chance.

She took one good long look at the dog's pleading eyes. "He does seem to be a good dog."

"I'd like to give him a chance."

Rocky whined once more, wagged his tail, and Claire melted. "Everyone needs a chance. Even dogs."

A few hours later, Tom parked his car in front of the apartment and introduced a new and improved Rocky to Amy.

"Oooh, Claire told me you had a new doggie," she called from her seat on the porch. "What's its name?"

"Rocky." Tom walked the dog over to her. "He's had a busy day. He's met Jeremiah, paid the vet a visit, made friends with a dog groomer, been deflead, deticked, washed, groomed, and is the new owner of matching food and water bowls and this snazzy new red dog collar and leash."

"He's so pretty."

Tom allowed Rocky to approach Amy.

Amy backed her wheelchair away from the card table and patted her lap. "Here, Rocky! Here, boy!"

Tom was glad he had bought a leash. He wasn't entirely sure what the dog would do. Some dogs didn't like children, but Rocky merely walked over, then sat down close to the wheelchair. When Amy reached out to pet him, he closed his eyes and accepted her caress like a gentleman.

"He's been hurt," Amy said.

"Yes, he has."

"Kind of like me and you."

Her comment surprised him.

"Yes, kinda like me and you."

"What kind of dog is he?"

"The vet said Rocky was Grand Pyrenees with some shepherd mixed in."

Amy continued to stroke Rocky's clean, white fur. "Do you think he'll make a good watchdog?"

"Maybe. The vet said Great Pyrenees were bred to be guard dogs, and that sometimes rescued strays are the most loyal dogs of all. He said that sometimes they seem to understand what you've done for them and love you even more."

"That's true." Amy grew pensive. "I'm kind of a rescued stray, and I love Claire to pieces. I know exactly how Rocky feels."

"Maybe you and he will be good friends."

"I know we will." Her face lit up. "I made you a present!"

"You did?"

"It's nice. You want to see?"

"I'd love to see it."

She picked up the card she had been coloring and handed it to him. He was surprised at the level of skill and artistry that had gone into it. It was much more advanced than what he would have thought a thirteen-year-old could do—but then, what did he know? He wasn't exactly an expert on children.

"That's an eagle on the front," she said. "I copied it out of a bird book Claire gave me."

"Why an eagle?"

"Because Grace said you were sometimes sad because you weren't flying helicopters anymore and so I thought I'd try to cheer you up. I wrote a poem just for you. Read it out loud."

He opened it and read the short verse:

To Tom, Our New Friend

Don't be sad.
Even birds walk sometimes
Instead of flying.
Walking isn't such a bad thing,
If you think about it.
Especially if all you can do is . . . sit.

The last line felt like a punch in the gut. He glanced up at her, sitting in her wheelchair, still stroking Rocky's fur, a look of calm acceptance in her eyes.

"Thank you for my poem. I'll put it on my bedside table to remind myself to be grateful for what I have."

"I like making cards," Amy said.

"Well, you are certainly good at it."

"We're all really glad you're here," Amy said. "Claire says that if we can get you to stay another couple months, she might have enough money to buy a new horse for our buggy—even if she is helping Rose. She says if she can get a new horse, we won't have to stop every mile to let Flora rest, which means we won't have to leave an hour earlier on church Sundays to get there on time."

Tom doubted that Claire wanted him to have all this information, but he was glad to know she was pleased he was here, even if it was only so that she could buy a new horse.

He also made a note never to let Amy know anything that he didn't want to have broadcast to the world.

A half hour later, the new dog bowl was on the floor in his kitchen and Rocky was sleeping beside his bed while he napped and gathered his strength from the unusually busy morning—and the conversation with Amy.

chapter TWENTY-ONE

Claire was returning from doing a routine checkup on Laura Yoder and asked Annette if she'd mind her stopping a few minutes to check on Rose. She hadn't heard from her sister in a few days and wanted to see how she was doing. Annette said she had a book she wanted to finish anyway, and would wait in the car.

She and her sister didn't bother knocking on each other's door. They let themselves in and half the time got involved with whatever project the other one was doing.

She opened the screen door, walked into Rose's kitchen, and stopped cold.

Rose was sitting at a table, her head buried in her folded arms, her shoulders shaking from silent sobs.

Claire flew to her sister's side. "What in the world is the matter, Rose? What can I do?"

Rose lifted a tear-stained face and immediately started to wipe it dry with her apron.

"N-nothing," she said. "Just a mood. It will pass." She looked around the kitchen, her voice suddenly a little too bright. "Can I fix you some tea?"

"Stop it!" Claire took Rose's face between her two palms. "This is me you're talking to! Tell me what is wrong."

"Henry went to town today to get another bank loan."

"Another one? What do you mean, *another* one?"

"A second mortgage on our house."

"A *second* mortgage? I never knew you had a first one. Didn't Henry inherit this place straight out from his father and mother?"

"Yes, he did." There was a faraway look in Rose's eyes. "For years we were debt free and he was bringing in a good income. If he can't get a loan today or an extension on the payments . . . we'll lose our home, Claire."

"What about our church? Surely the bishop would make arrangements to help you."

"Henry refuses to ask them for anything. I think he doesn't want the church to know where the money has been going or what he's been doing."

"And where *has* the money been going?"

"Henry won't tell me. He says it's his business and for me to stop nagging him. He says he's the man of the house and will take care of things. He gets so angry when I try to question him, I'm afraid to say anything."

"Have you looked in his checkbook?"

"He hid it."

"Oh, Rose. I'm so sorry." She wanted to try to cheer her sister up and tell her that things couldn't possibly be that bad— but things *were* that bad. "Could he have taken to drink?"

"I've thought about that. Henry had that wild streak when he was younger," Rose said. "I guess I don't have to tell you that. He drank and smoked when we first got married—back when we were still part of the Swartzentruber church, and alcohol and tobacco were not forbidden. After we became part of our Old Order church, the bishop frowned on such things, and Henry stopped smoking and pretty much gave up drinking, and I haven't smelled anything on him."

"Can you pinpoint when this behavior started?"

"No. I've thought back, and it's been so gradual, I can't remember when it started. All I know is, I don't think Henry loves me anymore."

She covered Claire's hand with her own, needing the human contact. "I think he's jumped the fence and gone against everything we've ever believed in or stood for. I think Henry has fallen for another woman."

A low growl awoke him. He'd been having a dream that he was flying over the mountains of Afghanistan, and for a couple of seconds, he couldn't understand why his motor had taken on that strange sound.

Then he heard the tap-tapping of Rocky's toenails on the wooden floor as the dog trotted over to the window, sat on his haunches, and every few seconds growled deep in his throat.

Tom had never been easily frightened, but he had also been physically capable of defending himself most of his adult life.

Now, after struggling to lift that twenty-five-pound bag of dog food, he knew that even though he was stronger, he would lose in a fair fight. He walked over to the window to investigate. The German paratrooper knife he always slept with was gripped tightly in his hand. The docs had attributed that little habit to PTSD as well, but in his opinion, sleeping with a weapon in his hands was merely the prudent thing to do.

As he scanned Claire's yard and house, he took stock. If someone was trying to break in here or at Claire's, he did have a Rossi .357 in the drawer beside his bedside table, but hoped he wouldn't have to use it.

His breath caught when he saw a shadow moving against

the white clapboards on the second story of Claire's house. There was a large oak beside it, with limbs growing close to the house. For a moment he thought someone was trying to climb into an upstairs window. Then he realized that someone was climbing out.

At that moment, he saw a sports car creep into the driveway, headlights off. A girl dressed in jeans and a bright tank top, her hair unbound and flowing down her back, slid down the tree and ran toward the car. The car door closed, and then whoever was driving it backed slowly out of the driveway.

A faint sound of rap music filtered back to him as the car drove away.

So Maddy was having a bit of *Rumspringa* again, was she? He just hoped she would use some common sense. There was a lot more trouble for kids to get into these days than when he was that age.

He and Claire had never gotten into anything when they were *Rumspringa* age. They'd been good kids. He was so in love with her back then, he probably would have continued to be a good kid, hoping he could talk her into marrying him someday. If that had happened, he most likely would have turned into a decent enough Amish husband and been content with that life.

Water over the dam, he told himself. No use crying over spilt milk. He tried to think of more clichés to comfort himself with, and couldn't. All he knew was that it hurt to think about the past, and so he did as little of it as possible.

"It's okay, boy." He tossed Rocky a treat. "You can go back to sleep now."

Instead of going back to sleep, he switched on the table lamp and selected another book of Levi's to read. His nephew had interesting taste. All of Mark Twain's works were there, right beside books on biblical archaeology and some autobiographies. There wasn't much else in the way of fiction, except for classics, but he did find an old, dog-eared Agatha Christie mystery. A cozy mystery was about his speed tonight. He put a couple of slices of bread into the toaster and, while waiting, made some cocoa.

There had been a lot of nights when he'd been awakened from a dead sleep, called for an emergency flight, and in the space of sixty seconds, was dressed and running—adrenaline pumping—to his helicopter, ready to do whatever was necessary.

Being awakened by Rocky's growl had brought on that same adrenaline rush, and he knew he would not get to sleep again until his hair-trigger trained response had calmed down.

Toast and cocoa and a good mystery was as good a way as any to put in time until he could close his eyes again. After a couple hours of *Murder on the Orient Express,* he had calmed down enough to crawl into bed again and drift off.

It seemed like he'd been asleep only a few minutes when Rocky started barking like crazy. He wasn't particularly worried. The sun had not yet risen. Perhaps the girl had returned and was going back to her bedroom the way she'd come out.

He went back to sleep, but a few seconds later, there was a knock on his door.

He jumped out of bed, yanked on some jeans, grabbed Rocky's collar, and opened the door. Claire stood there wearing a robe. Her hair hung over one shoulder in a loose, nighttime braid. There was a wild look in her eyes.

"Have you seen Maddy?" she asked. "She shares a room with Sarah. Sarah woke up in the middle of the night to use the bathroom and couldn't find her big sister. She came to get me. I checked and Maddy's bed has not been slept in."

He checked the clock. It was 2:15. "Rocky woke me up and I saw her climbing out her window and down the oak tree. A car picked her up. She was dressed *Englisch.*"

Claire's expression went from fear to accusation. "And you didn't *tell* me?"

"I figured she was on *Rumspringa* and you were turning a blind eye while she went through her 'running around' time."

"I don't 'turn a blind eye' when it comes to my children!" Claire said. "That might be some parents' choice, but not mine! I watch and I pray and I teach! You should have told me!"

"It was none of my business."

"How could it not be your business when you see a child endangering herself?" Claire said. "It should be everyone's business!"

"You'll have to excuse me. I've seen boys in uniform only two years older than Maddy engaged in house-to-house combat in Iraq."

"It's different with girls," she said. "They can be so silly and trusting at that age."

At that moment, her pager buzzed.

Claire yanked it from her robe. "I don't recognize the number."

"Here." He handed her his cell phone. "Use this."

Claire put her hands behind her back and shook her head. "I do not know how to use this device."

"Give me the number and I'll make the call."

After the first ring, he tried to hand it to Claire, but she put her hands behind her back.

He put the cell phone to his ear.

"Hello?" a young girl's voice whispered. "Claire?"

"This is Tom," he said.

"This is Maddy. I—I need a ride. I'm, um, locked inside an upstairs bathroom."

He did not bother to ask why she was locked inside a bathroom. He was afraid he knew. "Where is the house?"

She gave hurried directions.

"Stay where you are. Keep the door locked. I'll be there as fast as I can."

"Please hurry," she begged as he hung up.

"Where is she?" Claire said.

"I'll show you. We need to go."

"I should get dressed."

He hated to say it, but it was necessary. "I don't think we have time."

He jerked a T-shirt over his head, wondering if he should bring his revolver with him. If Maddy needed muscle to get her out of there, he didn't have it. On the other hand, it would probably scare Claire to death if she saw him carrying a gun.

His guess was that his Rossi would be overkill. It was probably nothing more than a *Rumspringa* party anyway, and he wasn't particularly worried about a bunch of drunken Amish teenagers getting violent, so he decided to risk it. Just to be on the safe side, he slipped the paratrooper knife into his pocket.

"Stay here, Rocky." He started to close the door and then changed his mind. Something told him it might be a good idea to have the dog along.

"Where is she?" Claire asked as they sped away.

"Maddy gave me directions to the old Tinker house near Fredericksburg. I used to be friends with a boy who lived there. I know where to go."

When they arrived, the house was derelict, and it looked like it had not been inhabited for many years. Nearly all the paint had peeled off the once lovely home.

The house certainly was not empty tonight. Dozens of cars were parked around it. Loud music poured out of broken windows. Someone had rigged lights to a generator.

"Please stay in the car, Claire," Tom said. "Keep the door locked. I'll leave Rocky here with you."

Claire nodded and huddled deeper into her robe, her eyes glued to the scene before her.

Rocky looked at him from the backseat and whined.

"Stay here," he said. "Protect Claire."

He knew the dog had no idea what he was saying, but he thought there was a chance Rocky would be a deterrent if someone tried to get into the car. Small chance of that happening, but still . . .

As he entered the house, he worked his way past several couples who apparently thought they were dancing but appeared to be basically holding each other up. There was no furniture. Old mattresses and sleeping bags were scattered about.

The Tinker place had once been a fine house. A wide staircase beckoned. Maddy said she was locked in the upstairs bathroom. Because of the age of the house, he was fairly certain there would be only one.

One thing he could tell was that this was definitely not a *Rumspringa* party. Amish kids, even when dressed *Englisch,* had a certain look. Someone who had grown up in Holmes County could tell. These were *Englisch* kids. Every one of them. Maddy had no business here at all.

One of the boys said, "Hey! No old men allowed! This is our party."

Tom saw the pistol grip of what looked to be a Glock 9mm peeking out from the waistband of the boy's low-riding jeans. He hoped the safety was on. There was a good chance that the kid was going to shoot himself in the leg if it wasn't.

"I'm looking for a girl named Maddy," Tom said. "She called and said she wants to go home. Her mom sent me to get her. Do you have a problem with that?"

"Dude." The boy was staring at his chest. "Chill out. I don't care if you take the Amish chick home."

"I intend to."

"Cool T-shirt, by the way."

Tom glanced down. In his haste, he had accidently grabbed an Army Special Forces T-shirt, a gift from an old Army buddy. It read, *We Do Bad Things To Bad People*. He'd been careful not to wear it since he came to Mt. Hope.

The kid went back to the party and Tom crept up the old stairs. Wallpaper hung in ribbons, and it was obvious by the rain stains on the wall that the roof needed attention. He was getting a bad feeling. It wasn't just from seeing the wacked-out kids downstairs, or the ruination of a formerly fine home. He was getting one of those bad feelings that only years of combat gave you.

If he had been in fighting form, he would not have asked for backup, not against a bunch of teenagers. The problem was, he couldn't box his way out of a paper bag right now. If Maddy truly needed help getting away, he wasn't sure he had the steam to do it. Not when he was unarmed and there were juveniles here who had guns stuck down their pants.

He paused on the landing and dialed 911. When the operator answered, he quickly gave the address and said, "This is Marine Captain Tom Miller. I've come to get a young friend out of a party that might turn bad before I can get her out of here. Could you send a police officer just in case?"

"We'll send someone over," the operator said. "Are you and your friend all right?"

"I don't know yet," Tom said. "I'm heading up the stairs to where she is, and I'd appreciate it if you'd keep this line open for a few minutes until I can evaluate the situation."

"No problem," the operator said. "I'll send one of our squad cars over right now."

"Thanks." He dropped his phone into his pants pocket without turning it off. It was a precaution he hoped wasn't necessary.

chapter TWENTY-TWO

Claire stared at the ruined house, wondering how Maddy could have allowed herself to go inside that evil-looking place. The longer she sat there, the angrier she got. What in the world had the girl been thinking? She had thought she and Maddy were close. Obviously, she was wrong. Right now she had no idea who Maddy was.

Tom should not have gone in there alone. He was big and could look intimidating, but she knew he was not yet a well man, nor a strong one.

Before he had pulled his T-shirt on this evening, she had a clear view of his bare chest. That sight would stay forever etched in her mind. Tom had been a soldier most of his life, and he most definitely still had a warrior's body, but the shrapnel had done more damage than she'd ever dreamed. There were multiple scars crisscrossing his chest. She could not even guess how many surgeries he'd endured.

Claire had seen something else before Tom had put on his shirt. On his left breastbone, directly above his heart, there was a tattoo. She did not approve of tattoos, but if a man had to have a tattoo, she could not imagine choosing a better one. There were no frills, pictures, or fancy swirls. Tom's tattoo was just seven bare, stark words.

For those I love, I will sacrifice.

It would be hard not to love a man who had chosen those words above all others to write permanently above his heart.

And now because of her foolish, foolish niece, that valiant man was going into that derelict house filled with who knows what, and he was doing it all alone.

What would Abraham would have done under the same circumstances?

She was afraid she knew exactly. Nothing until the child came home. Then, no matter how scared and contrite Maddy was, there would have been punishment.

Everything within her wanted to go inside that house in case Tom or Maddy needed her, but Tom had told her to stay here in the car, with the doors locked, and she had been trained to be obedient.

Everything within her wanted to go inside that house to be at the side of the man who was trying to protect her niece, but she was wearing her nightclothes and had no head covering. She had been trained that no respectable Amish woman could ever go out in public dressed as she was. "You're a good boy, aren't you, Rocky." She ruffled the dog's white fur, glad Tom had brought the dog along. It was a comfort having the animal with her.

She realized that her hair had come completely loose from its braid. She started to rebraid it when her attention was caught by something lying in the driver's seat. She picked it up. It was the knife Tom had stuck in his pocket when he thought she wasn't watching.

He now had no weapon upon him, and probably did not know it.

She disapproved of carrying weapons, but she most definitely approved of Tom.

No matter how she was dressed, or the fact that Tom had

told her to stay in a locked car, her girl was in there, and Tom. She could not make herself sit here one second longer.

She had just unlocked the door and stepped outside when she heard two gunshots, saw an upstairs window shatter, and heard a girl scream.

Her fear for Tom and Maddy gave her bare feet wings as she raced toward that house, a prayer on her lips as she burst through the door. She didn't notice that Rocky had leaped out of the car and was racing behind her, the new red leash trailing behind. She just ran.

Tom knew he was in trouble when he topped the staircase and saw a young man with a shaved head trying to pry open a heavy oak door.

"I told you to unlock it!" the young man shouted.

"I called some people." The girl inside was sobbing. "They'll be here any minute."

"*Your* people?" The boy laughed. "*Amish* people? What do you think they're gonna do? Hold hands and pray?"

Tom knew that there was an excellent chance that he was not going to get out of this mess without trouble. That tire iron the man was using and the muscle behind it were no joke. Hopefully the police would get here before anything happened to her or to him. Bluster and that paratrooper knife were the only weapons he had right now.

"*I'm* her people, boy," he said. "And I'd thank you to leave her alone."

The kid whirled, and his mouth dropped open in astonishment when he saw a six-foot-tall Marine standing in front of him. Tom had not planned it, but he hoped he looked enough like a soldier that the kid would decide he was more of a menace than he was.

"Where did *you* come from?" the kid said.

Tom kept his voice calm and deadly. "Most recently, Afghanistan."

This kid was no Amish boy on *Rumspringa*. Had he been, there was a chance he might listen to reason, but there was no Germanic lilt to his voice, no telltale white line around his neckline to indicate that he had recently traded his bowl haircut for an *Englisch* one.

Even more worrisome was the fact that he was beginning to grasp the tire iron as though he intended to use it as a weapon.

"Do it." A tall, skinny boy with no shirt and more tattoos than sense emerged from what had once been a bedroom. "You can take him." Tattoo-boy leaned against the open door-jamb and crossed his arms.

"Think about what you're doing, son," Tom said. "An underage Amish girl who's so frightened that she's locked herself in a bathroom isn't worth going to prison for. Let me take her home and you'll never see or hear from me again."

The boy with the tire iron hesitated and looked at the tattooed boy for direction.

Tom reached to pull out his paratrooper knife just in case . . . and discovered it wasn't there. Somewhere between here and the car, it had managed to fall out of his pocket. The only weapon he had to protect Maddy was his damaged, bare hands.

Tattoo-boy's eyes darted to something directly past his left shoulder.

He whirled just in time to see the low-trousered kid who had accosted him earlier point that Glock straight at him.

Adrenaline was a wonderful thing. Although his body was not strong, there was nothing wrong with his brain, and it went into overdrive. It felt as though time slowed down as he focused on how to get Maddy and him out of this alive.

The boy was a lefty, which complicated things. He grabbed the kid's left hand, and redirected it away from his body, but before he could gain total control, the kid got off one shot that blew out the window at the end of the hallway. Tattoo-boy ducked back inside the room and tire-iron-boy hit the floor as Tom and the kid wrestled over the gun. The kid pulled the trigger one last time before Tom used his larger body and superior height to shove the kid off-balance, and then he was able to wrest the gun away. The second bullet had buried itself in the drywall beside the bathroom. With his thumb, Tom released the magazine, allowing the remaining ammunition to drop to the floor where it could do no damage. He realized at that point that he had managed to get gun-boy's arm shoved behind his back in a position that God never intended an arm to go. Martial arts training was a wonderful thing.

"You come toward me," Tom told the other two boys, "and your buddy will be wearing a cast tomorrow."

He hoped the 911 operator was listening. If she had heard the gunshots, there should be multiple squad cars heading this direction.

These young men had the looks and actions of boys who had graduated from the hard-knock school of juvenile detention. Possibly they were part of a gang. If so, Tattoo-boy appeared to be the leader. All three were jazzed up on some sort of illegal pharmaceutical. His guess was cocaine. Probably selling grass and Ecstasy to the kids below, making money for their own, more expensive, habit.

He thanked God that Maddy had managed to lock herself in the bathroom and, like so many Amish teenagers on *Rumspringa,* had a forbidden cell phone that she was secretly spending a portion of her salary on each month. He also thanked God that the interior doors in this old place were made of solid wood with real cast-iron locks, not the hollowed-out shells that newer homes used to cut costs.

He still had the kid's arm twisted behind his back within a hairsbreadth of exploding out of its socket. This meant that gun-boy was staying very, very still. No sudden moves. No problem. His biggest fear was that the other two young hoodlums didn't share their friend's aversion to pain. Especially since it was gun-boy's pain and not their own.

He had his back plastered to the hallway wall now so that no one else could sneak up on him. His only hope was to keep them off-balance long enough for the cops to come.

"Does one of you own this place?" he asked, conversationally, trying to use words to distract them from the fact that he was still so weak that he was starting to tremble slightly from the effort of keeping gun-boy still.

Tattoo-boy had emerged from the bedroom now that the shooting had stopped. He didn't look quite as tough now. In fact, he was a little pale. With the bravado gone, he seemed a lot younger than Tom had originally thought.

Tom hoped the 911 operator had sent those squad cars. Unfortunately, in Holmes County, you never knew when you might round a curve too fast to avoid colliding with a buggy. The cops couldn't simply flick on their sirens and scream their way here, but every second he kept from getting jumped was one second closer to help arriving.

He pretended to look around. "I remember when this was a nice place. A rich guy lived here with his family." Tire-iron-boy was slowly getting to his feet. A natural follower, he kept looking back and forth between his two friends as though wishing they'd tell him what to do.

"What do you guys do?" Tom asked. "Run drugs from here when you aren't kidnapping little girls?"

Tire-iron-boy smiled at this. "I didn't kidnap nobody. Maddy came with me on her own free will. She knew what she was getting into. Your sweet little Amish girl ain't so innocent as you might think. This ain't her first party, friend."

"Let's get this over with." Tattoo-boy had managed to pull some of his confidence back together. What a waste of a life. One year with the Marine Corps, a different vision for his life, and the kid might turn into somebody. A boy with enough smarts and brass to make it as a gang leader could possibly turn out to be officer material once the Corps got him broken down and built back up.

"There are three of us up here, and only one of him," tattoo-boy said. "We can take him, you two know we can."

Tom could tell he was regretting his momentary show of weakness and was trying to win back the respect of the other two.

"Why are you making this so hard?" Tom asked. "All I wanted was to come take the lady home."

Now he actually did hear sirens in the distance, but far, far away.

Tire-iron-boy looked undecided and reluctant. Gun-boy was keeping his opinions to himself, which was wise, considering the position Tom was holding him in.

He figured he had just about two more minutes of enough strength left before he'd have to let the kid go. It was taking everything he had just to keep the kid's arm where it was. They wouldn't even have to call his bluff. A few more minutes of this standoff, and he would be close to collapse.

chapter TWENTY-THREE

Claire had never seen anything like it. Young people everywhere. More boys than girls. None looked familiar. All appeared to be *Englisch*. The thump, thump, thump of the music felt like it was thudding through her body, keeping time with the frantic beating of her heart.

It made no sense for her to go up those stairs. She was no fighter. There was nothing she could do to help, but she couldn't stay away. A force much stronger than her common sense propelled her up the stairs.

Rocky was plunging on ahead of her, sniffing out Tom's scent. She grabbed his leash so the dog's feet wouldn't get tangled in it.

There had been no more shots. No more windows breaking. But there were loud voices above her head. Very loud voices, and one of them was Tom's.

When Rocky heard Tom's voice, he tugged so hard against the leash, he almost jerked her off her feet.

Sweat had broken out on his brow, and he was starting to grow dizzy. The sirens were still far off. He needed help—and he needed it now. It would be ironic, after all the danger he'd come through as a pilot, to be beaten to death by three delinquents with a tire iron.

And then a vision appeared that brought a lump to his throat, even as his mind screamed at her to go away.

It was Claire and Rocky.

The minute that noble dog came up the stairs and saw what was going on, he took a wide-legged stance, ruffled his white fur, and began emitting a deep-in-the-throat snarl. It was the first time Tom had seen that behavior in Rocky. The vet had told him that Great Pyrenees had been bred to guard royalty. He believed it. At this moment, the dog had turned into a force of nature, and its attention was entirely focused on the boy with the tire iron.

Claire was directly behind the dog. At some point, her long hair had come completely undone. She had always had naturally curly hair. He remembered her fighting to keep it restrained beneath her prayer *Kapp* when she was a girl.

Now her fine, blond hair, frizzed by the night air, rose wildly from her head, curling in all directions. Her feet were bare, her face so pale it matched her white robe. To his astonishment, she held a wicked-looking knife in one hand while restraining a killer dog with the other hand Both were accidentally being spotlighted by a halogen light someone had rigged for the party.

Then Claire caught sight of Tom—and her eyes blazed.

It was the single most surreal thing he had ever seen in his life. She looked like an avenging angel with a supernatural guard dog standing right in front of her.

Tire-iron-boy, evidently possessing some residual Catholic training, crossed himself.

Claire had not been a mother of six for nothing. She cocked one eyebrow and with a low voice said, "How *dare* you threaten this good man!"

Had the situation not been so dire, he would have laughed. The Amish were most definitely pacifists, but that did not keep mothers from giving a child a good talking-to when a talking-to was warranted.

Her appearance as an avenging angel intensified as she and Rocky waded farther into the hallway. Tire-iron-boy stumbled backward to get away from her.

"Leave this man alone." She pointed the knife at them, sweeping all of their faces in one grand gesture. "And don't you ever bother my Maddy again!"

At that moment, Tom's strength finally gave way and he loosed his hold on gun-boy.

The three boys looked at one another, confused. The sirens were getting loud now, and he could see a blue light flashing through the window.

One minute the boys were there, the next minute they were gone, stumbling down the stairs, practically pushing one another down as they tried to get away.

Tom slid down the wall until he was sitting on the floor. Adrenaline could take a man only so far.

Claire held Rocky back from chasing after the boys. This was not at all what Rocky wanted. Then they heard a bolt being drawn and Maddy came out. It was obvious that the girl had been drinking.

"Maddy." Claire pulled the wayward girl into her arms. "Are you okay? Did they hurt you?"

"They tried," Maddy said. "But the Lord helped me."

"He certainly did," Claire agreed.

"No, I mean He really did. He was here. He spoke to me."

"I don't understand." Claire frowned. "How did He 'speak' to you?"

"He spoke to me in our language. He said, 'Get in the bathtub, Maddy.'"

"He said this in German?"

"Clear as a bell."

Uh-oh. Any second now, Claire was going to figure out that it was Tom speaking German to Maddy, not the Lord. He was far too drained to explain it. He wasn't even sure he understood it himself. He had no idea he had reverted to their common language when he shouted a warning to her.

"Let me get this straight," Claire said. "God spoke to you directly and told you to get in the bathtub?"

"Right before the bullet came through the wall."

Claire looked at Tom in alarm. "A bullet went through the wall?" All other thoughts had evidently been knocked from her mind by that one statement, and Tom was grateful.

"Yes," Maddy said. "It came through the wall right where I had been sitting. But I'd already jumped in the bathtub like God told me to do and I was okay."

"Do you know anything about this, Tom?" Claire asked.

Tom shrugged and rested the back of his head against the wall. Claire and Maddy were safe, that was all that mattered. He heard shouts downstairs and knew that the cops were handling things.

"It had to be God," Maddy insisted. "The only people out here were those guys and Tom. There was no one here who spoke the language, and only God would have known that a bullet would hit right where I was sitting. I think God saved me for a purpose, Claire."

Rocky whined and licked his face. He gathered the great dog into his arms and buried his face in its fur while relief washed over him. If Maddy wanted to believe that the Lord, Himself, had spoken directly to her in her own language—so be it. He did not remember shouting those words—but he did remember thinking them. The minute he saw the gun, he knew the bathtub would be the safest place for her. For all he knew, God *had* put it in his mind to yell those words to her. Because of the danger, he had evidently automatically reverted to his childhood language. His mind had done stranger things under pressure. The important thing was that Maddy was alive—and she'd come very close to not being so. If her fear-muddled mind wanted to attribute it to a direct communication with God—who was he to argue?

Besides, he was too weak to argue. It was hard being a warrior when you had no strength. Now that he knew Maddy was okay, the only thing he wanted was to get home and climb into bed.

The one thing he still had to do, though, was talk to the police. He knew Claire should not have to do it. Her people stayed as far away from the police as possible. It was practically bred into their DNA.

"Nice dog you have there," the police officer said after he'd gotten the information he needed. "I never saw that breed before."

"Great Pyrenees and shepherd mix. He was a stray."

"How do you know the Amish woman?"

How did he know Claire? There were so many things he could say. Instead, he gave the simplest answer he knew. "I rent an apartment from her."

Maddy climbed into the backseat, shivering so badly from fright, her teeth were chattering. Claire was beginning to think that raising teenage girls was a whole lot more complicated than she'd ever dreamed.

"I didn't mean for this to happen," Maddy said. "He told me we were going to a party. He named names that I knew. I thought it was safe to go."

"You would have been safe in your own bed, where you

belonged!" Claire was wrestling with such a tumult of feelings. Part of her wanted to hug Maddy, the other part wanted to smack her.

"I *am* sixteen," Maddy said with a small show of defiance.

"And how did being sixteen help you tonight?" Claire said. "Was it sixteen who rescued you?" She made a sound of disgust. "Sixteen does not give a girl the sense of a goose! I thought better of you than this."

"Did you never do anything wrong when you were my age, Claire?"

Claire's mind skittered back to a forbidden movie she had watched with *Englisch* friends, and her one night with Matthew . . .

"Of course I did." Claire knew her voice sounded irritated. Tonight had gotten on her last nerve. "That's why I can tell you that girls your age should not be let loose without a keeper!"

She did not want to talk to Maddy about this anymore. She wanted to hear what had happened between Tom and the police. She had been half afraid they would take Tom away to jail for some incomprehensible *Englisch* reason. "What did the police say?"

"They said that Maddy was a very lucky girl to have gotten away with no more than a good fright," Tom said, grimly. "Those two—the one with the tattoo and the one with the tire iron—are bad news."

"How bad?" Claire asked.

"According to the cop I talked to, the Mexican Mafia pretty much owns Ohio these days when it comes to the drug trade. These two had been pointed out to them by a couple Amish kids for trying to enlist some of them."

Claire turned to Maddy. "What have you gotten yourself into!"

"Nothing. I swear." Maddy wrapped her arms around her

waist and rocked back and forth. "He was really sweet when he was talking to me at the restaurant."

"You are finished working in the restaurant," Claire said.

The minute they pulled into the driveway and came to a stop, Maddy was out the door and into the house, where he assumed she would have a good cry.

Claire lingered, sitting in the backseat. He turned around, putting one elbow on the back of the seat.

"Are you all right?"

"No. I am *not* all right," she said. "My hair is all *schtruwwlich,* I am embarrassed by what I'm wearing. I'm shocked by the decision my silly niece made, and I am very ashamed of the way I acted tonight."

"Claire, don't worry about it. You were modestly covered from your ankles to your neck." He could laugh now, remembering the fear he'd seen on the boys' faces when the apparition of Claire had appeared. "But I was kind of wondering what you thought you were going to do with that paratrooper's knife."

"I wasn't thinking at all," she said. "I didn't even realize it was in my hand. That is the thing I am most upset about of all."

"You did nothing wrong, Claire."

"Oh, I do many things wrong," Claire said. "All the time. I pray God forgives me."

"Like what?" He found her contrition amusing. Whatever sins this lovely woman had committed could not be too heinous. From what he could see, the only thing she did all day and every day was work hard and care for her children and patients. "What things are you doing that are so wrong?"

Clair thought hard. "It was nearly eleven o'clock last Monday before I got my wash finished and hanging on the line."

After the strain of the past couple of hours, he couldn't help it. He burst out laughing.

"You make fun, but it is my job to be a good mother and homemaker and sometimes I fail at both."

"Sometimes we all fail," Tom said. "I've certainly had my share of failure."

"In what way?"

It was dark. They were alone. They had survived a traumatic evening together. He could no longer hold back. He took a tentative step into no-man's-land, hoping with all his heart that it would not turn into a minefield that would blow up in his face. "Many years ago I caused an accident that I've never forgiven myself for."

"That must be very hard to bear." Her eyes were compassionate. "What kind of an accident?"

"A car accident."

"Did someone die?"

"Yes." He struggled for the right words. He wanted to tell her it had been his brother, but the words stuck in his throat. "My . . . best friend was killed."

"Oh, Tom." She leaned forward and laid her hand on his arm. "Were you very young?"

The sound of tenderness in her voice nearly caused him to come undone. "I was not much older than Maddy."

"Ah." Claire nodded with understanding. "You were still stupid then."

"Yes." He smiled at her neat summing-up. "I was still very stupid."

"The sins of our youth. They are hard to bear sometimes." Claire looked out the window, as though seeing back through her own past. "But God's grace is sufficient."

"Maybe God's grace is sufficient, but my actions caused many people much heartache. No matter how hard I try, I cannot find peace or self-forgiveness for what I did."

"Self-forgiveness? Is this an *Englisch* word?"

"I don't know. It's a common term."

"This is not a word my people use. Self-forgiveness . . ." She lingered on it. "How does it work, this self-forgiveness?"

"I guess you find a way to forgive yourself for something you've done and then you go on with your life."

"But how is it possible to forgive yourself? What would be the point of trying? The Lord is the only one with the power to forgive our sins. Then you are forgiven indeed."

The concept was so pure, so biblical, its simplicity nearly took his breath away. Of course he couldn't forgive himself. He did not have the power.

"I had never thought of it that way. Thank you. That helps."

"I need to go inside now," she said. "It is not seemly for me to sit in this car with you."

Tom pulled his keys out of the ignition. "Good night, Claire."

He heard her laugh as she climbed out of the car. "You should be saying 'Good morning, Claire,'" she said. "Not 'good night.'"

He was grateful that she still had a sense of humor after what had happened tonight. She'd been through enough tonight to give some Amish women a nervous breakdown.

chapter TWENTY-FOUR

Claire tried to get some rest, but it eluded her. So many things to worry about. Maddy and her rebellion. Finding a new horse. Rose and Henry's continuing problems. Where would they go, she wondered? What would they do?

Claire simply had no more room, or she would have tried to take them in. She also wasn't sure she could live under the same roof as Henry without wanting to give him a piece of her mind! Rose might be married to him and under his leadership, but he wasn't the head of *her* house! He was not *her* husband. He wasn't even a leader in their church. She was under no obligation to allow him to be the head of anything in her life!

If only everything would calm down so she could get some peace!

She brushed and braided her hair once again, washed off her feet, and then crawled into her bed with a sigh of thanksgiving for her bed. The moment she closed her eyes, her pager went off. She checked the number. Fanny Yoder. The woman had been due these past three days. She needed to leave immediately.

Fortunately, Fanny lived only a mile away and had never wanted to use the birthing pool. With nothing more to carry than her bag of supplies, she could walk it in less time than it would take to hitch Flora to the buggy.

Most days it felt like she would never get caught up. It often seemed as though she had to fight her way through life, when many other women made it look easy.

The birth was an easy one—Fanny was quite the expert by now, and best of all, she had two competent sisters ready to take over the minute the baby was born. As Claire trudged back home, she was anticipating a leisurely breakfast with her family and then a long, long nap. It was their no-church Sunday and she was in desperate need of a true Sabbath rest. Last night, before going to bed, before the craziness with Maddy set in, she had made up a breakfast oatmeal casserole for this morning. With some cold milk, it would taste so good.

She wondered briefly about asking Tom to join them—he'd gone to so much effort and danger last night, she would like to say thank you, and her oatmeal casserole was truly delicious.

How Maddy would act today was a mystery. She might be surly or contrite or defensive. There was no telling.

She felt a little guilty about how much she enjoyed her no-church Sundays. *Englisch* people seemed to think it odd that the Amish had church only every other Sunday, but it had worked well for her people for hundreds of years. Of course, the Sundays they did have church, they certainly made it count. Sitting on hard, backless benches for three hours at a time—or more—was no joke.

As she walked home, she tried out several different conversations with her niece, preparing herself for whatever mood Maddy was in. She thought she was ready for anything Maddy could throw at her.

When she got to her driveway, there was a strange buggy parked in front of her house. This was not just any buggy. She could tell that it belonged to someone who was a member of the New Order Amish church. Instead of the rolled, strapped-up doors that her Old Order Amish church affected, this buggy had the sliding doors of the New Order *and* it had rubber tires!

What on earth was a New Order Amish person doing here?

The New Order people had been a thorn in Old Order people's flesh ever since they had pulled away because they didn't think the Old Order was "spiritual" enough. The New Order was so intent about personal spirituality, not only did they go to Sunday school on their "off" Sunday, they even held Bible studies in the middle of the week, as though the hours the Old Order church spent in services every other Sunday wasn't enough.

She even heard they talked about "having a relationship" with Jesus Christ—as though they deemed themselves worthy of such a thing! How could a lowly human have a relationship with Jesus Christ? It sounded very prideful to her, as did their claim that one could be "assured" of salvation! Oh, such a prideful belief! Everyone knew that you worked hard, tried to follow Jesus, and when you died, if you were very lucky, you got to go to heaven.

Those New Order people also made a big deal about what they called "clean courtship," eschewing bundling and any other sort of *Rumspringa* misconduct. That was all well and good, but from what little she'd seen, about the only thing their youngies did was study the Bible and go to hymn singings and highly chaperoned youth activities. That's why every other Amish sect called them the "goody-goodies."

The Old Order Amish did not shun them, but they shook

their heads sometimes over the New Order's enthusiasm for all things spiritual.

An *Englisch* woman had once asked her if the New Order Amish had electricity and cars. *Englisch* people could be so dense sometimes. Of *course* they didn't have electricity and cars. That was the *Beachy* Amish.

What did these New Order people want with her? She had not delivered any babies to New Order mothers. Perhaps one of them wanted her midwife services? She debated. Yes, she would deliver a New Order baby. Their money was as good as anyone else's.

She was astonished when Maddy came flying out the door dressed in her good church dress and climbed into the buggy.

"Where are you going?" Claire called.

"To church," Maddy said.

"Wait!" As tired as she was, Claire trotted toward them. A girl she'd never seen before turned the buggy around and walked the horse toward her. Maddy was sitting up front with her Bible in her lap.

"What's going on, Maddy? Who is your friend?"

"This is Joy. We work together at the restaurant."

The girl, not much older than Maddy, wore the caped dress of the New Order Amish and the ribbonless prayer *Kapp*.

"It's good to meet you," Joy said.

Maddy clutched her Bible against her stomach. "We're going to church."

"But this is our no-church Sunday," Claire protested.

"Not for Joy's church. They have church every Sunday."

Joy leaned forward. "It makes me feel better when I go to church every Sunday."

"But I was going to put my oatmeal casserole in the oven when I got back," Claire said. "I was looking forward to a nice, long Sunday breakfast."

"Oh, I already did that for you," Maddy said. "I got up early so I could help out. I know you didn't get any sleep last night because of me. Breakfast is warm and sitting on the table all ready for you. Everyone else is still asleep."

"But . . ." Claire said.

Maddy put her hand over Claire's, "I know this seems sudden, but I've been considering going to Joy's church for a long time. Last night, when God told me to get in the bathtub and when I heard the bullet hit and miss me, I promised Him that if I got out of that house alive, I'd start going to church with Joy. She's been asking me for a long time. Her church is like that. They talk to people about their souls. I texted her last night after we got home and asked her to pick me up. Joy is going to teach me how to have a relationship with Jesus so I'm not tempted to do anything as stupid as I did last night ever again. Joy says I need more accountability in my life and her church can help me with that."

Accountability? She had watched after Maddy as carefully as she knew how. Was Maddy sliding over to the New Order because she hadn't given her *enough* rules?

All she could manage was a weak "Come home soon."

She stood watching after the New Order buggy, remembering how hard it had been for her to leave the Swartzentruber church. So much soul-searching about giving up her church and much of her family. So much grief and prayer.

Once she made her decision, it took her months to get used to dressing in lighter, shorter dresses and to get used to the old hymns sung at a faster pace. It had been downright embarrassing the first time Rose took her to purchase store-bought underwear instead of the homemade underclothing required by Swartzentruber rules.

Of course there were great blessings when she crossed over to her twin sister's church. In addition to getting to fellowship with Rose again, Levi, who had left the Amish entirely, installed indoor plumbing for her. Oh, the joy of having a real flush toilet and shower! Hot and cold running water in the kitchen, too! She even had a nice graveled driveway now, instead of constantly tracking in dirt and mud. Now Maddy was exchanging one sect for another in the blink of an eye. Because God told her to get in the bathtub?

Kids these days!

"You look like you could use one of these." Tom held a coffee cup in each hand. "You can take your choice. You want it black?" He held up a cup. "Or with cream?" He held up the second cup. "There's a couple of packets in my pocket if you take it with sugar."

"Coffee is exactly what I need, but which do you prefer?"

"I can drink coffee any way it's possible to make it. When you spend as much time in the military as I have, you learn to drink anything hot you can find that even resembles coffee."

"Then I would like the one with the cream, please."

"Here you go."

She took the cup with both hands. "This is very nice of you. Thank you."

"I saw you leave this morning," Tom said. "When I was getting ready to go to Jeremiah's. I'm getting better at milking, so it didn't take us as long this time. I hit the start button the minute I saw you so it would be nice and fresh." He lifted one of the midwifery bags off her shoulder. "You look like you're going to fall over. Here, let me help you with this."

Claire felt tears start behind her eyes and blinked them away. She needed kindness right now, very much. This thoughtfulness couldn't have been any more timely.

"How did the birth go?" he said, as he followed her onto the porch.

"Fine." She hesitated.

"Have you had breakfast? Maddy tells me we have a warm oatmeal casserole sitting on the table right now."

"I would like that very much." Tom slung her bag over his shoulder and opened the door for her before she could reach for the handle.

He hadn't been expecting an invitation, but it was welcome. He hadn't had oatmeal casserole for breakfast since his mother died, and it had been a favorite of his.

Claire didn't go to any great lengths to serve him. One of the many things he admired about Amish women was their lack of fuss. She brought two bowls and two spoons to the table, got a pitcher of cold milk out of the refrigerator, sat down beside him, and bowed her head for a silent prayer. He responded by doing the same.

After a few minutes, she took a deep breath, as though finished with her prayer, and when he looked up, she was reaching for a spatula to place the oatmeal cake into his bowl.

"Oh, I forgot the applesauce." She jumped to her feet and brought a home-canned jar from the refrigerator.

"I saw Maddy leave a few minutes ago in a New Order buggy." He poured milk over the oatmeal cake. "That was different."

Her spoon was halfway to her mouth when he said this, and she paused with it still in midair. "You know the difference between Old and New Order buggies?"

He mentally chastised himself for having let down his guard. Most *Englisch* didn't know the difference, nor should he. "Jeremiah was talking about it."

That was true, but he didn't tell her that the conversation had taken place more than thirty years ago.

Claire swallowed the spoonful of oatmeal. "Maddy says

now that after God spoke to her in German, she wants to go to church every Sunday and learn how to 'have a relationship' with Jesus."

"There are worse ways for her to spend her time."

"Oh, and don't I know it after last night!" She shook her head. "I am having trouble believing everything that happened last night. These past couple of years, the only thing that mattered to me, besides being a good midwife, was creating a peaceful and happy home. I think I must be doing something wrong."

"One young girl's escapade doesn't make you a bad mother, Claire."

"Perhaps, but it does not make me a good one, either."

"With the exception of my own Mom, I think you're the best mother I've ever known."

His words hung there in the air, all shiny and golden. They were exactly the words she most needed to hear right now.

Those words also did something to her stomach that she didn't want to happen. Tom was becoming entirely too important to her life. And that was not acceptable. She could *not* get involved with this *Englisch* soldier, but his continual thoughtfulness, not to mention the unselfish courage he had shown last night, was wearing away her resolve.

How could a woman dismiss a man who wore the words *For those I love, I will sacrifice* above his heart?

The worry, lack of sleep, constant work, and danger they had been in last night had taken their toll. She laid her spoon on the table and dropped her head into her hands while tears flowed.

"Oh, Claire, sweetheart," Tom said. "I didn't mean to make you cry."

She gave a little shake of her head, wishing he wasn't here to see her break down.

"Come here, Claire." To her surprise, he grasped her hand, led her to the couch, and pulled her down beside him.

Claire was shocked. "I shouldn't . . ."

"Shhh." He put his left arm around her. "You remind me of a combat soldier who has been on the front lines too long without any chance to rest and regroup. It's time to regroup, Claire."

He pulled her close, drawing her head toward him until it rested against his chest.

"Tom . . ." For the life of her she couldn't stop crying, or make herself pull away from him.

"Just for a few minutes, Claire. Let someone take care of *you* for a change."

It had been so very long since anyone had held her. She closed her eyes, absorbing the comfort of it. Then she remembered where she was.

"The children . . . ." She began to pull away.

"Are asleep. If they wake, we'll hear them clattering down those wood stairs."

It felt so good to be held.

"I can't bear to see you beat up on yourself because your niece is acting like a normal teenager who doesn't have a brain in her head."

In spite of her tears, she choked out a laugh. That described Maddy perfectly.

"I've watched you, Claire. You take care of everyone and everything around you. Always. You've even taken on your sister's problems."

Tom's voice was gentle. It reminded her of the tone she always used to calm a panicked, laboring mother.

What she was allowing to happen was most assuredly not wise, but a knot deep inside her was loosening, and they were doing nothing morally wrong.

She gulped down a sob and allowed herself to relax within the circle of his arms. The rhythm of his great heart against her ear, his gentleness and healing words, the rawness of her own emotions—all worked together to draw her deeper into the comfort of his embrace.

"No one on earth works as hard as you or cares about everyone else as much as you. I remember how even when you were a little girl you were always . . . ."

He stopped abruptly, and she could feel him holding his breath.

Suddenly the pieces began to fall into place.

Tom could have bit off his tongue. This was not the time nor the place, but seeing her cry had lowered all his defenses. He had been remembering when they were children, how she had quietly started bringing an extra sandwich in her dinner pail each day to share with a girl whose food was not as plentiful. He still believed that he began falling in love with her the minute he realized what she was doing. They had been in the third grade.

Her tears stopped. She pulled away, placed one hand against the side of his face, and looked at him with wonder.

"Tobias?"

He let the breath he had been holding out on a sigh. There was no use trying to pretend. The barn cat was out of the bag, as his father would have said, and there was no use trying to put it back.

He nodded.

"Why didn't you tell me?"

"I meant to that first day. That was why I was there. To see you. To apologize for the damage I had done to your life. But then I got sick, and then Grace came and . . ."

"What do you mean?" Claire put a finger against his lips to stop the flow of words. "What do you mean you came to apologize?"

"For Matthew's death and what it did to you."

"You have taken all the blame for that on yourself all these years?"

"It was my fault. I am the one who killed my brother and subjected you to raising Levi alone and . . . ."

"I never blamed you for Matthew's death."

He could hardly believe his ears. "You should have. I was the one who ran off the road and rammed that electric pole."

"But Henry was the one who led the stallion out of the stable. My brother-in-law could be such a show-off when he was young. Henry even told me that he was the one who bet Matthew that he couldn't ride Ebony Sky. We both know Matthew could not pass up a dare like that, not even if it killed him. Each of you was to blame, and yet none of you were. You were all just kids—high on testosterone, thinking you were invincible."

"You're right," Tom said. "I wish you could have seen Matthew that night before the accident, the way he looked flying down the road on that magnificent animal. Riding Ebony Sky without a saddle as though he was glued to that horse's back. I was never so proud of anyone in my life."

"I knew that. I could envision every last detail—including the pride you felt watching your brother's expertise. You were always so proud of him. How could I blame you for the freak set of circumstances that caused Matthew's death?"

Oh, this was better than anything he had ever imagined when he decided to come back. She had not blamed him for Matthew's death or for ruining her life after all!

"Thank you for forgiving me, Claire." In his gratitude, he reached out to hug her. His heart was lighter than it had been in years.

"You think I have forgiven you?" She put one hand on his chest and stopped him. "You are mistaken about that."

He dropped his arms. "I don't understand."

"I saw your tattoo last night."

"Okay." What did this have to do with anything?

"'For those I love, I will sacrifice,'" Claire quoted. "That's what you have written there, right?"

"Yes. Why?"

She slowly shook her head. "That is an outright lie."

"I don't understand."

"I've never, ever blamed you for Matthew's death—but do you realize how much pain you caused by leaving and never coming back?"

"I couldn't come back. I was under the ban."

"You were not banned the day you ran away. You were banned later, for leaving the church. Not for hitting the electric pole. Yes, you would have had to confess and asked forgiveness for driving that vehicle, but you could have lived the rest of your life here and no one in our church would ever have held that night against you."

"My father blamed me."

"You father's grief was fathomless. He wasn't entirely sane for a few days. I know exactly what he said to you to cause you to leave. He repeated that story to me over and over, always with such regret."

"I didn't know he had regretted anything."

"How could we tell you? We did not know where you were. We did not know how to find you."

"As far as I could tell, no one ever tried." This statement surprised even him. All these years, had he actually been expecting his father to try to hunt for him?

"You have been too long among the *Englisch*," Claire said. "You forget what being Swartentruber means. What did you expect him to do? Call the police? Hire a private detective? Our people do not do things like that. He protected you and watched over you the only way he knew how—he prayed for you. He sat a place at the table every day for you, and he prayed for you!"

She was breaking his heart, and she knew it.

"I didn't think anyone would want me around."

"Really? Or were you just too proud to face us? You and I grew up together. We were friends. I was seventeen, Amish, and pregnant. I could have used a friend back then, Tom."

"I didn't feel worthy of even being around you."

"So—you abandoned me?"

"I thought it was the best thing for everyone if I just stayed out of your life."

She was so angry now that her face was flushed. "Did you know that Faye stood at the front window and watched for you? For weeks?"

"No."

"She was only eight, Tom, and that little girl had already lost her mother and a brother. She cried for days. Jeremiah could not comfort her. No one could. She kept insisting that you would come back. A light went out of her when months passed and you never showed up."

"Oh, Claire." He closed his eyes, sick at heart. To him, Faye had just been his little tattletale sister. Not once had he considered what this had done to her. "I am so sorry. I had no idea."

"So tell me—who did you love enough to sacrifice for, Tom? Because it surely was not any of us."

He could not take one more word. He had expected her to be angry, but he had never expected her to completely break his heart.

"What can I do?" He slid to his knees and gripped her

hands, desperate for an answer. "How can I make this up to everyone?"

"That is the thing." Her voice was unbearably sad. "You never can make up for it. Those are like years that the locusts have eaten. Only God, Himself, could give them back to you."

She had never been a vindictive person. That had been one of the many things he loved about her. Claire could get angry, very angry, but it never lasted.

That happened now. Compassion melted away her anger and she held out her arms.

"Come here."

Suddenly, this gentle Amish woman was holding him—a tough, seasoned Marine—as scalding, toxic tears that had been locked away behind a lifetime of regret bled from his body.

chapter TWENTY-FIVE

They heard the sound of Daniel's footsteps long before the child came down the wooden staircase. Tom had time to rise, wipe his eyes with the sleeve of his shirt, and walk over to the door before the toddler poked his head around the corner of the living room.

"Mommi!" Daniel raced across the floor in his little pajamas, and leaped onto her lap.

"Are you hungry, little one?" Claire asked, in German.

He nodded.

"I will feed you soon." She glanced up at Tom. "Are you going to be all right?"

"Eventually."

"What are you going to do?"

"I have no idea. I need time to think through all that you've told me."

"I will pray for you."

"And I will need those prayers."

As he climbed the stairs to his apartment, a part of him noted that it was a beautiful, cloudless day. The other part of him felt as though he were flying blind through a hailstorm.

Everything within him was shouting for him to leave. Right now. He hated this emotional stuff. He wanted to forget this whole mess. He could stuff that duffel bag in his car, drop a few hundred on the kitchen table in his apartment for Claire to find, head back to Washington, and accept whatever job the military wanted to give him. Even piloting a desk, no matter how much he hated the thought, would be less painful than one more minute of sticking around here where his heart seemed to get broken every time he turned around.

He had a life apart from this place. It would be so easy to walk away. Just like he'd done before.

Rocky had his nose pressed against the screen and was whining. His eagerness to shoot out the door made Tom feel even guiltier. He'd forgotten all about the dog while he was talking with Grace. He was good at that. Good at letting people down.

By the time Rocky was finished, he had decided to take a walk to Elizabeth's. She wouldn't know what he should do, either, but he needed someone to talk to now—someone who would have no angst about it. That conversation with Claire had just about killed him.

"Come on, Rocky," he called as he headed up the road. "Come on, boy."

He found Elizabeth sitting on the bench in the front yard wearing a floral dress, her pearls, and her best white tennis shoes. Her Sunday outfit.

She was not in a good mood and scowled when she saw him approaching. "Don't you start in on my tennis shoes, too."

"Too?"

"Last Sunday, Missy Perkins told me at church that they were having a nice sale on dress shoes at Payless this week."

"Why is that a problem?"

"Missy was a clerk in the clothing department store over in Wooster for years and always thought she had to dress nice. She's seventy-six years old and still wears high heels to church. Probably wears them to do her housecleaning in for all I know."

"I still don't understand why that's a problem."

"What's wrong with you? It's as clear as a bell to me. I've been thinking about it all week. She's been trying to tell me that my tennis shoes aren't good enough to come to church in!"

"Isn't she the one who picks you up for church sometimes? I thought she was your friend."

"She is my friend."

"But you're mad at her."

"I am now!"

"Why?"

"She called me this morning to say that she'd be here to pick me up and she asked if I'd gotten a chance to go to that shoe sale."

"But don't you have the right to wear anything you want?"

"I certainly do! If Missy wants to break a leg falling off of those high heels she wears, that's her business! It's not like anyone's going to mistake her for a fifty-year-old just because she dyes her hair red and wears her fancy shoes. My tennis shoes are comfortable, thank you very much. I have no intention of breaking a hip just because Missy doesn't approve of what I wear on my feet."

He didn't know whether to be amused or worried.

"I'm about ready to take Grace's car and drive myself. I still got a driver's license. Just because I stopped driving for a while because I was sick doesn't mean I can't get around now."

"I thought Levi told me there were some vision issues, as well." He said it as gently as he knew how.

"Levi needs to keep his nose out of my beeswax."

"Would you like for me to take you today instead?"

"Oh!" Elizabeth's demeanor changed completely. "Would you?"

"I'd be happy to."

"This is wonderful! You'll like our preacher, and our singing is real good—as long as Missy don't start screeching around on the high notes."

He'd just been offering her a ride to keep her from saying something she'd regret to her best friend. He had no intention of going inside with her.

But she was already on the phone, telling Missy that she had another ride to church and would be bringing a visitor with her.

He supposed it wouldn't hurt to go with her. He would just be sitting around anyway. Unless he decided to take off for good. "I'll go put Rocky inside the barn for now, and get the car."

"Better tuck in that shirttail while you're at it!"

"I will, Elizabeth."

As he walked back to the apartment, despite everything that had happened this morning, he smiled. Going to see Elizabeth had not turned out as he'd expected, but somehow he felt a little better anyway.

Thirty minutes later, they were inside of the church where Elizabeth went three times a week like clockwork. Four if you counted her ladies' class on Thursdays. Plenty of time for Missy to get on her nerves. Today was a good day for her, though. Elizabeth was as proud as punch about having him sitting beside of her.

The singing was good, but the preacher, Darren Stephens, was so young, he reminded Tom of a new, raw recruit.

"How old is that kid?" he whispered to Elizabeth.

"Doctor Stephens?" Elizabeth whispered back. "He's thirty-two."

"Oh." Tom paid a little more attention after that.

"I'll be preaching from I Timothy 5:8." Dr. Stephens said.

"The King James Version is my favorite translation of this particular passage."

Elizabeth shared her Bible with him, opening it at the assigned place.

Tom glanced down, found the passage, and read it. The preacher's voice faded into the background as Tom read it again. And again.

But if any provide not for his own, and specially for those of his own house, he hath denied the faith, and is worse than an infidel.

Tom had heard of things like this happening to other people—but it had never happened to him. And yet for the preacher to choose this particular passage today of all days when he was wrestling with the desire to pack up and leave . . . Well, it was uncanny.

He didn't hear another word the preacher said.

Claire was peeling potatoes for supper when he came back.

"Can we talk for a second?" he asked.

One look at his face, and she knew the potatoes could wait. "Maddy, would you keep an eye on Daniel and Sarah for me, please?"

Maddy was sitting at the table reading her Bible. She closed it now and turned to the two littles ones. "Want me to read you a story, Daniel? You, too, Sarah. I'll read any book you like."

She rinsed off her hands, dried them on her apron, and followed him out onto the porch.

"I saw your car leave," she said. "You were gone a long time. I was getting worried. Where did you go?"

"I drove Elizabeth to church. Then I dropped her back off and just drove around for a long time, thinking."

He looked so straight and tall standing there on the porch.

His scars had faded, but his eyes were troubled, and his hands were shoved deep into his pants pockets—a gesture she remembered from their childhood when he was upset about something. How could she not have recognized him all this time? The minute she knew he was Tobias, she could read the truth of it in every line of his body.

"I'll be honest with you. I seriously considered leaving and never coming back."

"I thought that might have been what happened, especially when I realized you'd put Rocky in the barn."

"I've served my country well, Claire, but you are right. I have sacrificed nothing for those I truly love. I made a decision today. Instead of asking for an extension of my sick leave, tomorrow I'm going to ask for a full retirement. When it comes through, I'll look near here for a place to live permanently. I have no earthly idea how to make amends to you, or Faye, or Levi, or *Daed*. All I know is that I have to stay here and try."

"Won't you miss your—what was it that Jesse called it—your Cobra?"

"I'll miss a lot of things, but right now, none of them seem very important to me."

She studied his face, his eyes, the set of his mouth. What she read there was that he was dead serious about this.

He would be living here. Near her. Quite possibly forever.

He had said he was willing to sacrifice for those he truly loved. It had not escaped her notice that her name was the first one on the list.

Did her heart *have* to start racing at the mere thought?

She would have to keep their relationship on a friendship level, and only a friendship level. Anything else would be disastrous.

"If this decision gives you peace, then I'm happy for you."

"It does give me peace. Now, is there anything you can tell me to do that would make your life easier?"

"Actually, there is a big thing you can do."

"Name it."

"You won't like it."

"Name it."

"I've asked Henry and Rose and their children over this evening for Sunday supper," Claire said. "I would appreciate it if you would join us."

"That's it?"

"That is a lot to ask. It is not easy for me to be around my brother-in-law these days," Claire said. "Having you there would be helpful to me."

"I'll be happy to come. Have things gotten worse?"

"Rose told me last week that they are for sure and certain losing their home. The bank will give them no more extensions."

Jesse came bounding out of the house, came to a skidding stop at seeing their serious faces, and asked, "What's wrong?"

"Nothing is wrong," she said. "I was inviting Tom to come to supper tonight with Rose and Henry and their children."

"Is Henry a bad man?" Jesse asked.

"Why do you ask?"

"Because every time you say his name now, your voice sounds like it does when you're mad with one of us."

Tom expected her to sugarcoat her answer. She did not.

"You are right. I am angry with Henry," she said. "And I have no idea if he's a bad man or not. That's what I hope to find out."

chapter TWENTY-SIX

Claire already regretted inviting Rose and Henry and their five children to supper. The invitation had been extended in a fit of compassion for her sister. Now she wondered how she could manage to show respect to her brother-in-law when she believed with all her heart that he was involved in something he should not be.

Had she been in Rose's shoes, she would not have stood for being kept in ignorance. But then again, she had never been in Rose's exact shoes. It was not possible to understand the intricacies of another's marriage. Abraham had not been an easy man to live with, but she had never had reason to doubt his faithfulness. Nor had he ever left them in want.

"They are here," Jesse called.

She also regretted her words earlier this morning when Jesse asked if Henry was a bad man. Who knew what the child might say at the supper table? She did not want Rose or her children getting their feelings hurt.

She did not care if Henry's feelings got hurt.

"You have made a feast," Rose said, as she and her family walked into the kitchen. "Thank you."

"Maddy helped a great deal. And Sarah." Claire said. " My girls are becoming very good cooks."

"Henry." She tried to be civil. "I am glad you could come."

"Is supper ready yet?" He fingered his beard, nervously, a habit she hated to see in a man.

"Are you in a hurry, Henry? Do you have someplace you need to be?" She tried to keep the sarcasm from her voice but did not succeed. It would be best, she decided, simply to keep her mouth shut.

"I wrote a poem for you today." Amy wheeled herself into the kitchen and handed a card to Rose. "I thought you might like it."

Claire saw that it was the card that Amy had been working on all day, ever since she found out that Rose's family was coming. She had looked over Amy's shoulder at one point and had been surprised to see that she was drawing a stark, barren tree with no leaves on its branches. That was not the kind of picture Amy usually drew.

"Read it out loud," Amy said.

"Thank you," Rose said. "I will be happy to."

Dreams

Dreams are made of heart and soul
More precious than diamonds or gold.
Some dreams get broken and frayed
Leaving your heart lonely and betrayed
Left not knowing where to stand
You reach up for a helping hand
A strong hand and maybe angels, too.
He said, "Follow, I'll lead you there.
I know it's hard to see it true
But I have better plans for you
The road may be long and rough,
But lean on me, and it won't be so tough.

Soon the sun will light your path,
And a dream will blossom,
One that will last.

Claire saw her sister's chin tremble.

"Thank you, Amy. I needed that poem today."

Amy, with eyes entirely too wise for her age, said, "I thought you might."

"These green beans are outstanding, Claire," Rose said. "How many quarts have you and the girls canned so far this year?"

"Only four dozen. I'll get another good picking in a few days and the girls and I should be able to double that."

"That's good."

Silence fell on the table, and it was not the first time. Tom could tell that Claire and her sister were struggling to keep a conversation going. Now they gave up and simply ate their meal. Even the children seemed subdued.

He had been introduced only as Claire's renter. Within those boundaries, there was little he could contribute to the dinner conversation. Henry didn't even try.

Tom had gone to the hardware store in Mt. Hope several times since he'd seen Henry catching a ride there, but had never caught him there again. He could still kick himself for having almost run out of gas that day. He didn't know what he could do about it if he found out what Henry was up to, but at least he could give Claire something to work with.

Henry finished his plate and pushed it aside. They had been seated next to each other, and Tom saw Henry, with his hands now unoccupied, flicking his right wrist beneath the table as he gazed out a window.

It was one of the oddest mannerisms he had ever seen, and

yet it was familiar. He had known a soldier who had developed the same strange behavior.

"How about me and you outside and walk off some of this good food?" he suggested. "While the women clean up the dishes."

"What?" Henry looked startled. "Oh. Sure."

Tom led him toward the barn, chatting about inconsequential things, but the minute they walked inside and were out of sight of the house, he slammed his cousin up against a stall.

"How dare you do this to your family?"

"Wh—what?" Henry looked dazed.

Tom grabbed him by the shirt collar and shook him. "How dare you allow your wife and children to go hungry? How dare you lose the good farm your father handed over to you free and clear? I thought you were smarter than that, Henry. I can't believe you've been this stupid."

"What are you talking about?" Henry struggled to get away. "Who are you, anyway?"

"Tell me how you lost it. Blackjack? Poker? Slot machines? Playing the ponies?"

Henry's eyes grew wide. "How did you know? And who are you?"

"That thing you were doing with your wrist at the supper table. You were throwing dice, weren't you? Visualizing it in your mind? Or is it because you've tossed so many dice you can't stop throwing them, even when they aren't there? I bet you can't even tell me what you were eating, and Claire's worked on that supper all day."

"Get off me!" Henry shoved him away.

Tom came right back at him, so furious he felt like he could tear the man apart. "You deserve a beating for what you've done. Do you know that?" He grabbed him by the collar again. "Do you realize your wife was here, trying to sell her favorite china to get enough money to buy groceries? Claire gave her four hundred dollars that she couldn't afford to give. How long did it take you to gamble that much away? Five minutes? Ten?"

Henry's eyes took on a hungry look. "Rose has four hundred dollars?"

That's when he hit him, with every last ounce of strength he had. Pain had never felt so satisfying as the sting he felt in his knuckles as Henry went down.

"Henry?" Rose appeared in the doorway of the barn. "Is that true?"

Tom half expected her to rush to her husband's aid, but Rose was beyond that. Instead, she walked over and stood looking down at him.

"I came out to see if you two were ready for dessert," she said.

Henry sat up and wiped a trickle of blood from the corner of his mouth.

"Is this true, Henry? Are the children and I losing our home because you gambled it away?"

"I—I had some debts."

"I just bet you did," Tom said.

Henry stood up, took a handkerchief out of his pocket, and dabbed at the cut on his mouth.

"Where have you been going?" Rose asked. "Where does an Amish man who should be home putting in crops go in order to gamble?"

"I didn't mean to," Henry said. "It was the horses."

"The horses?" she asked. "What about the horses?"

"I know horses. You know that. I've always known horses. An *Englisch* friend took me to Scioto Downs over near Columbus awhile back. He thought I might know horses well enough that I could help him place some bets."

"You lost everything betting on horses?" Tom was incredulous.

"No. Scioto Downs has a casino, too." Henry's eyes took on that faraway look. "Video games, slot machines, cards, you name it." He snapped to and seemed to realize that he had a wife listening to him rhapsodize. "I plan on getting it back, Rose. Honest. I was just on a losing streak there for a while. Tom says Claire gave you some money. If I could borrow some of it, I'm sure I could . . ."

Rose turned on her heel and walked away. A few minutes later, he and Henry heard buggy wheels crunching over gravel as she pulled out onto the road with the children.

"It's five miles to my house," Henry said. "Who's going to take me home?"

"Heck if I know," Tom said. "Maybe you should call a gambling buddy. One thing for sure—it's not going to be me or Claire."

"Henry told you that?" Claire was incredulous. "Scioto Downs? Horse racing? Casinos? What kind of Amish man loses his family's home by gambling?"

"My guess is probably not a very good one."

It was late. Now that the children were in bed, they could freely discuss what had happened. He had watched Claire wrestle with what to tell the children when they asked why Henry was walking home. Finally, she'd simply told them the truth. He liked that about her.

"At least we know now what was going on."

"Do you think Rose will leave him?"

"Leave him? Of course not. Don't you remember what you were taught as a child? Divorce is not an option? But I would not want to be Henry when he gets back inside that house."

"What do you think will happen?"

"Now that Rose knows what Henry has been involved in, she will go to the bishop and the church leaders will get involved."

"Will they intervene with the sale of the house?"

"Not as long as the children and Rose have shelter. It would take a great deal of money to save their property, and if Henry does not feel the true sting of loss, he may never seek to make a change within himself. I have heard that a gambling addiction is a powerful thing."

"Henry will need real help. Some sort of a recovery program. He might even have to get some in-house treatment," Tom said. "Will your bishop allow such a thing?"

"Our bishop?" Claire said. "Not only will Bishop Schrock allow it—to save one of our families, he would take money out of his own pocket to pay for it."

chapter TWENTY-SEVEN

It was almost dark when he saw it. He was coming home from the grocery store Monday evening, and saw someone sitting in the weeds beside the road, less than a mile from his apartment. He stopped the car and walked over to investigate. He was shocked when he saw that it was a young woman, and she appeared to be exceedingly pregnant.

Was this perhaps one of Claire's patients? Walking to see her and overcome with labor pains?

"Are you all right?" he asked.

It was a stupid thing to say. Of course she wasn't all right. She was sitting in the weeds beside the road and was at least eight months pregnant, if not more. She was a tiny thing, and her belly was so large in comparison to her body, it was almost grotesque.

One thing was for sure, she was not Amish. Dirty blond hair. A brightly colored tie-dyed top. Filthy white shorts, and lime-green flip-flops. A tattoo adorned her ankle. It was of a snake. Nope. Definitely not Amish.

"Do you need help?" he asked. "Can I call someone?"

She tried to stand up, and he helped steady her.

"The bus left me off in Mt. Eaton. I caught a ride to Mt. Hope. I'm trying to get to my parents' house, but I don't think this baby is going to wait."

The only thing he could think to do was get her to Claire's as fast as possible. Claire was a mile away, the nearest hospital maybe a half hour. He knew she would be home because she had told him this morning she planned on canning green beans all day.

"There's a midwife two minutes from here. Claire Shetler. I'm going to take you to her."

"Levi's *maam*?"

"Yes." He was puzzled. What could this ragged-looking *Englisch* woman possibly know about Levi and his mother?

"Okay."

He helped her into the backseat of his car, one side of which held two full grocery sacks. A package of cookies peeked out of one. He saw her eying it, hungrily.

"Help yourself," he said. "I don't mind."

The woman's features were nearly as beautiful as Maddy's, but that was where the comparison ended. Where Maddy had a look of youth and purity, this woman had led a hard life.

She tore open the package of cookies and wolfed them down, one after another, crumbs falling unheeded all over her and his car.

Then she grabbed her belly and let out a groan.

"What's wrong?" he asked.

"I don't know. I'm either in labor or I've got some really bad cramps."

He laid on the horn as he rounded the corner to Claire's and kept it blaring as he pulled into the driveway. He had never been so grateful in his life to see anyone as he was when Claire came running up to the car.

"What on earth is wrong?" Then she saw that he had a passenger in the backseat. "Oh!"

"This woman is half starved and in labor," he said. "I found her sitting along the side of the road."

"She wanted to see me?" Claire sounded confused. "I have no *Englisch* clients."

"She was trying to get to her parents. I was the one who suggested we come here. I didn't know what else to do."

The young woman was in the throes of another contraction when Claire opened the car door.

"It's okay," Claire soothed as she stroked the girls hair away from her face. "It's . . . ." She froze, staring, aghast. "Zillah?" Her voice rose high in astonishment.

"Can you call *Daadi* and *Mommi*?" the girl asked. "I want to see them again—really bad."

"Help me get her inside, Tom."

Albert, Jesse, Sarah, and Amy were playing Hearts in the front room. Maddy was sewing a dress on the treadle machine. Daniel was playing with building blocks on the floor. The games and the sewing machine stopped and they all gaped as he and Claire half carried the disheveled girl into the house and to the couch. Even Daniel seemed subdued by the hubbub.

"Maddy," Claire commanded. "Go out to the phone shanty and call Grace. Tell her we need her. Then call Bishop Schrock. His wife can hear the phone from her house. They are neighbors to Bishop Weaver and his wife and will know what to do."

"Who is Bishop Weaver?" Maddy asked.

"He's Zillah's father and bishop of the Swartzentruber church that Levi and I used to belong to before you came to live with us. Tell them that Zillah is here and is asking for her parents. Whatever you do, don't tell him she's pregnant. I don't know if he'll come if he knows that—and I think it might be very important for him to get here."

Maddy was out the door like a shot.

Tom helped Zillah lie back against the couch pillows as Claire pulled off the flip-flops. He couldn't help but notice the girl's filthy feet against the clean couch, but that appeared to be the least of Claire's worries. She seemed to be focused on the puffiness of the girl's feet and ankles.

"How far along are you?" Claire asked.

"I don't know." Zillah panted from the exertion of the last contraction. "Pretty far, I guess."

"When was the last time you saw a doctor?"

"I never saw a doctor."

"At all?"

Zillah shook her head.

"Albert, go get my midwife bag," Claire said. "Jesse, take Sarah and Daniel outside. Keep them there. Do you understand?"

"*Ja.*" Jesse did not hesitate. He quickly herded his little brother and sister outside.

"Here." Albert had brought his mother's midwife bag.

She grabbed a stethoscope out of her bag and frowned as she listened to the girl's heart. Then she grabbed a blood pressure cuff, pumped it up, and listened as she slowly let the air out. Her face grew pale.

"What's wrong?" he asked.

She ripped the blood pressure cuff off.

"How fast can you get us to the hospital?"

"A half hour if the roads are clear. More if I get behind too many buggies."

"We have to go." She tossed the cuffs and stethoscope into her bag. "Now."

At that moment, Grace came running in with Levi beside her. They stopped in their tracks, apparently as stunned as Claire when she first saw the girl.

"Zillah!" Grace exclaimed.

"What are *you* doing here?" Zillah said.

Levi turned on his heel and left the room.

Claire put her arm around Zillah and gave Grace a meaningful look. "Come on, honey. We need to get you to the hospital. Please stand up for me."

Before his eyes, he saw Grace shake off her shock and turn into a professional. "What do you know so far, Claire?"

"Full term. She's never seen a doctor."

She managed to get Zillah to her feet. Grace got beneath the girl's other arm, supporting her.

"I brought the baby home for *Maam* and *Daed*. I want them to keep it." Then Zillah staggered and went into another teeth-clenching contraction. When it was over, she gasped for breath before she said. "I don't want it."

"BP?" Grace asked. Claire answered that it was 220 over 130.

"Oh no!" Grace said under her breath.

"Levi!" Grace shouted. "Come back in here and help us lift her. Tom, bring the car as close to the house as you can. Maddy, grab an armload of clean towels, a sheet, anything you can find. Hurry!"

Tom rushed to bring the car right up to the house. He saw the women half carrying Zillah out to the porch. Then, at Grace's direction, Levi swept Zillah up in his arms and carried her down the porch stairs.

"I loved you," Zillah said, her arms wrapped around Levi's neck. "If you'd married me like I wanted, this wouldn't be happening."

"You never loved anyone on earth but yourself," Levi said with disgust, as he deposited her in the backseat.

It all came together now. He remembered Levi telling him, while they were working on the tractor together, about the bishop's daughter with the strange name who had tried to force him into marriage by pretending to be pregnant by him. The Swartzentruber church and her father had taken her word over Levi's. It had ultimately caused him to leave the church altogether—which had precipitated Claire's departure as well.

Grace climbed in beside Zillah. Claire sat backward on the front seat, leaning over the back to help Grace.

"Drive!" Grace commanded.

He spun gravel getting out of there.

"Try not to tense up, Zillah. Relax. Breathe." Claire was right beside his ear, coaching the girl. "Like this." Claire began to pant, demonstrating. "Short, shallow breaths. That's it. You are doing so good."

He concentrated hard on the road, driving so much faster than was safe. Praying hard that there would be no Swartzentruber buggy somewhere up ahead, practically invisible in the dark due to their rigid rules against reflective triangles or battery-operated lights.

Whether it was prayer, or the fact that no courting buggies were usually out on a Monday evening, he had nearly a clear shot all the way to Millersburg—having to swerve only once to avoid hitting a man riding horseback. The man had been wise enough to hang a couple of battery-operated blinking lights on his saddle. Claire nearly ended up in his lap, something he would welcome under other circumstances—but not tonight.

He heard a newborn cry, but could not allow himself to take his eyes off the road.

Guttural noises filled the car as Zillah strained.

"There's a second baby!" Grace cried. "Here, take the first one, Grace."

"I thought I heard two heartbeats, but I wasn't sure," Claire said.

"You're doing good, Zillah," Claire encouraged. "We're almost there."

"Here comes the next one," Grace cried. "Oh, she has a little girl and a little boy!"

A few seconds later, Claire turned around and sat facing the front with a naked, wet newborn baby in each arm.

"One more big push, Zillah," Grace said. "Then you're done, sweetie."

"I'm not your sweetie." Zillah then gave a loud grunt.

He tried not to think of the mess that was no doubt in his backseat right now. His job was to get them there safely, not worry about hygiene.

"Here are the towels Maddy put in." Claire threw two faded, clean towels over the seat.

With two babies squalling, Claire had to juggle to wrap each one in a towel. While the afterbirth was being expelled in the backseat of his new car, Tom just tried not to wreck it.

The babies, expertly wrapped into tiny terry-cloth cocoons, settled down. He heard the blood pressure cuff being pumped up again in the backseat, and then heard it being ripped off.

"What is it now?" Claire asked over her shoulder.

"Two thirty over one forty."

Claire gasped. He didn't blame her. Even with his limited training, he knew those were terrible numbers.

"What are you two talking about?" Zillah cried. "What do those numbers mean?"

"She's going into a seizure," Grace said. "Hurry, Tom."

They were approaching the middle of Millersburg now, only a few blocks from the hospital, but a red light blocked his way. He quickly glanced to either side and gunned the car through.

Just as he entered the drive leading up to the Pomerene Hospital ER, he heard Grace say, "We're losing her, Claire!"

Although Grace had saved her life the day she was shot, Claire remembered little of it. Her experience with Grace had always been in her own, small, domestic sphere, where Grace was nearly always at a disadvantage. This was the first time she had ever seen Grace fighting to save a life. It was obvious the moment they hit the portico of the ER that her daughter-in-law knew exactly what she was doing.

In the time it took Claire to maneuver herself and the babies safely out of the car, Grace had commandeered a gurney and two orderlies to help her lift Zillah's body upon it. Then, as Claire watched, her valiant, pregnant daughter-in-law climbed onto the gurney, straddled Zillah's body, placed both hands in the middle of her chest, and began to apply CPR.

"Come on, Zillah! Come on!" she heard Grace say. "Breathe!! You have two beautiful babies to raise. Breathe!"

Without missing a beat, she continued rhythmically compressing the girl's chest, fighting to save Zillah's life, as two orderlies, one on each side of the gurney, exploded through the ER doors.

Half in shock at everything that had transpired in the past few minutes, Claire stood there, a baby in each arm, knowing that for as long as she lived, she would never forget the image of Grace doing exactly what she had been trained to do—save lives.

"Looks to me like you've got an armful." She hadn't realized that a male nurse was beside her. "How about I take one of these little ones and we'll go up to the nursery and let the pediatrician on call take a look at them."

Gratefully, she handed the little boy baby over. The nurse leaned down and spoke through the open car door to Tom. "Sir, would you mind moving your car? We never know when someone else might need this spot in a hurry."

Tom decided that he had had his fill of hospitals. If he never saw the inside of another hospital, it would be fine with

him. Eventually, Claire came out of a back room. Her face
was expressionless and her shoulders sagged. She sat down
beside him.

"How is she?" He was afraid he knew the answer.

"If only these girls knew how important checkups are
when they are pregnant," Claire said. "All of this could have
been prevented. We could have saved her so easily if this had
been caught in time."

It was then that he knew Zillah, with her snake tattoo,
bright top, and lime-green flip-flops . . . in spite of Grace's
heroic efforts . . . had not made it.

"What about the babies?"

"They're fine." Claire said.

At that moment, Levi and two Amish people Tom had
never seen before came through the emergency room doors.
The man and his wife appeared to be in their late fifties
or early sixties. From the width of the man's hat, and the
oversize black bonnet of the woman, he knew they were
Swartzentruber.

"Hello, Mary." Claire rose and greeted them. "Bishop
Weaver."

"Our daughter?" Bishop Weaver asked. "She is here?"

"She is here," Claire said.

The bishop's wife leaned forward, eager for information.
"She is alive?"

"The doctors and nurses tried very hard, but they were not
able to save her."

There was a quick intake of breath as the bishop absorbed
this blow. His wife's face drained of color.

"How is it that my daughter died?"

Claire pressed her lips together for a moment, as though
wishing she did not have to say the words, but the words did
come.

"Eclampsia brought on by childbirth," she said.

"Our daughter was pregnant?" The bishop frowned and glanced at his wife.

Mary ignored him. She grasped Claire's arm and gave it a little shake. "Does the child live?"

Tom could only imagine the pain this careful, solemn man was feeling. He knew his people. The death of Bishop Weaver's wayward daughter was only slightly worse in the bishop's eyes than the fact that she was pregnant. Mary was another matter. According to what Levi had told him, Zillah had been an only child, born to parents old enough to have given up hope of ever having children. The fact that there might be a child was of utmost importance to Mary.

"We were able to save the babies," Grace said in a rush. "She had a little girl and a little boy. They are full-term and healthy."

The man and woman looked at each other as though they could not believe their ears.

"Twins?" They both spoke at once.

"She was trying to bring them home to you. She said that she wanted you to have them."

The bishop's wife grabbed her husband's hand.

"And her husband?" Bishop Weaver asked. "What of him?"

"We never learned who the . . . father is," Claire said. "Zillah would not tell us that. All she said was that she was trying to bring her baby back to you and her mother."

Bishop Weaver squared his shoulders. "May we see our daughter now . . . and these . . . grandchildren?"

"Of course," Claire said. "I will take you to Zillah first. Grace is upstairs in the nursery with the babies."

After they left, Levi collapsed with a sigh into the seat next to him.

"Something tells me there is a longer story than you told me behind all of this," Tom said.

Levi nodded. "Zillah was beautiful on the outside, but not so beautiful on the inside. I was never interested in her and she could not accept that from a man. She decided she was in love with me, but I knew I was simply a challenge. She plagued me for years. When she saw that her lies and the reality of the *Meidung* would not force me to marry her, she ran away and told her parents she was never coming back.

"Zillah's mind was not something I ever wanted to understand. I am guessing that she simply did not want the responsibility of caring for a child."

"Did all this happen before or after you met Grace?"

"The *Meidung* came after Grace came to live with Elizabeth. She and I were already friends. I think her presence in my life may have precipitated Zillah's lies."

"Grace knew all of this?"

"Grace knew everything. She and Elizabeth believed me and accepted me when no one else did. Even my mother reluctantly obeyed the bishop at first."

"After what I've seen tonight, I can understand why you fell in love with that wife of yours."

"Oh?" Levi glanced at him.

"I just watched her fight like a tiger to save the life of a woman who hated her and tried to destroy you. She was magnificent."

"Yes, that is my Grace." Levi's face softened. "She is something, that one is."

chapter TWENTY-EIGHT

After what had happened between Levi and Zillah, Claire had some major issues with Ezra Weaver, but never would she have wished something like this on the bishop and his wife.

He stood as still as a statue, staring at his daughter's body. There was a sheet draped over her chest and midsection, but the snake tattoo on her leg was exposed. Claire automatically reached to pull the sheet down to cover it.

"Don't," he said.

Mary started making a soft keening sound in the back of her throat. Zillah, as an only child, had been given more than most Swartzentruber children. Claire had never been able to decide if Zillah had become the person she was because they had spoiled her or if she was simply born with an ugliness inside her. Either way, it did not matter now. Nothing mattered now except the babies, and she was not sure the bishop would accept them.

Mary got control of herself, and the keening stopped. "Please, Claire," she said. "I want a basin of water and a cloth. Do they have something like that here?"

"Mary." The bishop's voice held a warning. "I do not think you should . . ."

Claire saw something she thought impossible.

Mary whirled on him, her face a mask of despair and grief. "You will not forbid me to wash my own child!"

Bishop Weaver backed down in the face of Mary's anger. "Is that permitted, Claire?"

She did not know. She looked for direction from the nurse who had been standing nearby.

The nurse, a young redhead about Grace's age with the name Karen on her badge, was struggling to hold her composure.

"Of course it is permitted. I will get everything you need."

The sight of Mary gently washing the dirt from her daughter's face was something Claire would never forget. Nor would she soon forget the sight of Bishop Weaver, standing ramrod stiff, expressionless, looking on as tears coursed down his cheeks.

"How is everything going back there?" Tom asked, as Claire sat down in a chair opposite him and Levi.

"Grace has taken Ezra and Mary up to the nursery to see the grandchildren."

"Are the babies all right?" Levi asked.

"They are healthy."

Tom could not remember Claire ever looking as wrung out as she was tonight, not even the night they brought Maddy back from the Tinker place.

"Can I get you something, Claire? Something to eat, maybe? Or drink?"

She shook her head. "I want nothing right now."

"How were the bishop and Mary?" Levi asked.

"Do you remember how humbled he was when he realized he had made a mistake in believing his daughter instead of you?"

"I will never forget that day."

"I believe he will walk with even greater humility before God and before his church after what I just witnessed."

"Zillah's death or her pregnancy?" Levi asked.

"Neither. Our former bishop and many of our people have sometimes judged non-Amish with yardsticks they should not."

"What do you mean?" Tom said, although he thought he knew where Claire was going with this.

"Those two babies Zillah brought home for Ezra and Mary to raise?"

"Yes."

"They are very beautiful, and by the grace of God, they are healthy, but I think the bishop will have to change his mind about some very important things."

"In what way?" Levi asked.

"If they are to love these babies as they deserve to be loved," Claire said, "the bishop and his wife will have to learn to love someone who does not share their own skin color."

"Oh." Levi absorbed this. "Do you think they can do it?"

"Mary will, and with no thought. Ezra?" Claire shrugged. "I do not know. It will be a tragedy if he cannot make himself bend."

"And if he cannot?" Tom said.

"Then someone else in their church might take them in if the bishop allows it. If no one else wishes to do so . . . I will ask permission to raise them."

Tom was practically speechless. "With all that you have to do, and all the children you already support, you would ask for these two babies?"

"Of course."

It was her unhesitant "of course" that broke down the last final floodgates of love he felt for this woman—and he knew exactly what he had to do about it.

chapter TWENTY-NINE

"Claire sent over some lentil soup." Tom handed a quart jar to Jeremiah, whom he'd found pitching hay down from the haymow. It was obvious from the overwhelming smell that his father had been mucking out manure earlier that morning. "She said you don't have to worry about getting the jar back to her."

"Set it over there." Jeremiah climbed down a ladder and began forking fresh, loose straw into a stable that had been shoveled out. "That girl always was the best cook. I'll have Faye warm it up when she sets our dinner out."

"Faye?"

He had not known that Faye was coming to visit.

"Faye's my only daughter," Jeremiah said. "She and her husband are visiting for a couple of days. They moved south to Gallia County a few years back." He threw another pitchfork full of hay into the stable. "The land's a lot cheaper down there, they say. They wanted me to sell this place and go with them, but I didn't."

"Why not?"

Jeremiah folded both hands over the top of the pitchfork handle and rested his chin on them. "Because I figure Tobias might come back and need it someday."

This was the moment he had been waiting for. He knew in his bones that this was the right time to tell his father that Tobias *had* come home, and that it wasn't necessary to try to keep the farm going for him anymore. It was going to be such a relief to have that off his chest and his conscience. His father might tell him to leave—but at least the truth would finally be out in the open. Then he would go in and see his baby sister and . . .

"Who is this?" a man said. "You did not tell us you were expecting company, Jeremiah." Tom saw a flicker of disdain in his father's eyes.

"This is Tom Miller, my neighbor." Jeremiah picked up his pitchfork and began tossing hay. Tom could tell that his father had contempt for the man, just by the way he turned his back on him. "And this is Faye's husband, Ephraim, my son-in-law."

Claire was taking laundry off the line when he got back home and she didn't see him at first. He watched her, enjoying the grace of the scene. If there was any prettier domestic task to find a woman involved in, he didn't know what it was. Fortunately, it was something he got to enjoy often. Claire had a lot of laundry.

"Need some help?" he asked.

"Hi, Tom. You can bring me that other empty laundry basket on the porch."

He grabbed the basket as he walked past it and sat it on the ground beside of her.

"How did it go?" she asked, folding a towel. "Did you tell him?"

"I wanted to." He picked up a wooden clothespin off the ground and handed it to her. "It was the perfect time, except for one thing."

"What's that?"

"Faye and her husband were there."

Claire's hands hesitated as she took this in, then she began her task once again. "I would think that would be a good time, when both of them were there."

"It didn't seem wise to start in on all of that in front of a man my father does not like."

"It was that obvious?"

"The son-in-law started telling me how much Jeremiah's farm is worth. He was practically licking his chops. I can see why Jeremiah isn't too thrilled with him."

"Did you get to see Faye?"

"I did, for a few minutes. She's changed a lot."

Claire smiled. "People do tend to change a bit between the ages of eight and thirty-five."

"My father said something right before my brother-in-law showed up and interrupted us."

"Really?" She unpinned a large flat sheet and handed him one end. "Help me fold this, please."

He grasped the two corners of the sheet. "He told me that my brother-in-law and sister want him to sell the farm and move to Gallia County with them."

"Oh? Is he considering it?"

"He said that he isn't . . . because he's trying to hang on to the farm for Tobias."

She stopped in the middle of folding the sheet and stared at him.

"It broke my heart, Claire."

"I'm sure it did." She finished folding the sheet and laid it in the empty basket. "But it won't be long now before he'll know everything. Faye and her husband never stay long. You can tell him then."

He helped her unpin and fold another sheet. "I'm looking forward to getting it off my chest—no matter what happens."

She began pulling a row of sun-bleached white pillowcases off the line. "Did you call about your retirement?"

"I started the process."

She laid the last folded pillowcase in the basket. "Are you still feeling okay about that decision?"

"I am."

The line was empty now. He reached for her hand before she could pick up one of the laundry baskets. "What are we going to do, Claire?"

She did not ask him to explain. She knew. They both knew. A man and a woman their age who lived this close to each other, spent this much time with each other, and cared this much for each other either fell in love and spent the rest of their lives together or they went their separate ways. They did not spend the rest of their lives being buddies.

He repeated his question. "What are we going to do?"

She did not play coy or pretend not to know what he was talking about. She was Claire. "I do not know." She looked at him with eyes as clear as the blue sky above them and answered honestly, "God help me. I do not know."

chapter THIRTY

T om went to the store to buy some more dog food and stopped in to check his post office box on his way back.

The most he expected to be in his box were a few circulars and maybe a bill or two. He certainly didn't expect any personal letters. So when he saw a long, official-looking envelope, he was surprised.

He opened it, scanned it, nearly dropped it, then went back and read every word, one by one, closely. Making sure he hadn't read something wrong. He was having trouble believing what he was looking at.

The letter was from the White House.

The fact that he had applied for retirement had become a nonissue. Retired or not, he was being called to active duty. The president of the United States had just specifically asked for him to become a pilot for *Marine One*. The president's personal helicopter. It was one of the highest honors in the world.

He was stunned. Becoming a *Marine One* pilot was the Holy Grail of every Marine helicopter pilot. A friend of his, highly qualified, had applied for the position year after year. Having watched his buddy try repeatedly and fail, Tom hadn't even bothered.

And now this? Was it a joke? A prank of some kind?

The letter gave him a number to call. He stepped outside the post office and dialed it on his cell phone, expecting to get an operator and being put on hold.

Instead, a man so high up on the president's staff it made Tom's brain spin, answered on the first ring.

"This is Tom Miller," he said. "I got your letter, and I don't understand. I'm honored, but I never applied for the job."

"We know, kid." The man on the other end of the phone chuckled. "This is a special request from the president. He asked for you personally."

This was the new president's first term. Tom had even voted for him. It made sense that he was handpicking some of his staff—but why him?

"How does he even know who I am?"

"You flew a junior senator a few years back. You probably don't remember it now. He's your new president. The way I understand it, he still believes that only your expertise saved your passengers' lives that day."

Tom tried to think back. He did remember a senator of some kind who had been especially wobbly going down the stairs after a tumultuous trip—but Tom had flown such missions so many times, it seemed almost routine to him.

"What had happened on that trip?"

"The president said something about how you safely had flown through an ice storm."

Ah, now he remembered.

When he was flying, nothing bothered him. It was almost like a drug, the feeling of being part of the machine, of being able to know—just by the touch of his hands on the instruments—if the motor was the slightest bit out of synch. Or whether or not the rotors were taking on ice. That had happened once, when that senator who was now the president had been on board.

Tom had been given wrong information about the weather by those who were paid to know. They had begun to take on ice, one of the most dangerous things a helicopter pilot could experience. He had seen the ice crystals beginning to form on the cockpit and knew the rotors were taking on ice as well. He could feel the helicopter growing heavier and knew it was only a matter of minutes before the rotors would stop altogether and they would plummet out of the sky, as heavy as a boulder.

He caught the danger just in time—in time to duck beneath the ice into slightly warmer weather. Then, before the weight could make them descend any farther, he had shaken the helicopter like a dog flinging off water, hoping to rid the rotors of the ice.

It had worked. They remained safely in the air and eventually made a routine landing. He remembered that the senator had looked a little green when they landed.

"Was that as bad as I thought?" the senator asked, as he staggered toward the door.

"Yes, sir," Tom said, "it was."

"Good job." Nothing else was said. The senator simply clapped him on the shoulder as he went past.

The incident had stuck in his mind because so many dignitaries he had flown were too self-important to speak to a mere pilot. That senator wasn't. Funny, he'd met the man who was to become the leader of the free world, and only now realized it.

A good leader was hard to find. A good leader who could withstand the scrutiny of running a national campaign was even rarer. Finding one who also noticed and praised the people who worked around him was a prize indeed.

"We checked out your background, of course. The president was impressed that you were born and raised Amish.

He said that from what he knew about the Amish, it would be impossible for them to be infiltrated by a terrorist organization."

There was a pause, as though the person on the other end had shifted gears or shifted papers. "You've been on sick leave for a while. How are you feeling?"

"Much stronger."

"Assuming you pass the physical then, we're offering you a job, my friend."

The military had surprised him a few times, but this was beyond anything that had happened before. It nearly rendered him speechless. "I don't know what to say."

"Then I guess I'll have to tell you. Say yes. We need your answer now so that I can get the paperwork started. We'll need you here tomorrow evening at the latest. "

Tom felt like his head was in a fog. In his mind and heart, when he awoke this morning, he was a retired soldier. His papers hadn't gone through yet, but that was just a matter of time and a few formalities. The big hurdle had been making that choice. It had not been easy, but once he made it, he made it with his whole heart.

"Could I have a few days to think this over?"

"The president has requested you." The man's voice grew cold. "According to our records, you have no dependents. I can see no reason for thought or discussion."

No dependents? He thought of Amy in her wheelchair, Jesse on top of the barn roof with a makeshift parachute, Albert chasing an irate rooster around the yard so he could put it back in the chicken pen, Levi and his struggles with his marriage, Maddy and her newfound religion, Jeremiah pitching hay in the barn while his son-in-law circled the farm like a vulture.

And Claire. Always Claire.

"What are we going to do?" he'd asked. She had known exactly what he was asking. Instead of feigning ignorance, she had replied, "I do not know."

He was no longer a lovesick boy. He was a man, and he knew exactly when a woman was interested in him. Over the past few weeks, a light had begun to flicker in Claire's eyes whenever they spent time together. Her face, so expressive, would brighten whenever he came near. Now that there were no secrets between them, that look of acceptance had deepened.

What *were* they going to do?

In one way or another, he had been pondering that ever since he'd arrived in Holmes County and discovered that she was free to remarry . . . but only an Amish man.

For those I love, I will sacrifice.

He could not ask her and the children to give up their faith, to become *Englisch*. But he could sacrifice the passion of his life, flying, for a passion he had held even longer—his love for Claire.

Retiring had been, in his mind, the beginning of the process of slowly building a new life for himself. He had nearly convinced himself that he was willing to go back to his roots, not by becoming Swartzentruber, but by embracing the gentler religion of the Old Order Amish.

And now, just as he thought he had made up his mind and could see the path of his life spread out before him, he received this summons.

Marine One pilots were not just the best of the best—they were the best. Period. If he accepted this position, he would be using his hard-earned skills to keep the president from harm.

He had been a soldier most of his life. There were things that had become hardwired within him. Things that were part of the fabric of his soul. *Semper Fi*—always faithful. No

Man Left Behind. There was one other thing that was embedded within him—patriotism. If his country called, he would answer. Even had he succeeded in retiring, every Marine, no matter how old, knew that if his country ever called, he would answer.

There was no such thing as an ex-Marine.

Tom unconsciously stood a little taller. "I'll be in Washington by tomorrow evening."

chapter THIRTY-ONE

C laire could not believe what was happening—and so quickly.

"I'm sorry," Tom said, after explaining the situation to her. "I have to go. I have to do this. I have no choice."

"But so soon?"

"Yes. So soon."

He seemed so distracted, so different from the laid-back friend who had always seemed to have all the time in the world to chat. He had a look in his eyes that seemed far away from her and this backward place. It seemed as though he was already flying the president in his mind, but his body had not yet caught up with his mind.

How could flying a helicopter be so *wunderbar*? To her it didn't seem wonderful at all. It seemed like a frightening and dangerous way to make a living.

He handed her a check. "Here's the rest of this month's rent . . . and a little extra."

The money was the last of her worries right at this moment. Tom was leaving. As far as she could tell, he would not be coming back.

What had happened to the thoughtful, compassionate man she knew? When had he been replaced with this . . . soldier? He was even standing straighter and taller.

He was not the Tobias she remembered from the past at all. Nothing of Tobias remained. He had turned into someone else entirely. The soldier, Tom Miller, was brisk and in charge and very much in a hurry.

He'd packed his duffel bag.

"Anything I've left behind, feel free to use. There's some canned goods and a few books I'm leaving. Oh, and I bought some work clothes I won't be needing. I think they might fit Levi if you take them up in the legs."

She could hardly bear to look him in the face, it hurt so badly to see the eagerness there. How boring they must all seem to him now. The scars had healed to the point that he simply looked rugged and masculine now. For the first time since he'd come, he was dressed in a uniform. If one liked uniforms, which she did not, he was an extremely impressive-looking man.

There would be many women interested in him—this man skilled enough to be handpicked by the president.

A simple Amish midwife could not hope to compete with all these exciting things coming into his life. She stared down at her hands, in which resided his check. A number caught her eye, and she gasped.

"This is not the right amount!" she said.

"I told you I'd added a little extra."

"This is much more than a little extra. This is extravagant."

"I can afford it, Clare," he said. "And after I leave, I want you to give that money to Levi and tell him I said for him to go buy you a decent horse. Something dependable."

"I cannot accept this much."

"Please. After all you've done for me, the least I can do is make certain you have dependable transportation. Besides that, you have no idea how much dog food Rocky can eat. I probably need to give you more just to take care of that!"

"We're happy to have Rocky. The children are already arguing over whose bedroom he will sleep in."

"None of them. He paces."

"What do you mean?"

"He was bred to be a guard dog. He'll go from one bedroom to another, all over the house. Making certain everyone is okay. He did a lot of that with just me to watch over. He'll be in his glory having so many to guard."

"Then he will certainly earn any dog food I get him," she said. "But please come and say good-bye to the children before you go. And what about your father?"

He glanced at his watch, a worried expression on his face. "I'll say good-bye to the children, and then swing by *Daed*'s. I'm not going to break it to him who I am. Not now when I have to leave so suddenly. I'll write him a letter and let him know that he's been spending time with Tobias after all. I'll let him know it's okay to move down to Gallia County with Faye if he wants to. He needs to know he doesn't have to try to preserve a home for me anymore."

Oh, how hard this was going to be on Jeremiah. As hard, if not harder, as it was on her and the children.

The only real regret she saw on Tom's face as he prepared to leave them was when he said good-bye to Amy and she began to cry.

"You're my friend!" Amy said. "You took care of me. I always knew you would keep me safe if anything bad happened."

"I'm so sorry, little one," he said. "But I have to go keep the president and his staff safe now."

"Do you love him more than you love me?" Amy asked.

Claire's heart echoed with the little girl's question.

"No," Tom said. "Of course not. I only met him once. But keeping him safe is my way of keeping you safe. He's a good man. From what I hear, he's trying hard to lead our country in a good direction. I need to help make sure nothing bad happens to him, and you'll have Rocky to watch over you."

"I guess," Amy said, doubtfully.

Claire walked him to his car and stood beside him while he slung his duffel into the backseat. Whatever bit of Amish she had seen in him had disappeared entirely.

"Keep safe and well," he said, as he climbed into the car. "And thank you for everything. Make sure you use that money."

She nodded, and then she turned her back on him and his car and his big, important hurry and began to weed the flowers beside the porch. She had no intention of giving him the satisfaction of waving good-bye. Those *Englisch*! She wasn't sure she would ever welcome one into her life ever again.

He knew she was hurt, but now that he knew what his life would become for the next few years, it would not be kind to give her false hope that he would be back.

Had Claire been any other woman, he would have asked to come with him. To marry him, live in Washington or Arlington, put the kids in school there. It would be possible to have a marriage under those circumstances. But not Claire. She would never leave. She would hate Washington.

Better that she find some good Amish man with whom to live out the rest of her life. The thought hurt—but he had no right to ask her to wait for him. She needed a good husband to help her raise those children, someone who would fit into her life.

As for him, he could no more say no to this call to duty for his country than Claire could cut her hair and wear shorts.

Saying good-bye to his father was going to be hard—but

he still believed his choice to keep quiet about his identity had been the best thing to do. He would write a long letter explaining everything to his father when he got a chance.

He planned to stop in and see his *daed* on his way out. He could tell him about the new job. Perhaps his father would be a little bit proud of him. That would be nice, to know that *Daed* was proud of him.

Faye, her husband, and Jeremiah were all sitting on the front porch when he pulled in. It appeared that he had interrupted a conversation that had not been going well. His father seemed relieved to see him.

"Why are you in uniform?" Jeremiah asked. "Are you going into the Army again? I thought you liked it here."

"It's the Marines, and I do like it here—but I got a letter yesterday that changed my plans."

In a few sentences he explained to his father where he was going and why. Jeremiah never once changed expressions.

"Got something I want to give you before you take off," Jeremiah said. "Come on back to the barn with me a minute."

When they got to the barn, Jeremiah led him to a work area where he kept a few tools and harnesses. Once there, the mask came off and Tom could see the worry in his father's face.

"Faye and Ephraim are trying again to talk me into leaving. Faye says she's worried about me here all by myself. The girl has always been softhearted like her mother."

"But you aren't going?"

"Faye misses her father." Jeremiah spit a thin stream of tobacco juice at a knothole. "But Ephraim has dollar signs in his eyes."

"You don't trust him?"

"I think he often wonders how soon I will leave this earth." Jeremiah took a square, green tin off a high shelf. "I will wait for Tobias. We will see how eager my son-in-law is to have me when I no longer possess eighty acres of prime Holmes County land."

He pulled a rusted, green tin box off a high shelf and pried the top off. Inside were some odds and ends, the kind of flotsam that floated around a working farm. Also inside was a small piece of chamois wrapped around an object. Jeremiah unwrapped it, and there lay a pocketknife with a carved bone handle.

"This is a good knife," he said. "It holds a sharpened edge longer than any I've ever owned. It's a Barlow. I don't need it anymore. I want you to take it."

He handed it to Tom. The thing was old, and extremely well made. It was also obviously something Jeremiah greatly treasured.

"It's beautiful." Tom turned it over and over in his hand. "Where did you get it?"

Jeremiah hesitated. "It belonged to my father."

"Are you sure you want me to have it?"

"You have been a good friend to me, *Englischer.*"

Tom slipped it into his pocket and grasped Jeremiah's hand in a firm handshake. "I'll carry it on me always."

"Good," Jeremiah said. "A man never knows when he might need a good, sharp pocketknife. You be careful out there."

His dad was right. A man never did know when he might need a good pocketknife. He also knew that this gift, a token of his father's care, would never leave his side from now on.

As soon as he got settled, he would write his father and tell him, truly, how much the pocketknife, and his friendship, had meant to him, Tobias.

chapter THIRTY-TWO

Although Tom had flown helicopters for many years, he had never flown *Marine One*. The protocol that had risen around the president's helicopter was enormous, and there was much to learn, much to observe. There were security measures beyond anything he had ever experienced, all to keep the most important person on the planet alive. He learned what countermeasures he should take to avoid a direct attack; he learned which men and women would be acting as his copilots; and he began to learn the personality of his new president, the president's family, and his staff.

Much of his job would be shuttling the president from the White House to *Air Force One,* the jet that had been so well outfitted from within and without that the president could run the country from it indefinitely if necessary.

He did not expect to become the president's friend. The only thing he wanted was to do a good job. There could be no errors. He could not afford to be distracted by personal issues. He existed, at least while he was the pilot for *Marine One,* for one reason only—to get the president from point A to point B as safely as possible.

He could not, for instance, allow himself to think about Claire. Or Amy. Or to wonder if Levi and Grace had ironed out their problems yet. He couldn't think about sweet little Sarah or the stalwart Albert, or mischievous Jesse. He couldn't allow himself to worry about Maddy and wonder if she was still determined to be part of the New Order "goody-goodies."

He shoved these thoughts aside every time he climbed into the cockpit, so that he could become one with his machine. Feeling every nuance. Anticipating the slightest bounce. Checking and rechecking to make certain the mechanics were perfect before taking off.

He also practiced, over and over, landing on the small landing pad by the White House. In some ways that was the thing he dreaded the most—trying to make a perfect landing on such a small space with the ground frequently littered by news people and White House staff alerted that the president was coming in.

He forced himself to ignore his longing to be back in Holmes County with the people he loved. He had to ignore it—that was what good soldiers did.

It helped a little that the president occasionally took the time to express his appreciation.

Claire was no stranger to grief, but this felt different. Matthew and Abraham had not chosen to leave her. Tom Miller had.

It took her a few days before she could steel herself to face going up to his apartment.

There was little for her to do. A hardback book, half read, was lying facedown on the floor beside the armchair. She picked it up and read the spine. It was one of Levi's innumerable books about history. This particular one was about an ancient Greek war. She could see no value in reading something like this, but that only underscored the vast difference between the two of them. On the other hand, she had enjoyed her conversations with him even more for that very reason. She closed the book and set it back on a shelf.

The apartment smelled different than when Levi lived there. There was a scent that had always lingered around Tom. It was subtle—he was not a man given to wearing cologne—but she had liked his woodsy-spice smell. As she went in to wipe down the bathroom and take the towels to launder, she found the source of that scent. It was nothing more than a dark-colored bar of soap. There was no longer any way to discern what brand it was. She held it to her nose and breathed deeply. Then she slipped the half-used bar of soap into her pocket.

She took everything out of the refrigerator. He liked to eat healthy. Some lean meats and vegetables were about all that was in there. He had developed a great affection for Mrs. Yoder's and ate there several times a week. She left the few canned goods behind. She knew where they were if she needed them.

He had already stripped the bed and folded the sheets and blankets. Never in her life had she wished for more work, but the fact that he had left so little sign that he had ever lived there was a disappointment to her. He had been a clean and organized man, used to living with little or no excess.

Perhaps that meant her and the children as well. Perhaps they were excess. Easily left behind. Perhaps she had made a mistake in confiding in him all her little problems. Her face burned as she thought about how she had treated him like an understanding friend, confiding to this very important pilot all the bits and pieces of her small world.

How foolish she must have appeared.

And how foolish she had been to allow him to become so close to Amy. That little girl had been hit hard by his leaving.

She didn't blame him for returning to his old life, flying his precious helicopters. What she blamed him for was ever coming here at all.

Claire had barely gotten the sheets and a few other whites soaking in the washtub at her house when Elizabeth pulled in. This surprised her. Elizabeth had not driven in more than two years, which might account for the erratic way the older woman had parked.

"The doctor has said you can drive again?" she asked.

"That doctor Grace took me to shouldn't even have a medical license. He looks like he should still be playing Little League."

"But he cleared you to drive?"

"I don't need a doctor telling me if I can drive or not. I have a perfectly good driver's license and I intend to use it."

Claire interpreted this to mean that the doctor had not cleared her, but Elizabeth had no intention of admitting it. "Can I bring you some tea?" she asked, as Elizabeth sat down on the porch to get her breath.

"That would be lovely," the older woman said. "Thank you. And then we need to talk."

That sounded ominous. She could not imagine anything all that serious that her old friend would want to talk to her about. Unless it was Levi and Grace. She hoped things hadn't gotten worse between them.

While she was at it, she made herself some tea, and then went out to face whatever bad news Elizabeth had to give her. Over the years, Claire had learned a significant fact—the more people you have in your life, the more crises you have to deal with.

Elizabeth took a sip and smiled. "You remembered that I like honey in it. You are so thoughtful."

Actually, Claire had not thought at all. They used honey for most things that needed sweetening. Their hives brought in enough every year to keep them well supplied with extra to sell. Besides that, she had heard that honey had some health benefits that sugar did not.

"I want to rent the apartment that Tom vacated," Elizabeth said.

Claire was surprised. That was the last thing she had expected to come out of Elizabeth's mouth.

"Who are you renting it for? Becky?"

"Becky will have to fend for herself next time she comes home," Elizabeth said. "I want to rent it for myself."

"I don't understand," Claire said. "Why would you want to leave your home?"

"Because your son and my granddaughter are driving me crazy," Elizabeth said. "I came to Mt. Hope for peace. I worked for it, and I deserve it. What I have right now are two hardheaded people who can't seem to work out any sort of a compromise, but still love each other too much to get a divorce." She took another sip of tea and shook her head. "I want out of it. I can hear their voices even in the *Daadi Haus*."

"They will be upset and embarrassed if they know they are the cause of your leaving your own home."

"Good!" Elizabeth said. "It would serve them right. I'll pay you the same amount that Tom was paying."

"What about the stairs?"

"I am much stronger. I go up and down the stairs all the time nowadays. Most of the time to get away from Grace and Levi."

"You are welcome, my old friend, to the use of my apartment—but I will not charge you rent."

"Of course you will."

"No, I won't. I mean it, Elizabeth."

"Maybe we could work out a trade," Elizabeth said. "Now

that I'm driving again, I'm going to do a lot of it. I'll take you on all your birthing calls and it won't cost you a cent."

Claire wasn't entirely sure what would be the most dangerous—her buggy or Elizabeth's driving. The woman had one wheel right now in the middle of one of her flower beds.

"We'll discuss that later. Right now I am most concerned about Levi and Grace. You're around them more than me. What in the world can we do to help those two?"

"Levi doesn't know how to be *Englisch,* and Grace doesn't want to be Amish. Each one of them has a foot firmly planted in the culture in which they were raised. Even their attempts to please each other seem to backfire."

"Like what?"

"Like that big-screen TV Levi dragged in. Grace had said she would like to be able to watch a show from time to time, and he overreacted. Now we've got that monstrosity up on the wall in our living room, and Levi is the only one watching it."

"My Levi?" Claire was incredulous. "Watching television?"

Elizabeth patted her hand. "He's practically addicted to it, Claire. It's the oddest thing. It's kind of like a disease. I think he never developed an immunity to it when he was little, and now he can't seem to take his eyes off it."

"What sort of things does he watch?" Claire was worried. This didn't sound like her son at all.

"Well, he decided to get satellite, and now he's got like a zillion stations to choose from. He keeps it on the History Channel and nature shows the most—you know how hungry he always was for learning."

"Always." Yes, she could understand how Levi could become addicted to such things. "How is Grace handling it?"

"Not well. I doubt that when she married Levi, she expected to have to compete with a television for his attention, but that's what it's come down to. I think it's also a sort of a cushion against the disaster of their marriage. Grace is a fighter. Levi is not. The more he watches, the less time he spends arguing with Grace."

"What do these two need to happen for things to get better?"

"I think they both need to be whopped upside the head with a two-by-four, myself, but moving out is the best idea I can come up with. Neither one of them is listening to a word I say. Last time Becky came home from college, she told them that unless they got their act together, she wasn't looking forward to coming home again. If I have to choose between Levi and Grace, right now, my choice is Becky."

"When do you want to move in?" Claire asked.

"I'm ready right now." Elizabeth stood up, and to Claire's astonishment, began to sing. "My bags are packed, I'm ready to go. I'm standing here outside your door. When you wake up . . . oh, never mind, you don't listen to the radio, do you?"

"No." There were times when she honestly had no idea what Elizabeth was talking about.

"Sorry, but that song has been playing in my head all morning." Elizabeth's voice suddenly sounded frail. "I'm wondering if they'll even notice that I'm not sitting at the supper table tonight."

When Levi came hunting Elizabeth, Claire was primed and ready for him.

"Hi, *Maam,*" Levi greeted her. "I haven't seen Elizabeth all day. I was coming down to ask if you'd seen her. Now I discover that her car's here. What's going on?"

"She's moved out."

"What?"

"She's moved out of her own house and into your old apartment."

"Why on earth would she do that? I built her a perfectly good *Daadi Haus*."

"I believe she's trying to make a point."

"And what would that point be?"

"That she can't bear to live with you and Grace anymore. She says you fight all the time."

Levi didn't meet her eyes. "Not all the time."

"You loved Grace enough to leave the religion of your forefathers for her."

"She wasn't the only reason," he argued.

"No, but the thoughts of getting to marry her certainly did not hurt, did it?"

"No. I love Grace."

"From what I can see, you're trying to change everything you loved about her."

"That's not true."

"It certainly looks like it to me."

"You don't understand. She won't follow my lead in anything. I'm supposed to be the head of our family—and Grace always wants to do something different from what I propose. Grace insists on trying to wear the pants in our family."

"Perhaps that is because Grace knows more about living in the *Englisch* world than you."

Levi looked like a thundercloud.

"I know I opposed your marriage, but Grace is the single most valiant woman I've ever known in my life, even if she isn't Amish. I wish you could have seen her fighting to save Zillah's life. . . ."

He wasn't listening. "She wants to help take care of our finances."

"So?"

"That's the husband's job."

Claire sighed. "Oh, Levi."

"Well, it is."

"Who says?"

"Everyone knows it is supposed to be that way, and Grace wants to work even after the baby comes."

"And why shouldn't she?"

"That is not the way it is supposed to be."

"Who says? I have a two-year-old. I work."

"That's different."

"No, it isn't. Grace has a God-given talent, and from what I've seen so far of her cooking and gardening, she has only one talent—but it's a big one. You cannot control Grace's actions, but you can control your own. You're one of the smartest men I've ever known, Levi. Use that good brain to figure out how to stay married—and how to be happy—with the woman you vowed to love and cherish forever."

"But, if Grace would just . . ."

Claire had loved her son from the moment she knew he had been conceived—but right now, she wanted to shake him.

"If Grace would just . . . nothing!" She stomped her foot. "*You* figure out what's wrong. *You* figure out a way to fix it. *You* figure out how to change you—and then maybe Grace won't feel like she's got to fight you for every inch of dignity she has left."

At that moment, Elizabeth walked into the room. "I saw your car," she said. "I figured you were coming to talk me into coming back. I'm not coming back. The two of you are driving me nuts."

"No," Levi said, "I think it would be best for you to stay here for now. I need to get some things straight with Grace. And it probably would be best if you were not there to hear it."

chapter THIRTY-THREE

His mission tonight was simple—fly the president of the United States from Andrews Air Force Base to the helipad at the White House.

At the moment, three decoy helicopters, exact replicas of the one he was flying, flew in tight formation around him, changing position at regular intervals, creating the shell game that he and the other *Marine One* pilots played every time they carried the leader of the free world.

Now you see *Marine One*. Now you don't.

It was an expensive and elaborate precaution the military put into place to protect their commander in chief from attack. At the very least, it gave the president a three-in-four chance of survival if terrorists guessed wrong.

Tonight, Rick Justice was his copilot and Tom was happy to have him beside him. Rick was a veteran with more than a thousand hours of flight time under his belt. Like Tom, much of that time had been logged flying into and over the unfriendly valleys of Afghanistan.

Several people rode with the president, including the staff seeing to his and the first lady's needs. If they wanted a grilled cheese sandwich or the special coffee the first couple preferred, it would be available. A doctor would be aboard, as well. In fact, the presidential jet, *Air Force One,* which had landed a few minutes earlier at Andrews Air Force Base, had a fully equipped operating room on board, just in case.

Until the president was safely inside the White House, neither Tom nor any of the other pilots would relax their vigilance. The small, elite group not only had years of training and experience, these men and women who had something more—some ingrained instinct, an extra something that made a helicopter feel like an extension of their own body.

"Clear sky tonight," Rick said through his mic.

"Great flying weather," Tom said.

The weather was not just clear, it was perfect. The star-lit sky was crystal clear. His bird, like all the other *Marine One* helicopters, was maintained and working—as always—with the precision of a Swiss watch.

Like the pilots, only the best of the best mechanics were chosen to care for the helicopters that transported the president.

Rick was right. It was wonderful flying weather. This was the kind of night in which Tom wished he could stay in the sky forever.

Tom had come to the conclusion that this particular president was going to do well. He might even have the wisdom to figure out a way to cool down the fever that always seemed to be raging in the Middle East—if they could keep him alive.

Yes, his mission was simple—to get the president safely from Andrews Air Force Base to the White House. And yet with every crackpot in the world wanting to kill your passenger—nothing was simple. Every second took complete focus and unending vigilance.

And that was the problem. Something had changed, and it wasn't physical. The change was more subtle, and had taken some time to figure out.

For most of his military life, he had only himself to consider. The fact that he had little to lose, combined with a razor-sharp intellect and well-trained instincts, had given him a fearlessness—an edge that many pilots with families couldn't achieve. It gave him an uncanny mastery over whatever craft he was flying. He could practically turn himself into a calculating machine when necessary. Clearheaded. Laser-beam focus. That ability was one of the many reasons he was able to perform so superbly.

Now when he flew, he couldn't stop seeing the faces of the people he'd left behind.

He had not written that letter to his father after all. Once he got to Washington and thought it through, it seemed like the coward's way out. He needed to look his father right in the eyes when he told him that he was Tobias. He did not want to die in a helicopter crash until he could do that. Amy would be devastated if anything happened to him, and that was one little girl who had endured enough heartache for a lifetime. And Claire—he had known he would miss her, but he'd had no earthly idea how much.

It was as though he had become a family man when he wasn't looking, and now his life mattered because *he* mattered to so many people.

The young man who rode up to her house looked familiar. It was Abel, Dorcas's husband, the young man she had been so impressed with. He was leading a horse behind him.

"Are Dorcas and the baby all right?" She could think of no other reason this young man should have come.

"*Ja*. They are fine. I have come because you delivered my son. I did not have the money to pay you then. I do not have the money to pay you now."

"That is okay, Abel. I know it is hard for young couples. I only take donations, and then only if a family can afford it."

"I have heard word that you are in need of a new horse? One that is younger than the standardbred you have now?" He glanced at Flora, standing near the fence.

"I am."

"I did some carpentry work for a man yesterday. When I knew you needed a horse, I asked for a young horse from him instead of my pay. He said he would be happy to give me this one. The horse's name is Copycat. Dorcas and I want you to have him for helping birth our son."

Like all Amish, she had dealt with horses her whole life and could see this one was *en guta Gaul,* a good horse, well muscled, and appeared to be a prize. She could not accept it from this young couple.

"This is *en guta Gaul*! It is worth much more than my midwife services," she said. "I cannot possibly accept him from you."

"That is all right, then." Abel grinned. "Because he is worth much more than the carpentry I did." He handed her the reins. "Please, he is yours. We are so grateful for our son. We wish to pay the woman who delivered him with such kindness and so skillfully."

The horse was beautiful. She could hardly tear her eyes away, she wanted it so badly. Best of all, if she accepted Copycat, she would be able to send Tom's big fat check, which she had not cashed, back to him. Thanks be to God, as well as a young Amish carpenter, she no longer needed that *Englisch* man's charity.

"I need to tell you, though, Copycat is not like any other horse I've ever known." Abel laughed.

"Oh, really? How?"

"Well, for one thing, he's smarter than most horses."

"In what way?"

"He likes to play hide-and-seek."

"I've never known a horse to do that."

"I don't think he believes he's a horse." Abel was still grinning as he wheeled his horse around. "He thinks you can't see him, even if he's hiding behind a skinny little tree."

That was indeed strange behavior, but she was not about to look a gift horse in the mouth, so to speak.

"I will accept this horse with thanks," she said. "But only if you agree that I can deliver your next baby for free."

"I will not turn that offer down," Abel said. *"Gut Gleck."*

"Good luck to you, too, Abel. And thanks."

When she led Copycat out into the pasture, he lay down, rolled over, and gave his back a good scratching by twisting and rolling around in the grass. Then he got up, shook his head, and began to crop the new, spring grass, completely ignoring old Flora.

Claire had to laugh because Flora gave her such a look when she saw Copycat cavorting around, as if to say, "You brought that into *my* pasture?"

Dear Tom,

(Shall I continue calling you Tom? Or would you prefer Tobias? Frankly, I think Tom better suits who you are now, don't you agree?)

A father of a baby I delivered brought me a new standardbred horse as payment. His name is Copycat and he is way too smart to be a horse. He has his own mind, and his own way of doing things, and I think he would happily run the family if I let him.

He does not particularly enjoy pulling the buggy, and hides behind anything he can find when he knows I'm coming out to get him. He has no idea he is too big to hide

behind a tree, and is always quite disappointed when I find
him. His head droops, and his body slumps as though to
say, "No! You found me? How can that be? I was hiding
behind the tree!"

He does have plenty of pep and enjoys prancing down
the road . . . for a while. When he gets tired, or bored—
I'm never quite sure which—he will develop a limp. I was
concerned until I kept coming home, checking all four
hooves, finding nothing at all wrong, and then would see
the limp magically disappear once Copycat got unhitched
and could romp in the pasture. Flora just puts up with
him like the tired old woman she is, but Rocky adores him,
and will give him kisses when Copycat puts his head down
close. They are great friends.

Copycat is also a scamp, and a seasoned escape artist,
and it takes a bit of surveillance to keep him from paying
visits to Jeremiah's vegetable garden. The slightest weakness in the fence or the smallest crack in the gate, and
Copycat is out exploring new worlds.

Keeping an eye on him is Amy's job, and one she thoroughly enjoys. I think, however, that Copycat has figured
out that she is the culprit who is tattling on him. He seems
to be eying her with suspicion. We are all enjoying him
immensely. I never saw a horse with so much personality.

And so, as you see, I will not be needing your check and
I am enclosing it.

Your friend,
Claire.

P.S. Elizabeth moved into your old apartment. She says
Levi and Grace are giving her hives.

P.P.S. Albert says that Jeremiah says he hopes you're still
carrying the knife he gave you.

Tom glanced at the check, tore it up, and threw it into the trash can. Sending it back to him was such a Claire thing to do. He was glad that he had sent his address back to them so they would be able to get in touch with him if they needed him, and he had to admit, indeed, it felt sweet, hearing the news from home. He appreciated Claire taking the time to tell him all about her new horse.

There was another envelope that had come with the mail. He recognized Amy's writing. Claire must have mailed it when she mailed her own letter. When he opened it, there was a hand-drawn picture of what was unmistakably Claire's house. Morning glories climbed up one side and a little girl sat in a wheelchair on the porch with a big dog lying beside her.

Inside was another Amy poem. It was the longest one he had ever known her to write.

Come Back Home

We long to see your face again,
To hear your voice and hold your hand.
Memories of you we hold so dear,
So come back home. We love you here!
I'm proud at the courage you have
To risk your life for another man
But please come home now, we need you here
Where friends and family love you so dear.
I'm sorry to see the path you chose.
Just know, the doors of home will never close.
Won't you please turn around and come back home?
Here with God, family, and friends—
Where you'll never be alone.

It took several deep breaths before he could steel himself to put that one away in a drawer. He sincerely doubted that anyone in Washington cared enough to write him a poem like that. Or send him a letter telling him about the antics of a crazy-smart horse they were enjoying. Or if he got sick, or disappeared, would anyone even particularly care one way or another? Not when there were at least a two hundred other excellent, well-trained pilots on a waiting list hoping to take his slot.

He considered writing Claire and Amy back immediately but couldn't face it. Not right now. He would have to wait for a moment when he could make himself match the tone of Claire's cheerful note, and Amy's poem sounded so forlorn, he had no idea how to respond. That picture of a little girl in a wheelchair—that child surely did know how to tug on his heartstrings.

He microwaved a TV dinner and did something he despised himself for: he watched a sitcom just for the company. He had never been so homesick in his life.

chapter THIRTY-FOUR

Claire was sitting on the porch gripping a bucket of freshly picked green beans between her knees. There was a bucket for discards on one side of her and a large cooking pot on the other. Before the end of the day, she would have another shelf of beans to feed her family. In the past, this sort of activity had always given her enjoyment. Today, she was feeling hurt and mad. She snapped handful after handful of beans in half, discarding any diseased ones, taking her anger at herself out on them.

It had been several days and Tom had not responded to her letter. She should never have sent it. She had worked entirely too hard to hit just the right note of cheerfulness, and he'd probably seen right through her pitiful attempt to pretend she did not miss him.

She had no idea what Amy had written him. That card was the first she had ever made that she had not shown her. It had already been sealed, addressed, and stamped before she handed it to her to mail.

Sarah sat on the floor in front of her with her own small pile of green beans, and Claire noticed that her actions exactly matched hers as the little girl snapped the beans and then threw them on the floor.

"Here." Claire moved the pot closer to her daughter and tried to stop her own jerky movements. "Toss them in here. You are a good helper."

She was angry at herself for another reason, as well. What had she expected to happen between her and Tom, anyway? Why couldn't she have been wise enough to protect her heart? And the hearts of her children. She was old enough to know better.

Inside, Maddy was singing one of her interminable praise songs that she was learning at the New Order youth singings. Annette, her driver, who attended a nearby Christian church, had recently called it a "seven-eleven" song. When Claire asked why, Annette had laughed and said that most of them had seven words sung over and over about eleven times.

Claire had thought Maddy's enthusiasm for her new religion would wear off, but it hadn't. If anything, Maddy was even more involved in Joy's church now than she was at the beginning. Claire did not feel a bit good about herself for being so annoyed with it all.

But then, she'd been annoyed with just about everything since Tom left. Oh, allowing him to live in Levi's apartment had been a mistake in so many, many ways! Last week, without her approval or knowledge, Jesse managed to get his hands on a plastic helicopter model set. He'd found it at a local garage sale and she hadn't known a thing until she followed the smell of airplane glue and found a half-finished model hidden beneath his bed.

With school dismissed for the summer, Albert had become the go-between between her family and Jeremiah. It was Albert who carried fresh loaves of bread, or extra fried chicken, or an occasional jar of tapioca pudding. There had never been anything but kind feelings between her and Jeremiah, and because he had lost a son, she knew he must understand her decision to become Old Order Amish in order to be able to fellowship with hers.

"*Maam!*" Albert came running back down the road. "There is something wrong with Levi's grandpa! He cannot speak!"

Every other thought went out of her head as she ran toward Jeremiah's.

Finding Tom's cell phone number was not a problem. He had written it alongside his address when he'd sent it to her. Getting him to answer that cell phone was another thing altogether. She left message after message. It took two weeks for him to respond. By that time, she was completely disgusted with him. She knew he was busy and important, but this was his father!

"How is he?" Tom asked the minute she answered the phone. She had been outside in her garden when it had begun to ring in her phone shanty. He did not apologize, explain, or even say hello.

"A little better. The stroke was bad, but he is a strong one and is holding his own."

"What is happening? Who is with him?"

"Faye was here for the first few days. Right now it's just nurses. Some people from church have come. Bishop Weaver asked me to stop in. Levi has gone in spite of Weaver telling him not to. Faye will be back next week, and Ephraim is coming with her. They are planning to make arrangements to auction off the farm and the contents of the house, and then they are moving him down with them."

A curse word came over the phone, followed by an immediate apology.

"I'm so sorry, Claire. The mission we were on was so top

secret, we weren't allowed personal phones. Mine was here in the apartment."

"Where have you been?"

"I can't tell you. I'm sorry, Claire, but I just can't. We're heading out again—soon. I can't tell you when over the phone—or where. It involves national security and . . ."

Oh, how important that one was! Too important to come home to see his father. Too important to stop his father's home from being sold to the highest bidder. Tom had been right about Jeremiah's son-in-law. Ephraim was circling that farm like a vulture, and Faye was too weak-willed to stop him. Only one person could stop him, and that was Tom, who had just let her know that he would not be coming home.

She no longer had any desire to talk to Tom Miller. She did something that she had never done in her life. She hung up.

When the phone began to ring again, she ignored it while she finished hoeing her vegetable garden.

It took a week to wrap everything up and go home. During that week, he kept tabs on his father by periodically calling the hospital to check on his status, and he had done more soul-searching than he had ever done in his life. The result of all that soul-searching was that once he went home, he would not be coming back to Washington.

It was not his father's stroke alone that was pulling him there, nor was it Claire—although both weighed heavily on his mind—but he had forced himself to face the facts. He was no longer the pilot he had once been. No one knew that but him, but a time would come when it would be apparent. He'd lost heart for the profession he'd once loved.

His country deserved to have the best pilots in the world protecting their president, and he could no longer claim that status. Not when all he could think about was the people he loved back in Mt. Hope, Ohio.

He was a Marine. He had sworn to protect the country from any and all dangers. It was one of the toughest things he had ever had to admit, but he had taken a good hard look at himself and faced the fact that he had become the danger from which he needed to protect his country. He should no longer be at the controls of *Marine One*. He was a good pilot, but he was no longer the best.

As he drove home, he made plans, devised actions, and organized everything in his mind in order of priority.

The first thing he did upon arriving in Holmes County Friday morning was to go see his father in the hospital.

Jeremiah was sleeping, but the nurse informed him that his condition had improved to the point that there was a good chance he would be going home when the doctor came in this morning. He would get to go back to his house with his daughter and son-in-law.

The next thing on his list was a visit to Bishop Ezra Weaver. After he got that out of the way, he would be free to go see Claire for a few minutes.

He had been to Ezra's farm many times over the years, usually whenever the bishop and his wife hosted church. Like most Swartzentruber homes, it looked run-down and the yard was scraggly. It would never do for the bishop to appear proud.

Today, there was an interestingly happy scenario on the porch. He found the bishop and his wife sitting on the porch, each with a chubby, brown baby on their laps, and they were smiling. He did not remember ever having seen the bishop smile . . .

"Hello," he said as he walked through the long grass to their house. "My name is Tom Miller. I'm the one who drove your daughter to the hospital."

"Did I ever thank you for that?" Bishop Weaver said.

"There was no need," Tom said. "I was glad to be able to help. It's good to see the babies are thriving."

The bishop's wife's face lit up when he mentioned the babies. "They are such good children!" she said.

"And beautiful," Tom ventured.

Instead of correcting him, the bishop smoothed the curly hair of the little boy on his lap. "I'm afraid most grandparents are a little prejudiced when it comes to our grandchildren, but Mary and I do believe they are exceptionally fine-looking children. Healthy and smart, too! This one here sat up all by himself the other day, and his sister said *Grohs Dawdi* the other day."

Mary laughed. "I am of the opinion that it was gas, but Ezra is quite certain she called him Grandfather."

"I am grateful our daughter wanted to bring them to us," Bishop Weaver said. "Even though the circumstances were regrettable."

"God can make triumph out of tragedy." Tom repeated something he'd heard come from his father's mouth so many times.

"That is true," the bishop said. "What brings you to our home, Tom?"

"I am in need of counsel, Bishop," Tom said.

The bishop's wife recognized that as her cue to leave the two men alone. Confession was serious business—and not for the wife's ears unless specifically asked to stay.

"I will take the children inside," she said. "It is time for their nap."

"You say you need counsel?"

"Yes. And I also need to make a confession."

"This sounds serious, and yet you are not of my flock."

"Do you remember a boy named Tobias Troyer?"

"Jeremiah's prodigal son? Oh yes, our church has prayed for him to return for many years, but there has been no word."

"The prayers of the church have brought him home, Bishop. To stay."

There was no one on the place to greet him when he got home. Not even Rocky. Then through the screen door, he saw Claire standing in the kitchen. She was canning, of course. That was no surprise. July and August were always the months for preserving food. No self-respecting Amish woman would consider allowing the summer to go by without filling her cellar and pantry to overflowing.

She was completely alone, her feet were bare, her work dress was stained with the blackberries from which she was making jam, her fingers also. Her prayer *Kapp* had been replaced with a choring kerchief. She was so absorbed in stirring the jam that she did not hear him open the screen door and step into the kitchen.

He stood there, listening to her humming to herself as she worked. The steamy kitchen smelled like heaven. He could remember few times when he had felt happier. His decisions and plans were made and he was at peace with them.

The steam from the kettle was causing her hair to do what it always did, try to make an escape from the braids and pins. There was a curl that had gotten away from her kerchief, and now lay on her neck right at the hairline.

He knew she was furious at him, but he didn't care. There was only one thing in the world he wanted to do right now, and so he did it.

"What on earth!" She whirled around and clapped a hand on the back of her neck. The spoon she had been stirring with was still grasped in her hand. He'd anticipated this reaction and had missed getting splattered with the spoon by stepping away from her the split second after he'd kissed her.

"Tom! When did you get here?" She was too astonished to remember that she was mad at him.

He saw the black liquid on the stove start to bubble up and he reached around her and turned the flame out beneath the pot. If he allowed her to burn a kettleful of jam, he really would be in trouble!

"Earlier today."

"Have you seen . . . ?"

"Yes, I've seen my father. He was asleep, so I didn't wake him, but I did have a chat with the nurse. He's being released today. Where are the children?"

"Amy's with Grace and Levi. Maddy and the others have taken a walk down by the river."

"Then that would explain Rocky's absence."

"He is a good snake finder. How long will you be staying?"

"Permanently."

"Do not tease me." She shook a finger at him.

"I'm not teasing, Claire." He stepped toward her. "By the way, that kiss was not a tease, either."

Her eyes were wide. "We cannot."

"You're right. But someday . . ." He drew her to him, looked deep into her eyes, and traced the curve of her cheek with one finger. "I know you don't understand, and I don't have time right now to explain everything—but please, if you've ever trusted anyone in your life—just know that you can trust me now. Everything is going to be okay. I promise."

• • •

The visit with Bishop Weaver had taken much longer than he expected. He had never considered Ezra Weaver a talkative man, but he had never gone to him for advice before. Bishop Weaver had a great deal to say, and Tom felt that, under the circumstances, it was wise to listen. If he was to accomplish all he wanted to accomplish, he needed the bishop in his corner.

By the time he got to his father's home later that day, the sun was beginning to set. An auctioneer's canopied truck was parked in the yard. Blue tarps covered tables filled with items. Household furniture had been brought out and piled around on the porch. Everything was in readiness for the auction Ephraim had set up.

If he liked his brother-in-law, he would probably be more sympathetic. A houseful of children three hours away. The responsibility of an old man who might or might not ever recover from a stroke. A house and farm to deal with. No doubt the man needed to get back to his own home as soon as possible.

But he didn't like him, and he was fairly certain that Ephraim was enjoying this situation a bit too much. He caught a glimpse of him coming out of the barn carrying a mowing scythe over one shoulder. At first, he thought Ephraim was getting ready to do some work on the fence row—then he saw him pile that ancient tool that had belonged to Tom's great-grandfather on top of one of the tables the auctioneers had placed outside. He nodded to Tom and headed back into the barn, presumably to drag out more of Jeremiah's tools.

Tom fingered the Barlow knife his father had given him and that he'd kept in his pocket ever since that moment in the barn. How many other treasures might be gone by tomorrow evening that could never be recovered?

The speed with which Ephraim had gotten the ball rolling for the auction was impressive. Unless he missed his guess, his brother-in-law had been fantasizing about this moment for years. Perhaps the very reason for his speed in setting this up was his fear that his father-in-law might recover sufficiently to thwart him.

Tom had done some checking. A farm like this would probably go for well over a half a million dollars—just for the acreage alone. No wonder the ranks of farmers were dwindling in this area. Who wouldn't be tempted to sell at prices like that? It took a man as iron-willed as his father to hold on.

He let himself into the front room through the kitchen. Swartzentruber houses were bare by nature, but there was hardly a stick of furniture or dishware left here. Nearly everything was already sitting out in the yard, on makeshift tables, covered with tarps. His father was sitting up in a twin bed someone had placed in the living room.

His sister had a straight-back chair pulled up to his father's bed and was coaxing him to eat some soup. Jeremiah had turned his head away from her and was watching Ephraim out the window.

"Please, *Daed,* you need to eat," she said. "We're going to take you home with us right after the auction tomorrow. It's a three-hour trip. You'll need your strength."

"Hello, Faye," Tom said. "Hello, Jeremiah, I see you got well enough to come home."

Jeremiah turned to see him, and although the left side of his face was drooping, his eyes lit up.

"Here?" He managed to say.

"Yes, I'm here. Washington didn't agree with me, so I came back. I'm afraid you people are going to be stuck with me for a long time." He looked around for something to sit on, but there was nothing.

"Here, you can have my seat," Faye said. "He's not eating anything anyway."

"Looks like you're taking real good care of him," Tom said.

"I am trying to." She glanced out the window where Ephraim was still making trips back and forth. "It is hard to do everything at once. I wish we could wait a few weeks before we had to do this, but my husband says no."

"Doesn't your father have to sign off on this sale before it can happen?"

"Oh, no." Faye got up. "He gave me power of attorney a long time ago when he was sick. But I have no business sense, so I'm just doing what my husband thinks best."

Well, that explained that.

"If someone were to offer you and your husband a lump sum for the whole place," Tom said, "do you think he would be interested?"

"Several people have already tried that. Some Old Order Amish farmer tried to buy it just yesterday. He made Ephraim a real good offer, but my husband wouldn't take it. He says it will bring more at auction."

For all Tom knew, Ephraim could be right. He was certainly no expert in the value of farmland.

Tom sat down and hooked one arm over the back of his chair. "Looks like you've gotten yourself in a fine mess, my old friend."

The pleading look in his father's eyes was more than he could take. While Faye was in the kitchen washing the dishes, Tom put his hand over his father's and leaned close. The time had come.

"Everything is going to be okay, *Daed*. Tobias just came home."

chapter THIRTY-FIVE

The next day was a gorgeous August Saturday. It would be a nice, clear day for Jeremiah's farm to go on the auction block.

Claire dreaded it. Auctions made her sad. They almost always came on the back of some old person getting sick or dying.

This one made her especially sad. Jeremiah had been her neighbor and friend for much of her life. Even when she was banned, she knew that if she needed him, Jeremiah would help her. He might not speak to her—but he would help her.

Now there would be a new neighbor on the property next to her. She prayed that whoever purchased the farm would be Amish. The last thing she wanted was another *Englisch* neighbor. Elizabeth was one thing, but who knew what a strange *Englisch* neighbor might bring to her doorstep? She had children to think of!

And yet—the draw to go to the auction was irresistible. Buggies started coming in. The weather was perfect. And there was a marble rolling pin that Jeremiah's wife had treasured, which Claire wouldn't mind having if it went for a good price. That was assuming Faye hadn't already taken possession of it.

The household items that had constituted Jeremiah and his family's life were now spread out all over the tables. Yet another thing that Claire disliked about auctions was that many of people's possessions looked kind of pitiful sitting out on a table in the hot sun with people fingering them. Jeremiah sat on the side, in a straight-back chair someone had brought out for him. He needed a wheelchair, but Ephraim had apparently been a little too preoccupied with arranging for the auction. Most of the Amish there knew him, and knew the circumstances. They were careful in how they dealt with his things, but there were several *Englisch* there who found it necessary to talk about the items, and some of the things they said were not flattering. She assumed they didn't know that the old man sitting in the chair had spent a lifetime using these items and could hear every word.

Of all the things that happened that morning while a hundred or more people waited for this prime piece of Holmes County real estate to be auctioned in front of the old man's eyes, she thought the thing she disliked most was an *Englisch* woman's loud excitement over some of the "primitives," as she called them.

These were things that Jeremiah or his father had made with their own hands. They had not been meant as decorations for an *Englisch* woman's home. They were honest household implements that had helped raise a family and run a farm. The fact that Jeremiah had to sit and listen to this was, in her eyes, one of the cruelest things she had ever seen. What could Faye be thinking, doing this to him so soon after his stroke?

There was almost a party atmosphere developing among the *Englisch,* some of whom appeared to be tourists who had stumbled upon the auction by accident. But she saw several older Amish men standing silently around Jeremiah, as though trying to cushion the emotional blow of this with their own bodies.

The auction finally started. The auctioneer began with the lesser items first. Jeremiah's wife's pots and pans, some little handmade pot holders.

Claire had her eye only on the marble rolling pin, and wasn't paying a lot of attention to the other items. It surprised her that Tom had not come. Perhaps it was too painful for him to watch. Or maybe he decided that he'd rather be in Washington after all.

A half hour into the auction, Tom pushed his way through the crowd to stand beside her. "What have I missed?"

"Canning jars and lids, boxes of your mother's quilt scraps, some pots and pans, a couple afghans. Why are you late?"

"I was staying in Millersburg and got caught behind an accident on my way here."

"Was anyone hurt?"

"No, but a livestock truck ended up sideways in the middle of the road. I couldn't get around it and traffic got so backed up, I couldn't turn back."

"Are you going to bid on anything, Tom?"

"Yes."

"What?"

"Hold on a minute." He held up a card with a number on it several times until he'd won an old, battered cream can.

"What do you want with a cream can?"

"It was my mother's. Hold on." He bid until he was the owner of an old-fashioned nonmotorized push lawn mower.

"You plan to use that to mow with? Even I use a gasoline-powered lawn mower."

"You don't understand. Hold on." He bid and won a crank washing machine. "I want everything."

"It would have been easier and cheaper to hand Ephraim a check."

"Faye told me that someone had already tried that, and Ephraim wasn't interested, so we're going to play it his way. Hold on." This time he captured a washboard with a hole rusted in the tin.

Then they moved to some heavy cast-iron Dutch ovens and hand-thrown bowls. Tom bought everything. Murmurs began to stir in the crowd, and people shifted from foot to foot. No one had ever been to an auction where one person managed to, or even wanted to, purchase every single item. At one point she caught a look at Jeremiah. She expected him to look devastated over what was happening. Instead of looking devastated, he looked exultant as he watched Tom bid on one thing after another.

"He knows, doesn't he?" she said during a pause in the bidding. She nodded toward his father.

"He does."

"I am so glad. Do Faye and Ephraim know?"

"They will soon."

The *Englisch* lady who loved the "primitives" tried hard to get the ones she had made such a fuss about, which left her husband red-faced and fuming over how far she was bidding over the maximum of what they had agreed to spend. At the end of the flurry of auctioning, Tom was still winning every bid.

They moved on to the furniture. Tom bid and won on everything that was not nailed down. Eventually, people caught on to the fact that no matter what anyone else bid, Tom would doggedly stay in the bidding until it was won. Several dropped out of bidding against him altogether.

Claire kept quiet. She didn't want to distract him. What Tom was trying to do here was admirable, even valiant. But it didn't make sense. What did he think he was going to do with all of his father's things once the auction was over? She hoped he didn't think he was going to store them in Levi's apartment. There wasn't room, for one thing. And she'd have to evict Elizabeth for another.

Two hours into the auction, it was time for the big event—the auctioning of the home and land. Several men who had not yet bid worked their way to the front. Most were Old Order Amish who owned businesses and who she knew were well-to-do. Two were *Englisch*. Everyone knew that serious money would have to be laid out to get Jeremiah's acres. Tom might have been able to snatch up every piece of kitchenware, tools, and quilts on the place, but he could not possibly hold out in a bidding war that could easily go beyond half a million.

"You're done now, right?" she asked.

He glanced at her. "I'm just getting started."

"Tom, you can't possibly outbid everyone on the farm itself. I don't know what a soldier makes, but farms like these—it will go for a half million or more. Land in Holmes County is expensive."

"I know exactly what land in Holmes County costs. I asked you to trust me, Claire."

And then the bidding for the land started. It was intense and the numbers began to get so high, they practically made her dizzy.

One by one, men dropped out of the bidding until it was just Tom and one *Englisch* man battling it out.

Tom folded his card and stuck it in his pocket. It had taken him a little more to buy back his birthright than he had expected, but he now had the legal right to do whatever he wanted with his father's property.

As he walked toward his father, a few *Englisch* people

tried to congratulate him on his win, but his goal was to get to his *daed*. His father's Amish friends, apparently sensing that something important was about to happen, quietly moved aside as he put one hand on his father's shoulder and announced to the crowd. "My name is Tobias Troyer. I am Jeremiah's son, and I've come home."

There was a quick intake of breath from the Amish men who had been standing around his father. Apparently they were Jeremiah's closest friends, so Tom knew that they were aware of the story. Everyone was. They all knew how long Jeremiah had waited and prayed for his prodigal to come home.

"You are Tobias?" Faye was standing only a few feet away. She resembled his mother so much, it made him ache. "My brother?"

"I am."

He watched as her face crumpled. He was reminded of the little girl she had once been. In two strides, he was holding his baby sister in his arms. He felt her shoulders shaking with sobs as her tears moistened his shirt.

She pulled away just long enough to look up at his face. "I don't understand. You have as much legal right to this as I. You were here just last night. Why did you not make us call the auction off?"

"The money will never make up for a little girl who stood at a window crying for her big brother who never came home—but it will make your family's life a little easier. You can go home now and finish raising your children. I will care for our father, here where he belongs."

She glanced at her father, a worried expression on her face. "Is this what you want, *Daed*?"

Jeremiah nodded. *"Gut!"*

"But you aren't Swartzentruber," Faye protested. You

aren't allowed to. *Daed* should be our responsibility. We've already built a room onto our home for him."

"Actually, I *am* allowed to," Tom said. "I have spoken to Bishop Weaver. He has given me special permission to stay and care for our father so that he can remain upon the land where he was born. The only home he has ever known."

"How did you get so much money?" Ephraim looked puzzled.

"If the check's good, does it really matter?"

"I guess not."

"Go home, Ephraim. I'll take care of my father. You take care of my sister and your children. You and Faye and your family are welcome to visit anytime you want. Next time, bring the children. I would like to meet my other nephews and nieces. If *Daed* starts feeling better, I'll bring him down for a short visit from time to time and he can make use of that room you were kind enough to build for him."

As the truth of who Tom was got repeated back through the crowd, the Amish began to do an interesting thing. All the items that Tom had bid on and won melted off the tables and into the crowd. One after another, the Amish made quiet, surreptitious trips into the house. By the time he got his father back into the home that yesterday Jeremiah had thought he was giving up forever, their neighbors and friends, Swartzentruber along with Old Order Amish, had quietly put everything back.

Everything was finally exactly where it belonged—including Tom.

Out the kitchen window, he saw the midwife who held his heart in her hands. She was walking home. That was as it should be. Today belonged to his father. He would talk to Claire tomorrow.

chapter THIRTY-SIX

With help from Grace, Elizabeth, Maddy, Rose, and Levi, Claire had made her home presentable for church Sunday. Since the weather was so warm, the men were able to set out the benches in Claire's newly swept barn. This was easier than moving the partitions that sectioned off the main floor of her house.

The dinner would be on two long tables made of sawhorses and plywood. They were already covered with every tablecloth Claire owned, all bleached a snowy white.

The children would be playing all over the place after services, which would include her upstairs—and there would be mothers going up to check on them. It was a great relief to her that every square inch of her house was clean—even if someone happened to peek inside a dresser drawer!

Sometimes she wondered if the Old Order Amish reputation for sparkling clean houses and lovely yards didn't come from the women's concern over hosting *Gmay*. Every woman she had ever known became slightly panicked as that date for church drew near.

This was going to be an especially good church day for her. Maddy had agreed to stay home from her New Order church for once, since the services were going to be held here. Amy was in her element with all the people around to talk to. And even Grace, Levi, and Elizabeth had agreed to come, but only because it was at her home. Levi had made a point of making certain she realized that there was no hope that he and Grace would ever turn away from being *Englisch*.

Everything was in readiness, and it felt so good.

Her thought was cut off by a sight that pushed all other thoughts from her mind. Tom was walking toward her house, and when he got there, he joined the other men for church.

The men sat on one side of the barn, the women on the other. Teenaged boys sat in the back, shredding pieces of straw, studiously ignoring the speaker or the singing. Old women sat in the back on the women's sides, where aching backs could obtain some support against the wall of the barn. Both groups faced each other. It felt so familiar. When he sang the old songs, he closed his eyes and sang some of them from memory, from his heart, hungry to join his voice with his people. There was one public confession that morning. Henry—broken and remorseful, asked the church to pray for him and the pride that had led him into a gambling addiction. He asked the church to forgive him for what he'd done to his family, and he asked for prayers for healing.

Tom was content to sit and listen and be among his people. It felt good to be back. Someday soon, he had every intention of becoming part of this—but not yet. Returning to the Amish was not a step to be taken lightly. There was a cost involved. A great cost.

It wasn't just a matter of wearing these clothes he had purchased yesterday at the Save & Serve thrift store. It wasn't just a matter of driving a horse and buggy. Or living without electricity or the other entrapments of modern society. That was the easy part. It wasn't even the sacrifice of never flying or being allowed to fly in a plane of any kind again.

It went deeper than that. To become Amish meant becoming a servant to God, to one's family, and to the church community. A man who became Amish was pledging himself, if chosen for leadership, to become a minister, or bishop, or deacon. Not for a season but for life. There was no training. No seminary. No certification one could take. It carried with it a responsibility for other people's souls—and that mantle could fall on anyone. There was no manipulating which one God might choose. No one really wanted this responsibility, but refusal was not an option.

He was no longer a sixteen-year-old boy trying to impress a girl. Once he made this commitment and accepted baptism, that commitment would be there for life.

For those I love, I will sacrifice. How little he'd realized, the night he had that sentence tattooed on his chest, what kind of sacrifices he would have to make. He had been twenty-seven and envisioning going down in a blaze of glory.

Now it meant committing himself to serve his people, his family, his church, and his Christ—day in and day out—for life.

Before he made that final commitment, he wanted to spend some time with Bishop Schrock. From the things Claire had said about him, he believed the man might have some wisdom to share about how to go the distance in this new, and old, life he was beginning.

Once church was over, he searched for Claire. She was busy helping get the meal laid out. As the hostess of this meal, she had heavy responsibilities.

"I'm not going to stay for the meal, Claire," he said.

"Ephraim and Faye are leaving this morning. She wants to get home to the children as soon as possible. I need to get home and take care of *Daed* so she can go."

"How did things go last night after everyone left?"

"It was wonderful, Claire. I owe God a great debt."

She smiled. "And it looks like you are on your way to paying Him back."

As he drove home, he mulled over the fact that he needed someone to help him care for his father, preferably some kind Amish woman. After this morning, he knew exactly whom to ask.

chapter THIRTY-SEVEN

Tom called Levi Monday around lunchtime to see if he could come sit with his father for a while. He doubted that Bishop Weaver was going to insist that a stroke victim could not be watched after from time to time by a grandson, even if that grandson was Levi.

The house Tom pulled up to a few minutes later was not large. Nor did it have a large yard. When he knocked, a young Amish woman came to the door with a baby on her hip. Over her shoulder, he saw a small front room cluttered with toys, children, and what appeared to be pallets made of blankets and pillows on the floor.

"My name is Tobias Troyer," he said. "Is your mother home?"

"Tom!" Rose had heard his voice, and came rushing in from the kitchen. "Won't you come in? Claire has told me everything. It is so good that you have come back."

He saw her glance around as though wondering if there would be a place clear enough for him to sit. He solved the dilemma for her.

"Could I talk to you out here for a few minutes, Rose?"

"Of course." She hurriedly put on her head covering before stepping outside the door.

"How are things going living here at your daughter's house?" he asked.

"Oh, we are all doing just fine." Her voice was unnaturally bright.

"Do you ever wish you could have your own home again, and not have to work at the restaurant anymore?"

"Of course, but I cannot see being able to get ahead enough to buy a home again, and we need the income from my job. Henry has only been able to find part-time work."

"What's he been doing?"

"Helping put new roofs on houses. He goes with a crew and sometimes they drive a very long way to find jobs."

"Does he enjoy it?"

"He is grateful to have employment, but does he enjoy his work? No. I am certain he does not."

"Do you think he'd like to farm again?"

"That will never happen," Rose's voice was bitter. "The farm that his father gave him is gone. We can never save enough to replace it. Not in our lifetime."

"Is Henry a good farmer?"

"Of course he is. You know that."

"How long have we known each other, Rose?"

"You used to push Claire and me on the swings at the schoolhouse when we were small scholars together."

"I've known you my whole life, Rose, and I trust you."

"Thank you, Tobias, but why do you feel the need to say this to me?"

"Here's the deal, Rose. You are one of the kindest women I've ever met, and one of the most competent," he said. "I'm planning to ask Claire to marry me. If she says yes, I know she and her children will want to be able to continue to live in their own home. So I need someone to watch after my dad when I'm not there, and I need someone to take care of my dad's farm—someone who would have the skill to do it well so that it will be a delight to his eyes as he watches. I know that Henry is that sort of farmer."

Her eyes widened as she began to understand what he was saying.

"I will make a deal with you and Henry. You quit your job at the restaurant, move into my father's home, and care for my dad when I'm gone. I'll try to be there every morning to help get him up. I'll come every evening to help him to bed. In return, Henry can do what he does best—till the land. *Daed* will love being able to watch and give advice, and who knows? Maybe he'll be able to recuperate enough to be of some help."

"But we are not Swartzentruber."

"A Swartzentruber no longer owns the property. I do. I also plan to have some plumbing and a refrigerator put in right away."

"I always liked your father," Rose said. "He was not as harsh with us when we left the church as some. Caring for him will not be difficult for me—not like waiting on tables. If there is any lifting to do, Henry can help me. He is still very strong."

"It is a large house. There will be enough bedrooms for your children, and I think my father is going to enjoy having so much life in his house," he said. "So you'll do it?"

"I think my Henry will jump at the chance, but I need to ask him before I commit. I will not disobey his headship even if he has made some mistakes."

"Of course not, but that brings up another question, Rose. Does Henry still take care of the finances in your home? I would hate for him to get into money troubles again."

Rose lifted her chin. "Henry has given me headship over our family's finances. He says it will help him to not falter if he does not have access to our money."

"Do you think he can stay away from the casino?"

"He is a good man, Tobias. He's been a good father to our children and a good husband to me. He made a prosperous living for us until Satan discovered the one vice that Henry could not fight alone." She squared her shoulders. "There are no secrets now and he is no longer alone in his battle. He has me beside him."

"He's a lucky man to have you. I'm hoping he'll soon be my brother-in-law and neighbor," he said. "Do you think Claire will have me?"

"She was distraught when you chose to leave, but she tried to hide it. Now that you're back, it is like the sun has come out again."

chapter THIRTY-EIGHT

"Y ou came to see me!" Amy cried. "I thought you'd never, ever come."

Rocky propelled himself off the porch at him and nearly knocked him down. "How are you doing, boy?" He ran his fingers through the dog's white fur. "I missed you, too."

He swung himself up onto the porch, his hand behind his back. "Well, I'm never going away again. You'll be sick of seeing me around so much."

"Never." She reached her arms up for a hug. "You know I love you—and you can stay forever. What do you have behind your back?"

"A present."

"For me?"

"Absolutely for you." He set a blue vase down in front of her with a small, exquisite pink orchid in it. "I thought you might enjoy painting a picture of this."

"Ooh!" She clapped her hands in glee. "I love it. Do you want me to put a poem with it?"

"I would like that very much."

"What kind of a poem do you want?"

"How about a love poem."

"There are all kinds of love poems," Amy said. "Who do you want to give it to?"

"How about Claire?"

"A love poem for Claire?" she said. "What kind?"

Claire's buggy was gone, so he knew he was safe in telling Amy his secret.

"How about helping me write a love poem asking her to marry me."

Amy's drawing pencil clattered to the table. "Please tell me you are not joking."

"I am not joking. Do you think she'll say yes?"

"I don't know," Amy said, picking up her pencil again. "But if I have anything to do with it she will!"

Claire came home, preoccupied, from a worrisome birth. It had been touch-and-go for a few minutes. The cord had been wrapped around the child's throat twice. Her body ached all over from the strain, and she badly needed a shower and a change of clothing.

"Hi!" Amy called. "I've made something for you!"

Claire loved Amy with all her heart, but sometimes she wished she could come home and soak in a tub without having to admire yet another of Amy's creations.

"What do you think?" Amy said, shoving a card beneath Claire's nose.

It was a lovely picture of an orchid. She wondered if Amy had copied it out of some book. Then she saw the vase sitting on her table.

"Where did that come from?"

"Tom came by and gave it to me," Amy answered. "Read the card."

"Tom came by?"

"Just read the card, Claire," Amy said. "Read it out loud. Slow."

Claire opened it and began to read.

To Claire

I loved you when we were children
Making daisy chains together in fields,
Playing hide-and-seek in firefly-lit meadows
Listening to your quick laughter.

There was an intake of breath as Claire realized that this poem was not from Amy. There was only one person from whom it could have come.

"Did Tom . . ."

"Shh," Amy said. "You're spoiling it, Claire. Just read. Out loud."

I loved you when you could not see
me for the bright light of my brother.
And later, with every mission
I flew,
In my heart,
I was protecting you.
I loved you when I opened my eyes
In your house—sick—believing
I was seeing an angel.
But it was no angel.
It was you standing there in plain clothes,
A house full of children,
A life that had known grief,
A life that had known great fear—
And you had faced that fear,
And made a life for your family.
I saw you—
No longer a young girl
But a woman who stole my breath
with your beauty and grace.
You touched my ravaged face,

With your healing hands,
And my heart was gone
I knew, in that instant,

A male voice joined with hers for the last line,

that I had never loved you more.

"Tom!" She whirled around. "I didn't know you where here."

"Do it like we practiced, Tom," Amy instructed.

"Who am I to disobey a professional poet?" Tom said. He got down on one knee. "Is this right?" he inquired of Amy.

"Yes, but now you have to take her hand in yours."

"Like this?"

"And gaze into her eyes."

He smiled up at Claire. "Like this?"

"That's good."

"Now . . ."

"I think I can take it from here, Amy." Tom stood back up and took both of Claire's hands in his own. "I have loved you silently for the first forty-four years of my life. Would you do me the honor of marrying me so that I can show my love openly for the next forty-four?"

"Does that mean you are going to stop loving me when we're eighty-eight?"

"You're spoiling it again, Claire," Amy warned.

"Are you saying that you're willing to put up with my strange hours, and my pager going off in the middle of the night?"

"I am so proud of what you do, Claire," he said. "I'll never stand in your way and I'll help you in any way I can."

"This is a noisy, busy family for a bachelor to move into, Tom. Daniel does not yet always sleep through the night. Albert has recently taken up the harmonica. Jesse got his hands on some firecrackers last week and scared us to death. Maddy goes around singing praise songs most of the time."

"I can handle it."

"Maybe, but it doesn't stop there. Elizabeth is still living in Levi's apartment and she likes to drop in for coffee every morning."

"I don't have a problem with that."

"At four o'clock in the morning. If I'm not awake, she'll make it herself."

"That could be a problem. What about Grace and Levi? Are they doing any better?"

"A little. They've found a church. The minister and his wife have a background similar to theirs. They've been getting together and talking. It seems to be helping. All I know is that my son and daughter-in-law aren't nearly as loud as they used to be. I'm warning you, though. Things could still blow up over there again."

"I've survived mortar attacks, Claire," Tom said. "I've survived suicide bombers. Surely I can survive any noise your family can make."

"If we marry, it won't be 'my' family, it will be 'ours.' Are you willing to take on that sort of responsibility, Tom?"

"Come over here and sit down on the swing with me," he said. "Amy, would you mind going into the house for a bit?"

"Well . . ." Amy looked from one to the other. "I guess my work here is done . . . for now."

She left, and he and Claire seated themselves on the swing.

"You are concerned about whether or not I'm willing to take on the responsibilities of a family," he said. "You need to know that I already have begun to do so."

"What do you mean?"

"How would you like to have Rose as a neighbor?" he said.

"I would love it. Why do you ask?"

"I've asked her and Henry to live in and work my father's farm in return for help caring for him. I'll move *Daed* into

Grandpa's old *Daadi Haus,* but as you know, it connects directly through the kitchen. Rose will be able to care for him, and I plan to help her with him a great deal."

"She and Henry agreed?" she asked.

"You should have seen Rose's eyes light up when I talked to her about it. She wants a chance to talk to Henry first, but I'll be surprised if they don't jump at it. It's a good deal, for everyone. Including my father."

"Thank you, Tom," she said with a break in her voice. "That is one of the most generous things I've ever heard of—with the exception of you buying the farm from your sister and brother-in-law in the first place.

"But . . . I just want to make absolutely sure I'm clear on something—you know we cannot marry unless you become Old Order Amish."

"That kind of goes without saying, doesn't it, Claire? Of course I know that. I intend to go see Bishop Schrock this week."

"You do realize that means you'll have to give up your flying, right? Are you sure you can do that? You have spent a lifetime honing that skill and you love it so."

"I'll miss it," Tom said. "I'll miss it greatly, but some things are worth sacrificing for. Flying will not get me to heaven. Flying will not keep me warm at night. Flying is exhilarating, but it does not feed my soul. And flying will keep me from having you.

"There's one other thing we need to discuss. Until Saturday, I was a wealthy man. Now, not so much. I'll need to get a job to supplement my retirement pay."

"What do you have in mind?" she asked.

"There is a flight training school a couple hours from here. I've already called. Once they learned about my credentials, they jumped at the chance for me to teach the basics. I won't be flying, but I can teach others some of what I know. I'll only be going there two days a week, but I'll be teaching back-to-back classes on those days."

"Do you think your students will be ready for an Amish teacher? They might not take you seriously."

"They'll take me seriously. Remember, I'm an Amish teacher who once flew the president. If they're smart, they'll listen to me. The pay isn't bad. I'll be able to help support you and the children."

"You do realize I haven't said yes yet," Claire said. "Right?"

He waved a dismissive hand. "A technicality," he said. "What woman could resist a love poem written by Amy and me?"

"Not me. I was ready to marry you after the first line." She laughed. "Tom, I knew I was in love with you the night I saw you go in after Maddy even though you were barely strong enough to climb those stairs."

"So it's a yes, then?" he asked.

"Well, I hate to disappoint Amy."

He heard a sound behind them, and they turned to see several pairs of eyes and noses pressed against the window.

"I think we're their entertainment for tonight," she said.

"Then let's give them something entertaining." He tipped her face up for a kiss.

The moment their lips touched, they heard a discordant "eww" from Albert and Jesse, and a romantic sigh from Amy and Sarah. Daniel pounded on the window with his hand and started to cry for his mother.

"And so it begins," Claire said. "You can back out now and I won't hold it against you."

Tom laughed with the sheer joy of a man who can hardly believe his dreams are coming true. "Claire, I have been waiting for this my whole life."

A Howard Reading Group Guide

Hidden Mercies
Serena B. Miller

When Tom Miller returns to his hometown of Mt. Hope, Ohio, after a twenty-seven-year absence, he discovers that nothing—and everything—has changed. He is still in love with Claire Shetler, his dead brother Matthew's widow, and still estranged from his father because of his part in the accident that led to Matthew's death. But Tom—formerly Tobias Troyer—is able to join the life of the town without revealing his identity because of war wounds he suffered during one of his tours as a Marine in Afghanistan. Tom rents a room from Claire and slowly becomes an integral part of her family life. As Claire and Tom begin to fall in love, Tom learns the true definition of homecoming and what it means to receive God's unconditional love.

Discussion Questions

1. "Remember not the sins of my youth, nor my transgressions: according to your mercy, remember thou me for thy goodness' sake, Oh Lord" (Psalm 25:7, KJV). How does this epigraph serve as a summary for the story? Consider the ways in which the characters in the novel are both sinners and saints, using Tom, Claire, Jeremiah, and Maddy as examples.

2. At the beginning of the story we learn of Matthew's death. Initially, Claire cannot believe that her soon-to-

be-husband has died, and she insists that her cousin is playing a trick on her with the news. "I have worked too hard on this wedding for you to spoil it with your tricks!" (6) insists Claire, and only later does she realize that the news of Matthew's death is no joke. Do you think Claire's reaction is a type of defense mechanism? In what ways does Claire experience the stages of grief upon hearing of Matthew's death? Have you had a similar reaction to horrible news?

3. Discuss the significance of Claire's vocation. How is helping to bring new life to the world reflective of God's love? Why do you think Matthew, Claire's deceased husband, did not allow Claire to practice this vocation? Compare Claire's vocation to Tom's. How are they alike? How are they different?

4. In what way or ways is Tom an outsider? Consider both his life as Tobias Troyer and his life as Tom Miller in your response. Does this outsider status contribute to Tom's life choices? How?

5. "There are only two things that matter in life—those you love and those who love you. Nothing else, except the good Lord, Himself, is worth a hill of beans" (66). This quote, said by Elizabeth to Tom, captures Elizabeth's spirit. Reflect on the ways in which Elizabeth acts as the voice of reason in the novel, especially for those characters most in need of guidance like Tom, Levi, and Grace. What advice does Elizabeth share with each of them?

6. Why do you think Grace and Levi have so many disagreements in their marriage? Do you think their differences stem largely from a difference in culture and religion, or are their problems common in any marriage?

7. When Tom initially confronts Jeremiah about his missing

son Tobias, Jeremiah says, "I have no son named Tobias" (106). Later, Jeremiah admits that he is waiting for his son to come home and that he even sets a place for his lost son each night at the dinner table. Why do you think Jeremiah initially told Tom he had no son? Do you think that Tom's presence softened Jeremiah's heart? Why or why not?

8. On page 107 a possible theme of the novel emerges when Claire tells Tom, "Without forgiveness, love cannot exist. Not with God, not with a family, not with a church." Do you agree? Can you think of an example from the novel where love was not possible without forgiveness? Why do you think the two emotions are so closely connected?

9. Discuss Tom and Claire's relationship. What, besides their shared history, do the two have in common? What attracts Tom to Claire, and vice versa? Do you think Claire had a relationship in mind when she rented the room to Tom, or was she merely thinking of finances?

10. Revisit the scene on pages 207–8 when Rocky comes into Tom's life. What does the dog symbolize for Tom? What does adopting Rocky reveal about Tom's character? In what way(s) is Rocky's homecoming like Tom's?

11. What do you think was Maddy's motivation for attending the dangerous party? Was she simply acting like a normal teenager? If Tom had not been there, what might have happened? Discuss how Maddy's decision to attend the party affected Maddy, Tom, and Claire. What changed for each character afterward?

12. How does Tom's moment of revelation to Claire act as a catharsis for both characters? Were you surprised at Claire's reaction? Why or why not?

13. In the end Tom decides to marry Claire and rejoin his

childhood faith. Do you think that Tom and Claire live happily ever after?

Additional Activities: Ways of Enhancing Your Book Club

1. So many moments in *Hidden Mercies* have at their center Amish food: what's being eaten, canned, baked, and preserved. On page 22, Tom longs for the food of his childhood, "comfort food—Holmes County soul food. Homemade egg noodles. Slow-roasted chicken. A custard pie with a crust so light it would melt in your mouth." Throw an Amish dinner party with your book club and use the food described in the novel as inspiration for your menu. Over dinner, chat with your book club about the importance of food in the story. What does this food symbolize for Tom? Share the comfort food from your childhood and culture. What is it that you like to eat and why? What type of comfort does this type of food bring?

2. Continue to delve into the world of the Amish tradition. Have your book club read Serena Miller's first Amish novel, *Love Finds You in Sugarcreek, Ohio* (Summerside, 2010). After reading, discuss with your book club the ways in which the Amish culture is presented in both novels. What similarities can you find between the two stories? What are the differences? Share with your group something that each of these novels taught you about faith and love for one's neighbor.

3. On page 108 Tom asks Claire during the middle of an intimate conversation, "What do you want out of life?" Claire is quick to respond that what she ultimately wants, above all else, is peace. If you had to answer Tom's question, what would you say? Is there one thing you want above all else? Share your answers with your group.

4. For Tom, Claire, and Grace, their calling in life is very clear. All three characters feel very strongly that they have a God-given talent and are called to share that talent with the world. For Tom, that talent is flying helicopters. For Claire, it is working as a midwife. And for Grace, her vocation is to work as a nurse. Vocations do not always have to be career choices, however, and sometimes our vocation is to listen to a friend in need or to be a good parent or sibling. Spend time with your group in prayer or meditation. Ask yourself the question, "Who am I called to be?" After a few minutes of silence, share your answers. To what vocation has God called you? How do you know?

Questions for Serena B. Miller

1. **You live in Minford, Ohio, near an Amish community, and though you are not Amish, you have many strong ties to the community. Describe what it is like to write about a community from the outside. Did you face any problems in your research? Did you make any surprising discoveries?**
The biggest problem I've run into from the outside is my own personal struggle with trying to portray the Amish community honestly but without doing any harm. It is hard to write a book like *Hidden Mercies,* which deals with a darker side of the Amish religion, without worrying that our friendship will be damaged. I try to balance things by also portraying the valuable things I see in their culture, many of which I believe we would benefit from by emulating. I did approach the leader of a support group of former Amish to see if any former Swartzentruber Amish would talk with me about their experience. They politely refused. I respect their reasons why. They don't know me, and they have no reason to trust me with what is a painful, personal journey. My biggest surprise has been discover-

ing the Amish sense of humor. I have never laughed so hard as when sitting around a kerosene-lit kitchen table sharing stories with some of my Amish friends.

2. **The point of view of the novel shifts from Claire to Tom frequently. In your opinion, whose story is *Hidden Mercies*? Why did you decide to tell the story from both points of view?**

I think the story tends to be Tom's. He is a man who has accomplished a great deal in his life, but coming home is such a mixed bag of emotions because it throws him back to a time when he was just a teenage boy making stupid decisions. He's extremely emotionally vulnerable in the beginning of the story because of his physical and emotional scars. Claire's story is strong too, though, which is why I chose to tell the story from both points of view. As a writer, I find spending time in both characters' heads, looking out at the world through their eyes, helps keep the writing fresh for both the reader and myself.

3. **What would you name as the major theme(s) of the novel? Would you agree that this is a story about homecoming, forgiveness, and unconditional love?**

All of the above, but it is also about dealing with shame. Everyone does stupid things when they're young. Pressing on without getting stuck in the past is a major theme not only of this book but also of the Bible.

4. **Were any of the characters based on people you've known in real life? On yourself? Which character do you relate to the most, and why?**

My Tom character came about after I read of a Swartzentruber Amish youth who joined the Marines, made a career of it, and then rejoined the Amish church and eventually became a bishop. One of my Amish friends is a midwife who helped me with Claire's everyday life and work. As far as which character I relate to most? Elizabeth. She's an observer, she's passionate about her family, and she's way too opinionated.

5. **This novel depicts a part of our community that we don't often see; that is, the Amish community living among us. How important was it to you to give a voice to this community? Were you hoping to break any stereotypes with the novel?**

Unless you've actually spent a lot of time with the Amish, it is easy to fall into quite a lot of media-driven stereotypes. I've had some disturbing conversations with non-Amish people. A woman once told me quite seriously that all Amish are dirty, dishonest, and run puppy mills. I couldn't help but compare her description with the Amish home I had just stayed that was clean and welcoming, the children well-cared for and happy, and the animals loved and treated like part of the family. I have actually been asked on two different Christian radio interviews if the Amish believe in Jesus. Considering the in-depth spiritual and biblical discussions I've had with my Amish friends, I'm astonished that these ideas exist. So yes, I was hoping to break some stereotypes with this novel. A couple of my Amish friends have expressed the wish that outsiders would realize that they are dealing with problems and struggles just like everyone else.

6. **How did you come to be a writer? Do you feel called by God to write, as Claire is called by God to work as a midwife?**

I absolutely feel called by God to write. That belief is validated every time someone tells me that they have been touched or strengthened by one of my stories. I wanted to be a writer my whole life, but I never knew a writer personally and I assumed they were people who were set apart somehow and were a whole lot smarter than me. Eventually I got the courage to join a professional writers' group and found the encouragement and tools I needed.

7. **All of the characters change throughout the course of the novel. In your mind, which character grew the most and why?**

It's tempting to say that Tom did, but I don't think so. Deep down, he just wanted to come home and be accepted. In my opinion, the person who grew the most was Bishop Weaver, the Swartzentruber bishop whose unmarried daughter came home pregnant. Too often Amish bishops are portrayed as stiff-necked and unyielding. Perhaps that is true to some extent, but I don't think people realize what an incredibly heavy burden becoming a bishop is. It is an unpaid, unsought, lifetime position that puts the responsibility of approximately two hundred people on a man's shoulders—a man who would, in most instances, prefer to be left alone to make a living for his family.

8. **Discuss the significance of the title. What "hidden mercies" are discovered in the novel?**

Tom thought he knew how things were going to be when he went home. His father was going to be stiff-necked and reject him, Claire was going to hate him for what he had done, and the Amish community was going to despise him. Without giving away the plot, the reality he discovered was an entirely different scenario than the one he built up in his mind. Another hidden mercy was that Claire, widowed, assumed that her life as a wife was over. She never dreamed that she would fall in love ever again. Of course, the title also rose from my own belief that life is filled with God's hidden mercies—so many of which we never realize and take for granted.

9. Why did you decide to tell Tom and Claire's story? Describe the journey from conception to publication.

An Amish friend told me about not being able to have any contact with a close relative because he had left the Amish church to join the Marines and had been shunned because of it. There was such sadness in her voice as she talked about him. He had become a helicopter mechanic who was so trusted and skilled he had even been allowed to work on *Marine One*. Soon after that, I also heard about that bishop who had once been a Marine and had come back to his church. Those two stories intrigued me. Then an Amish woman who had read *Love Finds You in Sugarcreek* called me from another state and told me she was a midwife, and that if I ever wanted to write about an Amish midwife, she would be happy to talk with me. She invited me to come stay at their home so that we could talk in depth. I was extremely impressed with her dedication and her love for the gift of ministering to the women of her county. The holiness in which she held her profession was incredibly inspiring. She also got permission for me to attend their worship with her that Sunday. Even though the church was Old Order Amish, they were kind enough to use English that Sunday, and I was able to enjoy the excellent lesson the bishop gave. I treasure my friendship with her and her wonderful family. It is a joy when she calls (her phone is in her barn) and tells me all that's going on with her family and church and about her "mothers" and the babies she helps birth. The latest news is that her church is growing to the point that they are in the process of having to establish another one several miles away.

10. Who is your favorite author? What are you reading now?

My favorite author? Probably Allan Eckert. The man was a genius at taking historical research and making it read like a novel. Reading now? I just started Laura Frantz's *The Colonel's Lady*.

11. What is next for you as a writer?

I'll be starting a third Amish book for Howard Books soon. The title will be *Fearless Hope* and will weave in some of the characters from *Hidden Mercies* and *An Uncommon Grace*.